"I LOVE YOU. ONLY YOU."

Cassie pulled Robert's tawny head down and reached to kiss him, full and open on the mouth. "I will marry you. I will be yours, right now."

He bent and lifted her again in his arms, trembling. Her soft, heated body beneath the gaping robe and thin shift gave off a faint but irresistibly erotic scent. "I—I want to make love to you, Cass. I have wanted you since the day I left you crying there in the city. But we must marry first."

"No! I want to belong to you, while . . . while no one can stop us. So no one can stop us later . . . please, Robbie."

He understood. He drew a deep breath and nudged the door closed with his knee. Then he carried her to her bed and sat down on the edge of it with her in his lap. She watched him, her face serious but calm, as he untied her robe.

"Kiss me again, Cass . . ."

Books by Jan McGowan

Flame in the Night
Heart of the Storm
Winds of Enchantment

Published by POCKET BOOKS

Flame in the Night

JAN McGOWAN

POCKET BOOKS

New York   London   Toronto   Sydney   Tokyo   Singapore

This book is a work of historical fiction. Names, characters, places and incidents relating to non-historical figures are either the product of the author's imagination or are used fictitiously. Any resemblance of such non-historical incidents, places or figures to actual events or locales or persons, living or dead, is entirely coincidental.

An *Original* Publication of POCKET BOOKS

POCKET BOOKS, a division of Simon & Schuster Inc.
1230 Avenue of the Americas, New York, NY 10020

Copyright © 1990 by Joanna McGauran
Cover art copyright © 1990 Lisa Falkenstern

ISBN: 0-671-70351-X

First Pocket Books printing March 1990

10 9 8 7 6 5 4 3 2 1

Printed in the U.S.A.

Flame in the Night

Book One

THE IRON MISTRESS

Prologue

Willie Harmon's funeral, held at the Eagle Forge Methodist Church on a bright June morning, was attended by a few farm families and his orphaned children. Willie had buried two wives, had neglected his farm and his family and spent his time and what money he had in the local saloon. In spite of his jolly nature and a fine singing voice, Willie would not be missed. But, as his neighbors agreed, something would have to be done about the children.

Standing in the deep green shade of the cemetery oaks behind the small church, the farmers squinted against the glare of sun and watched tall, fourteen-year-old Robert Harmon gather the other children, ten-year-old Cassie and four-year-old Lily, to start back to the old Harmon house.

The eyes of the farmers were speculative. Not all of them had sons, and Robert was a good hand in the fields, a rangy boy promising an early manhood. He was a product of Willie's first wife, Rebecca Thompson, who came from good stock. The Thompson men had all been big and strong as bulls, and there'd be no problem finding a home for the boy.

3

For one thing, the Harmon land would go with him, and it was whispered that there was even a possibility that the huge Thompson farm, now in the hands of a bachelor uncle, would someday be his.

The two girls, now, that was a different matter. The wives of the farmers discussed them as they walked along home, their faces red and perspiring under their bonnets, their full skirts and layers of petticoats raising puffs of dust on the road.

"Not to speak ill of the dead," Mame Tilburn said, "but there's a wild streak there. We all know that Cat Hayes had Cassie out of wedlock two years before she married Willie. As far as that goes, a pure stranger could take one look at her and know she's not a Harmon."

"She don't leave you wondering, though," Aunt Nora Sampson said. "No one likes to say it about Mrs. Andelet's brother, but it's as plain as the nose on your face that Cassie's one of Mark Gerard's by-blows. He was a real unusual-looking man, and even though she's undersized and scrawny, she looks just like him."

Everyone in the group nodded, and most of them turned to glance back south along the wide, shallow valley, where in the distance the large stone mansion of the Andelet family shone a muted silver gray in the noonday sun. Known as the manor, it boasted formal gardens and a fountain, along with the usual stables and a huge barn.

Like the farmers, the Andelets made their money from their land, though not in the same manner. The Andelets' five thousand acres of woodland were devoted to the manufacture of iron. Ore was mined on the property, and farther south, in the midst of thick forest, were the immense pyramidal furnace that melted the ore and the refining forge that gave the town its name. Turning back, one of the younger women sighed.

"And Mark Gerard's dead too," she said, breaking the short silence, "or so I heard. Killed in a duel." She said the last slowly, relishing the romantic sound of it.

"Two wild streaks, then," Mame said, wiping perspiration from her reddened forehead, loosening the high lace collar on her black funeral silk, "at least in Cassie. The sins of the

4

fathers, the Bible says, will be visited on their children. The sins of the mothers wouldn't be much different, I'd guess. Well, I know my Henry would like to have Robert, but I'll not take in Cassie, or even Lily. That Lily is Catherine Hayes's spittin' image. She could turn out the same, and I have my own girls to think of."

Chapter 1

"I must have her."

Having said that, Maria Andelet rose from her chair and, without a glance at the lean man propped against the ornate fireplace, proceeded down the length of the big room with an irritated swish of skirts. There, she stood at a bank of long windows draped in creamy brocade. Silently, she stared north toward the little church and the scattering of people leaving the grounds.

At thirty-one, Maria's petite figure was at its prime, her curves lush but her waist still small, her legs graceful and slender beneath her wide, layered and stiffened skirts. She was dressed in black silk, in mourning both for her elderly husband Armand and her beloved brother Mark. Still, above the black net ruffle around her throat, her white skin was luminous with health, her face strong and beautiful, her coiled topknot of thick black hair shining. But in the large, oddly set gray-green eyes there was a look of almost desperate loneliness.

John Kendall straightened, left the fireplace and joined

her at the window. As the family's legal advisor he had helped Maria take over after her husband and brother had both died within a year. Armand had been the ironmaster of Eagle Forge, and Maria had firmly refused to either sell or hire a new master. With Kendall's advice and the things she had learned from her husband, she kept the works going and found new markets that paid better than ever before. Still, Kendall felt deep concern for this small but autocratic woman. There were times—and no one knew it better than he—when those gray-green eyes could be soft as fog on a meadow. But behind the loneliness that filled them now, there was a will as strong and hard as the iron from her forge. He rested a hand on her shoulder, wondering where her will would lead her.

"I know your wish, Maria. And certainly the child would have more advantages living here with you than in any farm home. I explained that to her last night when I visited them. She listened and seemed to understand. She thanked me, but she said she would stay with her brother and sister."

Maria shrugged. "I have no interest in the other two." She glanced over at John, knitting her brows. "But surely that boy is old enough to realize what I am offering. Are you sure you made it plain to the dolt that Cassie is to come here as . . . as practically the daughter of the house?"

"Robert," John said, squeezing her shoulder gently. "That's the boy's name. Robert Harmon. He's not a dolt, Maria. In fact he's quite well-spoken and intelligent. He's bringing Cassie here this afternoon to see you. He wants her to have her chance, but he'll not force her to accept. If I were you, I wouldn't play grand lady of the manor with him. Robert wouldn't mind, but Cassie will notice and resent it for him."

He expected a flare of anger, but surprisingly, Maria's frown smoothed out and her tight lips relaxed into a smile. "Robert, then." She put a hand up and covered his. "I may sound the grand lady, but believe me, it's false courage. Are you absolutely sure there are no relatives who might claim her? Mark was all the family I had, and she's all that's left of Mark."

John bent his head and kissed the slender fingers that

covered his hand on her shoulder. He knew, as everyone who knew Maria had guessed, that there was little love lost between Maria and the other members of the Andelet family. All of Maria's love of family had been concentrated on Mark Gerard, her older brother, a man of great charm and even greater passions. Maria had actually refused to marry Armand Andelet until a place had been promised in his business, and in their life, for her brother. Thinking of that, John placed both hands on her shoulders and turned her to face him.

"Cassie has no relatives either, my dear. But I warn you, don't set your heart on having her. She will never agree to leave the other two." He smiled. "Surely, of all people, you can understand her love for her family."

Cassie Harmon had very dark, nearly black hair which sprang up and away from her small, intent face in stubborn curls, refusing to lie down no matter how hard she brushed it. Before starting for the Andelet's big stone house she had dampened the hair and brushed it back slickly, tying it at her nape with a faded scarf. Now, walking with tall Robert and little Lily, she could feel the warm breeze drying the short hair around her face and the teasing tickle as it loosened and sprang into curls again.

"I can't see why we're even going there," she said, turning to look at Robert. "It's a waste of time. You know very well it takes both of us to look after Lily."

Robert smiled. Though still reddened from crying, Cassie's enormous gray-green eyes were full of resolve, her voice steady. Robert was proud of her.

"We're going because I promised Mr. Kendall to bring you to see Mrs. Andelet," he said gently. "You don't have to live there if you don't want to."

Cassie wanted to ask him where they would live, but she knew he didn't know yet. At first she had thought—they had both thought—they could go on living in their own place. For a long time now Robert had been working and bringing home food and a little money, which they had hidden from their father. Cassie had cooked and taken care of Lily, and they had gotten along better than they ever had. But last night at the wake Reverend Wilson said that Robert, while a very fine, responsible young man, was not old enough to be the head of a household.

"Arrangements," he had said, looking around at the neighbors who had come to sit with the body, "must be made. It seems old Bob Thompson, Robert's uncle, is ailing and unwilling to take on any children to raise, even his own nephew. You must search your hearts."

Cassie hadn't known what he meant, but she remembered the silence in the room, the eyes darting toward her and sliding away. Mrs. Tilburn had pressed her mouth into a tight line and stared off into space. In spite of the warm June night there had been a chill mixed in with the gifts of food and sympathy. It had frightened her then, and now, glancing at Robert's serious face, she was still uneasy.

Maria stood again at the brocaded windows to watch the Harmon children coming down the road and then up the winding path toward her house. They came slowly, the two older ones suiting their pace to the four-year-old's legs, and as they turned up the long slope they joined hands, with Lily in the middle. There was no hesitation, no signal from Robert, just the hands reaching to help each other on the climb.

A lump came in Maria's throat, and with it an angry despair; an intimation of defeat. Those clasping hands might well be an unbreakable chain. She saw the children clearly now, the slanting sunlight touching the three shabby figures, robbing the faded color from their ragged clothes. It shone on the blond heads of the tall boy and the small girl, and lost itself in the deep sable of Cassie's springing hair.

Half hidden in the draperies, Maria stared thoughtfully at their faces, all serious yet calm; watched their glances as the two girls looked for guidance from the boy on the rocky path. They seemed so quiet, so close, as if they had lived apart from the rest of the world, as if they had learned to depend only on each other.

As of course they had, Maria thought, moving away from the window with a rustle of silk and settling into a wingback chair. Who else could they turn to but each other? The mother an invalid, the father a drunkard.

Oh, yes, she knew the details of their lives. Long ago, when she had heard that Catherine Hayes was pregnant with Mark's child, she began keeping track of her. She knew when she married, and wondered at her choice. She had heard the very day when Cat died, and had known it wouldn't be many years until Willie followed, considering his habits. She had wanted the child long before that foolish duel that ended Mark's life; now she felt she could never be content until she had her.

Maria sighed. Watching them together had convinced her that John was right. Cassie would never leave the other two, and the practice in the courts hereabouts was not to force orphaned children to part. Either someone would take them all or they'd end up over at Franklin in the orphanage.

Opening the door opposite her chair, John Kendall stepped in. "They are here, Maria. Where do you want them?"

"In the conservatory. Please tell Sallie to serve them sandwiches and punch. And then come back here and talk to me. I need a few minutes to think."

Ushered through the wide door and into a richly carpeted and paneled foyer hung with paintings and mirrors in elaborately carved frames, the Harmon children were silent, struck by awe.

The thin, stern-faced man, handsome with his thick brown hair, brown mustache, fancy silver-gray suit with a white waistcoat and shiny black boots, smiled gently and took them past an immense staircase, into a hall, and then through a door into a dazzling, large room blazing with sunlight and smelling of damp earth and fern, of roses and lilies and other things wonderfully sweet. The room was full of plants and flowers, like an indoor garden, and Cassie fell in love with it on sight.

"Sit here," the man said, and motioned to a small table and a set of chairs centered on the tiled floor. "Sallie will bring you some refreshments."

The two older children sat down obediently. Lily climbed into a chair beside Cassie and leaned on her, clutching an arm for confidence. Silently, they watched the dark man leave, and a few minutes later the rotund figure of Sallie Fernod appeared with a large tray.

Sallie, well known in the village by size and reputation, was an enormous black woman who spoke French, English, and Dutch, and was said to be the best cook in Pennsylvania. She gave the shabby children a long, sweeping glance and set the tray on the table, square in front of Cassie. It held a number of amazing things—a bell, a crystal pitcher of punch, a silver platter heaped with sandwiches, glasses, plates and napkins. There was also a silver knife with a long, long blade and a handle shaped like a running deer.

Sallie stood back, resting wide palms on billowing hips, her elbows out and her black eyes, fathomless in her round, brown face, fastened on Cassie.

"You, Miss, will serve the others. If there is more needed, you must ring the bell."

Cassie nodded and watched the huge woman sail from the room, gliding on feet neither seen under the long skirt nor heard on the carpet. Then she turned back to the platter of fancy, delicious-looking sandwiches, the glistening pink punch with slivers of ice floating in it, and gazed at it with awe.

"Robert," she whispered, "we must eat very fast before someone comes in, so we can save the food we have at home."

Quickly, she made Lily sit straight on her chair beside her and filled three plates with sandwiches, passing one across the table to Robert, putting the others in front of Lily and herself. Then she filled three glasses, her slender wrist trembling from the weight of the crystal pitcher, and they all began to eat. Not choosing among the varieties, only pushing the fresh bread, cheeses, and meats into their mouths, they chewed and swallowed rapidly, though both Robert and Cassie tried to be neat and Cassie brushed up the crumbs that Lily scattered.

A quarter hour later Maria Andelet smiled at John Kendall, nodded and rose.

"I know what you're thinking," she told him, "and you're right. My sister-in-law will take to her bed for a week and sulk for a month. But then, Geneva has always been her happiest when she has a grievance, and this one may last her for years. In any event, my mind is made up. Wait here—I may send for you."

"Maria." John Kendall's voice was gentle, as it always was when he addressed her. "You're sure you know what you're doing?"

She laughed a little and came to him, clutching his arm, resting her forehead on his shoulder. "No, of course not. All I really know is that I can't give up the last of the Gerard blood. Just don't talk me out of it, John. I would never forgive you."

His arms around her, Kendall held her gently, loosely, but the look of desire in his dark eyes would have given him away to the most casual witness. "In that case," he said, smiling faintly, "I won't say a word. I won't risk such pain as your displeasure would bring me."

Leaving Kendall in the drawing room, Maria made her way quietly to the open conservatory door and paused, looking in. The boy was standing at the wall of windows, his blond hair a nimbus of light around his well-shaped head, his blue eyes fixed on a field of flax in the distance. The two girls were still at the table, Lily's face shining with ecstatic greed as Cassie poured another cup of punch and let her choose between what was left of the fancy sandwiches. Bent toward the little girl, Cassie's face held a brooding tenderness, a patience far beyond her years.

Maria steadied herself with a hand against the doorway, battered by memories and pain. Even at a distance it had been plain that Cassie resembled her true father, but this was the first time Maria had been close to her, and it was like seeing the face of her dead brother on a child. The high, clear forehead and short, straight nose were Mark to a T, and so were the thick, long lashes and the intriguing little downward tilt at the outer corners of the huge eyes, eyes the same as Maria's in shape and color; the same as Mark's had been. Mark had grown up to be almost too beautiful for a man. Cassie, of course, wouldn't find that a problem.

"Good afternoon, Mrs. Andelet."

Maria started. She had been too busy staring at Cassie to

notice that Robert had turned around and was gazing at her with wondering respect. She looked at him now and managed a smile.

"Good afternoon, Robert. Thank you for bringing the girls to see me. Have you had a sandwich and some punch?"

"Punch," Lily said, quickly. "More, Cassie."

Cassie smiled at her and pulled her into her lap. "You've had enough, Lily. We have all eaten enough. Say thank you to Mrs. Andelet."

Lily stared at the floor and mumbled obediently.

"I thank you too," Cassie said, gazing at Maria with gratitude and also with Mark's eyes and a shy little ghost of Mark's smile. "The sandwiches were very, very good."

"I'm glad you enjoyed them," Maria began, and then stopped. She hadn't realized just how much this was going to affect her. She had a nearly uncontrollable wish to throw her arms around Mark's daughter and weep. In fact, tears were welling over on her cheeks, and suddenly she was horrified by the thought that she might break down. That would never do.

"Stay here," she added commandingly, and turned to the door. "Mr. Kendall, my lawyer, will come in and—and tell you my plans."

"Mrs. Andelet?" Cassie's soft voice, full of regret, caught her as she reached the door. "If it's about me staying here and being part of your family, I—just can't." As Maria turned back, Cassie caught sight of her tear-wet cheeks and went red as a beet herself. She put Lily down and went swiftly to the door and grasped Maria's hand, holding it tightly.

"Please, ma'am, don't feel bad. It's just that Robert and Lily and I are—are a family ourselves. We have to stay together."

Maria's slender fingers clutched the small, warm hand like a lifeline. "Yes," she said, struggling to keep her voice steady. "Yes, I do realize that. I can see how you feel about it. And, I think it's . . . well, I must say it's admirable."

"Oh, ma'am! Then it's all right. I—I hated to say no and have you think I was ungrateful."

"You will not say no," Maria said firmly. "The problem is

solved. I've instructed Mr. Kendall to make legal arrangements for the three of you to live here together." Feeling rather breathless, she smiled. "You will be my wards, which means I will take care of all your needs. Now, does that suit you?"

Speechless, Cassie looked at Robert, and, automatically, so did Maria, her eyes narrowing. So, here was the obstacle, no matter what John Kendall thought. Cassie would listen to this boy, so the boy was the one she must convince. Robert's face was pale beneath the sheaf of tawny gold hair, his young jaw set, his eyes on Maria.

"It would be a God's blessing for Cass and Lily," he said slowly, "and I'm grateful for that. But I'm able to do a man's work, and I'll not take charity."

"Nor I," Cassie said instantly. "I can work too. The two of us can take care of Lily, and—"

"But that's exactly what I had in mind," Maria broke in, putting her hands on her hips and staring from one to the other. "What did you think? That I wanted you to live here in luxury and not turn a hand? Of course you'll work, Robert, for I need you in my fields. And you, Cassie—you'll help in the house. Certainly there will be much you can do, and Lily too, as she grows older. Now, no more argument. This is the only house in the valley willing to take all three of you, and unless you want to be separated, you'll snap up the chance." She paused, watching the shocked, silent messages flickering back and forth in the eyes of the two older children. She smiled slightly and went on. "I'm sure you'll agree once you've given it thought. In the meantime, I'll send you back to your house with my man Noonan and the wagon. You will pack what you want and return here. Do you understand?"

Robert nodded slowly. "Yes, ma'am, I do. Thank you."

Suddenly bright-faced, Cassie looked at Lily and grinned, and Lily, always tuned to her feelings, stared, laughed and whirled around and around, dancing.

Cassie looked up at Maria and smiled. "She's happy too," she said shyly, "she just doesn't know why."

Behind Maria's shapely back John Kendall lounged in the doorway and watched her shepherd the three children out through another door and down the hall. When Maria wanted something badly, he thought, she went after it with all her formidable mind. When one channel closed, she opened another. Which meant that by the time it was settled, she'd have those children believing they were doing the best for everyone. And perhaps they were.

Kendall wandered down the hall and into the drawing room, standing at the bay windows and watching as Maria gave instructions to Noonan at the front door. Noonan, a heavy old man with a bald head fringed with silver hair, a red, kindly face, and wide, strong-looking shoulders, took the trio of children in hand and disappeared around the corner of the house, going toward the stables in the rear. Glancing up at the window, Maria saw John watching. She smiled widely, picked up her skirts with her small hands, ran up the steps and into the house.

"It went well, didn't it?" she asked breathlessly, coming into the drawing room, coming close to look up at his face. "I think they'll be glad to be here, once they think it over. Oh, John, isn't she lovely? So much like Mark . . ."

"So much like you," Kendall said. "Like her aunt." He grasped her shoulders and laughed softly, looking down into her clear eyes and smooth face. "An aunt! You look more like her sister."

"I am past thirty," Maria said briskly. "And I've been an aunt since I married Armand. Geneva's son Jacob is seventeen and her daughter Violet is fourteen. Which reminds me, I want my three wards to inherit shares of my estate equal to the amounts set aside for Geneva's children."

"You want the same amounts for all five of them?"

"Of course. There's more than enough. Oh, John, I am so thankful they agreed! That was a touchy moment when Robert spoke up. Somehow, I never expect the poor to have any pride. He wouldn't have come here if I hadn't caught on and said they would have to work."

His brows knitted, Kendall dropped his hands from her shoulders. "Geneva will be furious about them sharing the inheritance," he said. "How will you tell her?"

Maria shrugged. "Perhaps you should write to her, so she understands it is done legally. Why should she care? Armand left the money to me, and her own husband's wealth is far more than she and her two children will ever need."

"She will object strongly."

Maria gave a little laugh and turned away. "I know. But I try to ignore the fact that Geneva's greed is limitless. When you write to her, mention in the letter that I have already signed the papers accepting the children as my wards. Otherwise she will rush to my side and I will hear endless arguments."

"Perhaps," John said reluctantly, "you should give her that chance. After all, she is Armand's sister."

"No!" Maria whirled back in a twisting flutter of skirts. "Geneva thinks only of herself. She would never understand why I must have Cassie." She stared up at John's troubled face and then came close, putting her hands on his chest. "You will think I have no affection for Geneva, but I do. And pity too—for her greed and envy make her even more unhappy than they make me. But I'll not give in to her, John. That would make me miserable and her no happier. There is not enough money in the world to satisfy Geneva Bradford."

Kendall's opposition had melted as soon as she touched him. He quickly agreed, as they both knew he would. "You're a wise woman, Maria. I'll not argue with you on that." He took her hands from his chest and, holding them palm up, kissed them both. "There. I've sealed my pledge. I'll present the matter to the Bradfords as an accomplished fact, and stand with you against the onslaught."

"Spoken like a true friend," Maria said, chuckling, and tucked an arm in his. "Come, let us have a glass of wine. Do you know how I feel? I feel as if I am beginning again— beginning an entirely new life. And this time I'll be managing all of it myself!"

Chapter 2

꙰

It was late when Noonan drove up to the deserted Harmon house with the three children in the back of the wagon. But it didn't take long to bundle up their few belongings in three bags and clean out the foodstuffs in the larder. They were just coming out when Henry Tilburn arrived, puffing because he had run the last hundred yards.

"Lorda'mighty," he said to Robert, "I thought you'd stay the night at least. Listen . . ." He turned and drew Robert away from the wagon and out of earshot. "We ain't able to take all of you, you know, but Mame an' I will be glad to take *you*—an' treat you good too. No reason for a strappin' lad like yourself to git shut in an orphanage."

"I thank you for your kindness," Robert said stiffly, "but Mrs. Andelet is taking us all. We'll be working there, Cassie and I."

"Mrs. *Andelet?* She's taking all of you? *All?*"

"Yes, sir."

Henry Tilburn's face was suddenly congested with blood. "Why, she's a fool! Taking on three children she doesn't know, and what's worse, shaming her fine family with her wild brother's bastard. She's . . . why, she's crazy!"

Robert had gone crimson and then pale. He'd heard enough bits and pieces before to understand exactly who and what Tilburn was talking about when he said bastard, and he was suddenly, violently angry, half strangling on his own words.

"Don't you dare say that!"

"Why not? It's true, ain't it? Mark Gerard fathered Cassie, that's plain enough to anyone who ever seen 'em both! Besides, Cat Hayes had no more morals than a billy goat, an' her daughters likely will be the same—" Tilburn jumped back, throwing up his arms to block the wild swing of Robert's fist. "Now, you quit that, boy! I ain't insultin' *your* blood. The Thompsons were fine people—" He went down as the next blow connected with the side of his head, and then Cassie was there, kicking at his fat legs and shouting for him to leave, and Noonan was dragging him up out of the dirt. Cassie hadn't heard the quarrel, but she had seen Robert knock the man down, and jumped right in to help. To her frightened eyes, slim Robert was no match for heavy old Tilburn.

Now, tugging Robert toward the wagon, Cassie could hear the shocked Mr. Tilburn filling Noonan's ears.

"I sure never knew that boy had a temper like that, Noonan. Why, I believe he would've killed me if you hadn't stepped in, an' that Cassie would've helped him do it. You tell Miz Andelet to keep an eye on them."

"I'll do that," Noonan said smoothly, "but it's likely the boy will be all right once he gets over the shock of his father's death." Noonan had started toward them in time to hear some of it, and while he knew what Tilburn said was true, still he was proud of Robert for standing up for his sister. "I'll take him off before he starts anything else," he went on, brushing leaves and dirt from Tilburn's shirt. "No telling what a grief-struck boy will do."

"Well," Tilburn said, "I thank you for saving me. Here I was just trying to do my Christian duty . . ."

They drove back down the valley in the last of the long June day, Cassie sitting on the high wagon seat with

Noonan's broad body on one side and Robert's tall, boyish figure on the other. Sprawled in Cassie's lap, her golden head drooping on Cassie's thin chest, an exhausted Lily slept soundly.

"She ain't feverish, is she?" Noonan asked, troubled. "She's almighty pink-faced." A family man, he was soft on children and afraid of their illnesses.

"Just tired," Cassie said, easing Lily into a better position. "She gets so excited she wears herself out." She was almost worn out herself, her slender arms aching from Lily's weight, her own head nodding closer and closer to Robert's shoulder. But her gaze was fixed on the Andelet house, softly shadowed by the sunset, its long windows blazing like diamonds with reflected light. It seemed to beckon, to promise a strange and wonderful life. But she had learned even in her short years that things were not always as they seemed.

"Robert," she whispered, and saw his bright head bend toward her, listening. "What if we're unhappy there?"

He saw how tired she was and put an arm around her, pulling her over so he could take Lily's weight. "We'll be fine, wherever we are. Haven't we always got along?"

Cassie nodded but persisted, her whisper just a breath so Noonan wouldn't hear. "But if things we can't stand happen, what then?"

Robert forced a grin. "Then," he breathed, "we'll run away and live in the woods, eating nuts and berries."

Tired as she was, Cassie laughed. She knew how impossible that was, for nuts and berries were part of their food supply now, and they weren't nearly enough. But everything seemed possible when Robert said it, and she was comforted. She leaned into his enfolding arm, her huge eyes drooping shut. "I liked Mrs. Andelet," she said, yawning. "She's a nice lady. I think we're going to be all . . ." Her voice trailed off as her eyes closed. Robert reached for Lily's legs as Cassie's arms relaxed, drawing the small body into his lap, holding her steady while still keeping an arm around Cassie on the narrow seat. Settling himself to hold them both, he glanced up and saw Noonan watching him.

"Those two figure you'll keep 'em from harm, don't they? Most sisters ain't that trusting of a big, rough brother."

Robert smiled and nodded politely. He knew very little of other families and how they lived. His life had been more work than play, his family shunned by most of the villagers. It had hurt him to see Cassie's shy overtures of friendship ignored by the other girls at school, but it hadn't surprised him. He knew why. The village disapproved of both of their parents. His father had been kind enough sober, but when he was drunk, which was much more often, he punished his second wife by reciting her sins in full voice for all to hear. Cat Hayes had been a beautiful woman once, full of life, but she had wilted under an ugly torrent of shouted abuse, and died when she couldn't find reason to live.

"We trust each other, Cass and I," Robert said suddenly, breaking a long silence. "We're all Lily has. We're all *we* have."

They had turned up the hill and were nearing the circle of road around the house. Noonan clucked to the horses, encouraging them on the slope, and glanced again at the lanky boy, understanding in his faded eyes.

"I suspect it's been a hard row to hoe," he acknowledged. "Always is, for the children. But you've fallen on good times, Rob. There's no finer woman in the world than Maria Andelet, and she'll do her best for you." Sincerity made his words ring out, and Cassie awoke. She sat up, staring at the house, the gardens, the long, soft shadows of twilight growing around them, the lamplight glowing in the kitchen window as the wagon passed. The odor of roasting meat and fresh baked pie drifted after them, warm and tantalizing. Cassie turned and looked at Robert, and as she did, someone laughed inside the house. A deep laugh, rolling out thick and dark as molasses, full of good humor. Looking at each other, Cassie and Robert laughed too, not knowing why.

Noonan chuckled, pulling up at the back door, glancing over at them. "That Sallie Fernod laughs," he said, easing off the seat, "and everyone who hears it laughs with her. Now you two go right in at the kitchen and one of the maids will take you up to your rooms. Carry what you can and I'll bring the rest."

Going in, Robert carried Lily against one shoulder and a bundle of belongings in the other arm. Lily slept. Cassie, her dark hair springing loose in a wild tangle around her head, carried two bundles and stared over them with wide, dazed eyes. The kitchen was enormous, high-ceilinged, beamed with blackened timbers hung with copper pots, strings of onions and dried peppers, bacon and hams. The floor was paved with scrubbed flagstones of gray and blue-gray slate, polished by long use. A fireplace took up almost half of the north wall, but on this warm June evening it was empty and the delicious smells came from a huge black iron cookstove. Presiding there, stirring a pot of soup, Sallie Fernod suited the size of the kitchen. Massive, impressive in a long black dress and a wildly flowered red and blue turban, seeming to Cassie as high and as wide as a wall, she turned slowly as they came in and smiled, her big teeth snowy white.

"Good evening, Master, Miss. You, there, Adah, help with those bundles and show the young master and miss their rooms."

Adah, a tall young woman, thin and red-haired, came to them. She wore a black skirt, her blouse white and tucked into the waistband, her headdress a white cap trimmed with coarse lace. She took both of Cassie's bundles, and Cassie silently turned and took the bundle from Robert, so he could hold Lily safely in both arms. Their eyes met, questioned, and Robert shrugged.

"Go ahead," he said, nodding toward the maid, who was at a door and hesitating, looking back. "I'll follow."

Cassie went. If Robert thought it all right, it was. The maid led them through a short hall and up a long flight of stairs, explaining coolly, "These are the back stairs, Miss, much quicker than going through the house to the grand stairs, and not so much in the way. There's a dinner party going on tonight, with important people here to see the lady, which is why she isn't here to greet you. She has to be with her guests. Your rooms are up here on the south side." She smiled down at Cassie patronizingly. "The furnace will make you a light at night. Children don't like the black dark around, I know."

Cassie made herself smile back, though she was dazed and subdued by the size and grandeur of the house and understood little of what was said. Adah was nice enough. So were Noonan and Sallie Fernod. Yet there were tears in the back of her eyes, an ache in the back of her throat. She looked down at the steep steps, watching her scarred and broken shoes come up, one and then the other, carrying her into a new life. Behind her Robert came on steadily, bringing Lily. They had been happy in their own place, she thought, and suddenly she wanted to turn, grab Robert's hand and run.

They came to the top of the stairs and turned east in a carpeted hall with gas lights already lit. They stopped at the middle of three doors in a row. Adah put down one bundle and opened it. The room smelled of soap, lemon oil, and polish, the floors and windows sparkled in the light of more gas lamps. There was a large table and several chairs, a sofa and a piano. Bookcases lined one wall, full of books. Fresh-washed curtains fluttered in a soft night breeze.

"This is the old schoolroom, Miss. The mistress had all of us, even Sallie Fernod, up here cleaning these rooms today, just for you. Now step through this side door and you'll see where you and the little girl will sleep." Adah glanced back at Robert with a different look; almost coy. "You take the other side, Master Robert. Everything is ready for you."

Robert nodded and passed Lily to Cassie, taking the bundle of his clothes she was carrying. Lily awoke and stared around, her hands tightening on Cassie's neck. Catching sight of Adah, she stared at her and then at Robert.

"Where are we?"

Robert reached over Cassie's slim shoulder and ruffled Lily's golden curls. "A new place, Lily. A fine place. You'll see."

Lily's face cleared. She wriggled down from Cassie's arms and ran about, looking and laughing, until Cassie caught her hand and led her into the adjoining bedroom, where Adah was lighting a lamp. There were two beds in the room, beautiful beds, puffy with feather mattresses, fat with pillows, sleek with white linen sheets. Cassie stared, speechless, touching the thick woven coverlets of blue and white wool almost reverently.

"There is a tub and a water closet at the end of the hall," Adah said, "but you can wash up for your supper right here." She pointed at a large bowl and a ewer of water, soap and towels laid out on a chest. "Mrs. Andelet said to bring up your suppers tonight, for you were bound to be tired. You will eat in the schoolroom."

"Yes," Cassie said, dazed. "Yes. I'll tell Robert. That's good. Thank you very much. You're kind, Adah."

Adah laughed. "Not me," she said. "I'm following Mrs. Andelet's orders. She is the one who is kind. She'll be up after supper to see you. You can thank her then."

Cassie scrubbed both Lily and herself until their skin shone. Having nothing better, she put Lily in a cotton nightshift and herself in a faded blue calico gown made of one of her mother's old dresses. When they came out into the schoolroom Robert was already there, his skin shining from his own efforts. He had found a clean shirt with only two patches, but his tattered trousers were the best he had. He was standing at the bookcase when they came in, but he turned away to motion them to a window.

"Come look, Cass."

She went obediently, grasping Lily's hand as they neared the open square of night, then uttering a cry of surprise as she looked out. Miles and miles of dense forest stretched over the hills and dales south of the Andelet manor, a rolling dark sea against the starry sky. It looked as if it could swallow up anything in its way, but in the distance she saw an enormous intruder, a strange, astoundingly bright red flower that lighted the forest around it, that lit up the very air above it and, she saw as she looked at Robert, even reflected its red glare on their faces. She drew back, unconsciously touching her cheek, pulling Lily back with her but still watching.

"It can't be a fire, Robert. It isn't spreading."

He laughed. "It's a fire, all right. Hotter than any you've ever been near. It sends out a big, bright red light, but it can't spread. It's inside the fire bricks of the Andelet furnace, melting the iron."

"But Pa always said the furnace was two miles away."

"Yes. It only looks close. You can't see it daytimes."

Behind them the door opened and Adah came in, bearing a loaded tray. Behind her was an older woman, a solid, dignified woman with a calm, stern face, wearing a black gown with a white collar. She carried a loaf of bread, a cutting board, and knife, which she set down, before turning to Robert.

"I am Mrs. Brooke, Master Robert, the housekeeper here.

Mrs. Andelet has asked me to take over the care of Miss Lily. I am to see that she eats properly and then put her to bed." She bent down and held out a hand to Lily, who stood clutching Cassie's skirt. "Come, Lily. You and I will sit at the end of the table and you will have a good supper."

Cassie braced herself for Lily's howls of fright, and Robert moved forward.

"We can take care of her," he began, and stopped as Lily let go of Cassie's skirt and gravely took Mrs. Brooke's hand. She walked with her to the end of the table and scrambled into a chair with a confident smile.

"Supper," she said happily, watching Mrs. Brooke fill a plate from the tray. "A good supper. I am vewy hungwy."

"You are very hungry," Mrs. Brooke said pleasantly. "Say it right, Lily. Veh-ree hung-ree."

"Veh-ree," Lily said, and giggled. "Veh-ree hung-ree."

Lily was fed and put to bed before Maria Andelet came in. She came accompanied by Adah, who brought another tray, with a teapot, cups, and slices of rhubarb pie topped with clotted cream.

"I'm having dessert with you," Maria announced gaily, and smiled as both children scrambled to their feet. Cat Hayes, she thought, did teach them some manners. And proper English. It made her task simpler, and she was grateful. But her eyes ran over Cassie worriedly, noting the polite smile on a face hollow-eyed with fatigue. Maria's arms ached to hold her, yet she was still afraid to try. She sat down at the cluttered table and motioned to Adah to clear it. There was no food left, but she knew Sallie Fernod would have sent more than enough. She looked away, dismissing Adah with her tray of used dishes, smiling brightly at Robert.

"Sit down, please. This is a special pie. You must both try it." She waited while they sat down and each slowly and carefully took a bite of pie. This was harder than Maria had thought it would be, but she kept her smile as she went on, eating with them as she talked. "Most of the time, we will have our meals together. Tonight I had a formal dinner for friends from the city, a dinner planned months ago. Children are not expected to attend such affairs, and in any event you would have found it boring. How is the pie?"

"It is very good," Robert said gravely. "I think it's the best pie I ever ate."

Maria laughed. "How nice! I shall certainly tell Sallie Fernod that you approve. And you, Cassie? What do you think of the pie?"

"It's wonderful pie," Cassie replied, and then thought of what Adah had said. "You are very kind to us, Mrs. Andelet. Thank you."

The laughter faded from Maria's face. "Oh, Cassie," she said helplessly, "I should have been much kinder to you, for a much longer time." She stopped, knowing she could never explain what she meant, and perhaps it was better not to try. She began again lightly. "But you mustn't call me Mrs. Andelet. You are part of my family now. What will you call me? Aunt Maria or Auntie?"

They stared at her, shocked. Neither of them could imagine such familiarity. Yet the question had to be answered. Slowly, Cassie turned her puzzled face to Robert and waited.

"Aunt Maria," Robert said, his fair skin reddening, "for us. Auntie will be easier for Lily. Will that be all right, ma'am?"

"Of course it will. That is very good judgment, Robert." Maria stood up, her legs weak, and smiled brightly again as they stood up with her. "I must go back to my guests now, but I will see you tomorrow. I'll send Adah up for the rest of the dishes, and you may tell her or Mrs. Brooke if you need anything more." She hesitated, looking from one to the other, and then, in a flutter of laces and a drift of flower scent, she kissed their cheeks, first bending to Cassie and then finding Robert's cheek level with her own. "Good night, children," she said breathlessly, "sleep well."

"Good night," they chorused, and then Cassie, dazed by the soft kiss and sweet scent, looked up at the gray-green eyes so like hers, smiled her tired little ghost of a smile and added: "Good night, Aunt Maria."

Leaving, Maria felt warmed, happy, full of purpose. This was exactly what she needed. A house full of children.

"You're a brave, daring woman, Maria," John Kendall said. "I hope you never regret this day." He smiled at her quick, denying toss of head, and held up his brandy snifter. "To your three new family members, and may their lives be prosperous and happy."

Maria stretched out her slender legs with a whispering of crisp petticoats, leaned back on her velvet tufted lounge and swirled her own brandy, her face relaxed and dreaming. The dinner guests had retired early to prepare for an early departure tomorrow for Philadelphia. Alone, she and John sat in the small sitting room between her boudoir and the bedroom he used when he stayed at the manor, which was often, now that he was helping Maria with her business.

"I can see to their prosperity," she said, "and try hard for their happiness. Do you know, I really believe Cassie's stubbornness about leaving the others may be a blessing. Robert seems to be a very superior lad, and Lily is a darling, bright and happy. Considering Geneva's two children—no, I'll not say it. But the family may be the better for the new blood."

"Don't be unfair," John said gently. "Geneva's son Jacob may not be as strong and aggressive as his father would like, but he is a talented, sensitive boy."

Maria smiled ruefully. "I agree, and I was being unfair. I love Jacob, and if I could protect him from his father's demeaning remarks, I would. But . . ." She cocked her head at John pertly. "Please don't tell me you can see Jacob Bradford taking over Eagle Forge."

John laughed. Here, alone with Maria, he changed amazingly, his severe face softening, losing its look of cool detachment. "I won't. But then, I never considered helping to run a furnace and forge as an occupation for myself either—until a beautiful woman asked me for help."

"Beautiful, John?" The eyes looking at him now were soft and warm, inviting. "At over thirty?"

He slipped from his chair and sat on the edge of her lounge, taking her glass and setting it on the floor so he could hold her hands. "At any age, my love." He brought her hands to his lips, kissing the palms. "You have always been and will always be the most beautiful woman I have ever known."

Maria looked into his pale eyes, eyes called bits of winter ice by his opponents in court. They were anything but cold now. They were warm and wanting, sending a message deep into her body, bringing an eager response. From the start she had been amazed at her own desire, at the trembling pleasure this man gave her. In the first few years of her marriage to Armand, when he had still been able to exercise his husbandly rights, that business in bed had been a chore—embarrassing, invasive, boring. Not now. Oh, no, not now! She smiled slowly, feeling the spreading heat in her loins, the softening, the thrilling anticipation. "Such flattery," she said, her voice like velvet. "I don't believe it, but it's wonderful to hear. Take me to bed, Johnny."

He rose, pulling her up with him, feeling the rush and heat of passion as she moved into his arms, surprised again by the sense of extraordinary good fortune he had felt ever since that early spring day they first became lovers. Maria. So beautiful, so passionate. His heart pounded as they kissed. He was suddenly desperate to lie with her, to possess her again. There was so little time in a summer.

"Come," he said huskily, and turned her toward the door of her bedroom, sweeping her along in a susurration of taffeta ruffles, his own quickened breathing, her low, breathless laugh. He swung her through the door and shut it noiselessly behind them in a movement as graceful as a dance, then grasped her upper arms and kissed her again, a demanding, promising kiss that weakened her knees. She laughed and pulled away, her hands going to her hair, pulling out pins as she went toward her dressing table.

"Need help?" He was smiling, his eyes gleaming in the soft candlelight, his lean hands working the knot from his cravat.

Maria laughed and shook her head in answer. In truth, he already knew she'd refuse. Maria preferred to take off her own clothes, and she made an art of it. She knew just how to present her softly curved body in the exquisite sheer silks and laces beneath her elaborate gown, how to bend and sway and tempt as she slowly removed them. Watching her as he absently took off his own clothes, he felt his skin heating, his pulse beginning to race. *Maria.* Damn it, he wouldn't give her up. In Philadelphia, a city where the proper wife of one gentleman was often the clandestine mistress of another, there would be many places where they could be alone.

Halfway across the room from him, Maria marveled at the way he made her feel. Like a young girl. Soft. Yearning. She had known him always, and in the last year and a half since Armand had died, he'd become her friend, the good, staid man with the answers she needed in business.

It seemed unbelievable now, but for most of that time he had seemed as dry and dusty as his law books, useful but not interesting. Then came that day this spring, that wonderful, wonderful night . . . she turned as he came toward her, seeing again the body that had so surprised her. He was beautifully made under those conventionally dull, proper clothes. Strong, lean, smoothly sheathed in rippling muscle. And hung, she thought, amused by her own bawdy notion, like a veritable bull. And as virile. Her mouth curved as she noted the proof of that. She opened her arms to him and shivered with delight as she felt the heat of his skin on her own.

"Johnny, how I need you . . . how I will always, always need you."

He prayed that was true. He'd been married for twenty years, but he'd never been in love before.

Chapter 3

That first morning, waking in a soft, clean nest of linen sheets and feather bed, looking about with fresh, untired eyes at the silken curtains, the pictures and mirror, the thick wool carpet on the floor, Cassie was amazed at everything. It was like a dream, except that none of her dreams would have been so grand. Later, helping Lily use the water closet, which had been explained to her last night by Adah, she gazed at the bathtub, tried the faucet, then yielded to temptation. She ran water in and hastily stripped herself and Lily. They were splashing and giggling and soaping each other when Mrs. Brooke came in.

"She wasn't angry, she was nice," Cassie told Robert later as they went together down the back stairs. "She washed our hair for us and rinsed us with clean water, and then she dressed Lily and took her off to eat breakfast. But we aren't to take baths together here. She says it isn't right." She looked at him inquiringly. "What did she mean?"

"I guess she meant you shouldn't be naked together."

"But we're both girls!"

Robert shrugged, stepping down into the hall. "I should imagine she knows that. Ask Mrs. Andelet."

Cassie jumped from the steps and landed on his back, clasping him around the shoulders and laughing. "You mean ask Auntie Marieeeya! And I will too. She'll tell me, even if you won't."

Stopping, Robert unclasped her arms and let her slide down his back to the floor. "Don't act so wild," he said, his smile indulgent. "She'll throw us out."

Cassie caught his hand and turned him toward her, her laughing face suddenly sober. "Maybe she will. Maybe she'll get tired of having us around. I—I hope not. I really hope not, Robbie. It's nice here. And she—she's wonderful."

From laughter a moment past, she was close to tears. He was immediately concerned. He put his arms around her comfortingly. "I was teasing, Cass. She is wonderful, and she wouldn't think of giving you up."

Cassie rubbed her face against his chest, angry at her hot eyes. "Why? She never did say why she wanted me, did she?"

Robert swallowed. The knowledge of why Cassie was so dear to Maria Andelet burned in his mind. He pushed down fresh anger as he thought of Henry Tilburn's sneering remarks. "Why wouldn't she?" he asked, stroking Cassie's hair. "You're pretty and you're smart. If I were going to pick out a little girl to bring up, I'd pick you."

Cassie drew back and looked up at him suspiciously. "Little girl? I'm not *little!* You're teasing me again."

He broke into forced laughter, relieved that she hadn't pressed for an answer. "Maybe, though ten seems mighty little to me. But what I really think is she must have been awful lonely to take all three of us. Now let's go see if there's any breakfast."

There was breakfast. Thick slices of ham, fried apples, biscuits aswim in butter, quince jelly, mugs of milk thick with cream. They ate at the kitchen table under Sallie Fernod's watchful gaze, and learned to leave a bit on the plate so she wouldn't fill it again.

Robert hurried through the meal and left, on his way to the barn to find Noonan. "I want to get started on the work," he told Cassie. "That's what I'm here for."

31

But what was *she* here for? Cassie felt strange with nothing to do, and lonesome without Lily clinging to her skirts. She brightened a half hour later when Adah came to take her to Maria Andelet.

They went through the immense dining room with its stiffly formal furnishings and Oriental rugs, on into the big central hall where John Kendall had led them that first time, past the open doors of the sunlit conservatory, then on to the grand staircase that curved up and disappeared above.

Starting up, Adah took her hand, and Cassie wondered if Adah knew how scared she felt and was trying to help. But Adah said nothing and the silence grew, their footsteps muffled by the thick Turkey-red carpet on the steps. At the curve there was a niche in the plaster wall, and in the niche a marble statue of a lady with no clothes on. Cassie gasped and looked up at Adah's thin face, seeing a tiny smile appear.

"It's art," Adah whispered. "That makes it all right."

"Oh," Cassie said, and felt better.

The hall upstairs was as grand as the one below, carpeted the same, the walls covered with paintings and small, shaded lights. Cassie looked hard for the three doors she knew, but somehow they weren't there. Adah looked down at the shining fall of dark hair, swinging forward as the child craned to see the end of the wide hall.

"Remember the door halfway up the back stairs?" Adah asked as they went along. "If you opened it, you would be in this hall. This is only the second floor; your rooms are higher, on the third. That's why you can see so far through the windows."

Cassie's hand tightened on Adah's. "Thank you," she said, "I wondered." She could get lost in this house. Nothing had prepared her for all the turns and winding halls, the doors that all looked the same. "Where is . . . where is Aunt Maria?"

"Why," Adah said, shocked by the title even though she knew the incredible truth, "Mrs. Andelet's suite is right along here. She'll be in the sitting room." Glancing down at the thin, small-boned body, the shabby, often-patched dress, the broken shoes which were much too large for

Cassie's narrow feet, she sighed. *Aunt Maria.* What she wouldn't have given for a chance like this when she was a child. "We must knock, of course," she added, stopping at the door, "and wait until she calls out to enter. Remember that, Miss Cassie."

"I will." Cassie watched and listened, fascinated, as Adah went through the knocking, the announcement of who awaited, the formal entry after the gracious invitation to come in. It seemed a lot of bother within a family, but Cassie was determined to learn.

Maria was sitting on her velvet lounge, having coffee and rolls. Dressed in a pearly lavender silk robe, her long, dark hair loose on her shoulders, she drew Cassie to her and kissed her cheek.

"How fresh you look, Cassie. You must have slept well. And your hair is lovely and clean. Bring me the hairbrush from my room and I'll braid it for you while we talk."

Cassie went into Maria's boudoir with the feeling of entering a shrine. Her awed eyes traveled over the amber silk draperies of the huge bed, the satin coverlet, the tumbled pillows. On the dresser silver winked and glowed; a silver-backed mirror, carved silver handles on the brush, comb, and buttonhook, crystal flagons with silver lids. She took the brush in trembling fingers and went back.

What magic there was in Maria's hands, in her soothing voice. Cassie sat with her back to her, to let her brush and braid, to enjoy the sound of the soft voice flowing over her. She barely remembered to ask her question: "What am I to do, now that Mrs. Brooke is taking on Lily?"

"Why, you will study your books, you will sew, you will have lessons on the piano, and you will learn how to act in company. You will learn to ride a horse and drive a surrey, but that will come later. First of all, we must get new clothes for all of you. You will like that, won't you?"

Cassie blushed. She had sometimes dreamed of new dresses, pretty shoes. She knew it was vain and selfish, her father had told her so. Her eyes on her shoes, she nodded. "Yes, ma'am."

"Ma'am?"

Cassie peered around, half frightened. "Yes, Aunt Maria."

Maria hummed with subdued laughter. "That's better, dear. Don't worry, you'll soon become accustomed to it. Do you know the size of the shirts and trousers Robert wears?"

Cassie drew a deep, joyous breath. Robert was also to have new clothes. "I can tell by looking. I have always been the one to choose our clothes from the church barrel. Lily's too."

Maria was silent, envisioning Cassie picking through the villagers' castoffs for clothes for the three of them. At this moment she was very glad Willie Harmon had had the grace to die.

"Lily will be with us. We'll take Mrs. Brooke to look after her, and I'll drive in to Lynfield. We'll buy what we can and order some summer clothes made for you." Giving the top of Cassie's head a final pat, Maria stood up. "We'll wait until we move back to Philadelphia for the winter to order the rest. The materials and patterns are so much better in the city. Now, go and ask Mrs. Brooke to make ready. Even Lynfield is a long ride for a day."

"Yes, Aunt Maria," Cassie said, faint with excitement. She forced herself to walk slowly and calmly from the room, but once out, she went flying down the stairs and outside to find Robert. It would only take a minute to tell him the news about where they were going to spend the winter. *Philadelphia!* Before Lily was born, her mother used to tell Robert and her of that wondrous city, the beautiful buildings, the wide streets, the rich people—they lived like gods, her mother had said. And now they would see it themselves, even live there!

When Maria came looking for her, she was still in the barn, hanging over the door of a stall, talking and talking of Philadelphia while Robert worked. She looked up, saw Maria, and promptly turned white.

"I forgot," she said through stiff lips, and when Maria motioned sharply for her, she cringed away like a beaten puppy. "Oh, don't, please don't! I won't forget again, I promise."

Maria opened her mouth, but before she could speak, Robert opened the stall and came out, taking Cassie's hand and pulling her forward. "She wasn't going to hit you, Cass.

34

She just wants you to come with her." He turned to Maria. "She was telling me about going to Philadelphia, and the time went by."

"Who hit her?" At his look of surprise, Maria amplified, her soft voice stern. "I mean, who used to hit her?"

A wave of red went up over Robert's face. "My father drank, Mrs. Andelet. He was cruel at times."

Maria set her slim jaw. "Well, I'm not cruel, and will never be. But," she added, looking Robert in the eye and enunciating every syllable distinctly, "don't you dare call me Mrs. Andelet again."

"Yes, Aunt Maria," Robert said politely, but she saw the corner of his mouth twitch.

"Thank you. Now," she said as she took Cassie's hand from Robert's and turned toward the barn door, "you come along, young lady. When I give you something to do, I expect you to do it. Go into the house and find Mrs. Brooke . . ."

Her voice faded from Robert's hearing, and he turned back to his work with a half smile. Cassie was in for some needed lessons, he could see that.

The Harmons had never owned a horse, but Robert could ride, and ride well, having learned on his uncle's farm, where he helped out often. But he knew nothing of harnessing, and now, with the light surrey needed for the trip to Lynfield, he rushed to help Noonan harness the young bay. Harnessing was a useful skill, and Robert meant to learn everything he could.

"You picked that right up," Noonan said approvingly when they finished. "You've the hands for it, quick and able. Good with horses too, I judge."

"I like them, sir."

"That's what it takes." Noonan studied the good-looking and intelligent young face and thought to himself that Maria Andelet had done well to take Robert Harmon to raise along with her wild brother's daughter. In Noonan's opinion, Robert was a better man at fourteen than Jacob Bradford would be when he was full-grown.

"I'll tell you what," Noonan went on, "once the ladies

leave, we'll harness the horses to the wagon. I've got supplies to take down to the iron works and you can go along. I expect you'd like that."

"Yes, sir!"

At a signal from Adah at the back door, Noonan mounted the carriage seat, motioned Robert up beside him, and took the rig around to the front door. They both got down as the ladies emerged, first Maria, again holding Cassie's hand, then Mrs. Brooke, leading Lily.

Standing at the horse's head and holding him still, Robert stared at Cassie. She looked pretty but very odd in a pink dress that had clearly belonged to someone larger. It was much too long and it stood out around her stiffly. It was tucked and pleated, dripping with white lace, the waist sashed with pink silk ending in a large bow. The ends of the bow hung down to her heels as she stepped up into the carriage. Beneath the fluttering silk and ruffled skirt, which seemed to swallow her small body, scarred and broken shoes stepped along bravely. Robert's throat tightened with pity, thinking how she must feel, but then, catching his eye, Cassie kicked out a foot at him and winked. It was all Robert could do to keep from bursting into laughter. He looked down, struggling with himself.

"Robert."

His head shot up. Maria was sitting on the driver's seat, reins in hand. She smiled at him. "Please let the horse go, my boy, and stand aside. We're ready to leave."

"Yes, ma'am." He let go and then leaped out of the way as Maria sent the eager horse forward. Mrs. Brooke, with Lily in her lap, looked straight ahead in a dignified manner, but Cassie turned and knelt in the carriage seat to look back, waving and laughing as they went down the hill and turned north.

Grinning, Robert watched them out of sight. He was not envious. He had never seen Lynfield, but he'd never seen the iron works either.

"I figure we'll do this right," Noonan said as they rumbled away from the barn and turned south. "We'll begin at the beginning. I reckon you've already seen the men digging the iron ore off those slopes to the west."

Robert nodded. "I have. It looks like heavy work."

"It is. No part of making iron is easy. All of it's hard and some of it's dangerous. But it pays well."

Robert was silent, riding on. He knew a little about it from listening to men talk. He knew that the main reason the Andelets had settled here was because of Durmont Creek, which ran from springs high in the hills down past this section and on to the Schuylkill River. He knew the rapid creek turned the waterwheels that ran a blower for the furnace and the hammers for the forge. Widening and slowing as it passed the steeper slopes, the creek also floated the barges that carried the pig iron and the forged blooms to the Schuylkill and so to the city.

Coming down from the open woodland and pasture around the manor, the wagon rumbled into the deep shade of the forest. After a half mile or so, Noonan turned off on a narrow lane.

"See the smoke up ahead?" he asked Robert. "Right there's your first lesson. They're makin' the charcoal to feed the furnace. After a while there won't be any trees around here."

"They'll grow back," Robert said, unwilling to believe that. He stared ahead as the lane circled toward a clearing. "Those look like giant anthills, except they're smoking."

"They're stacks of winter-seasoned logs, leaning in a tight circle and covered with dried mud. Come spring, the men drop coals down inside and start them burning. They're hardwood, so they burn slow and even and make good charcoal."

Robert's eyes swept the wide, shallow glade ahead, treeless, glaring with heat and sunlight, the sweating men stripped to the waist while they worked. Dozens of the dried mud domes dotted the glade, each with its wisp of smoke trailing upward. Across the space men were loading finished charcoal from an opened dome into a wagon.

"Why charcoal?" he asked at last. "Why not just wood?"

"Wood won't melt the ore. Charcoal makes a hotter fire. We'll go back to the main road now and go on to the furnace."

Farther on the main road dropped down toward Durmont

Creek and the land sloped gently into open woodland and then a low, treeless section full of buildings, full of carts and wagons and men. The noise was deafening. First a penetrating, hollow roar that came from the tall stone chimney of the furnace, then the heavy, resounding pound of the forge hammers, the shouted orders, cracking whips, and creaking wheels. The rushing waters of Durmont Creek were nearly inaudible except near the bank. Then they made a gurgling, musical counterpoint to the harshness of the other sounds.

"It's a town," Robert said, astonished. "There must be a hundred men here. Where do they live?"

"Bachelors in a boardinghouse," Noonan said, driving on in a cloud of dust, gesturing at a far roof, "married men have cabins and gardens farther south along the valley. They've got about everything they need right here. Stores, friends, a meeting house, a church." He winked at Robert. "Liquor too, though the Andelets are against it for working men. They make their own, out of corn or apples. We'll tie up over here at the mule corral and walk the rest of it."

Robert jumped down as the wagon stopped and was tying the horse when a man came striding across the hard, barren ground from the furnace. Head up, unsmiling, the man stared at them. Robert felt a cold spot of challenge in the pit of his stomach as the hard eyes flicked over him and settled on Noonan. The man stopped a yard or two away, feet apart, hands on his hips. Robert looked him over warily. His arms looked as hard as oak. A shirt wet with sweat clung to a wide chest, ropy with muscles. The face showed a few scars that could have come from brawling, but none ever deep enough, Robert thought, to take the fight out of this man.

"No strangers here, unless Kendall brings you. Git!"

"Don't be hasty," Noonan said calmly. "Ask the other men. You're more of a stranger here than I am, and this boy's no stranger either. Him and his two sisters have been taken into the manor to be raised. You might be looking at your next ironmaster, Regan."

"How do you know my name?"

"Mr. Kendall told me he'd just hired an Irish straw boss named Regan. You've about got to be it. I'm Fred Noonan, handyman for the ironmistress, and Robert here is her ward."

Regan's head jerked around. His narrowed gray eyes met Robert's startled gaze, dropped to the patched shirt, the tattered pants and worn-out shoes. The corner of his mouth curled down in a sneer.

"A tall tale, Noonan. An ironmistress wouldn't let this one in her back door." He reached out in a swift movement and caught Robert's shirt, bunching it up in his fist and dragging him close. He smelled of acrid smoke and antagonism. "The old man's lying, isn't he, boy? Admit it, or take a beating from me."

Inwardly Robert quailed. The strength of the man's grip was parting the fibers of his shirt, the look in his eye begged a chance to throw a fist. He swallowed to wet his dry throat, planted his feet squarely and met Regan's gaze.

"Noonan told you the truth, Mr. Regan, and so will I. You may give me a beating, but you'll have your work cut out for you. I don't beat easy."

Regan laughed and let him go so suddenly he staggered. "I figured you were trying to put something over on me," he said to Noonan, "but the lad don't look dumb enough to take a beating just for a joke. It's true, then?"

"Yep," Noonan said, enjoying himself, and then, wisely or unwisely, added: "And he ain't easy to beat. He took on a grown man yesterday and sent him packing."

Regan's narrowed gaze swung back to Robert, searched him up and down and swung away again. "If you say so, Noonan. But I'd take the cub with a hand tied, and bet on it too. For now, keep him out of the men's way and out of harm. If the mistress is looking out for him, I don't want him hurt."

All afternoon Robert followed Noonan, looking and listening and asking a few questions. They started in the bridge house, a place of intense heat and noise that held the iron ore and other supplies used in charging the furnace, which lay below and thrust up its long chimney through the bridge house floor and again through the ceiling. There was a tightly closed opening in the wall of the chimney called a trunnel head, and a hundred times a day men opened it and poured in measured amounts of ore, charcoal, and limestone.

Once started, Noonan told Robert, the furnace ran twenty-four hours a day, and every six hours the taphole at the bottom was opened and the molten iron allowed to run out in a long trench called the sow. Smaller trenches to the sides were dug by a gutterman with a hoe, and the iron that ran into these and cooled made the "pigs," bars small enough to be easily handled.

"But it all starts up here," Noonan said, and introduced Robert to the two bridgemen, Ham and Lucius Biederman. The men looked exactly alike. They were huge, with powerful arms and backs, round-faced and grinning. "Ham and Lucius were raised here," Noonan told Robert. "Their father worked the furnace before them. They're twins, which means we got two of the best."

"Pretty words," Lucius said to Ham, winking. "Wonder what Noonan's got up his sleeve, butterin' us up like that. Let's load."

Standing back, Noonan and Robert watched the two strong men open the trunnel head to begin loading, and then one of them pushed the heavy container of ore along an overhead trolley to dump it in. The men wore leather aprons so their clothes wouldn't ignite from the heat, and stood well back themselves to dump and shovel. The heat gained a hundredfold, the noise intensified to a roar, the brilliant glare from the opening blinding as the rest of the load was dumped in. Noonan touched Robert's arm and led him outside.

"Too hot and too noisy, ain't it?" Noonan asked, going down the outside stairs. "It's no place to be. It takes months for a man to get used to working up there, and some of them never do. The forge is kinder, as you're about to see. There's fire in the forge, but not like that."

The forge was built right over the creek, to take full advantage of the twelve-foot waterwheels that powered the hammers. Robert stood with Noonan and watched as the men turned heat-softened iron again and again, allowing the huge hammer to pound it into malleable blooms for shipment on the barges.

"That machinery makes it look easy," Robert said as they left, "but what would they do if the creek dried up?"

Noonan laughed. "Take time off, I reckon. Which reminds

me that we may as well walk on downstream and take pleasure in the day. We've the time, and time to waste is rare."

They strolled along the pleasant, wooded bank until they could see the shine of the Schuylkill in the distance.

"Running southeast," Noonan said, squinting. "Heading for Philadelphia. Glad to go, seems like. You'll be heading for Philadelphia this fall. Will you be glad to go? If I know Mistress Andelet, you'll be stuck in a school when you get there. What will you study, young Rob? What will you be?"

Robert glanced at him soberly, considered the questions and then suddenly smiled. "Give me time, Mr. Noonan. Until yesterday I had no choice. Maybe I still don't, until I'm grown. I expect I'll do whatever it is that Mrs. Andelet wants me to do. I owe her that. I don't mind saying I was worried about Cass and Lily."

They were late getting back to the manor, but not so late as Maria and her riders, who came in after dark with the carriage lights lit. Watching for them, Robert was on hand to help them out and carry in the boxes and bags, while Noonan drove the carriage around to the barn. John Kendall came from the library with a book in his hand and spoke to Maria, his pale eyes concerned.

"A mishap on the road?"

Maria laughed and swept off her hat. "No mishaps, John. It was only that I was enjoying myself so thoroughly I hated to stop. And you must realize that the children all needed complete wardrobes. In a word, everything." Her eyes fell on Mrs. Brooke, carrying a soundly sleeping Lily and looking tired and wan. "Here," she added, stretching out her arms, "give me the little one, Brooke, and go rest yourself. Come, Robert, Cassie, pick up the boxes and bags and bring them along to your rooms. . . ."

The pink dress, wilted around Cassie's slender form, hung in drooping folds and dragged on the floor. The satin bow had come undone and the ends bounced along behind her as she whisked around picking up packages and loading Robert's outstretched arms.

"Wait," she whispered breathlessly. "Just wait, Robbie, till you see your handsome suit! We all have clothes, wonderful clothes. And shoes! Beautiful shoes, all of us. You never saw such a place as Lynfield."

Robert was grinning, trying not to laugh. She was so excited, her cheeks pink, the dress flopping around her. If his arms hadn't been full he'd have picked her up and swung her in circles and they would have rejoiced together as they always had. "That's *good,* Cass," he said, conscious that everyone was watching, smiling. "I'm glad. I'm glad you saw Lynfield too. Now, come on. You can carry the rest."

"I'll help," John Kendall said, and put his book down. "I haven't seen your schoolroom yet, and I'd like to."

Maria led the way with sleepy Lily on her shoulder, followed closely by Cassie and then Robert with his bulky load. John brought up the rear, several packages in his arms, his gaze on Maria's graceful back.

He had never seen Maria so happy. She had lost everything she valued when her wild, charming brother had died, and this was a miracle. These children had given her a purpose in life, a reason to live; the gift of laughter. Now, if only Geneva could be made to see that. He grimaced at his own soft sentimentality. Geneva Bradford wouldn't give a damn whether the children made Maria happy or not.

"I'll try to ease the shock," he told Maria later that night. "You can sign the papers tomorrow in the magistrate's court at Lynfield, and after I've made sure we've covered all the problems and solved them, I'll take them to Philadelphia and have them recorded. Then I'll visit the Bradfords and tell them."

Maria winced and then laughed wryly. "God help you. I hope your ears don't blister easily. If I weren't such a coward I'd go with you."

John smiled. "I'll take the first blast, my love, and I wish I could take them all. But Geneva won't give up easily."

"There's nothing she can do," Maria said confidently.

"Never say that," John answered. "Particularly about a determined woman."

Chapter 4

Geneva Andelet Bradford was a tall woman with a large bosom and wide hips, and a thick, sturdy waistline that refused to yield more than an inch or two when her maid tightened her corset strings. Geneva's hair was glorious; a golden red with deep waves and frisky curls that sprang out at her temples, curled around the edge of her purple bonnet and gave her plump and petulant face an air of gaiety completely out of character.

Especially now, Maria thought, watching Geneva emerge from John Kendall's carriage, which dipped with her weight on the step as she grasped John's arm. She wore an extremely fashionable gown in lavender cord, with an immense bell skirt, which Maria thought must be held out by at least a dozen petticoats. Geneva's expression was tight and bitter as she looked up at the stone mansion she had once called home. But then, Maria had expected both Geneva's uninvited presence and her obvious anger.

It was mid-July, and John had finished all the legal arrangements and safeguards necessary to make the three

Harmon children wards and heirs of Maria Andelet; arrangements irrevocable by anyone other than Maria. Then he had departed again for Philadelphia to tell Benedict and Geneva Bradford of their new family members. Soon after, John had sent word that Geneva was insisting on accompanying him on his return.

Resigned, Maria left the shelter of the draped window and went to the door, stepping out and embracing her sister-in-law as she came up the steps.

"Why, Geneva! What a delightful surprise."

Geneva kissed the air beside Maria's ear with a loud smack, then grasped the small woman's shoulders in her hands and held her away to look down at her. "I doubt it's a surprise, Maria, nor apt to be delightful for either of us. You must know I've come here to bring you to your senses."

"Do come in," Maria said calmly, guiding Geneva toward the door, "it's much cooler inside. Ah, there you are, Robert! See if you can help Mr. Kendall with Mrs. Bradford's luggage. She will have the room across the hall from mine."

Coming forward in the dark hall, his sun-bleached blond hair gleaming in the dim light, Robert nodded and strode past them to where John was struggling with several large bags.

"Robert?" Geneva exclaimed, looking after him. "Don't tell me that handsome young man is one of your *wards?*" Her pale blue eyes sped back, full of suspicion, and searched Maria's face. "Just how old is he, Maria? You know a young widow must guard her reputation diligently."

Maria nudged Geneva's bulk toward the staircase, like a small tugboat pushing an ocean liner into port. "I am sure," she said, "that you'll want to go up and refresh yourself with a wash in cool water after the hot trip. Then when you're comfortable, we'll have tea and a nice talk in the conservatory. Take your time, Gennie. I'll have a word with John while I wait for you."

"Well!" Geneva snorted, and started up the stairs. "I suppose I must do as you say if I expect to get any answers! You're as stubborn as ever, Maria."

Maria only smiled and turned to the front door again.

"Find Noonan," she said to Robert, "and the two of you can carry up Mrs. Bradford's belongings. Come, John, leave it to them. I'll speak to you alone."

From the turn of the stairs Geneva's round face looked down like a baleful moon. "No matter what plans you make with your lawyer," she said, "you needn't think Benedict and I will agree to them."

As usual, Maria pretended she hadn't heard. Chatting about the hot weather with John, she led him into the drawing room and shut the door.

"Advice, please," she said, and then laughed as he took advantage of the privacy and drew her into his arms. She had missed him, and she returned his kiss with frank enjoyment. They stood for a few moments in each other's arms, kissing again, caressing, murmuring endearments. Then, as their bodies reacted strongly, Maria whispered a warning.

"It's hard to imagine what Geneva would think if she came in," she added, drawing away. "She has already reminded me that a young widow must guard her reputation. Kissing a married man is hardly the way to do that. Now tell me quickly—what must I do to avoid a family quarrel?"

John shook his head. Beneath the softened look of passion his face was tired and hot, the stern lines in his flat cheeks deeper than usual. "I'm not sure you can, my love. Geneva considers that the money Armand left is for your use—your *careful* use—during your lifetime. Then, by some sort of divine right of blood, it belongs to her children—since you had none. She swears Armand told her it would be so before he died."

Maria stared at him thoughtfully. "He never told me."

"Nor me. And, more to the point, his will left everything to you, with no strings attached."

"Then there should be no trouble," Maria said slowly, "except . . . well, as Benedict's wife, Geneva has considerable influence in Philadelphia. I may find myself a social outcast for a time. What I cannot understand is why she came here."

"She thinks she can make you change your mind."

Maria laughed suddenly. "How strange, considering how stubborn she believes me to be. How is it she came alone?"

"Benedict and the children are behind us," John said. "They should be here in an hour or so. Geneva chose to ride with me and hone her arguments on my ears."

"So I'm in for a major family tussle—is that what you're telling me?"

"I am afraid so."

Maria shrugged and turned toward the door. "Come then, we must marshal our defenses for the first charge. I imagine Geneva is waiting, fully armed, in the conservatory."

"You must honor your husband's wishes," Geneva said, "whether you knew of them or not. It has always been understood in our family that Andelet money follows Andelet blood. To give Armand's fortune to unrelated people of the lower class is tantamount to treachery."

Maria was growing impatient. They had been in the conservatory for close to an hour, and except when Geneva was drinking her tea and eating Sallie Fernod's excellent small cakes, she had been repeating those sentiments over and over. Armand's fortune. Andelet money. Wifely duty. The good of the Family. Now, unrelated people of the lower class? Damn the woman for a high-nosed prig!

"Armand has no fortune," she said abruptly. "He is in his grave and the money is mine. I will do with it as I please."

Geneva's sharp intake of breath didn't bother Maria, but John's quick look told her she had spoken rashly. She hurried to add to her statement: "After all, the will was recent, and it left all to me."

"He thought you were pregnant!" Geneva said, red with anger. "You know he did!" She sat staring at Maria venomously, her hair a fiery aureole around her heavy face. "In fact," she added after a moment in which she seemed to puff up to the point of bursting, "it wouldn't surprise me at all to find out you told him you were with child so he would change his will. Deny that if you can!"

"I deny it all," Maria said contemptuously. "Had Armand thought me pregnant he would have also thought me unfaithful, and left me nothing."

Geneva collapsed back into her chair, staring. "Do you mean . . . ?"

"Exactly," Maria said. "Never, after the first few years."

"Ladies," John said hurriedly, "I believe I hear someone in the hall."

"I hope it's Benedict," Geneva said, confused. "I certainly don't understand enough . . . that is . . . Maria, I don't believe you! Armand seemed so much in *love.* . . .*"

There was a tap at the door and John rose to open it. A young girl stood in the hall, and after a startled look, John realized it was Cassie. She was lovely, slim and ethereal in an ankle-length dress of thin white lawn, her tiny waist accented with a narrow blue ribbon, her dark, wavy hair pulled back and tied with a matching ribbon. She looked up at him with eyes like the eyes he loved so well, and smiled.

"Mrs. Brooke sent me to say that another carriage is arriving, Mr. Kendall. Shall I call Robert to help again?"

"By all means," John said hastily, and stepped back to shut the door, to shut off the sight of the child from Geneva, who was staring at her with her mouth open.

"Wait," Geneva said loudly, "don't shut that door, John. Is *that* the older girl . . . what is her name? Cassandra? Good God! What will people *say?* She looks exactly like Maria!"

"It's only the eyes," John said, closing the door firmly. "The shape of the eyes. Odd, yes, but certainly not unique. Many people have eyes of that shape."

"The only two *I've* ever seen," Geneva said ominously, "are Maria and her late, rakish brother Mark." She turned back and looked at Maria, her green eyes glittering. "So that's it! You've been fool enough to take one of your brother's bastards into Armand's house."

"One more word," Maria said dangerously, "and much as I would hate to do it, I'll disown Jacob and Violet—and my entire fortune will go to my three wards."

"You *can't* do that!"

"Yes, she can," John said, angry at last, "and I would advise it if you continue your insults."

Geneva gave him a shocked look and rose to her feet. "Well! I'll talk to Benedict. This puts an entirely different face on the matter. I'm not at all sure we should stay here, especially since we have brought our innocent children." She sailed out, heading for the front door and the sounds of arrival.

Maria looked at John. "I said too much."

"You were sorely tried. What an irritating woman."

"But I intended to keep my temper."

John smiled. "And I mine. We didn't. Shall we go out and greet Benedict and your nephew and niece?"

Maria laughed and took his arm.

Benedict Bradford dominated the wide hall by sheer bulk. He was tall, but hardly tall enough to justify his immense belly and thick thighs, which were hidden somewhat by his knee-length coat, a thin, open garment intended to shed dust. The voice that emanated from his barrel chest alternately squeaked and reverberated hollowly.

"You, Jacob"—this to a dark young man as tall as Benedict but slim as a reed—"you can carry my valise. Don't drop it. And you—Robert, is it? You and Noonan can take Violet's trunk. It's full of gewgaws, light as a feather."

Off to one side a thin, sharp-featured girl with Geneva's red-gold hair and a pair of pretty green eyes giggled nervously, her fascinated gaze on Robert's broad shoulders and handsome face. Taking a protective stance beside the girl, Geneva scowled.

"If you will step over here and listen to me, Benedict, you may save yourself some trouble. Why transport the baggage upstairs if we aren't going to stay?"

Benedict's heavy face took on a patchy red flush and his voice rose to an irritated screech. "Now, don't start that! We *are* going to stay, Geneva. I didn't come all this way to turn around and start back because you can't get along with Maria! I told you to mind your tongue!"

"Shhh, now," Maria said kindly, coming forward. "It's all right, Benedict. A little disagreement, soon forgotten. Come in, come in, all of you. We are having tea and cakes in the conservatory, and I expect you can use a cup." She took Benedict's arm and smiled up at him, coaxing him along. He relaxed at once and went, grinning foolishly, rather like a large, overfed and friendly old dog that has been promised a bone.

Off to the side Cassie hesitated, and then, catching Maria's eye and the almost imperceptible shake of her head, she melted away toward the drawing room, warning Robert with a glance of her own. The rest went along to the conservatory, the slim, dark boy, the red-haired girl, and, with an impatient sigh, Geneva.

The argument, with only Geneva to keep it going, died before the evening was out. But the Bradfords stayed for five days, and by the third day Jacob was always with Cassie or Robert, either talking and laughing or lounging about and listening during their lessons. Even though it was summer, Maria had sent for a tutor, a young man named Arthur Masefield, who taught them all, even Lily, with great enthusiasm.

"It won't help, you know," Geneva told Maria one night at the dinner table. None of the young were present except Jacob, who was considered old enough to dine with adults, so she was free to speak of the others. "No matter how educated they become, they will never have the manners. That's a matter of birth."

"I believe you," Maria said mildly. "Violet's manners are very like yours. Her disposition too."

Jacob looked up. It took time to realize that Jacob was quite good-looking. His features were finely drawn, his face high-boned and slender, his dark eyes large and soft. His black hair was straight, with a shining elflock that fell across a high and intelligent forehead. Right now his troubled gaze was fixed on his mother.

"Cassie," he said, "is much more gracious than Violet. She is never rude, even when Violet tries to provoke her. And Robert is kind to everyone. Violet thinks he's wonderful. You should get to know them better, Mother."

Geneva opened her mouth, but Maria was ahead of her. "How nice of you, Jacob, to compliment my young wards. They speak well of you too. Cassie was quite impressed with your poetry, especially a sonnet she showed me, titled 'To a White Rose.' "

Jacob blushed with pleasure. "Ac-Actually, I wrote it for her. I think she's rather like one, you know. She has such a delicate air."

"Oh, for God's sake," Benedict said, disgusted. "Poetry! Be a man, Jacob. Not a blithering poet."

Jacob stared at his plate and said nothing. Benedict watched him a moment and then turned to Maria.

"Tomorrow will be our last day, my dear. Would it be possible to take Jacob over to the furnace and forge? He's never been introduced to the family enterprise."

Maria smiled. "Of course. I've reason to go myself. John wants me to meet and talk with the new overseer he hired and see if I approve of him. We'll make it a family visit."

The next day was pleasant, with a steady breeze and a cloudless sky. The weather, the welcome prospect of being rid of the Bradfords on the very next day, and a belated sense of hospitality combined to make Maria turn the outing into a full-fledged holiday. She had Sallie Fernod make up two huge picnic baskets, fill several jugs with cold apple cider and pack them in a box with ice and straw. These supplies all went in the wagon, along with a load of soft hay.

"There is transportation for all of you under thirty years of age," Maria said as Noonan brought the wagon around. She laughed as Masefield, the tutor, grabbed small Lily and climbed up beside Noonan on the driver's seat. Arthur Masefield had become a favorite with the whole family. Twenty-four, slim and blond, he was always pleasant and full of good humor. Lily hugged him, delighted to have the seat of honor.

"Now," Masefield said, grinning down at Jacob, Robert, Violet, and Cassie, "the rest of you can have the hay and the sneezes."

"It won't bother me," Robert said, vaulting in and turning to help the others up, "nor Cassie either."

"Nor me," Violet shrieked, and grabbed his hand. "I *love* hayrides! Pull me up, Robert. Oh! Oh, my! You're so *strong!*" She fell against him as he set her on her feet in the deep hay, and began giggling. Righting her again, he turned away and helped Cassie and Jacob in. Still giggling, Violet waited until everyone sat down and then snuggled into a place beside Robert, spreading her pink, lacy skirt out and leaning back with a satisfied sigh. "Oooh, *isn't* this fun!"

Cassie's huge eyes flicked to Robert's pained expression and then away, her lips tight and quivering, hiding a grin. Robert couldn't abide silly, giggling girls, though he'd put up with one forever rather than hurt her feelings. And anyway, Violet was Jacob's sister, and they were both fond of him. Turning, Cass stared wide-eyed at Maria, who was wearing a black riding habit with a white silk shirt and black boots. Beneath the folds of the long, gathered skirt were black and white striped pantalets, the newest fashion for riding and far more comfortable than the former bulky petticoats. Maria was mounted sidesaddle on a beautiful black mare and looked, Cassie thought, like a real queen. She was so perfect, and a wonderful rider besides, bringing her mount under control with no trouble at all. Cass gave her an adoring smile and Maria smiled back, waving as she and Mr. Kendall rode on to the head of the column. Behind the riders was the light surrey, with Benedict driving and Geneva beside him, and the wagon with food and young people brought up the rear. Cassie leaned back in the soft hay, satisfied. Where Maria Andelet led, she would follow.

They visited the shallow mines on the steep slopes near Durmont Creek, then proceeded to the smoking charcoal domes, where everyone dismounted or climbed down to look around and have a cup of cider. Jacob studied the domes and asked how many years it would be before the forests were destroyed by the need for fuel for the furnace.

"A shame," he said to John, "how we use the trees and never replant."

"That would mean another crew," Benedict broke in, "and more expense. If you had to raise the price of your iron to take care of that, you'd lose your customers. Be sensible, Jacob."

Jacob was silent. How many times he held his tongue rather than argue with his father, Maria thought. She was pleased with the boy for taking an interest in the problems. She had thought he'd be completely indifferent. She had always liked Jacob, and now she was in sympathy with him. He would never satisfy Benedict, for he would never be a big, bluff, and outgoing man. He would be an artist or writer. Perhaps a poet. His father would hate that. But couldn't the Bradfords and Andelets afford an artist or two?

She smiled, her expression so sympathetic and sweet that Benedict, glancing her way, felt an unaccustomed affection.

As the group rode into the large area around the furnace and forge, men began to gather. There was an almost feudal atmosphere on the Pennsylvania iron plantations. On the one hand there was the utter dependence of the workers on the owners; on the other, the owners took unusually good care of their skilled labor, for it was both expensive and time consuming to train new men. Mutual cooperation brought a family feeling to both sides. Now, dismounting to tie their horses at the corral, Maria and John Kendall were quickly surrounded by workers.

"Ten tons to a round this week, Mistress!"

"Three barges to the Schuylkill tomorrow!"

Maria laughed and called out praise for their efforts, and then John reached into the crowd and grabbed the shoulder of the new overseer, Payne Regan, and presented him to her. Maria turned, still laughing, and put out her hand.

"How do you do, Mr. Regan. It certainly sounds as if you've been pushing Eagle Forge to new heights. That's quite a record for a week."

Payne Regan took the hand, for once at a loss for words. His steel-gray eyes swept Maria's face and figure with disbelief.

"Thank you, Mistress. I'll do better."

Maria's laughter died away as he spoke, though she kept a smile. His gaze was so intense it made her uncomfortable, yet she thought it mostly surprise, not admiration. Undoubtedly, the new overseer had expected an elderly widow with perhaps little interest in the actual workings of the forge.

"Mr. Regan," she said, deciding at once to make the situation plain, "if you have problems while Mr. Kendall is away, don't try to solve them yourself. Come to me at the manor. I know the business well."

Regan's eyes flickered. "So do I, madam. I expect no trouble."

Stepping between them casually, John took Maria's arm. "We're bringing our visitors to the bridge house first," he told Regan, "but they'll want to see it all."

"Yes, sir." Regan said it automatically and turned, leading the way. The gathered men moved back and then scattered to their duties.

"Now, by Jove, you'll see something, Jacob." Puffing along behind Kendall and Regan, Benedict sounded breathless but gratified. "This is hard work, I am sure, but satisfying. Just listen to the roar of that furnace."

Jacob nodded. He held back politely as the others started up the outside steps of the bridge house, the ladies first, then the men, and last of all the children. On the platform inside men were readying the next charge of ore, charcoal, and limestone. The ladies stood well back and kept the children with them, though Benedict drew Jacob forward as John Kendall explained what the men were doing. John stepped back to let them watch as the men opened the trunnel head. Instantaneous, fiery heat swept them, the brilliant, orange-red glare like looking at the sun. Jacob gasped and retreated, shielding his eyes with one hand and peering with awe at the open trunnel. His father laughed and struck him a friendly blow on the shoulder.

"The red heart of the business," he shouted over the roar, nodding at the glare. "Impressive, isn't it?"

Maria was watching, suddenly concerned. Jacob's eyes held shock, his face glistening with perspiration. But he managed to mouth agreement. "Yes, it is. Very impressive. Like . . . a door into hell."

Only Maria read the last phrase on his pale lips. Benedict had seemed satisfied with the agreement and turned back, watching the men dump the load. Maria hurriedly sent the children out to clatter down the steps and then went to take Jacob's arm, conscious all at once that Payne Regan was aware of every move she made.

"It's too hot in here," she complained, ignoring Regan and whispering to Jacob. "Let's wait for them below."

Outside, Jacob gave her a grateful look. "I could never manage a place like this," he said, going slowly down the steps. "I'd hate it. I hope you're not counting on me. Mother says you are."

"Nonsense," Maria said cheerfully. "I can run it perfectly well myself, by hiring men and giving instructions. I'm hoping you'll do something entirely different—something wonderful. Every family should have at least one artist or poet—don't you think so?"

Jacob groaned. "I'm not good enough, Aunt Maria. I couldn't possibly—"

"Indeed you could! The poems you've written already show great talent, and you're only seventeen. Don't give up so easily."

The men were descending the steps behind them, and Jacob, glancing warily over his shoulder at his father, was silent. Maria understood, and, slowing, she waited for them.

"I was faint with the heat," she told Benedict as he came up, "and Jacob was nice enough to bring me out into the air. The forge will be more interesting, don't you think?"

Benedict laughed indulgently. "More comfortable, at any rate. No woman should have to bother with hard and dangerous work, my dear. You must begin thinking of a man who can take over as ironmaster. Someone of the family, honest and loyal . . ." He went on talking as they strolled along, the July sun beating down, the roar of the furnace and the swirling dust lessening as they neared the water. Robert had already led the other youngsters ahead, with Violet hanging leechlike on his arm. Cassie was taking Lily along the creek bank, collecting pretty stones. Here, the heavy, thumping pound of the hammers and the creaking noise of the waterwheels sounded almost pleasant in contrast to the furnace.

In the forge Maria watched Jacob carefully as he looked around and listened to his father trying to explain what was going on. Masefield had gathered the children and lined them up to listen and learn. When Maria noticed Jacob was also showing a mild interest, she left him with the others and went outside for a breath of fresh air.

The water of the creek was always cold, even in the middle of summer, and the air on the narrow bridge outside the forge was cool. Maria stood for a moment breathing it in, and then, taking off her snug riding cap, shaking back her hair, she rested her arms on the wooden railing and watched the rolling, burbling, hastening water beneath.

"Excuse me, Mistress."

She straightened and turned, looking with surprise at Payne Regan. "Yes?"

"Young Bradford will never make an ironmaster, Mistress. He's afraid of the furnace." Regan spoke in a rush of words, pouring them out faster as he saw her eyes grow cool.

"Jacob has his own talents, Mr. Regan. Not everyone is suited to becoming an ironmaster."

He moved closer to her, slowly; almost reluctantly, as if drawn against his will. He leaned one arm on the railing and watched the water as he spoke again. "There are plenty of iron plantations with a foreman doing the ordering and selling, and an ironmaster who does nothing but hunt and drink."

"Not this one," Maria said with spirit. "I'd sell it first. A family business prospers best in the hands of those who prosper from it. I'll keep my eye on it myself."

Still staring at the water, Regan let out his breath. "So, you intend to keep on. I've never taken orders from a woman."

Maria drew herself up. "I'll give you a chance to see if you like it," she said evenly. "My first order is that when you speak to me, you will confine your remarks to business. Now, if you have suddenly discovered that you don't like taking my orders, you may leave Eagle Forge immediately."

He straightened, a muscle rippling along his jaw, his eyes narrowing. "I'll not be leaving," he said abruptly. "Kendall hired me, and I like it here." He caught the sudden flare of irritation in her eyes and smiled sourly. "Sorry, Mistress. I didn't set out to be rude. I just didn't have you pegged as a bossy female. You sure don't look like one."

"That is a personal remark," Maria said coldly. "One more, and you'll have no choice about leaving."

His jaw hard, Regan gave her a scornful bow. "As you say, *Iron* Mistress."

"Precisely. I am the ironmistress, and the furnace and forge will be run as I say. I won't interfere with your part of it as long as things run smoothly here. But I will handle the ordering and selling. I know the markets."

Beside him the door opened and Cassie slipped out, her eyes wide as she noticed Maria's angry expression. She went

55

to her quickly and took her hand. "Mr. Kendall sent me to find you," she said. "We're ready for the picnic."

"Of course," Maria said, relieved. The small, lovely girl looking up at her drove away the irritation she had felt with Payne Regan. She turned her back on him and allowed Cassie to lead her inside again and out by the other door. The plan was to walk down to the Schuylkill River and dine al fresco on the shore. It would be cool there, and quiet, away from the roar of the furnace. With Cassie's hand in hers, she found herself looking forward to it with pleasure.

Chapter 5

❦

"I don't much like the new foreman, Johnny. He's too brash."

John Kendall looked over at Maria and smiled. After the picnic they had chosen to ride home along Durmont Creek and across the home fields, a much longer ride but very pleasant. Benedict and Geneva had preferred to take the shorter way along the road and stay with the youngsters in the hay wagon. Now, alone with Maria, riding along the murmuring creek in the shade of tall buttonwood trees, John was too contented to worry about Payne Regan.

"Is he? I thought you'd be impressed with his production. He's one of the best ironmen in the commonwealth."

"That may be so," Maria said, frowning, "but he's not the ironmaster here, nor will he be. I think he believed we'd be bringing Jacob in to run the place. He as much as suggested that *he* take over the ordering and selling, and leave the hunting and drinking to Jacob." She glanced across at John and smiled, her frown smoothing away. "Jacob would find those pursuits as distasteful as running the furnace, I fear."

John laughed. "I'm sure he would. I imagine you set

Regan straight as to who was boss at Eagle Forge, didn't you?"

For a moment Maria's carefully ladylike expression slipped and her temper showed. "Yes. He said he'd never taken orders from a woman before, and I told him if he objected to taking mine he could leave now. I certainly hope he knew I meant it." She settled herself more firmly in the saddle and spurred ahead to stop the conversation. She was uncomfortably conscious of having sounded like a shrew.

When they could see the chimneys of the manor they turned west, climbing the long, sloping bank of the creek, up into the sun and the long shadows of late afternoon. They relaxed as they rode through meadows full of fat white sheep, past the brilliant blue fields of flax in full bloom. As they drew near to the great house they could see Sallie Fernod moving with slow dignity through the kitchen garden, the sun dazzling on her brightly colored turban and ebony cheeks.

"I've always wondered," John said lazily, "where you found such an exotic servant. She wasn't a slave, was she?"

Maria chuckled. "With you, my love, I can be truthful. I told Armand that Sallie was a faithful old family retainer of the Maryland Gerards, for Armand was very conventional. But Sallie's past is much more interesting than that. My brother Mark found her working in a Baltimore tavern and was so impressed by her cooking and amazing command of languages that he brought her to me. Until I married Armand she was my only servant, and my only friend."

John looked across at her curiously, matching his horse's gait to hers. "You are still friends, aren't you? Sometimes I've seen you talking together alone, and the way you look—"

Laughing, Maria threw up a hand. "I see I can hide nothing from you, Johnny. Sallie Fernod is a rare woman, and yes, we are still friends. But Sallie wants to continue her role as a servant; she likes the obscurity. I am more than happy to oblige by keeping her on. She is one of the very few people in the world whom I trust."

John kept on looking at Maria's gaily amused face, her quick little gestures as she talked. His pale eyes grew thoughtful. "Perhaps," he said gently, "Sallie's past is more interesting than you have admitted to me. It sounds very much as if she is hiding from something or someone."

Maria's gray-green eyes widened. "Why, John! What a romantic idea! Perhaps she is. Perhaps somewhere a cruel husband, or a jealous lover, is still searching for her after all these years."

They were nearly there; Sallie Fernod had turned to watch them ride up, and John merely laughed at Maria's teasing and let it go. He told himself it was only his insatiable curiosity about Maria and Maria's life that had made him ask, for surely it didn't matter to him what Sallie might have done. He was keeping enough hidden in his own life to make him sympathetic to anyone else with the same problem.

That evening at dinner Maria tried to hold down the high spirits she felt when she thought of the Bradfords leaving in the morning. But her relief made her happy, and she was her most gracious, complimenting Geneva on her fine color after a day in the open; and later, as they finished dessert, nodding agreeably as Benedict expounded on the fortunes to be made by young men entering the iron business.

"I foresee the day," Benedict ended happily, looking meaningly at Jacob, "when there will be two furnaces and two forges on this land. I noticed a good site on the creek today as we rode down to the Schuylkill River. Imagine, Maria, how the money would roll in if you doubled your production."

"There's not enough woodland, Father." Jacob turned red as everyone looked toward him. "It's true," he added, glancing hopefully at Maria, "isn't it, Aunt Maria? You'd run out of trees for charcoal before you paid back the cost of a new foundry."

"That's perfectly true," Maria began, amazed by his perception, and was silenced by Benedict's irritated roar.

"By God, Jacob, I do believe you'd use any argument, no matter how stupid, to keep from working! What in hell do you intend to do with your life?"

"Benedict!" Geneva was rising from the table, her mouth twisted angrily. "Leave Jacob alone. Perhaps our son realizes something you evidently can't see—Maria has no intention of allowing him to take over Eagle Forge, now or ever."

Flinging himself back in his chair, Benedict glared at his wife. "And perhaps Maria realizes something *you* can't see, Geneva. You've coddled and petted the boy until he hasn't the courage to be an ironmaster. He's afraid of the furnace, for God's sake!" He turned, shoving his heavy face at Jacob. "Admit it! I saw the look on your face today. You're afraid!"

"So am I," John Kendall broke in calmly. "And so are most of the men. Only a few of them are suited to be bridgemen. The others who try soon give up." He smiled at Jacob, who looked pale, frozen with shame. "Frankly, it's my opinion that only a stolid man with no imagination can face that roar and glare without fear."

A shudder ran over Jacob's slim body. "I fear it," he said slowly, "I admit that. Father was right. But even if I didn't I wouldn't want to be an ironmaster. I want to write."

"Wonderful!" Maria burst forth. "That's exactly what you should do, Jacob. You have a brilliant mind and wonderful imagination. What a blessing to be so well suited for it!"

"And how convenient for you, Maria," Geneva said grimly, "not to have to share the business Armand left. I promise you will regret pushing my son aside."

"Be quiet," Benedict said, and stood up. "Be done with your quarreling, Geneva. I know my temper started it, but vengeful feelings have no place in a family. Come along, Jacob. Whatever your future, you need rest tonight. We leave early tomorrow."

Maria rose silently to see them to the stairs, and John followed her, quiet and unobtrusive as she wished them a good night. Sounds of voices and a hysterical giggling came up the hall from the conservatory, where Arthur Masefield presided over dinner for Robert, Violet, and Cassie. Geneva paused on the steps, listening.

"I can tell by the sound of her voice that Violet is overtired," she said stiffly. "Please send her up to me."

"Of course," Maria agreed. "Right away, Geneva." She smiled at John as she turned toward the hall, almost as happy to be getting rid of Violet as her parents.

Later, having brandy together in the drawing room—for

with the Bradfords in the house, John slept on a cot in the downstairs study—Maria and John discussed again her opinion of Payne Regan.

"If he makes you uncomfortable," John said, "you can do without the extra production. Heaven knows you don't need the money."

"But the workers also make more money when production goes up," Maria pointed out. "The pay goes by the ton. We'll try him, John. I'd hate to fire a good overseer just for a lack of manners."

John frowned. "There are men, my love, who can't accept a woman employer. If Regan is like that, he may work against you behind your back, even try to undermine your authority. That could make more trouble than you want."

Maria shook her head, smiling. "My men are loyal to me, John. You know that."

Warmed by the brandy, seduced by her smile, John laughed and relaxed. "This one is," he said, raising his glass, "and ever will be. Blast the Bradfords! I need to be in your bed again. I'm starved for you, darling."

Maria's gaze softened into a look of love. John wasn't the only one suffering from deprivation. She wanted him more every day, more than she had thought she could ever want any man. "I believe," she said carefully, "that I heard Robert and Cassie go up to bed a few minutes ago. No doubt Arthur will soon follow."

He looked at her, startled, and then laughed again, unsteadily. "No teasing, Maria. Even I know we can't take a chance with a gossip like Geneva in the house."

"She's dead to the world by now, after all the open air and walking." Maria rose, draining her glass and setting it down. "She'll never know what time I came up to my room." She turned to him as he stood up, and put her arms around his neck. "Your cot will hold us both, Johnny."

"No," he murmured, even as he kissed her hungrily. "We can't risk it. This house is full of people who might notice you wandering around in the wee hours and mention it. The slightest hint of anything clandestine will set Geneva off. And you know what that would mean."

Maria did know. John's wife Alice had been a victim of paralytic fever, and an invalid for many years, cared for by a nurse in constant attendance. But Alice's mind was clear, and she had friends who visited her. She would be badly hurt by gossip, and Maria would avoid that at any cost. She and John were safe now only because it was logical that John, the family lawyer and a close friend for years, would help and advise her after Armand's death. When they became lovers they were careful to keep up the appearance of simple friendship. But Geneva would be delighted to make more of it, and would, if she discovered any possible excuse to point a finger.

"I know you're right," Maria mourned, burrowing into his neck, breathing him in, "but, oh, how I'd like to have you next to me right now."

"Shhh, my little love. Don't say such things. You're torturing us both." Shaken by passion, John pulled away. "Go to bed before I weaken. They'll be gone tomorrow."

The Bradford carriage was brought around before daybreak the next morning, for Benedict liked to travel in the cool morning hours. Geneva, up early and ready to leave, had returned to her arguments.

"I hope you will come to a sensible decision soon, Maria," she was saying as they came down the stairs, Geneva in her traveling suit and bonnet, Maria still in her boudoir gown and robe. "I suppose I do understand your feelings. You were lonely, and these orphans appealed to your charitable nature. But really, a small dowry for each girl and a plain country education for Robert is all you could be expected to provide. Take it from me, you will only make them confused and unhappy if you elevate them above their natural station in life."

"Excuse me a moment, Gennie. I asked Sallie to make up a luncheon basket for you, let me see if she has it ready." Maria went rapidly down the hall and into the kitchen, making a perfectly horrible face at Sallie Fernod, who threw back her head and laughed soundlessly, big white teeth shining.

"The basket, madam," Sallie said loudly, and handed it to her. "All Mistress Bradford's favorites, just as you asked."

Geneva was smiling as Maria came back and handed Jacob the basket, kissing his cheek and turning to hug

Violet, who was sleepy and wan, disappointed by Robert's absence.

"You look very pretty in that green suit, Violet," Maria said kindly. "And Geneva, so nice you could all come for the visit. Do tell Benedict I appreciated his advice, and Jacob, I loved your poems. But don't let me keep you when Benedict is waiting in the carriage. He may become impatient."

She was turning away from the door and the sound of departing wheels outside when she saw the door to the study open and John Kendall peer out. He had evidently heard the sounds of the Bradfords leaving, for he had thrown on a pair of trousers and was buttoning a shirt; preparing, Maria was sure, to come out and make his farewells. She glanced around, seeing no one, hearing no sounds of others rising. They were alone. She laughed softly and ran, lightfooted, into his arms.

"Maria!" In one of his smooth, coordinated movements, John swung her inside the study and closed the door, holding her tightly. "My reckless darling! Someone could have seen you running to me in your bedgown."

"Who cares," she whispered, moving sensuously against him. "No one in this house now would betray me. The enemy has retreated." She hardly knew what she was saying, for the trousers he had pulled on were thin, the shirt half buttoned, and his scent and hard heat were making her want him more every moment. "Kiss me, Johnny, please. *Take* me . . ."

Afire, he covered her mouth with his, mauling her lips, his tongue thrusting inside again and again, his hands running over her breasts and scantily clad body hungrily, grasping her soft buttocks beneath the silk and lifting her to the thrust of his aroused loins. Maria moaned, a small, guttural noise deep in her throat. Her hands went purposefully to his narrow waist, her fingers fastening into the top of his trousers and trying to push them down. Failing, she sank to the soft rug, pulling him with her, her hands suddenly busy with the hidden buttons of his bulging fly. Her loose hair was tossed and tangled around her flushed, intent face, her mouth pink and bruised from his kiss. He had never wanted her more than he did at this moment, yet . . . on the floor?

"Maria . . ." Aching with passion, confused, it was in John's mind to at least get her to the cot. But even as he spoke his trousers sprang open and her hands grasped him, stroked him, held him between her kneading palms. He gasped, struggling for breath, and she looked up.

"Lie back," she said huskily, "and we'll manage very well."

With a deep shudder of pleasure, he lay back and lifted her over him, feeling her slender legs embrace his hips, feeling her lower herself so the hot, wet velvet of her inner flesh embraced his quivering shaft. Trembling herself, she bent down and kissed him, her tongue hot and busy. He reached beneath the flowing robe and gown and found her silky thighs, her small waist, the firm breasts and hardened nipples. He held the breasts in his palms and played with them as she moved up and down, discovering that this way he had more control, more time for the slow building of passion. He relaxed into a sea of sensuality, adoring her rhythmic body with gentle hands. "I love you," he murmured, his eyes shut. "I love this. It's heavenly . . ."

Gasping, she kissed him again, wildly, and he licked the panting, burrowing lips, soothing them with his tongue. She moved faster and faster, and then she trembled and cried out.

"Johnny, I—" Her small, curved body arched and he felt her flesh begin the throbbing, beating spasms of orgasm, squeezing down on him, rippling hard along his turgid length.

"Oh, God," he said, choked. "Oh, *God.*" His climax shook his whole body, deadening every other sense, until it seemed he was no longer lying on a rug but floating on a cloud. She was sprawled over him, her hot face buried in his neck, her fragrant hair strewn on his chest in disarray.

"Johnny," she whispered. "My darling Johnny. Never leave me."

"Never, my little love, never. You are forever mine."

Later, hearing the cheerful sounds of the children coming down for breakfast, the buoyant voice of Arthur Masefield, Maria waited until John reported them all at the kitchen table and engrossed in Sallie Fernod's fried ham and apples. Then she left the study, going rapidly up the front staircase and into her room, seeing no one but Adah, dusting in the hall. Adah, who was not a maid who saw her mistress when her mistress didn't want to be seen, calmly looked right through her.

Bathed and dressed, Maria went down for a late breakfast, alone. Sallie Fernod, moving steadily back and forth as she cleaned up from breakfast and started preparations for lunch, put a bowl of strawberries and cream in front of her and poured two cups of tea. She sat down with her for a moment, huge and thoughtful, her brown eyes studying Maria's relaxed and happy face.

"The new man was here this morning," she said abruptly. "The man named Regan. He came for Mr. Kendall, and I sent him off, with a promise that I'd tell Mr. Kendall when he woke up. He wouldn't say why it was so important, but he didn't like it when I refused to let him in. I think if he'd known which room to go to, he would have defied me."

Maria drew in her breath sharply. "He'd better not!"

Sallie's wide mouth flattened in a smile. "You know he'd never get by me to disturb you and your lover. But he may try. He thinks he's a bull. Why has he been brought here?"

"John says he's an excellent foreman who will greatly increase our production. Actually, he already has."

Sallie shrugged and rose, taking her cup with her as she went across the room, moving in her odd, floating way, her feet unseen beneath her wide skirt, soundless on the cool flagstones. She stood by the window, looking out as she finished her tea.

"He is the kind of man who makes a bad slavemaster," she said finally. "His heart is empty except for anger and pride. He will bring trouble along with the extra pigs of iron."

Turning in her chair, Maria stared at the broad, impervious back. "What kind of trouble?"

Peering around at her, Sallie Fernod laughed, the sound rolling from her massive chest, rich and melodious. "What? Don't tell me my little Maria still believes I can read the future. As I have told you many times, I can only read hearts. Your new man is trouble on two legs. Who knows what he will do?"

The sound of Sallie Fernod's laughter came faintly to the ears of two students in the schoolroom above. Cassie looked across the long table at Robert and smiled, knowing as he smiled back that he too was thinking of that June twilight when they had first come here in the wagon with Noonan, and Sallie's laughter had warmed their cold, frightened hearts.

Robert went back to the algebra problems he was solving, and Cassie took out a new, unsullied copybook and picked up her pen, ready to continue practicing the neat, graceful handwriting Arthur Masefield favored. But she still went on thinking of that night and the days that followed it. The wonder of enough food, new clothes, and kindness. Everything had changed, she thought, and especially Robert. Vaguely, she understood that the biggest burden had been on his shoulders, and Aunt Maria had lifted it off. Robert had taken his responsibilities hard. He had always been so serious, so tired from working from dawn to dark. He still worked hard, but now he had time off, he had things to do that he liked, he had lessons. Some day, Aunt Maria said, Robert would be an important man. Cass sighed with contentment. It was all wonderful to her. Looking back at those poor, sad days was like remembering another world.

"Very good, Cassie. Extremely neat. I see no mistakes at all. Not even a blot."

She started, for she hadn't seen Mr. Masefield move from his place at the end of the table. She looked down at the pen in her hand and the blank sheet of paper in her copybook. Blushing, she glanced up at the slim, boyish tutor, seeing the teasing humor in his clear hazel eyes.

"I'm sorry, Mr. Masefield. I was thinking . . ." She paused. Mr. Masefield liked his pupils to use the right words at all times. "No, I wasn't thinking, exactly. I was remembering the past, and so I forgot the present. I will do two pages to make up for it." She glanced across the table and found Robert looking at her approvingly. "That is," she amended, giving him her shy smile, "if Robbie will give me another riding lesson this afternoon."

Both Arthur and Robert laughed. "Take note," Arthur said to Robert, "of how a female of tender years learns to bargain and turn a situation to her advantage. That just may be the most important lesson of all."

"For which one?" Robert asked, winking at Cassie. "For the female or the male?"

Arthur laughed again, surprised. "An excellent question, Robert. Perhaps for both, but probably more important for the female, who must hold her own with domineering males."

"Remember that, Cass." Robert reached over and tousled Cassie's hair affectionately. "Always look for the bargaining point. Get those pages done, and I'll saddle two horses."

Chapter 6

The last week in August, when Robert was working in the flax fields with the men hired to cut and bundle the stalks for drying and then retting, to loosen the fiber, Noonan came out to tell him he was wanted at the house.

"Mrs. Andelet said you were to come to the study there at the back of the house. She's waiting for you."

Hot, sweaty, his loose cotton work clothes furred with flecks of leaves and chopped stalks, Robert wiped his flushed face with a sleeve and stared at Noonan. "Anything wrong?"

Noonan shook his head. "Nothing wrong, lad. She said take your time."

Robert took the time to brush himself off and wash his face and hands at the backyard pump. Then, running his damp fingers through tawny hair streaked pale gold by the summer sun, he went in and through the back hall to the study.

Maria had gradually put away her mourning black, and today was wearing a muslin gown in a soft lilac, cut with short sleeves and a low lace-trimmed neckline for coolness.

68

Seated at her desk near the back window, she had hiked up her skirt and the myriad of bulky petticoats to let the breeze cool her slender legs, hidden beneath the desktop. She had watched Robert come up from the field and thought about how much he had changed during the not quite three months since coming here. He had passed his fifteenth birthday a week ago, but because of his height and muscular development, he looked at least seventeen. Broad-shouldered and gaining weight rapidly, he promised to be a very large man. She looked up and smiled as he came in.

"I have some news for you, Robbie. Today, when I went through the letters Mr. Kendall brought me from Philadelphia, I found you'd been accepted by the preparatory school Arthur recommended for you. You leave tomorrow for Cambridge, Massachusetts."

He had looked seventeen only an instant ago; now his youth showed in his startled blue eyes.

"I'm *leaving?*"

Maria nodded. "Yes. I've put it off as long as I can. I enjoy having you here, and I know how Cassie is going to feel when she finds out you're going away, but I want you to be well-educated. Arthur will be going with you, dear, for he's going to teach in the school. He says you'll have no trouble keeping up with the other students, and within a year or so he believes you'll be ready for Harvard, which is an excellent little college there."

Robert stared, shaken but not unwilling. "I am to *live* in Massachusetts?" To Robert, who still hadn't journeyed even to Lynfield, the state called Massachusetts was as foreign as England or France.

Maria relaxed and smiled. She had heard the note of excitement. He wasn't frightened or upset, thank heaven. "Most of the next few years you'll be staying there," she answered, "but on holidays and vacations you'll be with us." She hesitated and then went on quickly. "You must remember to remind Cassie of holidays when you tell her you're going, so she won't feel so bereft. She will miss you."

"I'll miss her too. And Lily." Robert's excitement suddenly dimmed. "That part will seem very strange, Aunt Maria. I've always looked after them."

"You mustn't worry about Cassie or Lily," Maria said

sharply. "I'll take good care of them both. And Arthur will look after you—I've told him you must have everything you need."

Robert reddened but his head stayed high. "I wasn't worrying. I see what you do for them and I am grateful. Cassie and I will do whatever you think we should do."

Maria eased into a smile. Robert really was a fine young man, she thought. His naturally pleasant manner and handsome appearance would stand him in good stead later, when he entered the business world.

"I am sure," she said, "that when you are grown I will be very, very proud of all three of you. I intend to see that Cassie and Lily are also educated for their place in society. And now, why don't you find your sisters and break the news? I expect you can comfort Cassie better than I can."

In spite of her careless assurance, Maria felt guilty as Robert left. John Kendall had argued weeks ago that Robert and Cassie should be told of the coming separation. But Maria was sure she knew how Cassie would react.

"She'll mourn until she makes herself sick," she had told John one night. "This way it'll be over and he'll be gone before she has a chance to grieve."

"But is it necessary?" John had asked. "There are good schools in Philadelphia, and the university is there. Why Massachusetts?"

"The schools are better," Maria had said. "And Robert needs the experience of being on his own."

Part of the guilt Maria felt now was because she hadn't been honest with John. She should have admitted she simply wanted Robert out of the house for a time. Her attempts to win Cassie over had won her warm affection, but the child's primary loyalty still went to Robert and Lily. Especially Robert. Cassie looked up to Robert as to a hero. It would be a blow to the child to lose him even for a few months, but Maria had hardened her heart and told herself it was for Cassie's own good. And so, even while Maria insisted to John that Robert needed to be on his own, she was fully aware she was thinking only of herself. She wanted Cassie's whole heart and whole attention, and she would never have either with Robert around.

Cassie was outside with a willow switch, running back and forth in the huge kitchen garden, helping Sallie Fernod shoo the geese out of the ripe raspberries. Finding her there, Robert laughed at her ineffectual blows on the broad white backs of the geese, then grabbed a rake and swatted the hissing, belligerent gander. Waving the rake at the rest, he drove them all, flapping and complaining, down to the nearest stream.

"Well done," Sallie said in her deep voice. Immense in her voluminous black dress and tall, flowered turban, she wiped her gleaming ebony face with a clean kerchief and lavished her big smile on both of them. "I can't move fast enough in this weather to chase a turtle. You've earned raspberry cobbler for dessert."

Robert grinned. "That's a grand reward, Sallie. I'll stop by the springhouse and bring up some cream. Come on, Cass, walk with me. I've something important to tell you."

Cassie looked cool. Her dark hair was braided and pinned up and tied with a big white bow. Her ruffled and tiered blue gingham dress was airy and light around her ankles, and the short, embroidered apron she wore was the thinnest of thin white muslin. But standing there, still holding the switch, she was pale and quiet.

"I already know," she said as Sallie left them. Her voice was low and uneven. "You're going away. Mr. Masefield told me an hour ago. "It's . . . all right, Robbie. Lily and I will be fine, and you'll have Mr. Masefield and—and he said we'd all be together part of the time."

"Yes. As often as we can." Putting an arm around her shoulders, Robert drew her down the path to the spring. The thought of them being separated tightened his throat alarmingly. He made himself smile. "You'll be studying too, you know, in Philadelphia. Make me proud of you, Cass."

"I'll try." She looked up at him, and his heart dropped as he saw her huge gray-green eyes fogged with thick tears. "Robbie—why didn't Aunt Maria tell me herself? Doesn't she trust me?"

Robert swallowed. "Why, of course she trusts you! Who wouldn't? But she knew you wouldn't like it, Cass. She told me I could comfort you better than she could. It's probably

71

just that she loves you so much she can't bear to be the one who hurts you."

"But she *was,* Robbie. Don't you see? She was the one. I didn't like hearing that you were going away, and I'm going to miss you awfully, but what hurt the very most was her hiding it from me! I—I thought she was my friend."

That night, curled on her lounge with her nightcap of brandy, Maria admitted to John that he had been right. "I should have told Cassie ahead of time, just as you said. She is like a little ghost now, silently drifting about the house, and she won't even look at me. When I asked Robert what the matter was, he said she believes I didn't trust her."

"She's right," John said calmly. "You didn't. You thought she'd set up a howl that would last until Robert left." He smiled at Maria's indignant expression. "Oh, yes, my love, that's exactly what you thought. I think you were afraid if she became too upset you'd give in and let Robert stay."

Maria's smile was slightly lopsided. "Careful," she warned, only half teasing, "I may not want to be understood quite that well. But of course you're right, as so often you are." Her smile grew genuinely warm as she looked over at him, lounging in a nearby chair and wearing a blue silk robe over nothing at all. "Now that I think of it, Johnny," she added, sounding surprised, "of all the people I've ever loved in my life, you're the only one who has ever returned as much love as I gave."

"I almost wish that were true," John said ruefully. "But don't forget I was Armand's close friend for years. He loved you deeply."

Maria looked away. "I know. But he wasn't one of the people I loved. Armand was a dear man, John, and I never gave him cause to regret our marriage. But the truth is, my family had fallen on hard times and I married him solely for financial security, both for myself and for Mark. I thought you knew that."

John winced. "I suppose I should have, considering the difference in ages. But he was very happy with you, and, naturally, I thought—"

"Please don't talk about it, darling. I'm not proud of what

I did, though it saved Mark and me from poverty. Just remember, I honored my promises." She looked back at him, her huge eyes soft, pleading for understanding. "And now I want my own heart filled. I have cold and dutiful years to make up for, and I want it all."

"You have me. You will always have me."

"I know," she said passionately. "I know, and I thank heaven I do! You began my happiness, Johnny, and now I want more than anything to have a real family of my own. I was forced into taking Robert and Lily, I admit, but I'm truly glad now. I will do my very best for them. Cassie—" She faltered, tears suddenly glistening in her eyes. "Cassie is different. I don't think even you can understand what she means to me. She is Mark's. She carries our blood. She's *mine*. I want her to learn from me, to depend on me, to *love* me."

John frowned, swirling his brandy, watching the smooth amber liquid ride up in slow waves to coat the thin glass, to give off its rich odor. Whatever Maria wanted, he wanted her to have, but he felt she was making too much of this, asking too much from a ten-year-old child. From anyone. Love never came on demand.

"That may happen," he said carefully, "but don't be too set on what you want. Cassie has her own life to lead, her own loves to find. She is profoundly grateful to you and admires you very much. Perhaps you should let that be enough." He rose and came to her, grasping her hands and drawing her up against him. "We two have each other, Maria, and though I have love and duty to give to others, I need only you."

They were all up at dawn to see Robert and Arthur Masefield off. They were to go as far as Philadelphia with John as he went home, then cross the Delaware to Camden and take the Camden-Amboy train to South Amboy. There, Robert had explained to Cassie the night before, they would take a ferry to New York City and beyond, going up the Hudson River as far as Peekskill, and then take a stagecoach to Boston.

"Arthur's brother lives in Boston," he had told her, "and

he'll take us over to Cambridge, which is close to Boston. Arthur says when I come home to visit, I can take a steamer right from Boston to Philadelphia."

"In the *ocean?*" Cassie's eyes were wide. "Is that safe, Robbie?"

He laughed, excited, and took a turn around the schoolroom, stopping, hands in pockets, to stare out at the red glare of the furnace in the black night. "Of course. You mustn't worry about me, Cass. I'm almost a man."

Fear squeezed her heart. Looking at him, she could nearly believe it. He was already as big as some men. He was entering that other world, the world of grown-up people, and leaving her behind. Tears sprang to her eyes and her small face grew pink with the effort of not crying. "You aren't either! You're only fifteen!"

He turned back to her, his excitement turning to sympathy. He always knew how she felt and what bothered her. "You're growing up too, Cass. In another week you'll be eleven. What do you want for your birthday?"

She came close to him and put her arms around his waist, hiding her face in his shirt. "L-Letters. I want you to promise to write to me, Robbie." She sniffled and stepped back, wiping her face on her sleeve, a little ashamed of herself. "I'll write back, I really will, and tell you how Lily is."

"I promise," he said, and tousled her hair awkwardly. "A letter a week, and when you write back I'll want to know how you are too. Not just Lily."

Cassie had smiled then. If Robbie promised, he'd do it. She had gone to bed telling herself it would be all right; she'd have his letters and there would be holidays. But now, standing on the steps, holding Lily's hand and watching as the baggage was loaded into Uncle John's carriage, the thought of letters wasn't nearly as comforting as it had been last night. But at least Robbie didn't look like a grown-up beside Uncle John and Arthur Masefield, for they both wore tight-waisted frock coats that hung to their knees, fitted trousers, and tall top hats, shiny black. Robbie wore loose trousers, a jacket and cap, like any young boy. Cassie's eyes were brimming as they drove off, but she waved good-bye and managed a smile as Robbie and Arthur waved back.

Then, as they disappeared toward the village, she turned toward the house with Lily and went inside, followed by Maria and Mrs. Brooke.

"Robert will be back," she said in the echoing hall, both for herself and in case Lily felt sad, but Lily only laughed.

"I know *that*. Brooksie said he'd come back at Christmas and we're going to make him a present. Did you know we're going away too?"

"Cassie, I want you to come with me." Maria's soft voice interrupted them, her hand clasping Cassie's free one. "Lily, you may stay here with Mrs. Brooke and have your breakfast."

"Oh, good!" Lily loosed her hand from Cassie's and ran to Mrs. Brooke. "Can we have pancakes, Brooksie?"

Going up the staircase with her hand firmly held in Aunt Maria's grasp, Cassie stared at her feet and said nothing. Maria waited until they had topped the stairs and crossed the hall to her sitting room before she spoke.

"I'm sorry, Cassie." She sat down on her velvet lounge and pulled Cass down beside her, putting an arm about her thin shoulders. "I was wrong, darling. I should have told you weeks ago that Robert was going away. But I thought it might be easier for you if you didn't know."

Cass looked up, meeting the eyes so strangely like her own. "Why? I mean, why did you think that?"

Maria smiled. "I suppose I was thinking of how I would feel myself. I hate knowing ahead of time when something is going to make me sad. I'd rather find it out when it happens, and get it all over with at once."

"Oh." Cassie stared at her feet again, deep in thought. Then she heaved a long, surrendering sigh and leaned slowly into Maria's arms, nestling her head on a soft shoulder. "Maybe it is better for some people," she conceded. "But I like time to get used to things."

"Then you shall have it," Maria said, and hugged her, smoothing back her hair with a tender gesture. "I shall tell you now that we leave in a week for Philadelphia, and you and Lily are going to have a new teacher of your own, a young governess who Mr. Kendall says is a real bluestocking. Now that Robert is going to be a highly educated man, we must see to it that his sisters won't shame him."

"Yes. Robbie told me to make him proud." Pulling away from Maria's arms, Cassie stood up and shook out the full, ruffled skirt she was wearing. Only a day ago the announcement that they were going to Philadelphia would have had her speechless with excitement. But now she knew that when she got there Robert would have already seen all of that magic city and left it while he traveled on. She had wanted to share the magic with him. "What is a bluestocking, Aunt Maria?"

Maria laughed. "Why, a female intellectual, I suppose. A woman who is more interested in knowledge than she is in men. One who would rather study than flirt, and would rather teach than be married."

Cassie nodded. "I see. That sounds very sensible. I don't want to be married either. Perhaps I will be a bluestocking when I get older."

"Perhaps," Maria conceded, hiding fresh laughter. "Run along now and have your breakfast." She watched Cassie leave with a swish of skirt and glimpse of lace-trimmed pantalets, and thought how pretty she was, how beautiful she promised to be as she became a woman. A bluestocking? Some man would talk her out of that in her first season. Cassie's nature would never allow her to throw herself away on a scholar's life. Gerard blood was too hot for that.

Four days later, with most of the packing done and the house made ready for the winter, Maria had her mare saddled and rode down to the furnace and forge. Payne Regan saw her coming and met her at the donkey corral, doffing his hat politely. Puzzled, Maria looked around as she dismounted. There were several men in sight, going about their duties.

"How odd," she said to Regan as she tied her horse. "The men must be busy indeed if they don't come to greet me. I believe this is the first time that's happened since I have lived here."

Regan smiled tightly. "I put a stop to it, Mistress. It seemed that every visitor from the manor—be it you, Mr. Kendall, or even old Noonan—was an excuse to holiday for a half hour and talk. If you want more production, you cut the wasted time."

Maria glanced at his hard face, at the blue steel of his eyes and the faint sneer he could never quite hide. What he said was true enough, but still a shiver ran along her spine, chilly and frightening. She shook it off, angry at herself for letting him bother her. "I see," she said coolly. "But I hope you'll remember that the men are hard to replace. If you drive them too hard, they'll leave."

Regan gave a short laugh. "They won't quit. They're making more money every week—and so are you. Consider that and you may not need their bowing and scraping."

She stared at him angrily. His tone of voice was clearly contemptuous, as if he despised her for the way she was, the way she lived on the work of others. "Money isn't everything," she said, frowning.

"True." His cold gaze seemed to weigh her mood. "But it buys everything. Now, Mistress, how can I help you? Have you come only for a sentimental parting with your loyal workers? If so, I'll make an exception and gather them."

Furious at his further sarcasm, Maria straightened her back. "What were you doing when I arrived, Mr. Regan?"

He blinked, surprised. "I was supervising Ham and Lucius in the bridge house. Why?"

"Go back and finish your job," Maria said sharply. "I don't need a guide on my own property." She turned and left him, walking rapidly toward the one cobbled street and the company store there. The old man who ran it would give her a clear picture of what was going on and what the men were thinking.

John Kendall came in two days later, bringing his heavy traveling coach and a driver, Tom Watson, for the family trip back. He, Maria, Mrs. Brooke, and the two young girls would take Maria's light carriage, with Tom driving and a fresh horse tied on behind, and make the distance in one day, starting before daybreak and ending well after dark. Noonan, Adah, and Sallie would follow at a more leisurely pace in John's heavy coach, loaded with family belongings and the jars, jugs, and bags of food gleaned from the manor fields and garden.

At last Cassie was excited. She held the feeling off until

bedtime, convinced she should share it with Lily. But when she went upstairs she found Lily already fast asleep, her blond curls a halo around her angelic, peaceful face.

Laying out her blue linen dress and the striped pantalets she would wear on the trip, placing her narrow black slippers with them, Cassie turned down the lamp and watched the bright flame flicker and die. Then she crawled into bed and lay there with her eyes wide open in the dark. Tomorrow, though she was sure no one else knew it, was her eleventh birthday. The trip was like a present, a sign that she was entering a new part of her life. Tomorrow she would be following a path Robbie had made, to the city he had passed through. Why, even before she got his first letter she would see what he had seen, marvel at the same strange and wonderful things that her mother had told them of, years ago. She shut her eyes, trying to imagine the streets and ships, the tall buildings, the men and women in fancy clothes, riding in gold-trimmed carriages . . .

"Cassie?"

Her eyes flew open at the sound of Maria's soft voice. Carrying a candle that shone on her smooth forehead and rounded cheeks, her curved lips and tender, shadowed eyes, Maria stood in the dark doorway and peered in. "Did I wake you, darling?"

Cassie sat up. "I wasn't asleep, Aunt Maria. I was thinking with my eyes closed."

Maria laughed. "Good. I came up for a very special reason. First, to wish you a happy birthday tomorrow, and second to give you your birthday present from Robert."

"From *Robbie?*" Cassie gasped and scrambled from bed, rushing to light the lamp again. Turning back, she took the package from Maria's extended hand. "How?" she asked, holding it tightly in both hands, looking up at Maria's faintly rueful smile. "How could he get it here to me on time?"

"He insisted on stopping in Philadelphia long enough to buy it for you, dear. He gave it to John to deliver, and here it is." She patted Cassie's cheek. "It was very thoughtful of Robert, and I know you're pleased. I only wish I had known the correct day myself so I too could have given you a gift."

Staring down at her package, wishing wildly for a moment

alone to open it, Cassie answered absently. "You've already given us more than we can ever repay, Aunt Maria." She kept on looking at the package, wrapped in white paper and tied with red ribbon, the bow crooked and clumsy. She smoothed the bow, thinking of Robbie trying to tie it neatly. Then, conscious of a silence, she looked up. Aunt Maria was still smiling, but her eyes looked suspiciously wet.

"Cassie," she said, and shook her head despairingly. "Oh, Cassie. I don't give in order to be repaid. Aren't you ever going to think of me as part of your family?"

Her face red, knowing that somehow she had failed again to live up to Maria's expectations, Cassie put the package on the dresser and reached to hug her, feeling Maria's arms go around her, feeling her bend to put their cheeks together. Cassie's heart contracted as she felt the dampness on Maria's face. "Please," she whispered, "don't feel bad. We love you, Aunt Maria. It's just that we . . . we wish we *could* pay you back." She hugged her again and pulled away, looking over at Lily's round, peaceful face on her pillow. "Except Lily, maybe. Lily never worries about anything. She's just happy."

Maria was smiling again. "But that's what I want, darling. That's all I want, for all of us. To be happy and loving. Are you going to open your gift?"

Hesitating, Cassie touched the package with tentative fingers, fluffed the bow. "Perhaps I'll wait until morning. After all, it isn't my birthday yet."

Maria laughed and kissed her cheek. "Then I'll say good night, darling, and tell you I admire your patience. When I was your age, I tore presents open the moment I got my hands on them. Sleep well, you'll need your rest. We have a long trip tomorrow."

Cassie waited until Maria's light tread faded away toward the stairs. Then, her heart beating hard enough to feel in her throat, she took the package and sat down on the edge of her bed. The bow was tight, but she worked it loose carefully and removed the ribbon, smoothing it out. Unfolding the paper, she gazed down at a book, a beautiful book, bound in dark red leather. The title and author's name were printed in gold: *Oliver Twist,* and then, "By Charles Dickens."

Cassie drew a deep, satisfied breath and opened the book

carefully. Inside Robbie had written: "For my beloved Cassie, on the occasion of her eleventh birthday. Make me proud, Cass. Robert."

She held the book to her chest and hugged it, tears of happiness beading her lashes. "I will," she whispered, "I really will. You'll see." In a moment she got up and took the lamp from the dresser and put it on the bedside table, glancing over to make sure it didn't shine on Lily's sleeping face. Then, plumping her pillow and leaning it against the head of the bed, she got in and opened her book.

Chapter 7

Later, in the dimly lit boudoir below, Maria and John lay naked together on silken sheets, their bodies entwined. They murmured to each other, their voices hushed and husky, laden with feeling. They had made love; they waited now for their blaze of passion to cool and then grow hungry again so they could make love once more. It never took long.

"We'll find a place, darling. We must. I can no longer do without you more than a few days."

It was John speaking, but Maria nodded. Had it been her, she would have been saying the same. They would have to find a safe place in the city for their meetings, for their illicit lovemaking. There was no use now to say, as they had in the beginning, that they must stay apart in the city and wait for the move to the country again. No, she thought, never. She would die of longing. She reached up and traced the line of his stern lips, then raised herself over him, straddling his narrow flanks. Bending, allowing her breasts to touch him, she brushed his half-open mouth with a taut nipple. As he began to suckle she let out her breath and closed her eyes, feeling the shuddering pleasure stab through her from breast to loins. "I love you," she whispered. "Love you, Johnny. Always." She felt his hands move down to play in her patch of dark curls, and eased away to make room for them. Each knew so well, now, what pleased the other. Before they slept, he knew her mouth and tongue would give him the rare ecstasy he had found only with her.

This second time they were all over the bed, playing, laughing, trying to keep from making too much noise. There was a childlike freedom between them, a quality of openness, a lack of false modesty that John could hardly credit when he knew most husbands and wives made love silently with their nightshirt and nightgown on. What had happened between them to make it so he didn't know—nor care, for that matter, as long as they kept on feeling that way. With a swoop of long arms and lean body, he captured her and held her down, murmuring erotic threats in her ears, wild fancies that made her first laugh and then grow still, listening, running the tip of her tongue over her full lips, beginning to breathe faster. Then she eased over him again, caressing him with her eyes and hot, trembling hands, pressing him down on his back, using her agile tongue and soft mouth to make some of his wild fancies come true, then lying open to him while he did the same and she cried out in ecstasy.

Sated at last, they were still awake when September ushered itself in at midnight with the first fall storm, so that the heavy draperies billowed in the wind and rain and John had to rise and shut the windows. She warmed him in her arms when he came back to bed, and they talked of ordinary things, chiefly of the furnace and forge and how soon it should be shut down for the winter.

"I still do not like your rude and opinionated overseer," Maria said in the end, "but I must admit he has increased our production by at least a third. And the men respect him, though from what the storekeeper says, they don't like him any better than I do."

"Get rid of him, then," John said drowsily.

Maria yawned. "Not yet. He may settle in. At least he'll not be able to say we didn't give him a chance." She waited, but only deep, regular breathing answered her. She smiled and snuggled down to sleep. Not until next spring would they be able to spend a whole night together again, and she wanted to make the most of this.

The trip to the city was miserable, made so by cold wind and blowing rain that found its way through the hurriedly curtained windows of the carriage, dampening everyone's clothes and spirits. Cassie was exhausted. She had read her book the night before until her lamp faded from lack of oil and went out, long after midnight. Now she was silent, her huge eyes swollen from strain and from tears shed over poor Oliver's plight. Lily, who never whined, whined all day, pushing her bright head into Mrs. Brooke's shoulder, begging for sweets and sulking when she couldn't have them. Maria shone, patient and sweetly reasonable with everyone.

"You're a wonder," John told her when they stopped for dinner at an inn along the way. "Not one complaint. I'm ashamed of my grousing about the weather."

Maria smiled. They were alone at a table, for Mrs. Brooke had taken both girls into a washroom to clean their hands and faces and help them change into dry clothes.

"You shouldn't be," she said, "you've a perfect right to grouse, considering you've had to put up with four females, one of whom has been at her worst. But it's nearly over, Johnny. Only another two hours or so, and we'll . . ." Her voice died away at the warning look on his face. "Johnny?"

"Shhh." He turned slightly in his chair. "Wait a moment," he said in a low tone, "and then look at our friend in the window bay. The woman with him isn't his wife, but I can't be sure who it is. Her bonnet hides her face."

Maria did as she was told. Her sharp intake of breath brought another warning glance from John. She met it with dancing, mischievous eyes. "Never mind," she whispered, "they're leaving."

Both of them kept their eyes averted until the outside door opened and closed again, the couple gone. Then Maria chuckled. "Piers Von Graaf," she said, marveling, "and I recognized the woman as they left the table. Melainie Scott. I've suspected them for a year! A pity he's married to that termagant cousin of his. For all her seminary education and talk of independence, Melainie's head over heels in love with Piers. Her eyes have always given her away."

"I thought it was her," John said, looking uncomfortable. "And I wish it weren't. I had no idea she was interested in a married man. I'm afraid I've put you in a difficult position. She's the applicant I hired as your children's governess."

"Oh?" Maria laughed a little and then was silent as she heard Lily's voice. Mrs. Brooke was approaching with both children, and the serving maid behind them carried a full tray of steaming food.

It was still misting rain and blowing when they left the inn for Bryn Mawr and then on to Philadelphia. Lily was asleep in Mrs. Brooke's lap before they left the inn's courtyard, and Cassie's eyes were drooping shut. Mrs. Brooke settled herself in a corner and put her other arm around Cassie. The soft warmth of Brooksie's maternal body and the gentle swaying of the carriage in the black night soothed her into sleep. She slept for two hours and then, wakened by the clicking of the carriage wheels on stone, sat up to peer out into the black night. She stared, awed, at the endless rising and falling line of wet, gleaming roofs along stormswept streets and the flaring gas lights. Then the enormous buildings suddenly appeared on both sides, turreted and towering, for all the world like dark, ominous mountains leaning over a narrow, wet valley.

"We're here," she whispered, so low only Mrs. Brooke heard. "We're in Philadelphia." She clutched the window frame and went on staring, at the shining, raindark cobblestones on the streets, at the large coaches pulled by high-stepping horses, streaming past with their outside lamps lit. There were a few figures of people hurrying along in hooded cloaks, and she marveled that they would be out so late. Then she remembered that Robert had seen this, all of this. He had even stopped on one of these streets and had gone into a store in one of these immense buildings, to buy her wonderful book. If only she could have been with him, she thought wistfully, if only they could have discovered the city together.

She braced herself and held on as the carriage swayed and turned, and then she was seeing the black silhouettes of four-story houses, set close together and close to the street, but with the glow from their windows half obscured by the black, waving branches of huge old trees planted in rows in front of them.

"We're almost home," Mrs. Brooke said softly. "Almost there. Another corner to turn."

Cassie drew in her breath and looked over at the dim figures in the other seat, wanting confirmation. But Aunt Maria was asleep. Cass could see in the gloom that her bonnet was off and her glossy head on Mr. Kendall's shoulder. And Mr. Kendall's arm was around her, his cheek resting on her hair. Cassie swallowed and looked away, looked again at the big houses, the big trees that overhung the narrow street, the white steps gleaming in the darkness. When they slowed and stopped she drew in her breath again, for this house was not only big and handsome, it was full of light. Light in the windows, upstairs and downstairs, light pouring out as the wide door flew open and welcoming voices called out.

"Good heavens," Maria said sleepily, sitting up. "We're here. That wasn't too bad, now, was it?"

Recalling the arrival later, Cassie would remember only confusion, excitement, gabbling voices, hands helping her out, exclaiming over the pretty young miss and the plump, golden-haired child in Emma Brooke's arms. They were all rushed through the door, into a vestibule, through another door that opened into a wide hall. Inside, the place seemed full of noise and people; Cassie was trapped amongst bodies she didn't know well enough to push past. It seemed a crowd, and she was amazed when she straightened everyone out and found that Mr. Kendall had gone to his own home and there were only three new people: an old man named Dickon, with white side whiskers and a friendly look to him; and two maids, one short and stout, named Betty, and one thin and red-haired, named Maud. Maud looked like Adah, and when Cassie shyly said so, Maud laughed and said of course she did, for they were sisters.

Then, with everyone busy with baggage and Maria giving orders, Cassie could look around. The hall they were in was narrower than the one at Eagle Forge, but very fancy, with carved chests along the walls and bowlegged chairs covered all over with wine-red plush and trimmed with rows and rows of tiny tassels. Tables held marvelous oil lamps over two feet high, their chimneys made of fine rose-colored glass, etched with graceful stems and flowers and circled by snowy glass shades. It was no wonder light had poured out in a flood when the doors were opened, for the huge lamps were all lit, casting dazzling brightness into every corner. Silent, awed by such grandeur, Cassie felt Aunt Maria's hand slip into hers.

"Come along, dear, and I'll show you your bedroom. Maud will bring your valise and help you get ready for bed. What we all need first is sleep."

Mrs. Brooke was already halfway up the stairs, Lily in her arms; the maids were bustling after, laden with baggage, and Dickon was closing the entrance door. Cassie looked back, thinking of the city out there in the dark night. Everything seemed frightening without Robert to comfort her. Swallowing a sudden lump in her throat, she went with Maria to the stairs. The carpeting on the steps was heavy and quiet, but the stairs were narrow and steep, with tiny landings and sharp turns as they ascended. On the second floor was a long and well-lighted hall, stretching the full length of the house, with a window at each end.

"First," Maria said, "I will show you which door is mine, so if you are frightened or ill, you can easily find me. It is here, with the small table beside it. Your room is toward the front . . . there, where Maud is taking in your valise. Lily will be in a room at the opposite end of the hall, beside Mrs. Brooke's room."

Cassie stopped. "Lily won't be with *me?* But she'll be lonesome, Aunt Maria, and frightened if I'm not there."

Maria smiled, though her huge eyes were smudged with weariness. "I don't think so, darling. Lily is very fond of Mrs. Brooke, and their rooms adjoin. Lily will be quite content. Do come on."

"Oh." Suddenly subdued, Cassie went on, thinking that what she had said was probably true. From the very beginning Lily had loved being with Mrs. Brooke. So it was all right, except that now, with Robbie gone, maybe she'd lost Lily too. She looked up at Maria as they turned in through the doorway where Maud had gone and asked hesitantly: "Will I still be able to see Lily every day?"

Maria came to a stop in the middle of the room and laughed, giving Cass a quick hug. "Why, of course, darling! You'll be living in the same house. Now, what do you say about this?" She swept a hand in a grand gesture. "I had the room done over for you. You must look around and tell me if you like it."

Cassie turned obediently and looked. It was a small, cozy room, which she liked, and it had three windows, all on one side. Under their feet was a soft cream-colored carpet, patterned with pink roses and green leaves. The windows had rose-colored, silken curtains, looped and ruffled, and on the four-poster bed was an intricate white lace bedspread and rose-pink draperies. The furniture reminded her of the bedrooms in the manor at Eagle Forge; large, plain chests and dressers of thick, polished maple, made by country craftsmen. There was a maple rocking chair too, padded and set near the windows, and against the opposite wall a desk and another chair, dark wood with curved legs like those downstairs, only this one was covered with white brocade and fringed instead of tasseled.

"It's beautiful," Cassie said softly, "very, very beautiful, Aunt Maria."

"Yes," Maria breathed, studying the room carefully. "The decorator John hired did a wonderful job. The more I look, the better I like it. It matches you, darling."

Pleased with the room in spite of the strangeness of being far from everything she knew and loved, Cassie flung her hands wide and broke out in soft, clear laughter. "That's silly, Aunt Maria! How can a room match me?"

Startled and thrilled by Cassie's sudden happiness, Maria grabbed her hands and swung them both in a circle, skirts swirling like ruffled clouds. "I don't know, Cass! I only know it does." She let her go after another hug. "In any event, it's yours, and you look as if you belong in it. I hope you will always be happy here."

"Sure now, she will be, Miss Maria," Maud said, smiling at the high jinks, and came to them, bringing Cassie's nightdress. "Why, even a princess would be happy in this room."

Tucked into the feather bed, the lamps out but a narrow, comforting band of light showing under the door, the wind and rain muffled by stout walls, Cassie reminded herself that she was now eleven years old, and that was far too old to be afraid of being alone. A few years more and she'd be a woman. A teacher perhaps. A bluestocking. Would that make Robbie proud? She smiled in the darkness, burrowing deeper. Wait. And study hard. A person must have to know a lot to teach.

Melainie Scott was tall and slender, her blond hair parted in the middle and drawn straight down the sides of her well-shaped head to a cluster of curls over her ears. In back, the hair was also smooth and tucked in, but several thick golden curls dangled from the knot on her nape. It was a style nearly everyone wore, since it went well with the coal-scuttle bonnets. The bonnets came straight down on both sides and back, and straight forward along the top and sides of the head. They allowed the curls to escape below, and were generally draped over with a pretty wisp of colored silk to tie beneath the chin. But their most notable and sometimes very useful feature was the fact that they protruded far enough forward to hide a lady's face and expression from view unless she chose to look squarely into someone's face.

Ushered into one of Maria Andelet's double parlors the next morning by Dickon, who left her there while he reported her arrival to Maria, Melainie fidgeted, sat down, stood up, and walked to the windows. She stood there, staring out into the walled back garden and then to the right side, where the wall had sections of iron bars and a gate, through which she could see the property owned by Benedict Bradford next door. Melainie hardly knew either family, but she didn't envy Maria's position in this case. Geneva Bradford was universally feared and disliked, both for her power and her tongue, and it was well known that Geneva had never cared for her brother's wife, and cared even less for her now as his widow.

"Good morning!" Maria's cheerful voice startled Melainie, who jumped and turned, mumbled a greeting and then stood watching as Maria directed Betty, who came in behind her carrying a tray with a pot of coffee, cups, and sweet cakes.

"On the desk will be fine, Betty, and you may go. Miss Scott and I will serve ourselves. Thank you, and do let me know when Sallie Fernod arrives." She turned back to Melainie, smiling, as Betty shut the door.

"I must apologize, Melainie. Mr. Kendall told me you would be coming in this morning, so I cannot plead ignorance. I simply overslept, after a long, horrible, stormy ride from Eagle Forge. But now that we are together, do sit down over here. We'll have coffee and cakes before we talk."

Stiffly, Melainie came and sat in the chair beside the desk that Maria had indicated, averting her face a little. Normally, Melainie was vivacious and charming; today her expression of unease was painfully apparent. "I believe I am the one who should apologize," she said, bravely raising her chin, "for coming here and wasting your time. I—I know you saw us last night, Mrs. Andelet."

Maria handed her a cup of coffee and pushed the small tray of cakes closer. "These are quite good," she said. "The best are the ones with the tiny seeds on top. Do try one."

"Th-Thank you." At a loss, Melainie took a cake and placed it on her saucer. She sipped her coffee and put the cup down in sudden decision. "I didn't come here to ask you to forget what you saw," she said, "nor to beg for the position of governess in spite of it! I came only because I had said I would come, and I thought it would be rude to leave you waiting and wondering."

Maria smiled, took a bite of cake and a sip of coffee before she spoke again. "I am quite sure you will like Cassie, Melainie. She is very bright, very likable, and she is looking forward to having lessons. In another year or so you'll be able to take on Lily too. She is a sweet, pretty little thing. When do you think you can start?"

"Stop!" Melainie leaned forward, her voice shaking. "Stop pretending there is nothing wrong! You don't have to be polite to *me,* Mrs. Andelet! You know what I've done. I—I don't want you hiring me and then firing me on some pretext, just to avoid bringing out the truth now! You surely must feel that I'm not fit to teach your children. *Say* it!"

Maria looked up, locking her soft gray-green eyes on Melainie's frantic blue ones, setting her jaw firmly. "My dear," she said, her voice calm, "I have no idea what you're talking about. But no matter, for I am sure it will make no difference between us. Do I make myself clear?"

Caught, Melainie stared into the warm depths of Maria's understanding eyes. Finally she looked away, her young face soft again, shining with a tremendous, soaring relief.

"Yes," she said, "you do. Thank you. I'll need a day or so to gather some suitable textbooks and other materials. If it's not too soon, I'd like to begin next Monday."

"That will be fine. Cassie will settle in by then, I'm sure, and be ready for lessons. Now, do have some of these seed cakes."

Coming downstairs a short time later, dressed in lace pantalets and a pale yellow muslin dress with a huge skirt and what seemed to her to be a dozen starched and ruffled petticoats put on her by Maud in spite of her protestations, Cassie saw Maria at the main door, bidding good-bye to a tall young woman with a pleasant smile.

Shutting the door, turning back, Maria looked up. "Oh, there you are, darling. That was your governess, Miss Scott."

"It was?" Cassie ran down the rest of the steps and to the window, peering out. "I see her, getting into a gig. She's pretty, Aunt Maria. When is she coming back?"

Maria laughed. "Monday, dear. I hope your enthusiasm continues. Most children aren't that anxious for lessons."

"Most children," Cassie said seriously, "don't want to be teachers. I do. May I go outside?"

"If you stay inside our garden, you may go out at any time. Have you had breakfast?"

"Yes. I ate with Mrs. Brooke and Lily." Cassie paused, her eyes meeting Maria's and then sliding away. "You were right. Lily likes having her own room with Brooksie next door. She didn't mind even a little bit that I was so far away. I . . . well, I'm going now." She whirled, skirts fluttering, and ran down the hall to the back door.

Maria sighed. She knew how Cassie felt. First Robert and now Lily had deserted her. She was thankful that Cass couldn't know that she had planned it all herself and made it happen. But it had to be. Those children had been entirely too close, too completely dependent on each other, as if they lived on a desert island and ignored the rest of the world. It was wrong, she thought, going back upstairs, wrong no matter how you looked at it. Besides, Cassie was *hers,* whether she knew it yet or not.

Outside, Cassie stared enchanted at the garden. There were late roses still blooming on the bushes near the kitchens, carefully tended beds of herbs, a massive grape arbor along the high back wall, and narrow brick paths that circled two large, grassy plots where apple and cherry trees grew. The cherries were gone, of course, but several apples still hung on the tree. She picked one, munching on it as she wandered over to breathe in the fragrance of a late rose. It was lovely here, but nothing like home. No geese nor cows, no sheep, not even a horse. Both the horses and the carriages were kept two streets away in a livery stable, Maud had said, and sent for when needed. She sighed and picked up a stick to rattle along the iron bars of the fence.

"Never mind," she said, half aloud, "we'll go home and stay there when we grow up."

"Cassie, is that *you?*"

She jumped at the sound of a familiar voice and turned around. Leaning on the other side of the fence and looking in at her was a tall young man with a lock of silky black hair falling across his white forehead, shy, dark eyes, and a slowly dawning smile. "Jacob! Where did you come from?" She rushed to the fence and put both hands through to take his. "Oh, Jacob! It's lovely to see you! Were you coming to visit us and lost your way?"

He laughed, his face pink with pleasure. "No, I live here, on this side of the fence." He gestured behind him at a large brick house. "Would you like to come through and visit us? There's a gate down there at the corner."

Cassie clapped her hands lightly, smiling. "You *live* there! That's wonderful! I thought everyone around would be a stranger. But I can't come through, Jacob. Aunt Maria said I could go outside whenever I pleased, but I must stay within the garden."

Jacob felt full of unaccustomed warmth and easy affection. He had felt that way before at Eagle Forge, whenever he'd been around Cassie or Robert. "We'll have to change that," he said, still holding her hands. "We're as good as cousins, and cousins can visit back and forth. I'll speak to my father. He gets along well with Aunt Maria."

"All right. But what difference does it make? We can talk right here." Pulling her hands from his, Cassie dropped down and sat on the velvety grass, her skirts around her like an enormous mushroom, and looked at him happily through the bars. "You sit down too, and tell me about your latest poems! I'm dying to read them."

Maria found them an hour later, still sitting and talking with the fence between them. She told Cassie the dressmaker had arrived and was waiting for her, and smiled at Jacob.

"Tell your parents," she said to him, "that I'll be receiving every day this week at tea, and I'd love to see them. And Jacob—as usual, you are welcome any time."

Chapter 8

"This whim of yours becomes irritating," Geneva said, giving Maria a cool embrace. "I was sure you would tire of it by now. But from what Jacob tells me, you are still playing Lady Bountiful to those orphans—with Armand's money."

"Let me take your shawl," Maria said, taking it, "and your hat and walking stick, Benedict. There. I'll put them all here on the stand. Now, you must join us in the back parlor for tea. John Kendall and Jacob are already here."

"Good," Benedict said, pleased. "I've wanted a word with Kendall about the railroad stock. I'll just go on." He lumbered across the hall and into the drawing room, closing the door smartly behind him.

Staring into the hall mirror, Geneva smoothed her red-gold hair, which was done up in more curls than usual. "I couldn't believe my ears," she said, "when Jacob told me you had sent that boy off to a school in Cambridge! You know, of course, that you're throwing money away."

"Come," Maria said, taking Geneva's arm. "I've acquired a chest of Gunpowder tea from the Yankee clipper just into port, and I want you to try it."

"Stop evading the subject," Geneva snapped, and pulled away. "You do that to me all the time, Maria, and I'm sick of it. Are you going to continue with this foolish charity of yours? I know what the school fees at Cambridge are, and Armand would turn in his grave if he knew you were paying them for a—a farm boy! You can't make a gentleman out of a country bumpkin, Maria."

Maria smiled. "Oh, I wouldn't say that. Great changes can be made. For instance, you're doing very well at making a mean-mouthed termagant out of a lady."

"Maria!"

"Hush," Maria said, taking her arm again and leading her toward the drawing-room door. "Come taste the Gunpowder tea, and don't tempt me to go on trading insults with you. You know you always get the worst of it. Did I tell you I invested in one of the new clipper ships they are building? I hear it's a wonderful opportunity."

"You'll lose every penny," Geneva said, recovering with a smirk and patting her hair. "Benedict bought shares in one last year. I told him the cursed thing would sink on the way to China, and it did."

"What a pity," Maria said, standing back to allow her to enter the parlor first and then following her in. "So many young lives are lost in the trades now. The world has gone mad over commerce. Sit over here, Geneva."

As Geneva came in, Cassie put down her cup of cambric tea and slipped through the door that led into the dining room, escaping the tea party. Aunt Maria had told her that if Violet came along she would have to stay and amuse her, but Violet hadn't, so she was free to go. In a way, she would have liked staying in the cheerful, fire-lit room and listening to the grown-up talk, especially with Jacob there, but she couldn't bear to be in the same room as his mother. She had seen the scornful dislike in Geneva's green eyes when she looked at her, or even at little Lily.

She shivered slightly as she passed into cooler air, for Betty hadn't lit the fire in here yet. The same as all the other rooms in this house, the dining room was long and narrow. Oil paintings, including one of a brace of dead ducks, one of a bowl of fruit, and two of landscapes, hung on the walls, dimmed by coal smoke and age. The rest of the room was cheerful, even luxurious, with a carved Renaissance cabinet from France, the polished glow of a long, narrow table and tall-backed chairs upholstered in wine-red plush. But what fascinated Cassie was the intricate arrangement of candle holders and tinkling cut-glass prisms that hung over the table like a glittering upside-down fountain. She could hardly wait to see it lit for a party.

Passing through a swinging door, she went into the kitchen. Sallie Fernod had arrived at last, along with Adah and Noonan, and it seemed like a breath of air from home, just seeing them. She exchanged smiles with the immense Sallie and went through to the short back hall, opening doors until she found the back stairs. She ran up to the second-floor hall and into her room. Taking her book from the top of her dresser, she went to the padded maple rocker by the windows and curled up to read with the aid of the late afternoon light.

There was, after all, one good thing about Mrs. Bradford, she thought, opening to her bookmark, and that was the way she kept Aunt Maria occupied. This was the first free moment she'd had since talking to Jacob this morning. Ever since then Maria had kept her busy; talking, choosing new materials for clothes, trying new ways of braiding or curling her hair. Which was fine, she supposed, but not with Oliver Twist still in Fagin's clutches, waiting to be rescued.

It seemed to Cassie during the next weeks that all at once she was running, faster and faster, into the future. Not that she minded, for it brought Christmas and Robbie closer. Time sped by, for there weren't enough hours in the day to do everything Aunt Maria planned for her.

Lessons were paramount. From eight in the morning until noon Cassie was closeted with Melainie Scott in a sun-room on the third floor that had been made into a cheerful schoolroom. It took another hour and a half during the afternoon to complete the arithmetic problems and write the essays Melainie asked for. But Cassie didn't mind that either. She loved Miss Scott and loved studying all the new things Miss Scott thought she should know, like the rules of etiquette, music appreciation, and French. She even loved Philadelphia, especially when Maria took her and Miss

Scott along on a trip to the docks on the Delaware River. Maria owned a light, open gig and a city-trained gelding, a bored but obedient horse who shied at nothing and even ignored the train whistles. Maria drove the gig herself, expertly.

"Most of the Andelet fortune came from the sea trade," Maria told them, bowling along crowded Water Street in the crisp fall air, "back when Philadelphia was the greatest port in our country. Now, New York far surpasses us in number of ships and goods, but our warehouses still turn many a penny here, buying from the southern coastal steamers and selling to the north." She smiled. "If my venture into the China trade is successful, I'll take a profit in New York too."

Melainie Scott chatted with Maria and Cassie listened, but mostly she watched the tall ships with their clouds of sail, the dock laborers with their barrows skipping nimbly between the tangle of carts and wagons, all bent on transporting goods either to the ships loading or from the ones that had brought cargo from other places. A confusion of foreign tongues filled the air, sometimes harsh, sometimes melodious, but to Cassie, always magical.

At the bottom of High Street Maria pointed out the ferry that crossed the Delaware to Camden, which Robert and Arthur Masefield had taken on their way to Massachusetts. "We'll cross over someday," she told Cassie, "and go to New York. It's a pleasant way to travel."

They stopped at the Jersey Market on the way back, where barrow loads of melon, meats, butter, eggs, and game had been sent up from small boats at the docks, and oysters and crabs from the Chesapeake Bay had been brought by fishermen. Maria loaded her baskets and then took the long way home, for the bright, cool weather tempted her to stay outside.

"I'll show you the streets where the best Philadelphians live," she said to Cassie, and laughed as she caught Melainie's eye. "Or, at least that's their opinion." She drove up and down the lines of red-brick houses, each with its set of white marble steps, its white shutters on the downstairs windows, its green shutters above. The streets were shaded by lines of tall old trees and named for other trees, Chestnut,

Walnut, Locust, Spruce, and Pine. Heading home to their own house on Spruce, Maria asked Cassie what she thought of it.

"So many big houses," Cassie marveled. "So many *bricks.* Do the best Philadelphians live here in the summer too?"

"A good many of them have a house in the country, like we do," Maria said. "The city is uncomfortably hot in summer, and diseases breed. It's best to leave if you can afford it."

Cassie sat up and smiled. "Good. I like Philadelphia, but I'm glad we'll all be together in Eagle Forge in the summer. I'll tell Robbie when I write to him—he misses the country as much as I do."

Melainie patted her hand. "That's thoughtful, Cassie." She turned to Maria, looking pleased. "Cassie is so faithful in her letters to her brother. She never misses answering his weekly letter. She writes well too."

Maria's smile dimmed. Slapping the reins to hurry the horse on, she managed to bring back its brightness again. "That's fine, Cassie. Writing is a useful skill."

"It's easy to write to Robbie," Cassie said. "It's like talking. He told me this week that he and Arthur had stayed overnight with one of Arthur's friends at Harvard. He said the Harvard men drink cider for breakfast, and if they don't get it right away they all bang their cups on the table until they do. Robbie says it makes an awful racket."

The two women laughed. "Boys," Maria said with gentle scorn, and raised her brows. "You wouldn't act like that, would you, Cassie?"

"No," Cassie said, "I wouldn't. Neither would Robbie. We don't like cider."

We. Maria glanced at Cassie's young face and saw the faraway look, the wistfulness that always came at the mention of Robert; the loneliness in the big eyes, the drooping corners of the soft lips. Maria glanced away, feeling again the same angry despair, the same intimation of defeat that she had felt when she first saw the three of them together, shabby children holding hands and coming up the path to the manor. Then, she had seen the clasping hands as an unbreakable chain, and perhaps they were. Perhaps she would never be able to loosen the links and take Mark's child for her own.

Past Spruce to the south was Pine Street, and between them to the east was a sprawling section of unnamed streets, little more than alleys, where some of the gardeners and grooms who served the well-to-do families found lodgings in boardinghouses. There were also empty houses to let, some well built. It was one of these that John Kendall had bought soon after Maria had returned to the city, and had seen to it that it was cleaned and refurbished, and a commodious stable built in back—large enough to hold, and hide, a horse and a gig.

As Maria said, no one would be apt to see them except for the servants who lived around there, and servants always knew all the gossip in any case. It had been a careless thing to say, but by the time the house was ready for them she had been so full of desire, so hungry for John's lean, strong body that she really didn't care.

Since John had taken over the legal matters concerning all of Maria's different interests, and stopped by her house every morning for a short conference, it was easy to arrange the time of their meetings. They had only one strict rule—never at night. Unless he was out of town, John spent his evenings in the company of his invalid wife Alice. Confident of his love, and warmly sympathetic to Alice, Maria approved of his decision, and in early November decided herself to pay Alice Kendall a visit. They had been very friendly in the past, and if she neglected Alice now people might wonder why.

Visits were commonly made in midday, and at two o'clock Maria gathered up both Cassie and Lily in her gig and drove to the Kendalls' splendid brick house on Walnut Street. It was a bright, windy day, but the snow was deep and the air freezing cold. All three of them were dressed in warm, woolen gowns, flannel petticoats, laced leather boots, and fur tippets with hoods. Sitting together on the open seat of the gig, they were pink-cheeked and talking gaily as they drew up at the door.

Alice saw them from her window. Years back, she had

chosen the broad living-room window as her station, and her chaise longue had been placed there, along with a table for her tonics and food. She watched the world go by, and looked eagerly for visitors. She smiled now and called to Vera, her maid, to come and see.

"Maria Andelet is bringing two of her wards for me to meet! Aren't they beautiful, Vera? So full of life. Look at that darling little girl with the golden hair, and the other, older child—why, she's the picture of Maria's br—" She stopped, blood rising in a wave in her pale, thin face. "Do go and greet them," she went on hurriedly, "and tell Forman to throw a blanket or two over the horse until they're ready to return. It's terribly cold."

Maria led her children in proudly, confident that Alice would find them both interesting and lovable. They had removed their hooded tippets in the hall, and with her shining sable hair showing, Cassie's likeness to Mark Gerard was even more striking. Alice, who had been raised in Maryland near the Gerard plantation, had at one time thought Mark the handsomest man in the world. Now she could hardly keep her eyes off Cassie.

"How kind you are, Maria, to come out on a miserably cold day and bring me such charming company! Do come close, you darlings, and give me a kiss."

Lily ran to the chaise longue immediately and kissed Alice's cheek, receiving a hug in return. Cassie, her huge eyes soft, came more slowly and knelt to hug the thin but smiling lady. "I'm Cassie," she said, "and she's Lily. We are happy to meet you."

"Thank you, Cassie. I'm so glad you came." Looking up at Maria, Alice saw the fiercely possessive pride in her eyes as she watched Cassie. It was true, then. Somehow, the child was Mark's. Maria had always been the same way about him, proud and possessive. However, it was not something one would discuss in front of the child. Alice turned to Vera.

"Tell Cook we'll need hot chocolate and cookies with our tea. And, later"—she looked at Cassie and smiled—"later you'll take the children to the pantry and show them our new kittens."

"Oh!" Cassie's eyes flew to Maria. "Kittens!"

Maria laughed, choosing a chair. "First your tea. Then, *if* the kittens are old enough, and *if* Mrs. Kendall is willing to part with one—"

"You may have whichever one you want," Alice said, "and take it today." She smiled at two delighted faces. "Those kittens need someone to play with."

Sitting alone later, over empty teacups, Maria and Alice talked, at first of others and then of Maria's wards.

"Few people here remember Mark in his youth," Maria said, "except you. And so I'll not explain to anyone else why I took these children. But I saw your face when we came in, and I know you understand. John knows too. I felt I had to explain to him, for as my legal advisor he was strongly against it."

"Was he?" Alice smiled sadly. "How foolish of him. How I have wished for children of my own, and I suspect he has felt the same, though he would never say so and risk hurting my feelings. I would have gladly adopted one, had I strength enough to be a proper mother. I think you did a very, very good thing, both for the children and for yourself." She laughed a little. "Still, it was brave to take all three. Surely, the other two weren't . . ."

"No, only Cassie is my brother's child," Maria admitted. "Though Lily is her half sister, through the mother. Then, Robert is half brother to Lily since they share a father, but Robert and Cassie aren't related at all."

"Yet you are having him educated! You deserve a great deal of credit for your charitable nature, Maria."

Maria flushed. For some reason, she couldn't accept undeserved praise from this woman. "No, I don't. I'm . . . not the angel you think I am. I intended to take only Cassie, but she wouldn't leave the other two."

"But you seem so happy to have them!"

"I am, now. They are charming and intelligent children, and I am truly fond of them both."

Hesitating just outside the door, a kitten in her arms, Cassie was shocked almost to tears, her face flaming. *Cassie is my brother's child.* Things she had heard in the past came back to her. Lies her drunken father had yelled at her mother. Her father? He wasn't her father, and the things he had yelled were true. She wanted to cry, but instead she wiped her eyes on her sleeve and petted the nervous kitten, comforting him. Then, turning, she went back to the pantry and sat down on the floor again with Lily, who was happily playing with the other kittens.

"Does Aunt Maria like the kitty?" Lily asked, stroking him as he lay, contented, in Cassie's lap. "Does she want to have him at our house?"

Cassie swallowed. "They were talking about—about grown-up things. I decided I shouldn't go in. But she'll like him, Lily. Don't worry. She'll let him live at her house. She . . . she's very kind."

It was snowing a day or so later, a light, feathery snow that melted into a rising vapor as it touched the warm back of the horse that pulled Maria's gig. He was trotting through the alleys between Spruce and Pine, taking a route he had learned well in the past few weeks. There was shelter at the place where they were going, and an elderly stableman to give him a nose bag of oats, and he needed no coaxing.

Rounding the last corner, Maria saw the smoke rising from a chimney and smiled. Since the weather had become bitter, John made it a point to arrive ahead of her and warm the rooms with fires. Driving directly into the stable, she hopped down and gave the old man a bit of money.

"Wipe him dry," she said, "so he won't take a chill."

"I'll surely do that, madam. The weather is raw."

She smiled and left him, going through a side door of the stable that led into the house. The light there was dim; she gave a little scream and then laughed as John appeared from nowhere and swept her up in his arms.

"Heavens," she said, teasingly, "have you no time for greetings?"

"No. I'll not pretend there is anything on my mind but making love. The sooner I strip you bare, the better I will like it." While he talked, John was carrying her into the room he had furnished with everything needed for a lovers' rendezvous. There was a lovely big bed with linen sheets and a goose-down comforter, a bright burning fire in a wide fireplace, comfortable chairs, a thick rug, and even a spirit lamp on a corner table if they cared to make coffee or a hot toddy. The old house was low-beamed and cozy, the windows small and protected from prying eyes by shutters.

Maria sighed with pleasure as he put her down and took off her hooded fur tippet. Tossing it to a chair, he took her cold, pink cheeks in his palms and kissed the smiling mouth.

"Each time I wait here and you come to me," he said, his voice suddenly unsteady, "it seems a miracle. Why do you come? I can offer you only my love and myself, and there must be a dozen good men in Philadelphia who would jump at the chance to marry—"

Maria's fingers touched his lips and closed them. She was laughing, her eyes merry. "You have brought me here on false pretenses," she scolded. "To lecture me instead of to make love! I shall leave if you keep trying to marry me off to some other man."

John brightened and laughed with her. "Never! I may say you should, but only to hear you deny it. Here, let me . . ."

His fingers, Maria decided, were as agile as any lady's maid. And much more exciting as he helped her with her heavy outer clothes. But she still preferred to take off her silken lingerie herself, to tease and pose and evade his reaching hands until his breathing grew ragged, his control began to slip. When he grasped her and pulled her to the bed, she caught fire from his excitement and rolled with him in passionate abandon, her legs wrapped around his lean flanks as she urged him on.

"That was hunger," she said afterward, sitting up. "The next time will be love." She smiled slowly and stretched, arms over her head and her breasts rising like ivory moons. "Lasting love, my darling, for we have the whole afternoon. I shall undertake to make you cry for mercy."

He had never known a woman so sensuous, so wise in the ways of heightening desire. She used every sense, of sight, of odor, of touch and hearing, whispering erotic words, tonguing them into his ears, playing adoring slave to his rapidly hardening arousal. And then she held off, laughing softly as she whispered: "Not yet, love. Not yet."

"I cry mercy," he said huskily. "Mercy, or I burst."

For all her teasing, her own heart was pounding thunderously, her loins aching to be filled. She turned at last and opened her thighs for him. "All right," she said, with a fine carelessness. "I'll not keep you waiting longer."

He pushed in slowly, feeling her shudder and tremble

with delight, feeling her strong, pulsing climax begin before he was fully mated with her. And then he was helpless, caught in the shattering glory of his own release. But still he smiled secretly as he floated down from the peak, knowing she had been as close to the edge of madness as he, wanting him as much as he had wanted her.

Chapter 9

❧

It was nearly Christmas, and Maria, in sudden rebellion against the wintry scene outside, the drab streets and bare trees, began early and decorated the entire downstairs of the house with wreaths of fragrant pine, swags of red ribbon and what seemed to be dozens of candles. She opened the folding doors between the two parlors, set up a magnificent Christmas tree tall enough to brush the twelve-foot-high ceiling, and covered it with ornaments. Colored balls, toy trumpets, and bright tin whistles were stuck amongst the needles; carved wooden angels, painted in bright colors, hung in frozen flight on the branches; silver bells tinkled and candy canes swung and were coveted both by the kitten, Boots, who batted them with his tiny paws, and by Lily's bright, greedy eyes.

Cassie helped. In her mind, the decorating and the odors of cookies and candies coming from the kitchens were all in honor of Robert's return, expected daily. Arthur Masefield was coming with him, for Maria had insisted, saying that since the holiday was too short for Arthur to travel to South

Carolina where his family lived, he could celebrate with them.

"And," Maria said to Sallie Fernod in private, "it will give Robert company as he enjoys the city and winter sports. A boy his age will certainly prefer male company."

Rolling out dough, Sallie smiled indulgently. She knew Maria like the back of her hand, and she understood jealousy. "Maybe. But he's fond of Cassie and he may take her along. Why worry about it? It's only for a few days."

"Yes, of course." But Maria was unconvinced. When Robert did arrive, bounding up the steps and into the house like a healthy young lion, bigger than ever and bursting with vitality, it was all Maria could do to stand aside as Cassie flung herself at him, hugging him hard, laughing and weeping with joy. Behind him Arthur Masefield grinned at them as he dragged in the luggage. Then he dropped the bags and picked up excited, babbling Lily himself, giving her a hug.

"As you can see," he said to Maria as he put her down, "we've missed the girls. How Lily has grown!" He came forward and took Maria's hands. "You were wonderfully generous to ask me here for Christmas, Mrs. Andelet. I would have been lonely in my own digs. No one hangs around school on the holidays."

Maria smiled, struck by the gratitude in his eyes, the remembered enthusiasm and naiveté that made him seem almost as young as Robert in spite of his age and superior education.

"We will enjoy having you—" she began, and stopped as Robert, now holding Lily in his arms, came over to them, trailed by an adoring Cassie.

"Merry Christmas, Aunt Maria," he said, smiling, and bent his tawny gold head to kiss her cheek.

Maria felt the warmth of his lips, the faint bristle of young beard on his cold skin, caught the warm, musky scent of a healthy male. As he put Lily on her feet again, Maria stared up at him, for once unsure of herself.

"Merry Christmas, Robert," she said through stiff lips. "You—You've grown. Are your studies going well?" She could see Cassie's upturned face at Robert's side, the pride and happiness in her eyes.

"Galloping," Arthur answered beside her. "He soaks up knowledge like a sponge. I'd wager he could be through college by the age most students begin. It's true, Mrs. Andelet. He's eager and very able to learn."

Robert laughed with easy warmth, turning away to pick up the bags. "Masefield exaggerates, Aunt Maria. I do study hard, as anyone would who had the opportunity you've given me. But I'm no genius."

And no farm boy either, Maria thought, amazed by the change. A scant three and a half months, and the uncertain boy was a confident young man. Arthur was right: Robert Harmon was quick to learn. But perhaps that was all to the good. It would take some thinking, though, to turn it to advantage. "Dickon will show you your rooms," she said, turning toward the back of the house. "I'll call him."

Cassie caught her arm. "Let Dickon rest, Aunt Maria. I helped Maud and Adah with the rooms, so I know where they are. Come on, Robbie, and you too, Mr. Masefield. Did you know I have a bluestocking to teach me now?"

"A bluestocking?" Arthur groaned and they all grabbed pieces of baggage and went up the stairs in a wave of joking and laughter, leaving Maria and Lily to follow or not, as they pleased. Maria shrugged and held out a hand to the child.

"Come, Lily. Let's see what Sallie Fernod is baking. It smells good."

In the kitchen she put cookies on a small plate and set out a glass of milk to occupy Lily.

"Christmas just arrived for Cassie," Maria told Sallie ruefully. "She won't require anything else. Her face glows like the sun in June, and Robert is just as pleased to see her."

Sallie's chuckle rumbled deep in her throat. "What did you expect?"

"Frankly, I had hoped he would become bored with her. Most fifteen-year-old brothers consider an eleven-year-old sister to be nothing more than a nuisance."

"Their life was different from most," Sallie pointed out.

"Well, it isn't now!" Maria's voice was sharp. She heard the sharpness herself and shook her head. "It won't help to be angry, I suppose. As you said, it's only for a few days."

* * *

A few days never to be forgotten. The gaiety and happiness Robert brought with him was a magnet to everyone. As his part of the holiday, Arthur Masefield chartered a large, horse-drawn sleigh for their daily use, and it was always filled to the limit when it left the house. Jacob and Violet Bradford joined the crowd, Melainie Scott went along as a chaperon, Lily sat on Cassie's lap, and Arthur sat up on the driver's seat with Robert, who drove. They were bundled to the ears in warm clothes, and swathed with wool lap robes against the bitter cold.

Often the party ended up on the Schuylkill, ice skating with the other intrepid Philadelphians who braved the winter wind. Skating was a passion of Cassie's; she would have gone there every day. But she also loved coasting on borrowed sleds down long snowy slopes in the parks, and Lily could join in on that, clinging to Cassie's waist and screaming with joy.

Home again in near darkness as the long winter nights came on, the whole group trooped into the Andelet house. Neither Jacob nor Violet could tear themselves away from the warmth and noise and fun and go next door to the quiet Bradford residence. Maria shrugged, laughed, and told Sallie Fernod to cook enough for two more.

Christmas, when it came, was almost overlooked because of the day itself, which dawned with rare blue skies and bright sun in below-zero weather. The Bradford family came in force for the rituals of giving and receiving gifts, most of which were either to be worn or eaten, for the old Quaker values of usefulness still ruled custom. That over, everyone except Lily, who had a new doll to play with, agreed the weather was perfect for skating. John Kendall brought a sleigh, and the Bradfords and Maria joined him for the trip to the river.

"Only to watch, of course," Geneva said, pulling her furs around her and settling down for the ride. "It's been years since Benedict and I have skated. But it will be a pleasure to see Violet skimming lightly over the ice."

Kendall's sleigh moved away, and in the sleigh behind, Robert's amused gaze slid wickedly to Cassie's carefully sedate face, which lowered and turned pink as she struggled not to laugh at such a description of Violet's skating, which was far more stumble and screech than skimming. Melainie leaned forward between Violet and Cassie to hide Cassie and the giggle she was sure would bubble out sooner or later. Arthur, who by now had exchanged his seat beside Robert for one beside Melainie, gave Melainie a look of fervent approval for this intervention. Then Jacob spoke and ruined it all.

"You heard that, Violet," he said. "Today you must skim instead of scream."

Except for Violet, everyone broke out in uncontrollable laughter. Tears came to eyes and were wiped away quickly, lest they freeze. Violet turned pale with rage, her freckles standing out and her green eyes blazing. "I don't *scream,*" she shrilled at the top of her voice, "and I'd skate as well as any of you if you'd teach me like you teach Cassie! All of you take her out on the ice twice as often as you take me!"

"Teach her?" Jacob was still laughing. "She skates better than I do. I take her out for the pure pleasure of it."

"Never mind," Robert said, sobering and driving on. "Perhaps we haven't been fair. I'll help you today, Vi."

Violet shut her open mouth and settled back, purring and satisfied. "Thank you, Robert. It's nice to have one gentleman in the crowd, at least."

Under the lap robe Arthur Masefield squeezed Melainie's hand. "And one lovely, thoughtful lady," he whispered, and watched her color come up to the roots of the pale blond hair inside her velvet bonnet.

The Bradfords owned a boathouse and landing pier on the Schuylkill north of Market Street, which provided shelter from the wind and a good view of the skaters for Benedict and Geneva. The others sat on the small pier to put on their skates and then swoop away to join the brightly dressed crowd of skaters already on the ice. Cass was the first out, a bright spot in her claret wool gown and white mittens, the sable fur of her hooded tippet setting off the pink and ivory of her face, the warm gray green of her huge eyes.

Maria, seated on the pier while John Kendall helped her put on her skates, saw Cassie join the group of other skaters. Watching her, studying the line of her clear profile, the turn of her head, the grace of the small, slim body swinging the tilting layers of skirt and petticoats through the intricacies of a tight figure eight, Maria felt a rush of pride.

"Just look at her, John," she said. "She's the best of the lot. Cassie is going to excel at anything she does."

John smiled. "She's a beautiful, agile, charming girl. That's enough. Don't ask her to be the best at everything."

Maria stood up, balancing on the skates. "I don't have to ask," she said, crossing her arms and offering him her hands in the skaters' hold. "She just is. Like Mark, she does everything well."

"There goes Jacob, chasing her down," John pointed out. "Let's follow."

With a nervous giggle, Violet sailed past, held securely by Robert's strong arms. "Isn't this fun, Aunt Maria? I do wish my parents would join in!"

"Heaven forbid," Maria muttered, head down as she matched her strokes to John's long legs. "The Schuylkill would have to freeze top to bottom to hold Benedict." Her face came up, growing rosy with effort, her eyes laughing into his. "But the silly little fool is right. This *is* fun!"

They skated; Robert with Violet, Jacob with Cassie, John with Maria, and Arthur with Melainie, in and out of the spaces along the line of boathouses and piers, amongst the other skaters and back, waving as they swooped past the Bradfords, who sat in the sun and watched benignly. They skated until the sun dropped sharply west, and then bundled into the sleighs and went back for Maria's Christmas supper.

Leaving both horse and sleigh in the livery stable south of Pine, the young people walked back to the house. But John Kendall delivered Maria and the Bradfords to her front door and then jingled off in the sleigh alone, saying Alice would expect him home.

"Kendall must not know what a supper you serve, Maria," Benedict said jovially, going inside. "Or he'd let his wife wait a bit. I trust you're having the frizzled beef and the smoked salmon?"

"I'd never dare ask you to attend otherwise," Maria answered. "And we're also having oyster stew. Ah, there you are, Cassie. Come up with us, and I'll brush your hair. It tangled in the wind."

Going up the stairs, Geneva ignored Cassie's presence

entirely. "John Kendall is always here, isn't he?" she asked Maria. "Hardly a day goes by I don't see him at your door. Honestly, if it were any other man, I'd say you were being foolish to allow him to come so often. In fact, the way he looks at you . . ."

"Oh, please," Maria said, half chuckling. *"John?* Come now, Gennie—don't tell me you suspect John Kendall of an illicit yearning for me?"

Geneva tried to keep her face straight, but an unwilling laugh broke through. "I'll have to admit he's as dry as dust, Maria. And you're hardly the kind of woman he'd want, with his precise ways. Besides, everyone knows how faithful he is to poor Alice. He rushes home every night to sit with her and talk. No, I cannot suspect anything between you two but business, though Lord knows there's been plenty of that. He's making you a rich woman, Benedict says."

"Oh, yes," Maria said carelessly. "He's given me good advice, but after all, I pay well for it." She chattered on, and behind them on the stairs Cassie followed the swish of their voluminous skirts and tried not to think of Aunt Maria's head on Mr. Kendall's shoulder, nor of how easily and quickly she had laughed off Mrs. Bradford's faint suspicion. Especially that last. Why, Aunt Maria was better at deceiving someone than that crook Fagin in Oliver Twist!

On New Year's Day the Bradford family observed the old custom of calling on their friends, and Jacob and Violet were forced to go along. It was the last day in Philadelphia for Robert and Arthur Masefield, and they chose to celebrate it by taking Cassie and Melainie Scott on one more trip to the Schuylkill for skating. Watching the sleigh jingle away on new-fallen snow, Maria smiled. Cassie's small, red-clad figure sat erect on the driver's seat beside Robert's bulk. On the wide seat behind them, two more figures sat close together and bundled beneath a lap robe. Maria would have bet her fortune that under that robe were entwined hands. By now, everyone in the house knew Arthur had lost his heart to Melainie.

Wandering back to the kitchen, Maria spoke to Sallie Fernod, who always knew all the gossip. "Piers Von Graaf may lose his lovely bit on the side," she said, sitting down and pouring a cup of tea from Sallie's pot. "I wouldn't be at all surprised if Arthur proposed today."

"The lady may refuse."

"Oh, no. I believe she's transferred her affections. She seems as entranced with Arthur as he is with her."

"Entranced but sad," Sallie said, regret in her rich voice. "Our—what do you call her, our bluestocking?—is a woman of high ideals. She'll either refuse or confess her sin, to give him a chance to forgive her or back out. Either way, she'll not be a bride."

Maria gazed at the broad, black face, fascinated. "You truly believe that, don't you? You think Arthur Masefield would actually withdraw his proposal if she told him about Piers?"

"Yes. Your Arthur is not a man of the world. He will be badly shocked, and Miss Scott will see it. She will then say she understands how he feels and offer to forget the proposal. He, the poor fool, will weakly agree. And sorely regret it later, when he realizes that women as beautiful and intelligent as Melainie Scott are as rare as diamonds."

"Or, when he marries a virgin who hates to be touched and lies beneath him like a block of ice."

Sallie laughed, deep and merry. "It would serve him right."

They sat together in perfect understanding and silence until Maria finished her tea and stood up. "I wish I had taken time to talk to Melainie," she said. "I've been too engrossed in my own problems. Did I tell you that Arthur and I have decided to push Robert's education ahead with summer studies?"

Sallie gave her a wry, knowing glance. "No, but it doesn't surprise me. Will you let him come home at all during the summer?"

"He will have ten days between summer and fall sessions. I would presume he'd spend some of them in Eagle Forge."

Silently, Sallie rose and glided to the iron sink, carrying the teapot and cups. Emptying the dregs from the pot, she frowned. "She'll never forget him, you know."

"Of course not," Maria said, her voice a little too high and shrill. "I wouldn't want her to. I simply want to raise her without him—without his influence."

For a moment Sallie looked as if she would say more, but then she shrugged and let it go. She was another one who knew the iron will inside Maria Andelet's softly curved body.

She had greeted him with laughter and tears, but the next morning Cassie bade Robert good-bye quietly, her head bent, her huge eyes shadowed by long, black lashes, her hands clinging to his until the last moment. She knew she wouldn't see him again until mid-August, for he had told her himself last night and had tried to convince her that it was better this way.

"Those extra two months or so every summer will make the time shorter in the end," he had said. "I'll be on my own and making money that much sooner. Don't you see, Cass? I need to be able to make a living for us."

She had seen the sense in that, and had tried to smile. "I'll help, Robbie. I'll be a teacher, like Miss Scott." The thought of being like her idol had cheered her, though Melainie had looked utterly miserable at dinner last night and had gone to bed directly afterward.

Now, conscious of the time, she loosed Robbie's hands and gave him a final hug around his waist, stepped back and smiled, the effect slightly marred by a quivering lower lip.

"Tell Mr. Masefield good-bye for me," she said. "He went through here so fast I hadn't time to tell him myself. You will write, won't you?"

Robert's strong face softened into tenderness. "You know I will, Cass. Every week, and I want you to do the same. We're still us in those letters, talking to each other, no matter how far apart we are. Kiss Lily for me, and . . . and keep on making me proud." He touched the top of her head awkwardly, smoothing her hair, and he was gone.

Maria and the maids took down the Christmas decorations the next day and stored them in the attic. The day after that Mrs. Brooke assumed command of a thorough housecleaning. Melainie and Cassie took over the care of Lily for a time, turning the schoolroom into a kindergarten. Melainie, who seemed rather quiet and sad after the holiday, threw herself into the task of teaching Lily her letters and numbers. A week later, called on to listen to Lily reciting the alphabet on the third floor, Maria was holding the playful black and white kitten in her lap and applauding Lily's stumbling recitation when John Kendall sent Adah to bring her down to the first-floor study.

It was so unlike John, who was always willing to sit down with a cup of tea and wait, that Maria found herself hurrying down the stairs with a feeling of dread in her stomach.

"What has happened? Is anyone hurt?" She blurted the questions as she opened the door. He was standing at the back window and staring out at the snow-covered garden and stark, leafless trees. He turned immediately to reassure her. "No one is hurt or ill, Maria. I didn't mean to frighten you. It's only business."

She smiled with relief. "Oh. Well, that can't be too bad. The way you've scattered our funds among so many ventures, we can bear a loss here and there. Wait, I'll ask Sallie to send in coffee for us both."

Over the coffee she discovered why John was so upset. It wasn't the loss, which could be easily borne, it was because it looked as if Payne Regan was responsible, and John felt guilty because he had hired him.

"I have always prided myself on knowing an honest man," John said. "If this is true, I won't know whether to trust my judgment again. Somewhere between Eagle Forge and the ironworks here on the Schuylkill, we seem to be losing iron. As you know, production is up. So are prices. We're making money, but not much more than we were before. I've gone over the shipping records a dozen times, both Regan's and those from the ironworks, and I've talked to the bargemen. They all say they're as puzzled as I am."

"Have you talked to Regan?"

"No," John said slowly, "and perhaps I won't. If he is stealing from you, I want to know how. I'll talk to Noonan and a couple more men I can trust, and put them to watch when the furnace starts up again."

Maria was silent, thinking of Payne Regan and how he made her feel. She could feel now the faint echo of chilly foreboding, see the sneer on his thin mouth. "Fire him," she said suddenly. "Get rid of him. Sallie Fernod warned me about Regan. She said he was trouble on two legs, and it looks as if she was right."

"We need to catch him," John said gently. "We need to see that he's punished. Fire him, and he'll only victimize someone else."

Maria opened her mouth to protest, and then closed it again. John was right, of course. A thief should be caught and brought to justice.

"All right. Handle it any way you believe is right. But be careful. I have my instincts about people too. And I believe Payne Regan is a dangerous man."

Chapter 10

In mid-April they were back at the manor again. The hired men were now plowing the fields for corn, wheat, and flax, after first plowing the big kitchen garden for the women and children to plant. The plow had disturbed a nest of field mice near the house, tiny things that leaped and scrambled over the furrows of black, fertile soil and drove the kitten into a frenzy of leaping and scrambling in pursuit. Boots didn't catch any of them, and came back to the kitchen door with his white feet, nose, and chest as black as the rest of him, mewing piteously.

Raking down the furrows, copying the efforts of Adah and Sallie, Cassie watched Lily wash the squalling, furious kitten at the backyard pump, getting herself thoroughly wet while doing so. Cassie laughed, thinking of how she'd describe the scene in her letter to Robert. She had made up her mind when he left at New Year's that if they must be apart most of the time, her letters would stay cheerful and full of news. Robbie was working hard for them all, and the least she could do was keep up her spirits. Aunt Maria had made that a lot easier by giving Cassie her own mare and teaching her how to ride. The mare, Dawn, was a bright golden-red chestnut with a white star on her forehead, and Cassie adored her. She was already planning to surprise Robbie with her riding skill when he came in August.

"Cassie?"

The sound came from above, and Cass looked up, shading her eyes. Melainie smiled down at her from a second-story window, her pale blond hair a silver halo in the April sun.

"Lessons! If we finish in time we can go to the village with Brooksie and Lily this afternoon."

Coming out the back door, Maria smiled as Cassie dashed to put up the rake and hurry inside. She stopped her to kiss her cheek and smooth her hair.

"I'll be at the forge most of the day, Cassie, going over the books. If you see ribbons you like in the village, Melainie will buy them for you."

"Thank you. But I have plenty of ribbons. Is Noonan going with you?"

"Yes, he has a wagonload of supplies to go out. But he'll harness the bay to the surrey before he goes."

"I can do that. Robbie showed me how."

"Noonan will do it," Maria said crisply. "It isn't work for a girl. Now, hurry along. Melainie is waiting." Crossing the yard and the garden space, heading for the stables, Maria thought that possibly what she planned to do wasn't work for a female either. John Kendall, tied up this week in court appearances, had told her to leave the books alone until he could go through them. But it would be another four days before he could leave the city, and that was too long. If Payne Regan found out John had questioned the bargemen —and he'd be seeing them soon, now that the furnace was working again—he'd have time to hide or change any evidence he'd left around.

Noonan was waiting, horses hitched, the wagon loaded and Maria's mare, Diamond, saddled. Maria talked with him for a moment; Noonan, like Sallie Fernod, was in her confidence.

"I don't know what we'll find," she ended, "but whatever is there, we say nothing until John can come down. That's a promise I made John."

116

The habitual sneer that played around his thin mouth deepened into an unpleasant smile. "You surprise me, Mistress. I wouldn't have thought you gave a damn about propriety. I've eyes in my head, you know."

She could feel the heat of blood creeping up her cheeks. She had known that the men who worked for her would wonder about John Kendall; she had counted on their loyalty to keep their mouths shut. But this man was not hers like the others were, not loyal to the ironmistress. Nor would he be here long, she decided suddenly, even if the records proved him innocent. She raised her chin.

"Bring the books and other records to the office *now,*" she said crisply. "I will wait in the store."

In the end it surprised her how little time it took to figure out the method Regan had used to cover his tracks. There was one bargeman involved, she was sure. But then she'd been sure of that once Noonan had told her about the bargeman who knew Regan, and both of them members of the Revenue Marine! In her youth near Baltimore, Maria had known a good deal about the men of the Revenue Marine, and given a chance to steal, none of them were angels.

Anyway, what Regan was doing was simple. Every so often, maybe once every two or three weeks, he had noted in the shipping records that he had sent one barge downstream when in reality it had been two; one, evidently, to the ironworks that bought from the Andelets, and one to someone else, who undoubtedly paid the bargeman in cash. It was easy to see, if you knew how to add up the daily production, the inventory on hand, and then divide it by bargeloads.

Sitting at the rough desk, alone in the small room, she leaned back and laughed a little. It was a marvelous scheme, really. No one but John Kendall, who studied profit and loss constantly, would have ever wondered about it. The men who loaded the barges never saw the records. John, who saw the records, never saw the barges loaded.

In any case, she had the proof. Sorting through the papers, she picked out several that showed production and inventory, several that showed shipping for the same times. Enough, she knew, to prove her accusation when she made it. She put the rest away and, papers in hand, went into the store. It was past noon, which meant a new shift, and there were several men there, buying supplies before going home. She spoke to them, smiling, and then went to Martin.

"Put these in your safe, Abel, and don't give them to anyone except Mr. Kendall or me."

Abel nodded, looking at her with wide, questioning eyes, then glancing down at the papers when she handed them to him. He hurried to the safe under the end of his counter and put them in, slammed the door and spun the lock. Coming back, he nodded again.

"He won't get them, Mistress."

Maria smiled. "Good." There was no reason to ask who "he" was. She went out, and met Regan coming up the wide steps. He stopped, looking at her directly, questioningly. She met his gaze, and in her strange, down-tilted eyes there must have been a look of triumph, for suddenly, for the second time that day, his face turned red.

"Well," he said, trying for an even tone, "it didn't take you long to get tired of those records you wanted so badly."

Maria gave him a dazzling smile. "That's true. I found what I wanted almost immediately." She went past him toward the furnace, and he turned and went with her, catching up and matching his stride to hers. He took her arm and spoke, keeping his voice low.

"If you're thinking of bringing charges against me," he said, "remember what I can do to you. You'd be ruined if I told what I know."

"I don't know what you're talking about, Mr. Regan. Please take your hand off my arm."

They had reached the stairs that went up to the bridge house, and he swung her around and beneath the steps, pushing his face close to hers. "Don't you play cat and mouse with *me,*" he said hotly. "You're looking for a chance to take me to court, and I'm telling you you'd regret it!"

"Would I? Why?" She sounded contemptuous, for it had come to her that no one of any importance would listen to an accused thief on a matter of who was sleeping with whom. They would simply put it down to a juvenile attempt at revenge, if, indeed, they ever heard it. If her affair with John was all he had for blackmail, she'd risk it.

Regan suddenly let her go, though he still had her trapped between his muscular body and the steps. "The penalties are stiff," he said, almost whispering, "for harboring an escaped slave. I suspect they're even worse for aiding and abetting an escaped murderess. Now, does that buy me out?"

Shock coursed through Maria's body, but at the same time she caught at his last words. *He wasn't sure.* If he were sure, he wouldn't have needed to ask. He wouldn't have asked at all. He would have gone straight to the police. The reward for Sallie would be enough to offset losing a job.

"This time," she said finally, thankful for the gloom beneath the steps that shadowed her face, "I truly don't know what you're talking about. Who is it that is harboring runaway slaves and helping murderers?"

"I said *murderess!*"

"Oh. I misunderstood. Anyway, the question still stands. Frankly, I thought you were threatening to spread gossip about John Kendall and me, which is ridiculous. After all, he's my lawyer, and he manages my businesses, and I must see him often because—"

"Shut up!" Regan made a nervous gesture. "You talk like a fool! No one would listen to me about that. But the police will listen to what I know about that big black woman in your kitchen! She's been wanted for fifteen years, ever since I worked in the Revenue Marine."

"You mean my *cook?*" Maria asked incredulously. "Why, Sallie's been with my family ever since she was born and she's never even thought of escaping! As for hurting someone, that's almost funny. Sallie wouldn't hurt a flea."

Regan looked belligerent but far from sure of himself. It was apparent he had doubts. "She could have a hard time clearing herself if I name her, innocent or not! There aren't many women that size, and damn few slaves who speak English as well as a Philadelphia lawyer—"

"Now, *you* listen," Maria said sharply. "Stop grasping at straws and trying to blackmail me with something so stupid! It isn't at all necessary, anyway. You took too much for granted. I've never had any intention of taking you to court."

He stared, angry but confused. "Then what in hell *were* you planning?"

Maria shrugged. "I'm planning on giving you notice. I know you've been getting away with some pig iron on your own, but I've no way to prove it. When Mr. Kendall gets here next week, he'll work it out with you."

Slowly, Regan relaxed. He seemed eager to believe she meant what she said. "That's better," he admitted, and shifted away from her. "Maybe I can talk sense with Kendall. A man will know everyone takes a little of the extra around a business like this. I'm no different, though maybe I have been a little too greedy—"

Maria slipped out between the steps and his body and turned to climb up to the bridge house. She was shaken and deeply frightened under her outward calm. "Just talk to him," she said, trying to sound reassuring. "He'll know what to do." She hoped to God he would, anyway. John really knew nothing about Sallie's past, and she'd have to tell him now. She entered the bridge house just as the trunnel-head door was opened. Gasping, she turned away, putting a hand over her eyes to shield them from the heat and glare.

A half hour later, having made all of her official calls, Maria went back to the corral and mounted Diamond again, worried but determined. Somehow she was sure Regan would keep on sniffing around Sallie Fernod's past, and if he did she'd be forced to send Sallie somewhere else— somewhere safe. She hated even thinking of it, for Sallie was her true friend, the one person in the world who knew all that had happened to Maria Gerard Andelet, all that had made her who she was. She would be lost without Sallie.

Brooding, she rode slowly through the woods until she was nearly to the open space and the road that led up to the manor. Entering a small glade, Diamond stepped skittishly and blew, whuffling air through her velvety nose. Alerted, Maria looked around and saw another horse, tied to a tree. Then Regan stepped out from the brush and grabbed Diamond's halter.

"I mean you no harm," he said, with an attempt at a smile. "I wanted a few words without others around."

It was the others around that had made Maria brave. Now her heart began beating thunderously. Still, she controlled herself.

"I don't like this," she said stiffly. "We've already talked. You are to take your complaints and excuses to Mr. Kendall from now on."

Regan ignored what she said. "I've been thinking since we talked, Mistress. I want you to reconsider. I want your promise to keep me on."

She stared at him in amazement. "Are you crazy? You *stole* from me! Watch your step, Regan. You'll end up in jail yet."

"No, I won't. I've figured one thing out—you're afraid of me." He laughed, his eyes glittering. "I'm not sure why, but when I find out I'll use it. Then we'll see who runs Eagle Forge."

Afraid? Maria despised the word. Furious, she tried to jerk the mare away from his gripping hand, and the mare reared, frightened. Regan pulled her down, cursing.

"Get your hands off my horse!" Maria raged. "Let her go, I say!" She raised her crop and cracked it down hard across Regan's shoulders. He gritted his teeth and grabbed it, snatching it out of her hand. Tossing it away, he wound a hand in Maria's skirt and pulled. She gasped and kicked the mare, hard.

"Go, Diamond! Go!"

The mare reared again, desperate, and pulled her bridle free from Regan's hand. Coming down, she spurted forward from her bunched hindquarters, and the leap, combined with Regan's grip on her skirt, threw Maria to the ground. She scrambled to her feet as the terrified horse disappeared, crashing through the woods.

"Damn you! Haven't you sense enough to know how to treat a blooded mare? Go back to the forge and send someone with a wagon to take me home!"

Regan stared at her, and then he threw back his head and laughed. The sound rang through the small glade, echoed off the hill, a strange, mirthless snarl.

"By God," he said as the echo died away, "no one can fault you for lack of nerve. Have you forgotten you fired me, and threatened to put me in jail?"

"And why wouldn't I, you fool? You threatened me with blackmail! And, on top of that, you're a thief and a liar!"

"And a man," Regan said grimly, "who no longer has to take orders from you." He reached out suddenly and grabbed the broad belt that circled her waist, jerking her close. His gaze ran over the shape of her breasts under the silk shirt, moved up slowly to probe her furious eyes. "Maybe I'll try giving you some orders, *Mistress*. Maybe I'll see what you're like naked and on your back. The way Kendall hangs around your skirts, it must be good."

The first tendril of real fear curled sickeningly in Maria's stomach. She leaned away from him and looked him in the eye. "You leave me alone or I'll make you sorry you didn't. Someone will soon see my horse and come looking for me."

Regan laughed again, beginning to breathe hard. She could smell his excitement. "Who will? Old Noonan? He's still at the forge." His free hand snaked forward and grabbed the front of her shirt, tearing it open and exposing the tops of her breasts. Maria set her jaw and swung, her palm striking the side of his face with a resounding crack.

"Damn you!" she cried again. "I—" Knocked off her feet by a hard blow from his fist, she fell to the ground and crumpled as Regan threw himself on her, grabbing her throat.

"You hit me again," he said hoarsely, "and I'll kill you. You're nothing but a slut, anyway." Still holding her throat, he inched up along her body and stared down into her eyes. "You want to die?"

His eyes were hot, an animal excitement building in their depths. Maria swallowed the acid taste of fear, her throat aching from the pressure of his fingers.

"No, I don't want to die."

Regan grimaced, his lips flattening, stretching thin in a parody of a smile. "Then pull up your skirts for me."

Her anger was gone, swallowed up by danger. She was thinking again, her mind honed to a fine edge. Diamond would be home now. If she could hold him off for a little while . . . She moved, reaching down as if to catch hold of her skirts, and he eased away to give her room, grinning now like an animal baring its teeth. She flashed up and was gone, running through the woods straight toward the manor, hearing him curse and start up, then his feet pounding behind her. Dodging, putting trees between them, dodging again, she caught sight of the manor through the trees. Then she shrieked, feeling him grab her shoulder, shrieked again as he hit her with his fist and sent her flying against a tree. He lunged for her, and she wrapped her arms around the rough bark and kicked hard, her booted heel catching him low in the belly. Howling with pain, he bent double and she kicked again, grazing the side of his head. He turned a face near black with fury and stared at her, insane hatred in his eyes.

"You devil bitch," he whispered. "Now I'll kill you."

She screamed again as he caught her flailing foot and pulled her from the tree. Scrambling away, trying to get up, she screamed once more when his heavy boot slammed into her side. Then she was quiet except for the sobbing in and out of her tortured breath, and Regan screamed, a scream half pain and half anger. Maria's breathing grew easier as she watched him struggle helplessly in Sallie Fernod's grip. Sallie had his arms crossed and bent up his back, putting a strain on the shoulder sockets. She used one hand to hold him, her long fingers clasping his crossed wrists. He jerked and flailed, an expression of frantic disbelief on his strained face.

"I knew you would come," Maria said when she got her breath. "I didn't know if you'd be in time. He's crazy."

"It only took the sight of your mare. Noonan had told me enough to make me watchful. Are you badly hurt?"

"Bad enough. A broken rib, I think." She sat up, wincing, and then struggled to her feet, holding her side. "That and bruises," she said, catching her breath. "Nothing to what would have happened if you hadn't come."

"It was good you kept screaming," Sallie said. "The noise led me and deafened him to my arrival." She swung Regan around in the circle of her arm and looked at him curiously.

The fury in his eyes had faded; he stared back at her in dawning fear. She laughed without mirth, her eyes like dark ice. "Still feeling mean, little man?"

"He wasn't sure, Sallie, but he threatened blackmail."

Sallie shrugged. "It makes little difference now, Maria, what he planned. He shouldn't have touched you."

She came, bringing Regan along, to offer her other arm to Maria. She took it, limping as they left the woods and came out on the road. Sallie looked up the long slope to the manor, her wide brow furrowed.

"Shall I go after Noonan and the wagon?"

"I can walk."

"What in hell are you going to do with me?" Regan asked, his voice trembling with angry fear and frustration.

Sallie looked at him, surprised. "Tie you up until Noonan gets back. Did you think I'd let you go?"

He cursed and kicked at her, then cried out as she ignored the kick and lifted him off his feet, straight up with his crossed wrists, so his weight tore at the ligaments of his shoulders. Tears of anger and pain ran down his flat cheeks as she lowered him to his feet again.

"I know you had to try it," she said calmly. "But don't try anything else. I'll break your neck if you cause me a minute of trouble, now or later."

They took it slow, the man walking slightly ahead to ease the strain on his arms, the big woman holding him securely but with most of her attention on the small figure by her side. Once Maria coughed, grimaced and spit, and Sallie stopped, staring at a fleck of blood on Maria's lip.

"Blood! Could that broken rib have pierced your lung?"

"No," Maria said, wiping it off. "It's from a loosened tooth, I suppose. It's not bad. The rib hurts like fury, but nothing bubbles inside." She glanced up at the house. It was closer. Thank heaven, Cassie had gone with the others to the village. She would have hated having Cassie frightened. Pray God they wouldn't come back until this was settled. She glanced sideways at Payne Regan, whose dark face had turned gray and stiff, the wild anger cooled by fear and helplessness. He knew now, Maria thought, all he needed to know about Sallie Fernod.

Adah came hurrying from the front door as they crossed the lawn. "Oh, my dear Lord save us! What has happened?"

"I took a tumble from my horse," Maria said rapidly, "that is all." Her eyes flicked up at Sallie's broad face and met the dark eyes, calm and merciless. "But you can help me, Adah, and let Sallie take care of Mr. Regan."

Chapter 11

It was past midnight when Sallie Fernod came up the broad staircase on her silent feet and through the hall to the suite of rooms Maria used. Going noiselessly through the sitting room, she tapped once at Maria's bedroom door and then slipped in, flowing through the door like a dark cloud. She saw by the light of a flickering candle that Maria's huge eyes were open, her expression strained but calm, waiting.

Moving to the side of the bed, Sallie put a wide palm on Maria's forehead and frowned. Bruises on Maria's cheek and chin had gotten worse, her ivory skin crushed and darkened like petals on a windblown flower. But the forehead was cool.

"I'm all right," Maria said, her voice soft and low. "Tell me what happened."

"We're safe," Sallie said, "unless he had mentioned his suspicions to some other."

"He wouldn't. He'd be afraid they'd get the reward." Searching the broad, dark face looming above her, Maria took in a deep breath. "You . . . he's dead, isn't he?"

128

"There was no other way."

Letting out the breath, Maria nodded, her mouth quivering and then firming. "Who else knows?"

"Noonan. The Biederman brothers were close by, but I am sure they suspected nothing."

"The Biedermans?" Maria sat up, wincing but distracted. "Why go near anyone? That could make trouble, Sallie—"

"We needed a place to put him. A freshly dug grave would be dangerous if a search were made. And no one saw us. We went to the furnace long after dark, and Noonan had a bottle. I waited under the steps with Regan, and Noonan went up and brought the Biedermans down to drink. I took Regan up and was down and away before they returned. It was easy enough to do, though I scorched my skirt opening the trunnel head."

"Oh, dear God," Maria said faintly, and lay down again. In her mind she could see the red glare and hear the roar that leaped out when the trunnel head was opened, see the body with the stiff, gray face sliding in. What was it Jacob had said? *Like a door into hell.* She shuddered and rubbed her eyes. "I suppose it was best," she said finally. "Certainly there will be nothing left. Are you sure the Biedermans neither saw nor heard anything suspicious?"

"I am sure," Sallie said, straightening the covers around Maria with tender care. "They couldn't see from where they were, and you know I make no noise. As for Mr. Regan, he couldn't make a sound. I gagged him well when I tied him up."

Maria turned white, but she held out until Sallie had gone, and then, her side shooting flaming arrows of pain through her chest, she crawled from the bed, pulled the chamberpot out from underneath and vomited into it, weeping with pain and horror. She had thought Sallie would kill quickly and then dispose of the body. It was terrible, *awful,* to imagine how it had been, the torture of lying there, unable to move or scream, watching that great dark form pulling aside the trunnel head. Seeing . . . knowing . . . when the blaze and roar leaped out. Being dragged over toward the orange glare, the blistering heat . . . She leaned, gasping, against the side of the bed and wept for the agony and terror of Payne Regan's evil soul. Sallie Fernod had shown him not one drop of mercy. But then, Sallie had always loved and hated with equal strength.

Later, when time had passed and she could think again, Maria knew there was no use in trying to hide it all from John. He would never believe her injuries came from a simple fall, and he had to have some explanation about the records and Regan. But there were things he must never know.

In the next two days Maria planned carefully, and was ready for John before he came. Parts of it she hated: most of all, deceiving John. It was strange how much that bothered her. When she had been married to Armand she routinely kept anything that might irritate or annoy him to herself, and in fact prided herself on how well she did it. But then, she had never shared her thoughts with Armand, nor her secret hopes and dreams. Gradually, she had given all those things to John, and in the end, her complete love and trust. She knew they were fully returned. But it would never be the same again, for now she must, for Sallie's sake, hide from him the worst sin of all—murder. She hadn't committed it, but she had condoned it. John would never understand that.

Another problem was the necessity of swearing Noonan to secrecy. He was troubled by the affair and had done what he did only for her. Regan had been no threat to him. Still, he shook his silvered head when she apologized for getting him into it.

"I'd do it again, Mistress. He would have killed you, if Sallie hadn't come. Besides, he was headed for hell anyway. All we did was shorten his trip."

It was a gallant speech, and Maria was warmed by his affection, but she felt his sorrow. Noonan would have much rather turned the man over to the authorities. Even so, she trusted him not to reveal what had happened.

When John Kendall did arrive, Maria took the precaution of remaining in bed, for she knew her apparent weakness, along with her bruises and wan appearance, would keep him from badgering her with questions she might have trouble answering.

It worked out well. Once John satisfied himself that she was mending and in no danger, she told him the truth, but not the whole truth. She went from the beginning when she lost her temper with Regan, which she admitted was foolish, right on to the fight in the woods and Sallie rescuing her from what appeared to be certain death at the hands of a guilty and enraged thief. Except she left out Regan's remarks about harboring escaped slaves and murderesses, and failed to mention that Sallie had captured Regan. She let John believe Regan had run away when Sallie arrived.

John became more and more upset as she talked. He paced back and forth, unable to remain seated, and shot question after question at her.

"You do know he hasn't been seen since?"

"Yes. I've been told."

"Has he ever mentioned a home or family? Friends?"

"Not to me."

"Do you have any idea where he might go?"

"No, John. And I don't care either! I—I never want to see anyone who even looks like him ever, ever again."

John groaned and came quickly to the side of the bed, leaning down, taking her hand and kissing her cheek. "I know, darling. It was horrible, and I shouldn't keep reminding you. It's just that I want him punished. He tried to murder you!"

"I know," Maria said, looking aside. "And if I had done something like that, and got away, I'd put as many miles as possible between me and the place where I did it."

"I suppose that's it. But he left everything. His clothes and other belongings, even some money."

"We know he's been stealing," Maria pointed out. "He could have had a cache of money somewhere else, just in case he had to run."

"Of course." John blew out his breath, disgusted with himself. "Why didn't I realize that? I suppose I just want to get my hands on him. Damn his soul! I'd like to kill him for what he did to you."

Kill him. Maria closed her eyes and sank back in her pillows, feeling heat under her eyelids and a sharp pang of guilt. "What I'd like to do is forget it," she said, "and get on with our own lives. It's over, Johnny. Let it be."

Finally, John let himself be persuaded to put it behind him. It was wasted time, and he was loaded with duties at the furnace. Without an overseer and with Maria unable to help, the paperwork kept him busy. He began looking among the older, trusted men for a new overseer.

In the meantime, Cassie and Melainie vied for the chance to fetch and carry, to read aloud or otherwise amuse Maria as she healed. The three of them became very close, and Maria purposely put off her return to activity and reveled in the affectionate attention Cassie lavished on her. But still she insisted that Cassie ride every morning, practicing her horsemanship on Dawn. The little mare was very smart and responsive.

"So few women really ride well," Maria told Melainie, "but Cassie is a natural rider. Besides, she has the slender, erect figure that looks so marvelous on a horse."

Melainie smiled. "I see you mean to make sure Cass has every advantage she would have had if you were her mother. It's wonderful of you, Maria."

Maria shook her head. "No, it's my pleasure. I'm living through her and I love it. She's doing for me what I couldn't do when I was young. We were too poor to have any advantages. I want Cassie to have a wonderful time as she grows up, and then make an excellent marriage."

Melainie sighed and looked away, her fine-boned face sad. "Just before my mother died, she told me her dearest wish for me was a good, kind man to marry. Perhaps if she'd lived I wouldn't have been so foolish. I ruined my life when I fancied myself in love with Piers."

"One mistake doesn't ruin a life, my dear. Some good, kind man will still come along for you."

Melainie stood up, taking the tray she had brought, ready to leave Maria's bedroom. "One did," she said. "One perfect man for me. But he didn't want an adulteress."

"Oh, Melainie! I know you mean Arthur, and Arthur is madly in love with you! He'll come around, really he will. But why in the world did you *tell* him?"

"He had the right to know he'd be getting damaged goods," Melainie said. "I remember my father saying once he'd rather his son never married than to marry damaged goods."

"How would he know?"

"My father?"

"Arthur."

Melainie blushed. "I've heard they can tell. But that isn't the reason I told Arthur the truth. It's just that I—I love him too much to deceive him. It was awful, Maria. He was so shocked he couldn't say a word. I had to just say that now he knew why we couldn't marry and then get up and leave. And he . . . oh, Maria, he l-looked s-so h-h-hurt." She was suddenly crying, her face twisted, tears dripping down on the tray she was holding. Maria threw back the covers and climbed out of bed, taking the tray and putting it down, then hugging Melainie to comfort her.

"Never mind, dear. He'll be back, I swear it. You'll see. He loves you as much as you love him, and he'll not be able to stay away."

The next day Maria was dressed and down for breakfast, and life at the manor resumed a normal pace. Alone with Sallie in the kitchen, Maria sat by a wide window and enjoyed the sights and scents of a countryside in May. Lilacs bloomed just outside, the black soil of the kitchen garden was alive with green shoots and leaves, and the sky was pure blue, without a cloud in sight. In the meadows lambs leaped and played, butting each other with their woolly heads and then running to hide behind their calm mothers. Maria sighed with contentment.

"I'll write to Arthur," she told Sallie, "and suggest he begin a correspondence with Melainie. I'm sure he will jump at the chance. I can send it along with John to be mailed. No one should be miserable in May."

"Ordinarily I think people should be left to cure their own ills," Sallie said. "But in this case I believe you're right. Play Cupid, by all means." She glanced past Maria and smiled. "Look, Maria. You'll enjoy the sight."

Maria turned to the open window again. Topping the far rise of the land where it bordered the unseen creek, the bright chestnut mare flowed over the ridge with Cassie on her back. Graceful and strong, the mare came on, down into the deep green grass, her head stretched forward in a fast canter, sleek sides shining like gold in the sun. Blue skirts fluttering, dark, loosened hair flying back in a whipping flag, Cassie urged her on, scattering the sheep. Even from here Maria could see Cassie toss back her head and laugh.

"She rides as well as any man," Maria said. "But then, she does everything well. It's just that she's so quiet and unobtrusive about it that no one notices. She'll begin this fall at the Dancing Class, and I'll wager she'll be the best on the floor in the Assembly when she's old enough to go."

"The Philadelphia Assembly?" Sallie laughed richly. "As I recall, even your fine old Maryland family didn't get you into that dance. You had to marry an Andelet. As for Cassie, it will take either a brilliant marriage or a miracle to get her an invitation."

Still watching Cassie through the window, Maria shrugged. "So? All that means is that I must manage one or the other. I suppose the marriage would be the easier. It has been said that a member of the Assembly can bring his cook to the annual dance, if first he weds her."

"At times I despair of you," Sallie said shortly, and glided away to begin the day's pies; still dried apple and mince, for the earliest of the fresh fruit and berries were weeks away.

Soon they were back to the easy ways and the tempo of summer, the irritation that Regan had brought to the forge was gone. John Kendall elevated one of the older bridgemen to the position of overseer. Production, which had dropped, settled and stayed steady. John, who had stayed overlong because of the trouble, was overdue for Philadelphia and his legal cases.

"I've learned a lesson," he told Maria the night before he left. "From now on we stay with the tried and true at Eagle Forge. We'll take our risks on other investments."

They lay naked in the darkness, the cool, lilac-scented air drifting across them from the open windows. Maria yawned and snuggled closer. "Are you sure you want to talk about business, Johnny?"

He laughed and drew her into the circle of his arm. "What about that rib?"

"The pain is nearly gone."

"I'll be very careful."

His slow, tender lovemaking was exactly what she needed now. His care for her, for her feelings, brought tears to her eyes. Until John, she hadn't known a man like him, had never thought there could be a man who put a woman's needs ahead of his own. "Lovely," she whispered. "Oh, lovely, Johnny. That's wonderful. Now, let me."

Both of them were wary of her side with the broken rib, both were careful and much less demanding than usual. But when they came together in the end, the darkness seemed alive with color and spiraling light, and the rush of passion coursing through Maria rose and fell like giant waves on the ocean, sweeping away the past, the fears and lies and problems. She felt renewed, somehow shriven of all her sins and forgiven absolutely. Weak with emotion, she held his face between her palms and kissed him over and over again.

"I love you, Johnny. I love you so much."

Then it was June again, and, sitting in the conservatory, Maria saw Cassie coming in through the back hall from a ride on Dawn, her thin shirtwaist wet with perspiration and clinging to her chest. There was a faint rounding there, the shadows of darkening nipples. Noticing the changes, Maria felt a sad tenderness, a sorrow for all young and carefree girls who must pass from the simple happiness of childhood into the bewildering maze of new emotions, disturbing physical changes, fears and strange thoughts. She watched Cassie run up the stairs, agile and strong as a boy, yet smoothly, delicately feminine in appearance. Three more months and she would be twelve. Some girls began their periods even before that age. Sighing, Maria set aside the book she was reading and rose from her chair. Unless she knew to expect it, Cassie could be frightened out of her wits by a show of blood. It would be best to tell her now.

"I knew it would happen," Cassie said later. She had had a bath and dressed, and now sat on the white brocade chair while Maria brushed and braided her hair. "But I didn't know when it might start. Thank you for telling me."

"I will always tell you the things you should know, darling. But how did you learn of it? Did Adah or Sallie tell you?"

"No. I've known for a long time. I had to help my mother,

135

you know. She was sick, and too weak to do things for herself."

Maria thought back. She had heard that Cat Hayes had never got up after Lily was born, yet she'd lived for another three years. Cassie was six when Lily arrived, nine when her mother died. For three years the child had tended a bedfast woman. Maria's heart hurt with pity.

"That's no work for a child. Surely, someone else could have done it. Didn't the village women help out?"

"They wouldn't come near our house," Cassie said matter-of-factly. "Robbie helped—he lifted her for me. But when it came to her monthlies, she didn't want him around."

"Oh, the poor soul." Maria was struck by her first pity for Cat Hayes. "How miserably unhappy she must have been."

"Not when she had the monthlies," Cassie said, handing up a ribbon for the braid. "She was happy then, because it meant no baby. She said another baby would kill her."

Maria's hands went still, the bow half tied. She stared down at the curve of young cheek she could see, the thick fan of black lashes. How much did this child know? What had she seen and heard in that miserable hut? "But Cassie . . . your mother was very ill. Surely her husband didn't . . ."

"When he wasn't too drunk he did. She screamed and cried, but he slapped her hard and did it anyway. He . . . he hit me when I tried to make him stop. Robbie would come in and take Lily and me outside, but . . . but I could still hear her, Aunt Maria. I could still hear her . . . begging him to leave her alone, and crying, crying . . ."

Dear Lord, no wonder the child swore she would never marry. Aghast, Maria stared at the cheek and the blinking lashes and the tears rolling down, and then she was around the chair and kneeling, pulling Cassie into her arms. "Oh, Cassie, my dear. My poor little girl. You must try to forget it, darling. Pretend it was only a bad, bad dream."

"I'm all right," Cassie said, leaning against her and wiping her eyes. "I'm fine, Aunt Maria. It's over. That's what Robbie said when Ma died—just remember that it's all over and nothing bad can ever happen to her again."

Robbie. Holding the warm, slender young body close,

Maria felt the familiar jealousy, the despair of ever really having Cassie for her own. How old had that boy been then? Twelve, thirteen? Yet he had thought and acted like a man. But then, both of them had been pushed into an unusual maturity. "Try to forget it," she said again, and forced herself to add: "Robert was right. It is over. But you shouldn't even think of it, ever. Think of happy things, my darling, happy, happy things like friends and fun. Store them up while you are young. They'll be nice to remember, later."

And then it was July, and when John Kendall came from the city and brought the usual sack of mail, which always included the letters from Robert to Cassie, there was another letter from Cambridge, a thick one, addressed to Melainie in a much neater handwriting. Sorting the mail at the breakfast table, Maria tossed the envelope to Melainie with a smile and a soft remark.

"I have no doubt you'll find this interesting, Melly."

Melainie drew in her breath, barely touching the envelope with her fingertips, as if she thought it might disappear. Then, looking stunned, she stood up, took the letter gingerly and slid it into a pocket.

"Excuse me," she said, shakily. "I'll be upstairs . . . in the schoolroom, Cassie. But . . . don't hurry, please. Read your letters—t-take your time."

"Yes, Miss Melly." Immersed in the pages of Robbie's first letter, Cassie didn't bother to look up.

Chapter 12

By mid-August Cassie could think of nothing except Robbie's arrival. In his last letter he'd said he had made arrangements to get to Philadelphia by train and come out to Eagle Forge with John Kendall on his usual middle of the month visit, and, much to Melainie's delight, he had said also that Arthur had suddenly decided to come with him.

Not wanting to miss a moment of the few days she expected him to stay, Cassie rode each morning and afternoon across the meadows and creek to the eastern borders of Andelet property. For several miles the border touched the high road that led to Philadelphia, and, though she was obedient to Maria's orders to stay away from strangers, Cassie rode along the section at a safe distance and watched for Mr. Kendall's coach. The fine coach would be easy to see in the sparse traffic of farm wagons, gigs, and the neat, plain carriages of the Amish and their trotting horses.

Her patience was finally rewarded late one afternoon by the sight of Kendall's coach and Robbie's hatless, tawny head, broad shoulders, and his big body on the driver's seat.

In a rush of wild happiness Cassie put Dawn in a gallop down from the ridge, sailed over a ditch and swept by the coach, waving and laughing. Robbie yelled and cracked the whip to come up to her, a wide grin on his face.

"Pull up! We'll tie that fancy beauty on the back and you can ride with me!"

"Nothing would suit me better!" Cassie called back, and reined Dawn in as Robbie stopped the team. Both John Kendall and Arthur Masefield got out on the dusty road while Robbie took Dawn to the back of the coach and tied her there. The two of them greeted Cassie warmly, complimented her riding and asked about the rest of the family.

"And Miss Scott?" Arthur added as they got back in. "She's still with you, isn't she?"

"Oh, yes. She's looking forward to your visit." Cassie felt safe in saying that, since Melainie talked of nothing else. Then she turned to Robbie as he came back to climb up to the driver's seat, caught his hand and sprang up beside him. Alone, their eyes met, clung for a moment in mutual delight at being together again, and then Robert grinned and started the team.

"That chestnut mare yours?"

"Yes. Her name is Dawn. I can ride her all right."

"I saw. You're growing up, Cass. You handle her well, for all you're so long-legged and skinny."

She gasped and then laughed ruefully. "I really am, aren't I? But Aunt Maria says I'll fill out."

"You look fine. I just figured it was my duty to tease you a little. I think I'll get a saddle horse while I'm here and we'll ride together. Would you like that?"

"Of course! But you won't have much time."

"Sure I will! Plenty. It's two weeks, maybe longer, before we leave."

"Two weeks!" Cassie's heart soared. "Oh, Robbie, that's wonderful. I thought you had to be there as soon as school opened."

"Why, no. I thought you knew—" He stopped talking to negotiate a turn off the road, through a shallow ditch and up to a lane that led around the ridge to the manor. Once on the lane he settled back again and looked at her puzzled face. "I guess Aunt Maria didn't tell you what we've planned. Do you remember she said last fall that she'd put up money to build a clipper ship?"

Cassie smiled. "Yes. It has a name now—the *Sea Sprite*. She talks about it often."

"That's it. It's finished." Robbie took a deep breath and laughed. "Art and I went to see it in Boston before we started home. She's beautiful, Cass. They say she's the fastest yet, and they've hired one of the toughest and best captains in America for her first voyage. Now, listen to this! Art and I are signed on as petty officers, and we leave for Cape Horn around the first of October. What do you think of that?"

She stared at him, paling. "Robbie . . . the clipper ships go to *China*. That's on the other side of the world."

"I know. Now, don't worry. All the old salts around the port say she's a good ship, well-made and seaworthy. I don't intend to keep on being a sailor all my life, and neither does Art, but we can't turn down the chance of a fortune. A couple of good trips and we'll be set. Then we can study again and be whatever we want to be."

"It takes a *year*," Cassie said faintly, "a whole year to go and come back."

"Not in a clipper, Cass. Why, one made it to Frisco and back in eighty-nine days, and a lot of them now make the whole trip to Canton and back in no more than nine or ten months. Don't think about the time it takes. Think of the money we'll make and the things we'll see!"

She clung to the seat as the coach rocked around a corner and started up the slope to the manor, which shone in the sunset light. At sight of the house hope sprang in her heart. "Just the same," she said, "you're only sixteen, no matter how big you are. I'll wager Aunt Maria won't let you go."

"Ah, Cass, please don't feel so bad about it. Trust me to keep myself safe. Anyway, Aunt Maria won't object. It was her idea."

"Her idea?"

"Of course. How else would we manage to get a berth? I'm to be her supercargo. She says I can finish college any time, and I'd better get my adventuring over with first." He reached over and capped Cassie's shining head in his palm, stroked down and grasped her braid. Pulling it around, he tickled her under the chin with the curly end, coaxing for a laugh. "Just think," he added, "where I'm going, it's the men who wear these pigtails."

Cassie tried to smile, but inside she was full of icy fear. Since Aunt Maria had begun talking of the *Sea Sprite,* Cassie had taken an interest in the China trade. She had read the harrowing accounts of shipwrecks and accidents at sea, the trials and tribulations of the sea traders. What Robbie planned to do was cruelly dangerous. Every clipper ship, in common with all the oceangoing fleets of traders, suffered casualties on every trip. The storms were awful going around Cape Horn, and there were men whose backs or legs or necks were broken in falls from a swaying mast. There were men missing and presumed drowned, men dying from foreign fevers or murdered in a foreign port. And, on some of the ships, men keelhauled or beaten to death by the fierce downeaster mates, because of a mistake or a fancied insult. She knew Robbie was strong, stronger than many men, and quick-thinking, but . . . oh, *how* could Aunt Maria let him go? As Robbie brought the coach to a stop in front of the house, she reached over and clasped his thick forearm in both of her small hands.

"Robbie, I must know—is your mind truly made up?"

He turned to her and she saw before he spoke that it was, that he would go. "Yes, truly. Aunt Maria said she must have someone aboard to look out for her interests. It's a good way to pay back a favor or two. And it's the quickest way for me to earn enough money to take care of the three of us." He dropped his voice as Kendall and Masefield climbed out below and Noonan came hurrying around the house to take the coach and team. "Please understand, Cass. I don't want to keep on taking charity from her forever."

Cassie nodded, holding down desperation. "Neither do I," she whispered. "But please—don't let anything bad happen to you. I'd want to die." Then she was dropping down, skirts ballooning around her striped riding pantalets, smiling as the front door was flung open and Maria swept out to greet the travelers. Stepping out of Noonan's way, Cassie moved to untie Dawn and ride her around to the stables.

Welcoming the three men and preceding them into the house, Maria glanced at Cassie, riding away. From the droop of her slender shoulders and the tight look of her smile, Maria knew Robert had told her about his planned voyage. She was taking it well, then. No tears. Maria knew a moment of rueful pride in that, and thought perhaps Cassie wasn't as wrapped up in her brother as she had been. Maria wondered a moment if indeed the new plan had been necessary, and then forgot it, busy in directing the two young men to their rooms on the third floor.

"And Arthur," she ended, "I know Melainie would like to welcome you herself when you have the time. She's in the schoolroom. I'm sure you remember where that is."

Agreeing with an incoherent but happy mumble, Arthur picked up his bags and went rapidly up the stairs. Robert set his bags by the newel post and asked for Lily.

"I suspect she's at the barn," Maria answered. "That black and white kitten she got last winter just had kittens herself, and that's where they are. I imagine Cassie will bring her in when she comes back."

"Thank you. I'll go to meet them." He was gone, his long stride carrying him swiftly to the rear of the house.

Maria turned to John, laying the tips of her fingers on his wrist. "Would you care for tea? There's a tray in the conservatory."

"Anywhere," John said, his voice suddenly husky. "Anywhere we can be alone. I've missed you, darling."

Leading the way down the hall, skirts rustling, Maria entered the conservatory with John close behind her. She turned and shut the door, laughing a little, and moved into his arms. The scent of late roses, of damp earth and green growing things drifted around them as they kissed, murmured to each other and kissed again, with playful nips and licks.

"I'm home," John said softly, leaning away to look at her flushed, dreamy face. "This has become home to me. This house is full of love, my sweet."

Maria smiled and moved away, going to the tea tray. "It is now. I can imagine the warm words and little caresses going on upstairs." Pouring tea as John sat down, she gave him a cup and laughed. "Melanie has been beside herself ever since she knew Arthur was coming with Robert."

John nodded. "I received a full report on Miss Scott's beauty, accomplishments, and general excellence on the trip from Philadelphia. Masefield can talk of nothing else. What a blow to the poor girl to find out he leaves within a month for the Orient."

"It shouldn't be. He will have a share of the profits. It will more than pay her to wait for a year or two and wed a wealthy man instead of a schoolmaster."

John set down his cup. For a moment he simply looked at Maria in surprise. Then he shook his head. "I suspect Miss Scott would settle for the schoolmaster's salary and Masefield here, in her arms and safe from the dangers of such voyages. I wondered at you when I learned you'd set Robert to be your supercargo. Perhaps you should think it over a bit more."

"Oh, come now, Johnny." Maria laughed and waved a hand carelessly. "Don't speak of doom. The *Sea Sprite* is perfectly safe. I've been on her myself, and she is excellently made and very well appointed."

"Most any ship is safe tied to a dock," John said. "Sailing around the Horn is a different matter. Men are lost even in much stronger ships with seasoned crews. As I told you in the beginning, a lot depends on the weather when you invest in a China clipper. They depend on speed for their success, and therefore are made of light woods and carry an immense spread of sails. A bad storm can cripple or sink—"

"Johnny!" Interrupting him, Maria looked angrily a-mazed and distraught. "For heaven's sake, don't call down disaster on our heads with your gloomy forecasts! I thought you'd be pleased to hear they were going. Where's your spirit of adventure?"

John gave her a wry smile. "How old is your man who is to captain the *Sea Sprite,* Maria?"

"Why, I believe he's twenty-one, or nearly. But then I've been told all the clipper captains are young."

"How old is the oldest member of the crew?"

She flushed. "You know I can't tell you that until the trip begins. They round up a crew at the last minute—"

"They *buy* drunk sailors and derelicts from the docks," John corrected, "from the crimps who drag them aboard. Their petty officers are all untried youths with their heads full of sea stories and the hope of adventure and profit. Granted, it works out fine if the ship survives—the master can retire before he's thirty. And he will. He'll have enough sense by then not to go again."

"Really, John, you make it sound impossible! Please stop such dreary thoughts." Soft mouth twisted, Maria was clearly angry now. "If Arthur or Robert heard you I'm sure they'd feel very depressed. They might even change their minds."

John gave her another searching glance. Her voice was too high, there were spots of hectic color on her cheeks, her eyes avoided his. This was obviously not a subject she liked.

He shook his head and stood up, walking away from her toward the tiers of potted plants, suddenly knowing the origin and reason for the plan. Staring unseeingly at the ferns, he spoke quietly. "You're sending Robert on that ship to make his separation from Cassie complete, aren't you, Maria?" He turned and looked at her when she didn't answer, and found her staring at the floor, pale and stubbornly silent. "I hope," he added, his voice still softer, "you aren't counting on an accident at sea to make it permanent."

Maria jumped to her feet. "How can you say that to me? Haven't I always done the best I could for him? Why do you think I'm sending Arthur along? He has promised me to look out for Robert and keep him safe!"

"Perhaps I was wrong," John said gently. "I know you aren't cruel. But you must admit your obsession with Cassie leads you to extreme measures. As for Arthur keeping Robert safe aboard a ship, the chances are strong that it would be the other way around."

There were tears in Maria's eyes, brimming over. She wiped them away, turning her face from him. "Then you talk to them, Johnny. Tell them everything. I don't want you to think I'm so heartless."

He embraced her, his own heart aching with remorse. "I'd never think that, love. I'm sure it's only that a woman can't truly understand the dangers. Don't cry, my darling."

But she had understood the dangers, always. She had only

shoved them into the back of her mind with the other things she didn't want to think about. Guiltily, she hid her face in his shoulder. "All right. It's just that I want you to think well of me, Johnny. It hurts when you suspect me of something so vile."

Acquiring a saddle horse was Robert's first task. He had a good sum of money, since he had saved nearly all the allowance Maria sent him, so he borrowed the wagon from Noonan and went to the old Thompson farm to see if his uncle, a man noted for his love of good horses, had one he wanted to sell. He came back with a fine big bay tied to the back of the wagon and wearing a good saddle. In spite of threatening clouds Cassie promptly left her studies and saddled Dawn while Robert unhitched the team from the wagon and rubbed them down. They rode away from the barn together and took off at a canter toward the meadow and the rolling land that led down to Durmont Creek, glancing at each other and laughing from sheer pleasure.

Along the creek the buttonwoods were too close together for running horses. They slowed and began to talk.

"Was your uncle in good health, Robbie? I remember seeing him years ago in the village. He was a very tall man with a stoop, who spoke softly to others but not at all to me."

Robert frowned, watching the creek. "He is the same, a little thinner. But he's been ailing for a long time. There's a woman, Mrs. Hinton, who does for him. She says he won't eat." He looked around at Cassie. "Would you go to see him before we leave? He asked me to come and to bring you."

"Of course. Why ever not?"

Robert looked away again. "Uncle Caleb was . . . unkind about your mother, Cass. He regrets it now, but if you decided to refuse his invitation, I'll understand it."

"I won't refuse." She met his eyes as he turned to her again. "I know about my mother, Robbie, and I know who my father was. I heard Aunt Maria talking about it once— when I wasn't supposed to be listening."

"Aw, Cass . . ." Robert stopped his horse, looking at her helplessly, and then when she stopped beside him, he reached over with one long arm and gave her a quick hug. "I'm sorry, dear girl. I wish now I'd told you myself."

"It's all right. It has nothing to do with us, Robbie." She held him a moment and then let go, managing a rueful smile as they rode on. "At least I know now why my eyes look like Aunt Maria's."

Robert nodded. "And why she wanted you badly enough to take in Lily and me too. Of course, Lily is related to you—but I'm not."

"I know, but I couldn't have been happy here without you."

He nodded again, thoughtfully. "I feel the same. We've always depended on each other, Cass. You've been my one and only true friend, and you'll always be dearer to me than anyone else in the world."

There were tears of happiness seeping down Cassie's cheeks. He had said exactly what she wanted to hear. "Then nothing else matters," she burst out, "nothing at all! I don't even mind having Aunt Maria's eyes."

"You shouldn't," Robert said, laughing. "They're pretty. Besides, you must never forget what she's done for us all, Cass. She loves you very much."

"Does she, Robbie? Do you really think she does?" Cassie glanced over, her eyes full of doubt. "Sometimes when she looks at me it's almost as if she is seeing someone else."

"Such fancies," Robert scoffed. "Of course she loves you—enough to put up with Lily and me besides. There's the forge ahead, Cass. Let's go take a look."

"Yes, let's. It's much more pleasant now to visit the works. The men are like family since Mr. Regan left."

Robert laughed. "I'm glad he's gone. I thought I'd have to fight him someday. Where did he go?"

Cassie shrugged. "No one knows. He just disappeared. Adah says he was stealing from the company and Aunt Maria found it out. I suppose he was afraid he'd go to prison."

"He probably went west," Robert said carelessly. "Come on, it's clear enough for a gallop along here."

That evening John Kendall asked both Robert and Arthur to join him in the study for a time. Methodical as always, he had gathered facts and figures on the clipper ships, their perils and problems, and had brought them with him to go over with Maria before her own ship left port. Now, without emotion, he went through all the information with Arthur and Robert.

"Neither of you come from seafaring families," he concluded. "Otherwise I wouldn't feel obligated to tell you these things. You'd know. Well, now you do know, and can make your final decision based on all the factors. Think about it for a day or two."

In spite of the difference in their ages, Robert and Arthur had become the best of friends. They looked at each other now and saw the same determination they felt personally reflected in the other pair of eyes.

"We knew a good bit of what you've told us, sir," Robert began. "But we've learned more tonight. It was good of you to tell us. It helps to be forewarned. I know, and I think Art does too, that what we're going to do is dangerous. But we've thought about it for a considerable time, and we figure it's worth the risk."

John's pale eyes moved to Arthur. "Do you second that?"

Art smiled and stood up. "I have more reason than ever now to wrest a fortune from the sea trade. Melainie's family has fallen on hard times during the last few years, but she was raised in luxury. She has accepted my proposal of marriage, and I'd like to be able to give her a wonderful life."

"My congratulations," John said warmly, and stood up to shake Arthur's hand. He turned to Robert, who had also risen, and smiled. He was fond of Robert. "What's your excuse, then?"

"It's a way of returning a little of the favor Aunt Maria has shown me, sir. And perhaps relieving her from further expense for Cassie and Lily. And besides . . ." Robert's wide grin came, brightening his strong young face. "I'll like the chance to adventure a bit, and I imagine Art will too."

"Ah," John said, laughing, "now I hear the truth. Come, let us have a glass or two of brandy and discuss the various adventures available in the Orient."

The time was long to Maria. Cassie demanded freedom from her studies until Robert left, and Melainie was very willing to let her go so she could be with Arthur. Maria saw her influence over Cassie waning every day. She and Mrs. Brooke both found themselves with little to do as the three Harmons celebrated their reunion.

With Lily on the saddle in front of one of them, a basket of food strapped on with the other, Cassie and Robert escaped from the activity and confusion of the harvesting and picnicked away from the house and farm. Sitting in the flickering sun and shadow of a forest glade or on the bank of the creek, they would talk together while watching Lily play amongst the trees or at the water's edge. They had always talked; it was one of the things both of them missed most when they were apart. In their days in the hut Robert had spun stories of magic or miracles to keep their spirits up, or stories of comical happenings to make Cassie smile. Now he wove tales of the Orient. Stories of showers of gold that rained on visitors, of magicians who transformed rocks into glittering jewels, of animals who talked and sang to home-sick sailors. Tales so utterly ridiculous and told with such a straight face that Lily gasped in wonder and Cassie laughed until she cried.

With only a few days before Robert was to sail, he and Cassie made the trip to the Thompson farm, taking Lily along because Robert had said there were puppies there and she begged to go. She chattered most of the way, perched on the saddle in front of Robert in a ruffled yellow dress and yellow and white pantalets, the yellows made pale by the glory of her golden hair, shining in the fall sunshine.

They rode through untilled fields overgrown with weeds, past a dairy barn with only two or three cows, past an empty hog pen and, nearing a big log house, through a barnyard with a few fluttering, squawking hens scattering before their horses. In the stables there were two horses thrusting their heads out to whinny at Robert's bay, and a trio of farm dogs, the only animals on the farm that looked well cared for.

"I see the puppies!" Lily exclaimed. "Right there in the stable door! They're peeking out at us. Let me down, Robbie."

"First we go in and see Uncle Caleb," Robbie said firmly, "and you must ask if you can play with his puppies."

"And I will ask if I can come out with you and see those horses," Cassie said. "They're handsome." She smiled at

Lily, glad to have her along. She felt odd, here in this place owned by the part of Robbie's family she had never known.

Silent as they neared the house, Cass slipped down from her sidesaddle, straightened her long skirt, and helped Lily down as Robert dismounted and tied the horses. She held Lily's hand and followed Robert to the back door.

Caleb Thompson opened the door himself. Thin and bent, yet with a big, rawboned frame that spoke of former strength, he had thick silver hair and eyes as blue as Robbie's. His face wrinkled into a smile at the sight of Lily.

"Good. I hoped you'd bring the little one. Folks told me she was a beauty, and I see she is." His eyes left Lily's smile and traveled up to Cassie's huge, serious eyes. "Well," he added slowly, "they didn't lie about you either. You do look like Mark. Come in, then. I'll have a talk with you both."

Lily grabbed his hand and swung it, asking for attention. "Uncle Caleb! Can I stay out here and play with your puppies?"

Caleb's laugh was rusty from disuse, but genuine. "I'm afraid you'd get that pretty dress dirty in my stables, Miss. But if you'd like, you can bring one of the puppies into the kitchen."

"I'll help her," Cassie said quickly, and took Lily's hand. "She might have trouble catching one, and I want to see the horses too." Her eyes flew up to Robert's. "You go on in, Robbie. We'll be along."

Robert looked distressed. He knew she was upset by what his uncle had said to her about "Mark," and she wanted a moment or two to recover. Half running, she took off for the stables with Lily, then pulled her down to a walk so they wouldn't scare the puppies. Stroking the horses' velvety noses and talking to them, she calmed down. When they went back to the house, Lily carrying a puppy in her arms, they found wiry, middle-aged Mrs. Hinton in the kitchen, a big, clean place with a black iron stove and an iron sink with faucets, which meant running water. Cassie looked around, impressed. In the manor those things were commonplace, but not in a farmhouse. Now she knew why the Thompsons were so well respected. They had done much more than the other farm families. She felt a sudden pride in Robbie's ancestry.

"Here," Mrs. Hinton said, and handed Cassie a plate of cookies. "Take them in to the men. The tea is already there. And you, Miss, you stay here with me. That puppy's not getting in there on the rugs."

Plate in hand, Cassie went through a dark hall, following the sound of voices. The men were in a large parlor, lavishly furnished and full of light from large windows. She entered timidly, plate in hand, and went toward Robert, who sat in a wingback chair with a footstool. A teapot and cups were on a table nearby. She put the plate there and sat down on the stool, facing Uncle Caleb in the opposite chair.

"Well," Caleb said, staring at her, "how do you like the house?"

"It's a splendid house," Cassie said shyly. "I like it very much." If he said no more about her real father she thought she could like him too.

"You'd better like it," Caleb said, his blue eyes staring at her intensely. "I'm leaving it to you when I die. Robert gets the farm and you get the house. He wants it that way in case something happens to him. The farm's gone down since I lost my strength, but Robert will bring it up again once he's home from the sea. I figure leaving it to you two will help make up for what I haven't done before. Now pour us some tea and pass those cookies."

Cassie did as she was told and then sat down again and let the conversation between Robbie and his uncle flow past like a deeply murmuring stream. Her mind was far in the future, when she was grown-up and keeping house for Robbie and Lily. *Here.* In this beautiful big house. A line from the Bible came into her mind and she repeated it soundlessly. *My cup runneth over.* Oh, indeed it did.

Maria had put off the return to Philadelphia because Cassie wanted to stay at Eagle Forge until Robert left.

"It wouldn't be the same in the city, Aunt Maria. Robbie and I feel more at home here, and no one bothers us."

Robbie and I. Scalded by jealousy, Maria could do nothing but smile stiffly and nod.

"I'll wait," she told Sallie one morning in the kitchen. "If I insist on leaving now, Cassie will never forgive me."

Sallie raised her brows. She was solemn these days, her laugh gone, her big face set in pensive lines.

"Quite true. Nor will she forgive you if he's lost at sea."

Maria whirled. "Damn it, Sallie, don't you turn on me! Why does everyone think I'm sending that boy to his death?"

Peering through the window, Sallie shrugged massive shoulders. "Part of it, I suppose, is your evident desire to get rid of him. In any case, here he comes, with Cassie on one side and a stranger on the other."

Maria hurried to the window. "You're right. I've never seen that man before. I don't like strangers wandering around our land. I wonder what he wants."

"It looks very much as if you'll find out soon. Robert's bringing him to this door."

Dismounting and coming in, Robert shepherded Cassie in front of him and let the stranger bring up the rear.

"Titus Hammand, Aunt Maria. He was down at the forge, looking for Payne Regan, and he was asking for someone to bring him up here. He says he's just passing through and in a hurry."

"I see," Maria said stiffly. She didn't like what she saw. The man was dressed well enough, and clean, but quick-eyed, foxy, and . . . *staring at Sallie.* "You can leave him with me, Robert, and take Cassie on for your ride. Sit down, Mr. Hammand, and have a cup of tea."

Hammand smiled, revealing bad teeth. "After you, madam."

Maria sat down as Robert took Cassie out, and the man took a chair opposite her. Sallie moved slowly to bring cups and the teapot. The man watched her, fascinated, as she poured. Sallie's broad face was blank, incurious; her eyes, always so full of life, now looked dull and empty.

"I'm afraid I can't help you," Maria said into the silence. "No one here has seen Mr. Regan since he left."

"Sometimes the servants around a house see more than the owners," Hammand said, sipping tea. He smiled at Sallie. "Isn't that true, Miss?"

Sallie shuffled her feet. "Yassuh," she said, bobbing her turbaned head. "Ah reckon it is if'n you say so."

Hammand studied her for a full minute. "Well, then," he said, "what can you tell me about Mr. Regan?"

"Nuthin, suh," Sallie said, embarrassed and servile, "'cept he gone."

The man sighed, his fascination with Sallie fading. "I wish someone could tell me more. He owes me a great deal of money. Ah, well, I'll leave my card. If you do hear anything, Mrs. Andelet, I'd appreciate it if you'd drop me a line."

Maria shut her open mouth and stopped staring at Sallie. "Of course, we're soon leaving here and traveling to Philadelphia. However, I'll keep the card." She waited until the man finished his tea and rose, then stood up and walked with him to the kitchen door. Outside, putting on his hat, he glanced back through the kitchen door at Sallie and smiled again, his quick eyes running over her thoughtfully.

"Bonjour, Mademoiselle Hecate," he said smoothly.

Placidly, Sallie shuffled past the door and picked up the cups and the teapot, taking them to the sink. Hammand shrugged and switched his derisive smile to Maria. "Just a little joke," he said. "I was wishing her a good day, but she didn't understand. When I first came in I thought I knew who she was, but evidently I was wrong. She's the right size, but not the right woman. Good day to you too, Mrs. Andelet."

"Thank you," Maria said. "I'll let you know if I hear from Mr. Regan." She stood in the door until he mounted and rode out of sight. Then she went to the table and sat down again, putting her hands on her hot cheeks, staring at Sallie.

"He was here to take a look at you," she whispered. "Regan did mention his suspicion to someone, then. I thought I'd faint when he spoke to you in French! And he knew your old name!"

"Yassum," Sallie drawled. "He sho' did." Her broad face slowly broke into a mocking smile. "The right size," she said in her normal tone, "but not the right woman. Hah! What did he think Hecate would do when he spoke her name? Hold out her wrists for the shackles?"

Maria shuddered, looking up at the large form, the broad face. "Don't even think of it, Sallie. Even after sixteen years those French pirates would torture you for what you did. What will we do if he comes back?"

"There is only one thing I can do if he sniffs too close at my heels, Maria. I can't kill a slave hunter—his absence would be noted, his track followed. You and I would both be in trouble then. I must leave."

"No! I will hide you!"

Sallie stared. "How? Stand in front of me?" Her laugh rolled out, deep and rich, pouring its vibrant sound through the house. In the study John Kendall looked up for a moment from his papers and listened, smiling. He often wondered about Sallie Fernod, what she was and what she had been. But when she laughed he was glad to have her around.

Book Two

NEW YORK
HARBOR

Chapter 13

September 13, 1848

The *Sea Sprite,* weather-beaten and in need of paint, polish, and new rigging, drifted closer to her usual place on New York's South Street wharf. Her cargo, of tea and silks from China, sisal from Manila, spices from Sumatra, gold and ivory from the Guinea coast, had been offloaded yesterday onto a guarded dock in the Hudson River. Now the crew of the *Sprite* wanted shore time, none more than Robert Harmon. Ending five years on the clipper, the last year and a half as the captain, Robert was more than ready to leave the life at sea. He stood now behind the helmsman and watched critically as his men warped the scarred but still handsome hull of the ship in toward the wooden seawall.

At twenty-one, Robert looked closer to thirty. His strong face was burnt to the color of teak, furrowed by frown lines and sprayed with crinkles at the outside corners of his eyes, which were a surprising bright blue in his brown face. He was taller; he was over six feet by two or three inches, and heavier, for the promise of strength once apparent in a rangy sixteen-year-old was fulfilled now in wide, thick shoulders, deep chest, and powerful thighs. The last difference was in his expression. Calm and self-possessed, he no longer looked like a country boy.

His ship secure, Robert let his gaze rove over the familiar scene. There were enough ships in port, including the newest Andelet clipper, *Sea Racer,* to make a forest of masts and spars, with canopies of drooping sails, and rigging dangling like leafless vines from trees. Thick jib booms stretched halfway across crowded South Street. Even now, in late afternoon, the noise was constant on the street, rising and falling like a wave. Horses trotted by, pulling rattling drays loaded until they groaned; barrels were being rolled on the cobblestones; barrows full of bales and boxes creaked past, pushed by straining men; a donkey engine wheezed and steamed. Men and boys of all sizes and ages worked, yelled, cursed, fought, and laughed. Watching, his ears assaulted, Robert thought of the quiet of the rolling pastures on the Thompson farm, the cool green grass, the sound of bees in the clover. Joy rose inside him. Soon, he thought, and smiled.

"Thinking of home." There was amusement but no question in Arthur Masefield's voice as he stopped beside Robert and eyed his smile. Arthur had changed too, though he'd been mature when the voyages began. He had grown thinner, more muscular, nearly as sunburnt as Robert, and honed like a blade. But he hadn't taken to the life of a sailor, nor to the skills. Robert had done that, and risen rapidly to the position of mate and then, when Captain Keith was killed in a Hong Kong brawl, to captain. Then he'd made Arthur the supercargo, the bargainer, and thereby increased the fortunes of everyone involved. Arthur knew values.

"I am," Robert said now, admitting to sentiment. "Of home and my family. Thank God this is over and we've both survived." He grinned and punched Arthur lightly on the shoulder. "There were times—like when that gale pushed us into the ice pack below Cape Horn—when I doubted we would. But here we are, and the gangplank just went down. Let's go home."

"I'll get my records. Maria will want to go over them." Arthur was turning away when Robert's hand shot out and stopped him.

"Look. Isn't that Maria's carriage with Noonan driving?" He laughed. "What's this? Couldn't she wait to see the final summing up? God knows, she should be satisfied with this trip."

"She will be," Arthur promised, and led the way down the gangplank to escort Maria aboard. Robert followed more slowly. It had occurred to him that Maria Andelet might have more than one reason for showing up now on the New York wharf. Eighteen months ago, when he'd announced that this was to be his last trip, she had argued that he was throwing away a "fascinating and lucrative career" to waste his life on a farm, and tried to persuade him to change his mind. He hadn't, nor would he now, but it was hard to refuse to listen when she'd done so much for him and for Cass and Lily.

Stepping from the carriage into confusion, noise, and lecherous stares, Maria looked cool and exquisite. Beneath the beribboned, lacy capote cap every curl of shining black hair was in place, her ivory skin smooth and youthful, her color still high. Her gown of rose sateen had a low neckline edged in lace, short puff sleeves, and a snug bodice that accented the shape of her firm breasts. The layered, scalloped and ruffled bell skirt swept the street with a fine disregard for the dirt lodged between the cobblestones. She smiled as the two young men pushed through the crowd to greet her, and embraced them both, chattering the while.

"You are both well? No, don't bother to answer, I can see you're in excellent health. Nothing like sea air, I've always heard, to keep a man in shape. I've just come from the Hudson docks, Robert, and I must congratulate you at once! You've made a real killing this time."

"Lay the credit for that on Arthur's sharp bargaining," Robert said, grinning at his friend. "All I did was sail the ship and pick up freight where he pointed it out."

Arthur burst out laughing. "That's carrying humility a bit too far, Rob. Fortunately, we all know where the major part of the credit lies. Come, Maria. The captain's quarters aboard are far cleaner than this street, and there's a tot or two of brandy left in his decanter."

Robert let Arthur escort Maria to the ship while he helped

Noonan find a hitching post in the shade for his horses. The affection that had sprung up between the old man and the orphaned boy in the beginning had ripened into a confidence in each other that allowed them to speak frankly.

"Why is she here, Noonan?"

Noonan grinned, his red cheeks bunching up like wrinkled apples. "Got you worried, has she? She'd like to talk you into staying on the ship, but I'd say she's given that up." Tying the horses, Noonan climbed up and set the brake on the coach. Climbing down again, he joined Robert to push through the crowds to the ship, which he'd never seen. His eyes snapped with excitement, staring at the graceful hull. "But come to think of it," he added, "I did hear her tell Sallie she had a favor to ask of you, now that you were free."

"What kind of a favor?"

Noonan shrugged. "She didn't say. But it must be important. Sallie asked her if she would be taking Cassie or the Bradford girl with her to greet you, and she said no, it was business this time, not pleasure."

Starting up the gangplank, Robert laughed. "I would have loved to see Cassie, but pleasure isn't a word I would use for Violet Bradford's company. Is she still as forward as she was the last time I was home?"

"Hard to say with no men around but Jacob and John Kendall," Noonan replied, grinning again. "But I can swear her voice is louder." He stepped down on the deck, staring up at the towering masts and the men still clambering around the rigging like monkeys, taking down the drooping sails. "Suffering saints! What if they fall?"

"Step out of the way," Robert advised, laughing. "In the meantime, help yourself to a drink from the grog barrel." He went on, his face sobering as he neared the cabin and heard Maria's voice inside. A favor? Perhaps he had only thought himself free to go home . . .

It took another half hour before Maria brought forth her request, carefully sandwiched between two warmly extravagant compliments.

"I am very proud of you, Robert. In a position of frightful responsibility you've done better than many a man twice your age. And now I think you'll be able to solve my present dilemma. You know Frederick Barclay of our shipping office in London, don't you?"

"Yes, of course."

Maria sighed. "The poor man isn't well, and he's asked for a year's leave. I'd be glad to help him, but I can't find anyone willing to take over. I know you plan to go into farming, Rob, but this is only for a year. You'd help a sick man, and take a worry off my mind." She smiled brightly. "I can trust you implicitly."

Robert sat staring at her for a long moment. He was no longer as easily convinced of the merit in Maria's motives as he once had been. He had met Fred Barclay when he last visited London, and while he thought little of Barclay's ability, the man's health had seemed fine. But for the life of him he couldn't see what other reason Maria might have for the request. He tried another tack.

"Are you positive you need that office, Aunt Maria? Our shipping in London has been handled profitably for years by Laing and Baggett. More profitably than now, when you must bear with the added expense of an office and staff. I don't want to give up my own plans for a position you'll soon find unprofitable."

Maria flushed, her skin blotching red over her creamy neck and cheeks. She never liked anyone to question her judgment, but this time she seemed unusually angry. "I fully realize you've reached your majority, Robert," she said, her tone deadly cold. "I couldn't order you to London if I wished. But then, if you can refuse to help me after what I've done for you and your sisters, I wouldn't want you there anyway."

Arthur got to his feet, murmured something to the effect that they might want privacy for their talk, and left the cabin. Robert continued to study Maria. After a time he spoke again.

"You know I won't refuse you, even though I think your request unnecessary and in fact foolish. When do you want me to go?"

Maria took a deep breath and rose, straightening her crumpled skirt. Anger still showed in her tight lips, but Robert thought there was also relief in her eyes. She puzzled him, but then, she always had.

"As soon as possible," she said. "I've hired Captain Benjamin Close to take over the *Sea Sprite* immediately, so that's off your mind. And a packet to Europe leaves the day after tomorrow. I'll give you a bank draft now for your passage money and your first six months' pay—"

Robert stopped the flow of hurried words with a gesture. "I need no money yet, Aunt Maria. I've plenty of my own."

She nodded. "Good. But I assure you your pay will be adequate and more. I'll leave you now—I'm sure you'll have much to do in the next twenty-four hours."

He watched her sail out of the cabin, collect Noonan with a peremptory wave of one hand, nod to Arthur and step up to the gangplank. He went to the cabin door and saw the lace and ribbon capote cap bobbing down the gangplank and through the crowded street, heading for the patch of shade where her coach was standing. Turning to Arthur, who looked distraught, Robert spread his hands.

"How could I refuse? She took us in when we were poor and hungry."

Arthur shook his head. "I know. But the question in my mind is: How could she *ask?* You've risked your life to double her income for the past five years, and any man with a head for business could take that useless office over. Are you going to leave right away?"

"Hell, no! She thinks I am, but I'm going to see Cassie and Lily first. We've had little enough time together since I started sailing, and after a long year and a half this time, I think we deserve a day."

Two days later, stepping from the front door for her morning walk, Melainie saw a rented gig come bowling along Spruce Street with two tanned and familiar men in it, luggage piled behind them. It was her cry of joy that alerted Maria. When Robert left Arthur and Melainie entwined and murmuring in the gig, picked up his bags and came up the steps, it was Maria who opened the door, not waiting for Dickon, who was coming slowly down the hall.

"Well, Robert! This is a surprise. I was sure you wouldn't have time for a visit before leaving for London."

"I took time," Robert said calmly. "I couldn't go away again without seeing Cass and Lily. Where are they?"

"Upstairs. I sent Adah up to tell them you were here."
Maria studied him warily, remembering their conversation
on the ship. Robert was no longer easy to manage. "I expect
you'll find Cassie has matured greatly in the last year and a
half. She's seventeen, you know, and very pretty. You'll be
proud of your sister."

"I've always been proud of Cassie," Robert answered, and
gave Dickon his bags. "And Lily? She's eleven, isn't she? It's
hard to believe. How—" A flutter of footsteps on the stairs
made him look up. A vision paused at the landing, all lovely
curves in lace and cream-colored silk, a clear, beautiful face
with shining gray-green eyes, a mass of loose, sable waves
sweeping over her shoulders. "Good Lord," he added softly,
"don't tell me that's *Cass.*"

"Robbie! It *is* you! I couldn't believe Adah!" Rushing
down the stairs, Cassie flung herself into Robert's arms and
hugged him, tears of happiness in her eyes. "Aunt Maria
thought it would be another month, but here you are, and
you look just wonderful, and now—oh, Robbie, *now* you
don't have to leave again! Ever! We'll all be together and
happy!" She whirled to look up the stairs, and her unbound
hair flew out and brushed his chin, fragrant and silky. She
laughed as she saw Lily peering over the landing, big-eyed
and awed. "Lily! Come down, you goose, and let our Robbie
see how big you are."

Maria stood off to one side, watching as the three of them
came together in a laughing, talking, hugging muddle, then
silently left the hall, joining Sallie Fernod in the open
dining-room door, passing through and closing it behind
her. She stared up into Sallie's face with tears in her own
eyes, but not from happiness.

"This time I truly thought she had changed, Sallie, but she
hasn't. Once she saw Robert, I was again an outsider, as I've
always been. She ran past me without a word or glance and
straight into his arms. Even when she turned to call Lily
down, I'd swear she never even saw me standing there. They
are her family, her loved ones, and I—I am only her friend."

Sallie's eyes were thoughtful. "Her jealous friend?"

Maria clenched her fists. "Yes, damn it! Thank God,
Robert must leave again tomorrow."

"Absence diminishes small passions," Sallie said, quoting, "but increases great ones, as wind blows out a candle but fans a fire into leaping flame. There is a very strong tie between them. So, I doubt another separation will help. It may even worsen the situation."

"Perhaps you are right," Maria admitted, staring at her, "but I must try. That was a very unusual thing to say, Sallie. I didn't know you were capable of such a turn of phrase."

"I'm not. La Rochefoucauld made that observation two hundred years ago, or one very like it. Has it ever occurred to you that deep in her lonely little heart your darling Cassie may blame you for sending Robert away?"

"Of course not! She understands. She knows Robert is a man and must be concerned with business."

"The mind understands. The heart feels."

Maria snorted. "Oh, come now. Did La Rochefoucauld say that too?"

"No, I did." Sallie's deep laugh reverberated through the room. "But it's true, nonetheless. Now tell me—does your heart feel for Cassie?"

Maria looked suddenly desolate. "Oh, Sallie, you know it does! Can you look at her and not think of Mark? She is his very image, and I love her dearly. I want so much to have her turn to me, to truly love me."

"I know. You have felt that way from the beginning. But don't you hear your own words, Maria? You love her for Mark. When you love her for Cassie, she will love you back."

"Oh, don't be silly," Maria said, impatient. "Of course I love her for Mark—she's *his*. She's all that is left of him. The problem is solely the habit she has of clinging to Robert. Once she realizes I am more her family than he is, that will stop."

Sallie shook her head. "Once she discovers that you knew Robert had returned yet you said nothing to her, once she hears that you saw him in New York and forced him to agree to stay away for another year, Cassie may never trust you again."

"I shall simply say I kept it from her because I knew it would make her unhappy," Maria said lamely. "Besides, I didn't force him. Why did you think I did?"

"I know you did. Had he felt he had a choice, he wouldn't have agreed."

"Cassie doesn't know that."

"Maria, I warn you. The girl will hate you in the end."

Maria raised her chin, staring up at Sallie's broad face, her own face proud and determined. "When she is old enough to understand and appreciate all I've done for her, she will *love* me."

The southwest sky, as usual, was stained with smoke from the factories along the Schuylkill. The sun had dropped down far enough to tint the smoke a dirty red before Cassie slowed her pace. Still wearing the lace-trimmed gown of cream silk that set off the curves of her diminutive figure, and now a light green velveteen bonnet with a wreath of pink roses around the edge, she looked lovely, gentle, and sweet. In truth, she was furious and heartsore. When, over a late lunch of sandwiches and tea in the kitchen, Robert had told her he could only stay a day, and told her why, she had grabbed her bonnet and his hand and left the house, too upset to speak.

"I know you must be tired," she said now. "I've walked you all over the city, trying to wear off my temper. I'm sorry, truly. Let's go back."

"I'm not tired, Cass." Still, he turned as she turned and they began walking slowly east along Rittenhouse Square. Glancing at her, he felt his throat grow tight. His beloved little girl had turned into a beautiful woman without any warning at all. Small but perfectly proportioned, delicate but strong, she amazed and disconcerted him. He knew her so well, and yet he felt now as if he didn't know her at all. But he could feel her despair and he understood it. Like him, she wanted to go home. Home to Eagle Forge; home to being their own family again. "You're not being fair," he added abruptly. "I guess you know that."

Inside the shadow of her bonnet, Cassie frowned. "Fair? Is it fair for Aunt Maria to lie?"

"Did she lie?"

Cass hesitated. "No. But you know what I meant. She didn't tell me you were back; she never mentioned the shipping office in London. If you'd done what she wanted, I wouldn't even have seen you for another year! She kept all of that from me, and I don't even know why."

"I think she's afraid, Cass."

"Afraid?" Cassie shook her head. "Oh, no. Aunt Maria's not afraid of the Devil himself."

"She's afraid she'll lose you."

Cassie stopped and faced him, standing in a long bar of sunlight that reached between the trees and lay along the street. Lighted, her huge, gray-green eyes were like clear water, amazement suspended in their depths. *"Lose* me? What am I, then? A trinket, a plaything? She doesn't own me, Robbie. I own myself."

"In the long run, yes." He was reluctant to say it, but he had to. "But you're forgetting that until you're twenty-one she controls what you do. I have finally reached that age and I give her credit, she asked this time. She didn't order me to London."

"Then why are you going?" Suddenly excited, Cassie seized his arm. "Robbie! Tell her you've changed your mind! You can begin on the farm, and in the summer I can ride over and—"

"No! I already owe her an apology, which I will see that she gets before I leave, for arguing about it. Stop and think, will you? Don't you remember how cold and hungry we used to be? Don't you remember the clothes from the church barrel, the few scrawny potatoes we grew, the bone and rancid fat from the butcher's leavings? Come on, Cass—you tell me how I could refuse to help Maria Andelet!"

Cassie looked away, ashamed. "I'm sorry. You're right and I am very wrong. I was being most ungrateful. I just wish she'd . . . no, there's no excuse for my thoughts."

Robert put an arm around her and turned her toward home. "On the contrary, I think you've had plenty of reasons for your thoughts. She's a—a managing woman. But she is still your guardian for four more years. Learn to bend, Cass, so you won't break."

They arrived home to find the house lighted and festive, the Bradfords there as guests, a fine late supper being laid. Melainie could be heard in the distance, directing Adah as to seating the guests. Where Melainie was, undoubtedly was Arthur. Everyone else came out as they heard the door open. Violet's voice as she greeted Robert rose into a delighted little scream.

"Oooh, you look just like an Arabian *sheik,* Robert! How romantic! I'll wager you've had a marvelous time on some of those Pacific islands I've read about." Tall and very thin, Violet was wearing a gold satin dress that combined with her red hair to give a brilliant sunset effect. She smiled roguishly after her last remark, leaned forward and put up her fan to hide her lips from the others. "Is it true," she added in a whisper, "that the women go swimming half dressed?"

"No," Robert whispered back, "they take everything off."

"Oooh!" Violet giggled and fanned herself rapidly. "That would be such *fun!* I'd love to do that."

"Do what?" Geneva joined them in the hall, looking stern. "Oh, never mind. You never tell me the truth anyway. Benedict, do come and greet Robert. . . ."

Tired, morose, Cassie hung back. She took off her bonnet and smoothed her hair, wondering if she had time enough to go up to her room, then smiled as Jacob came up and slipped an arm around her. He smiled back and kissed her cheek.

"Happy?" He knew how she had missed Robert.

Tears sprang to her eyes and she wiped them away with a quick, embarrassed gesture. "Very. But he leaves again tomorrow."

Shocked sympathy made Jacob's eyes even darker, ebony against his naturally clear white skin. "I'm sorry. Can't he put it off for a time?"

Cassie shook her head. "Aunt Maria wanted him to leave yesterday. It's some sort of a position in London." She looked up at Robert, who was being greeted by enormously fat, dignified Benedict and tall, proper Geneva, who simpered when Robert kissed her cheek. Cassie sighed. "He's twenty-one," she said in a low tone, "he could have said no. But he still feels he owes Aunt Maria. Where is she now?"

Jacob gave her a peculiar smile, almost conspiratorial. "I believe she's sulking."

"Sulking?"

Geneva raised her voice. "Do come along, children. Supper is laid in the back parlor, and the tea will be cold."

"Yes, sulking." Jacob's arm brought her along as the others began to move, his voice whispering in her ear. "You knew she asked my mother to get you a bid from the Assembly?"

"Oh, that." Cassie lost interest. For a year now Maria had been trying to get her an invitation to the Assembly dances. To Cass it was foolish to make a fuss about something so useless. "Who cares?"

"She does. She thinks it's important, and she wants the best for you. But there's been another refusal. She truly feels struck down, Cassie. Be kind."

Cass slowed, leaned her head against Jacob's wiry shoulder and sighed. "I will, of course. But it's strange to me that lives can be changed in an instant by a woman's whim, yet something as trivial as a dull dance can be so important that years are spent in trying to get into it!"

"How odd," Jacob said. "You've just described all of Philadelphia society perfectly. You don't know how lucky you are that you haven't been admitted to its most sacred rite. It is, as you said, a very dull dance. Now start walking, or Maria's smoked oysters will all be gone."

Cassie hardly slept that night. Everyone had stayed late, enthralled by Arthur's stories of the adventures and mishaps of the long and successful voyage. And then discussion turned to the wedding of Arthur and Melainie, planned a week hence since neither could be persuaded to wait longer, and toasts were drunk. Too many toasts, Cassie thought, though even with a whirling head she didn't sleep. Things Robbie had said, and Jacob too, kept running through her mind.

Robert had said: *Remember how cold and hungry we were.* But what Cassie remembered now was the freedom they'd had and how close they had been, always together. There were things worse than hunger, worse than cold.

Jacob had said: *She wants the best for you.* But Cassie didn't believe it. Aunt Maria wanted the best for herself; it was her pride that demanded that invitation for her "ward." Tossing on her pillow, Cassie wondered how many knew by now that Mark Gerard was her father. A bastard would never be invited to that dance, no matter how many strings Maria pulled.

Be kind. Jacob had said that, bless him. Jacob was always kind. Kind and sweet, with a quirk of wonderful wit. She would try hard to be kind, because Robbie was right—they owed a lot to Aunt Maria. But she remembered something else that Robbie had said that was very important: *Bend, Cass, so you won't break.* So she would bend. She would be unbroken when Robbie came home for good, and ready to help run a farm. She punched her pillow again and prayed for sleep.

"Cass?"

Cassie was up and dressed, sitting by her window and staring out at the leaves fluttering to the ground. Her mood matched the day, autumnal and sad. Robert's voice outside her door only deepened her dreary thoughts. He was leaving, then.

"Yes. Come in if you like."

She glanced around as the door opened and saw him standing there, his big body filling the doorway, his blue eyes staring at her with a worried expression. Then he came on in, closing the door, and gave her a searching glance.

"Aunt Maria said you didn't feel well enough to come downstairs," he said. "So I came up to say good-bye. Are you all right?"

"Oh, yes." She tried hard to make it sound right; she looked up at him and smiled. But seeing the dearly familiar face, the solid strength and warmth she had always known, she thought with utter despair of the ocean that would lie between them again, and burst into tears. Collapsing forward on her knees, she put her hands over her face and fought for breath with rasping, tearing sobs and words so broken Robert couldn't make them out.

"Oh, Cassie, don't. *Don't.* Please . . ." He picked her up and sat down in the chair with her in his arms, holding her tight against him, rubbing his cheek on her hair and feeling tears in his own eyes. "Come on, Cass. It's only a year. We've been apart that long and longer before. We can do it again."

Cassie didn't even try to answer. The flood gates had opened and her grief was spilling out. Her hot, streaming face in his neck, her arms straining to hold him, she cried until she could cry no more. His throat tight, Robert stroked her hair, her back, murmured to her and waited. Finally her sobs ceased and she managed to get her breath.

"I'm sorry," she got out, still hiding her face. "I promised myself I wouldn't do this."

"It's all right. I don't like leaving you either." It was true. He hated leaving her again, knowing how sad she'd be, how lonely they'd both be. His chest hurt just thinking about it; in a way, he envied her the tears a woman could shed. He felt her arms tighten around his shoulders.

"Robbie . . . I could go with you! You'll want a place to stay, a house or rooms. I can cook and clean, you know I can. And I'm grown now. I could be a help to you."

He shook his head. "She'd never let you." He was becoming painfully tense, increasingly aware of her warm breath on his neck, of her softness in his arms, the alluring femininity of her scent. "You aren't that grown-up in any case," he added almost harshly. "Not on the inside, Cass."

Calmer, Cassie leaned back to look up at his face. "That isn't so," she said. "Inside, I was always grown-up." Her wet eyes were soft, her lips tremulous. Reaching up, she smoothed a lock of his thick, tawny hair back from his face, her hand soft and gentle. "You know I'm right, Robbie. Neither of us ever had time to be a child."

What it was, Robert never knew. Perhaps the look in her eyes, the gentle touch of her hand on his hair, or the warm, sweet weight of her in his arms. Whatever it was, it nearly burst his heart with love, tightened his arms around her and brought his whole body alive with a yearning desire. He drew in his breath as he felt the sudden throbbing of his blood, the heat and stiffening in his loins, and then he was on his feet and setting her aside.

"Don't be foolish! I don't need anyone to take care of me. Even if I did, your place is here, finishing your studies and . . . and setting an example for Lily." He was babbling, he knew. But he couldn't look at her; or dare to touch her again. Love and desire battled inside and he fought them both, denied them both. "Promise me," he went on wildly, "that you won't cry any more." He reached out to her, wiping away the tearstains on her cheeks with a trembling thumb. "Promise?" She was so sweet, so loving. He couldn't bear the thought of her being unhappy.

"I'll try not to," Cass said faintly. "I really will." It frightened her to see Robert so upset, and she felt it must be her fault. She went close to him again and put her arms around his waist, burrowing in his shirt as she always had, breathing in his familiar odor. "I'll be braver," she whispered. "I meant to, before, but I acted like a baby. Good-bye, Robbie."

Her small breasts against his chest were firm and warm, moving as she breathed. "Good-bye," he got out, trembling, and tore himself away. He was halfway down the stairs before he thought of his baggage, left in the hall beside Cassie's door. He sent Adah up for it, afraid of what he might do or say if he went up himself.

Chapter 14

It was unlike Geneva Bradford to seek someone out in private for a personal talk—she prided herself on saying things out in the open and letting the barbs fly where they would. But ten days after the Masefield-Scott wedding, which they had all attended at Christ Church, Geneva came alone to the Andelet house in midmorning and asked Maria for a "few minutes" of her time.

Intrigued but on her guard, Maria agreed and led Geneva to the study. Ordering tea and the tiny, white-iced cakes Philadelphians adored, Maria settled down to listen.

"I'm not going to beat around the bush," Geneva said. "You and I both know that if the name of Benedict Bradford won't get Cassandra Harmon an invitation to the Assembly, nothing will. You may as well give up that idea."

Maria eyed her. There was a certain amount of malicious satisfaction in Geneva's voice, but Maria had expected that. At the same time, she knew Geneva had tried hard, had pulled every string, to get Cassie in. That too would be a matter of pride. In any event, Geneva had more to say. She wouldn't have made this effort just to gloat.

"I suppose you're right," Maria said. "Fortunately, Cassie doesn't mind a bit, except she's sorry for me. I'm terribly disappointed."

Geneva leaned forward. "There is a way, you know. An open sesame every bit as good as Ali Baba's. Your Cassie could be inside the Assembly crowd in the wink of an eye. And not as a barely tolerated 'new' member, hanging on the fringe, but as a member of the inner circle."

"How?" Maria asked, but she asked automatically, for somehow she knew the answer. It came to her in a revelation. Geneva would suggest a solution that would benefit her.

"By changing her name," Geneva said smugly, "from Harmon to Bradford. She would make a lovely little bride for Jacob."

Maria laughed out loud; she couldn't help it. It was so like Geneva to figure that out. Next, no doubt, she'd offer Violet for Robert, and Andelet money would follow Andelet blood after all, except for Lily's inheritance. Unfortunately, Geneva had no son to offer for Lily. She wiped her eyes and saw Geneva's insulted expression.

"Oh, Geneva . . . I'm truly sorry. No, no, don't look like that—I'm not saying it won't happen. I approve heartily of Jacob, you know I do. He seems very fond of Cassie, and I know Cassie likes him—better, really, than anyone except her own family. But I don't think they have the sort of feelings that, well . . . that lead to marriage."

Geneva snorted. "A person of property must marry well, or be a fool and lose all. It is very seldom that money and hot attraction come together."

"True," Maria agreed. She was busy with a new thought of her own. Cassie liked Jacob, but she didn't love him. Marriage to Jacob would be a safe haven with a gentle, wealthy man and an assured place in the Philadelphia world. And . . . *it would distance her from Robert.* With a husband of her own, Cassie would have to leave off that silly adoration of her "Robbie." And surely—oh, *surely*—when Cassie began the long and confusing life of a grown woman, with a formal engagement and wedding, the first years of marriage, the babies, then she would leave her childhood loyalties behind and turn to her Aunt Maria for advice and companionship. Drawing a deep breath, Maria raised her eyes to Geneva and smiled. "Actually," she said, "it's a wonderful idea. Let's see if we can work it out."

One of the most lovable traits John Kendall possessed was his thoughtfulness. Each time Maria visited the hidden house between Spruce and Pine there was some new thing, some little touch that greeted her—a vase of roses in her favorite dark red, a new French wine in a crystal decanter, dipped chocolates from Schrafft's. Today it was roses and wine, and on the soft, wide bed a set of gloriously sensuous peach-colored satin sheets, turned back invitingly.

"Lovely, darling. You think of everything! And, oh, I do need you after the last two days. So many problems—"

John swept her into his arms and kissed her deeply. Then he took her shawl and brought back one of the soft robes she wore in this place. He was already wearing his silver-gray silk dressing robe and slippers. Long ago they had decided that this was the way they wanted to be in this cozy house. Completely relaxed together, not throwing off their clothes for a hurried coupling, dressing again and rushing away. After years of afternoons spent together here, they felt safe in staying, safe in dressing as they wished. If anyone knew of their hideaway, he was in no hurry to expose them.

Her street clothes laid over the back of a chair, the soft, cherry-red robe wrapped around her small but lush figure, Maria poured wine, handing John a glass. He took it and set it down, keeping hold of her hand, bending to kiss the palm.

"I'll listen to your problems," he said, smiling, "but first I'll tell you the size of the profit young Robert Harmon brought you. Your problems may look smaller then."

"Oh, do." Maria sat down and leaned forward, lips parting, her attention fully concentrated. "The gold . . . how did it assay? And the ivory—it looked prime. I was amazed at how much there was."

John laughed and took a folded page from the pocket of his robe. "I have it all, right here at my fingertips. I knew you'd be anxious to know." He let out his breath, looking at the bottom of the long page he held. "It's hard to believe. But I promise you, you won't be disappointed."

When they made love later, Maria's excitement over the list of treasures made her even more passionate. She was hot with wanting, coaxing him over her, whimpering with need. John had meant to prolong the preliminary lovemaking, to take her to the farthest edge of sensation and then ease back to start again. But always her passion ignited his, swept away his control. He took her, and this time, beneath his usually gentle caresses, Maria sensed a lean and hungry wolf. His long fingers gripped her soft buttocks tightly, lifting her to his strong thrusts. He seemed to want to bury himself in her softness, driving in again and again in a turbulent climax. She lay looking at him when it was over, her large, oddly shaped eyes full of wonderment. Then she smiled.

"For a moment," she said, "you almost frightened me. You . . . seemed different, darling. Not that I minded at all."

John sighed and rolled over, staring up at the low-beamed ceiling. "I wanted you so much I lost control, love. I'm beginning to feel as if I will never truly have you for my own. I hate this life. No matter how wonderful it is to be with you here, I still must leave you to go home."

"As I must too."

"Oh, I know, I do know . . ." He turned and held her, his lips against her cheek. "You've given up much more than I, for you could have had a normal life with someone else. At times you must wish you had chosen a different path, and married again."

But she didn't. She gazed at him, wondering how he'd feel if she told him she had no desire at all to marry anyone. The sudden thought of having a man controlling her businesses, her decisions, her very life, was utterly repellent to her. John might not like hearing that, but it would be only fair to tell him enough to quash any hope he might have for the future. Alice wasn't well; the time might come when he'd be free. She twisted away and sat up.

"I find many things to rebel against in this world," she said cheerfully, "but the single state is not among them. I love being single! I will never marry again." She slid from the bed and began to dress, glancing at John and suddenly straightening to stare. "You're not surprised?"

"Should I be? Haven't you always said whatever was most likely to ease my heart? You are forever trying to take away the feeling I have of guilt."

Maria sighed. He thought she would lie to make him feel better. Well, she had lied many times for various reasons, but she wasn't lying now, and he'd better know it.

"I'm quite serious, Johnny. You see, I've grown used to handling my own affairs and making my own decisions. A husband would take over—and I would hate it." She glanced at him and away, pulling on her gloves. The glance had shown her his shocked displeasure, but she still added, firmly: "No matter who it was, I would hate it."

On her way home, the gig spanking along, the trotting horse tossing his head in the cool fall air, Maria was half smiling. Johnny had acted like a little boy after that speech, accusing her of fickleness, insisting that if she really loved him she would marry him, if and when it became possible. She had let him talk it out, and then, in a soft and reasonable tone, told him that she did love him, that she had been faithful to him for six years, and that a woman bent on marriage would have long ago given up on him or driven him mad with her nagging.

"As it is, we have all the best of it," she had concluded, laughing. "All the romance, the thrill of secret meetings, the zest of danger. Instead of dying of boredom, our love will last forever!"

Later, when she talked it over in the kitchen with Sallie Fernod, Maria told her, "I made it amusing, but I meant it. He laughed and afterward he admitted it was foolish to argue about anything so far in the future, when one or both of us may change our minds."

"If he believes you may change yours," Sallie said, "he is blinded by love. You grow more stubborn and imperious every day. Have you noticed how sober and silent Cassie has become since Robert's departure?"

"Yes. But just the same, I was right, and I've had a note from Robert, written before he even left our shores, apologizing for arguing with me and saying he hoped Cassie would remember that her Aunt Maria always has her best interests at heart."

Sallie gave Maria a derisive look. "I suppose you rushed right in and made her read it. No wonder she's subdued."

"I did not, though I've kept the letter in case of need. I had no wish to make her feel worse than she already did. Girls of seventeen are full of moods. But don't worry. I have plans for her that will take care of that." She laughed and whirled in a rustle of skirts, hugging herself in sheer pleasure. "She will soon be swept into the most exciting time of a young woman's life, Sallie! I've decided to bring her out at the first Dancing Class evening this fall, and she'll be surrounded by beaux all winter."

Sallie had been putting together a Yorkshire pudding, and now she pulled a sizzling beef roast from the oven, poured the pudding into the pan beneath it to bake, closed the oven and came to lower her immense bulk into a chair at the kitchen table. She reached for the pot that was always there and poured one of her interminable cups of tea. "I remember you at seventeen," she said. "That was the year Mark brought me to you—to save us both, I think. You were alone in that great, echoing house, crying your heart out because you had no gown to wear to a dance."

"Was I?" Maria laughed and sat down, tossing her shawl aside and reaching for a cup. "I don't remember it, but it's probably true. Mark did the best he could to take care of me, but there was no money for dancing gowns."

"So this Dancing Class evening will be your first coming out." Sallie sipped her tea, the cup tiny in her huge hand, her dark eyes watching Maria. "Does it suit Cassie?"

Maria poured tea, her eyes dreamy. "Oh, I'm sure it will. I would have much rather presented her at the Assembly, but I doubt she'll care one way or the other."

Sallie smiled suddenly. "It's really your coming out party, isn't it? The one you never had."

"It's ours," Maria said, her voice soft. "Cassie's, really, but I'll enjoy every minute of it. She's so young, Sallie, and so beautiful and carefree. Mark's daughter! How I wish he could see her."

Sallie pushed back her chair and got up, moving silently to the oven to look at the roast and the Yorkshire pudding. "Mark Gerard," she said, her back to Maria, "was not a man to appreciate fatherhood. He dropped Catherine Hayes as soon as she told him she was pregnant, and took up with Abigail Weston." She shut the oven and glanced at Maria. "Nor did he ever show any interest in his child after she was born. You did, I know, but he did not."

Maria leaped to her feet, spilling tea across the table, her hands trembling as she wiped it up. "You always criticized Mark," she said, her voice uneven. "It was the women, Sallie. The women wouldn't let him alone."

Sallie sighed. "He would have been bitterly disappointed if they had. I'm not criticizing, Maria. Mark was Mark, and he was good to you, in his way. But stop making a hero of him. The man you have now is far superior to your brother. You don't give John Kendall his due."

"I appreciate your kindness," Cassie said, managing a weak smile, "but I really don't wish to attend a Dancing Class evening, especially if you plan to have old Richard Simon present me to everyone. That's tantamount to being placed on an auction block."

"Cassie!"

"It's true, isn't it?"

Maria, seated in the tiny sun-room at the southeast corner of the Spruce Street house, had sent Betty to summon Cassie so they could plan together what Cassie would wear, what they would serve as refreshments after the dance. She had fully expected Cassie to be happily excited at the prospect, and overjoyed when she heard that the dancing master, Richard Simon, had consented to do the honors, even to dancing the first dance with the honoree. Of course, he was old and rather boring, but it was considered a mark of society's favor if Simon even noticed a pupil. She gazed at Cassie now and wondered how Mark Gerard's daughter could be so uninterested in society.

"No," Maria said after her long pause, "it is simply a case of being . . . ah, introduced to your peers. And to their parents, of course. It's a ceremony about coming of age—a coming out from girlhood to womanhood, you might say." She smiled, glad she had taken time to think it out and say it sensibly. At times Cassie could be very confusing. "Sit down, dear," she added, "and we'll discuss it pleasantly."

Cassie swept to a chair opposite Maria, smoothed her billowing skirts and sat. Her slim torso rose from a rustling field of taffeta like the stem of a flower, blossoming into high, rounded breasts and perfectly modeled shoulders and arms. Maria, studying her, noticed once more the velvety texture of skin, the delicately beautiful but proud features, and the thick, shining dark hair that sprang in waves from a rounded forehead. She could hardly wait to take Cassie to her first evening dance. There were mothers who would grit their teeth in dismay when they saw her there, competing with their dull and colorless daughters.

"This is foolish," Cassie said, suddenly making up her mind. "It's not even honest, nor fair. No matter how you put it, a coming out isn't just a ceremony about leaving childhood. Everyone takes it for granted that it means you're ready to be courted. And I'm not. I have no intention of marrying."

"You would be an old maid?" Maria's tone was indulgent.

Cassie smiled. "I would be a spinster. And a teacher, I hope."

"Ah. Well, perhaps you know your own mind. But humor me in this one season, darling. It's a pleasure for me to have you presented, and an obligation to our society to follow the rules. What you say to the young gentlemen who may ask permission to call is your own affair. Refuse them if you wish, but please don't refuse me."

Bend, don't break. Cassie's lips compressed and held in a surge of argumentative remarks. She looked up and met Maria's eyes. "If it is that important to you, Aunt Maria, I will go."

Maria drew in her breath. Their eyes were still locked, and it was as if she were young again, pure again, looking into a mirror. She turned away, looking out at the frostbitten garden. The illusion of youth was gone; the reality was in the fall scene outside. She let out her breath and smiled, too brightly. "Fine! I will send a note to Mistress Anna Lane, the dressmaker, and say we wish to see her materials and a pattern for a beautiful ball gown. And then we must remember to tell your friend Jacob. He will want to be there and dance with you on your night."

"Oh, yes! Dear Jacob!" There was great relief in Cassie's

tone. It was clear that Jacob's presence was one thing that would make the occasion more bearable. Jacob was older and experienced in society. He would be a great help in getting through the evening.

Rising, reconciled to the idea, Cassie smiled, and memory stabbed Maria's heart. *So like Mark.* Mark's smile had given him the same look of intense sweetness, of charming gaiety, that Cassie wore now. But Mark had known he was irresistible when he smiled; Cassie didn't, yet. Watching her leave the room, Maria felt her own lips curve up. Heaven help the young men, she thought, when Cassie finds out.

That afternoon Maria called on Geneva to report the progress of their plan. They sat in her front parlor, which was richly decorated with large paintings, embroidered damask hangings, and enormous mirrors. The room was brilliant with light from candelabra and chandeliers, heavy with carved tables and chests. The love seats they sat on were covered in luxurious, pale green satin. Geneva, as elaborately dressed as if she were to attend a royal reception, her red-gold hair in fat side curls and a huge bun in back, served tepid tea and stale cakes. Speaking, her tone was complaining, her expression tight and discontented.

"I can't imagine why Cassandra would object to a coming out, Maria. Why, she should be profoundly grateful to you."

Maria frowned. She intended to be diplomatic, but she hoped there would be no more remarks like that. To Geneva, Cassie was still the poor orphan of a low-class family and phenomenally, undeservedly—even unfairly—fortunate to be where she was, in the bosom of the Andelet family.

"She seems a bit shy," Maria said, controlling her irritation. "And serious. She isn't interested in young men at all, and swears she will never marry. Of course, that is only her innocence talking."

"In that case, she and Jacob should match very well," Geneva said dryly. "He's twenty-four now, and I've been encouraging him to marry for the past two years. He only laughs and says he has plenty of time. Ah, well, they do say the cooler the head, the better the marriage."

"There is one thing I must ask you," Maria said. She

spoke slowly, feeling her way, for the question was sensitive. "I have said Cassie is innocent; perhaps I should add that she doesn't accept many of the things more worldly people take for granted. I understand that Jacob must have a mistress by now, and certainly I don't mean to object. But what is the woman like? Do you think she'll cause trouble when he becomes engaged?" She waited, startled and amused by the flush of bright red that climbed Geneva's cheeks, amazed by the difficulty Geneva found in speaking.

"Not at all," Geneva got out after a struggle. "There will be no trouble from that direction. Put your mind at ease." She settled back on the small love seat and breathed deeply. "Now tell me the particulars, Maria. I'd like to hear your plans for the evening, and what you plan to wear . . ."

They chatted for an hour, and then Maria escaped, glad to leave the ornate, overdecorated room with its heavy odor of scented candles and potpourri. She hurried to her own door, for a misty rain had begun to fall and the air was sharp. Still, she wore a small smile, a smile perhaps a little malicious. It was seldom in a lifetime that anyone saw Geneva Bradford embarrassed, let alone unable to speak! Jacob must have a perfectly scandalous affair going, one that would cause a great deal of gossip if it were found out. A married woman, of course—but then, that was all to the good. The unmarried ones were the ones who resented sharing.

Chapter 15

"Maria," Geneva said in her loud whisper, "I must indeed congratulate you. Cassandra looked lovely when Richard Simon presented her, and she behaved like an angel. And now, with Jacob leading her, she dances as well as anyone here. You've done a miraculous turnabout with the little country maid."

"Shhh. When you whisper in my ear I cannot hear the music of the violins. But you're right, Geneva, and they do look beautiful together."

That was further than Maria meant to go in complimenting Jacob, but it slipped out. Anyway, it was true. She leaned back in her chair and looked around, noting the large crowd. It was a pleasant, cool night, and it seemed everyone had come to watch and to listen to the music of the string orchestra. They filled the ballroom, which had been refurbished and decorated for the Dancing Class evening with swathes of green ribbon and bouquets of yellow chrysanthemums.

"It's really too bad," Geneva said, staring at the dancers again, "that she couldn't come out at the Assembly. Especially since she's to marry Jacob. I do hope he won't mind that she had such a poor start."

Maria gave her a slow, knowing smile. "You mustn't worry about it for a minute. If Jacob objects, Cassie can easily marry someone else. After all, everyone will know she'll have a fine dowry."

Geneva's face fell. "Heavens, Maria, don't jump to conclusions! Jacob is the last person in the world to be snobbish. I suppose he takes after Benedict. You know how Benedict is—never a thought of a man's background, only whether he's honest and fair. Why, he'll talk for hours to a common laborer . . ."

Maria let Geneva's chatter go in one ear and out the other while she watched and listened, and gloated. Seamstress Anna Lane had outdone herself on Cassie's gown. Pink silk, the color of dawn, light as a cloud, shaped around high, young breasts, banded across smooth upper arms, leaving Cassie's perfect shoulders bare except for dark, satiny curls that hung down the nape of her neck and made her warm ivory skin glow brighter. And the skirt was lovely! Three tiers that made a hugely spreading array of silk, the top layer caught up on one side and held with a spray of sweetheart roses and trailing ivy, and at the back a tiny, ruffled train that swept the floor as Cassie dipped and swayed in a waltz.

Maria dreamed, trying to imagine how Cassie felt with so many eyes fastened on her, paying tribute to her beauty.

"She was born to waltz," Maria murmured, as much to herself as to Geneva. "Light as a feather, and always in perfect balance." Like Mark, she thought, but didn't say.

Not hearing, Geneva talked on. Not listening, Maria watched, more and more entranced by the dream, beginning to see more than she had seen before. Cassie was caught up in the waltz, in the swooping, sliding, whirling, dipping, in the rhythm, the intoxicating freedom and grace. She had abandoned herself to the dance, to the ecstasy of swinging movement. For these moments, Maria felt, Cassie had escaped from reality and into a passionate dream of her own. And she *is* passionate, Maria thought with a sudden wrench, she will have her own way if she can. Oh, if I can only turn her to me . . .

Jacob, dressed in his best, was clearly inspired by his

partner. One hand on her waist, the other holding her hand high, he whirled her around the dance floor with consummate mastery. Jacob was always handsome and serene, but Maria had never seen him looking so sure of himself, so happy, with his shining lock of black hair falling across his white forehead, his cheeks flushed with pleasure. She leaned toward Geneva and interrupted her flow of words.

"Jacob looks quite pleased."

Geneva raised her brows. "Naturally. His manners are superb. Besides, I have told him our plans, and he wants his future wife to be accepted."

Maria drew in her breath. "You *told* him? Shouldn't you rather have sounded him out? What if he didn't care for the idea?" But even as she asked she knew it was unnecessary to question Jacob. He might have superb manners, but the happiness she saw in his face was real. She relaxed and leaned back again. "Oh, never mind. I expect we can all set our fears to rest. It looks very much as if Cassie has got in nicely."

Geneva nodded. The music had stopped and Cassie was nearly hidden by a circle of young men crowding close to ask for a dance. And, across the room, Richard Simon looked over and nodded majestically, a smile on his autocratic old face.

"Motherrrr, I've been looking everywhere for you!" Wearing ruffled white lace trimmed in rose-colored ribbons, her long, thin face irritated, Violet Bradford sat down on the other side of Geneva and tapped her mother's arm with her fan. "When is Jacob going to leave off dancing with Cassie long enough to take me out on the floor? I've had two dances, both with that horridly shy Martin Bosley who works for father, and I'm tired of—"

"Hush," Geneva said, and beckoned to Jacob. "He'll dance with you now. But don't keep him at it all evening. He'll want to dance with Cassandra again, and you must be gracious to Martin, you know. I believe the boy is becoming serious."

Rising to go and meet Jacob, Violet sniffed. "Martin can be as serious as he wants, Mama, but I'll not have him. I have my cap set for someone much nicer." She gave Maria an abashed smirk and hurried off.

Maria glanced at Geneva and smiled. "Violet looks lovely tonight," she said generously. She felt she could afford generosity now that Cassie was such a rousing success. "Did you say Martin Bosley is smitten?"

Geneva sighed. "The girl's a fool," she said abruptly. "I hate to say it about my own, but Violet hasn't a practical thought in her head. Martin would make her a very good husband, you know, but she's utterly determined to have Robert."

"Oh? So that's the someone much nicer!" Maria laughed, then softened the laugh with diplomacy. "Well, who knows? Once Jacob and Cassie have wed, no doubt Robert and Violet will see a good deal of each other."

"In their case," Geneva said, "it won't make a particle of difference if they see each other every day. Violet will flirt madly and Robert will ignore her. He's always courteous, but he wouldn't marry Violet if she were the last woman on earth. Oh, do stop staring at me, Maria! I'm not entirely blind when it comes to my children."

Cassie, swinging past with one of the Wharton men, caught Maria's proud smile and smiled back brightly, half ashamed of how unappreciative she had been when Maria was planning this party. After all her reluctance, she was having a wonderful time! She turned the smile on Harry Wharton, and Harry stumbled and missed a step, laughed, recovered and whirled her around.

"You're a marvelous dancer, Miss Harmon! I do believe you're the best partner I've had this evening, and certainly the prettiest."

Catching her breath, Cassie laughed. She supposed it would please Aunt Maria to see her with one of the Wharton family. The Whartons were one of the oldest families in the city, and very well thought of. "You're a wonderful partner yourself, Mr. Wharton, and one of the most flattering. Please, don't turn my head with compliments."

Staring down at her, Wharton examined her minutely, from the unusual eyes to the white teeth in her laughing mouth, from her glossy dark hair to her ivory velvet skin. It might be very satisfactory, he thought, to turn this young lady's head. She was a real beauty. He looked up and saw

Maria Andelet's gaze fixed on him, caustic enough to burn that thought right out of his mind. He grimaced and whirled Cassie around again, presenting his back to Maria. "Indeed I won't, you're much too lovely to spoil. May I take you in to supper, or have you already promised young Bradford?"

"I have," Cassie said, smiling again. "He's looking out for me this evening. But it was lovely of you to ask."

Wharton sighed. She was really too young, and too naive. But there was a warmth about her, an unconscious sensuality that led a man on like a promise. If, as he'd already guessed, there was a wedding being planned by Maria Andelet and Geneva Andelet Bradford, over there with their heads together, then Jacob Bradford would be getting more than he could handle. The thought excited him and he tightened his hold on Cassie's uncorseted waist, feeling her supple muscles give sweetly and obediently as he swept into another turn, his long legs covered by her swirling skirt. Sudden heat ran through him.

"Perhaps another time, then," he said smoothly. "I am often at these fall dances, and I would like to know you better."

"The little affair was quite nice," Geneva pronounced on the way back to Spruce Street. "Entirely adequate, including the fine supper." The five of them had traveled to the dance hall in the large, luxurious Bradford coach, and at midnight were traveling back in it, tired but content.

"It was lovely," Cassie said, and slipped her hand into Maria's. She was seated between Maria and Geneva on one seat, facing Jacob and Violet on the other. "I thank you, Aunt Maria. I enjoyed the dancing very much."

"You certainly looked as if you did," Violet said. "You even flirted with that wicked Harry Wharton! You'd just better watch how you act around him. You'll get a name for yourself if you don't."

"Come, now," Maria said comfortably, "Harry isn't wicked, Violet. He just has an eye for beauty. Cassie's age and innocence would keep Harry at bay. He's no fool." In the darkness she squeezed Cassie's hand. "You didn't really flirt with him, did you, Cassie?"

"I don't know," Cass said, genuinely bewildered, and

everyone, even Jacob, laughed. "Well, I *don't* know," she insisted. "I tried to be nice. I smiled. I told him he was a wonderful dancer and asked him not to turn my head with compliments. Is that flirting?"

"When you *smile,* you're flirting," Violet said with utter conviction. "I've noticed that in you before."

"So have I," Jacob said, his voice laced with amusement. "It's a lovely way to flirt, Cassie, and no one can blame you. Smiling is allowed in all the best circles. And, Harry Wharton will take no liberties unless you let him. He's a gentleman."

"Thank you, Jacob," Cassie said, and smiled.

It was a lovely fall; a lovely holiday season, full of dances and parties. Lily was delighted to be invited to some of the afternoon affairs. At eleven, going on twelve, Lily was charmingly eager and amusingly awkward, like a colt. She was going to be tall, for she outgrew everything she owned in a matter of months. Cassie spent a deal of time helping Maria and Lucy, the new governess, cope with energetic Lily.

At Thanksgiving, Sallie Fernod took Cassie in hand and taught her how to make pastries and yeast rolls.

"You'll have a home of your own before long, and servants to train," Sallie said. "You can't teach what you don't know."

Cassie listened eagerly and worked hard for the same light touch Sallie had. She dreamed constantly of living in the Thompson home, with Robert and Lily to cook for.

Arthur and Melainie came for Thanksgiving dinner, their happiness like a radiance around them. Speaking to Cassie apart from the others, Melainie mentioned Robert.

"How wonderful it would be if he could be here too," she said, and gave Cassie an impulsive hug. "Lily was young enough to accept a different family, but I know you love Robert most and miss him terribly."

Cassie hugged her back, glad of an understanding friend. "Oh, Melly, you do know, don't you?" There were tears in her eyes, but they were tears of gratitude. "No one else realizes how close Robbie and I are, and I'm so glad you do. And yes, I do love him most, the very most." It was true;

though at times she felt it was selfish to love him more than Lily. Sweet, pretty Lily, who now clung to her, adored her, and wanted to be just like her.

As Christmas approached, and the new year of 1849 loomed just ahead, Cassie shone. Maria put it down to the gaiety of the season, the fun Cassie was having with all the other young people, perhaps even the beginning of a romance with Jacob. But to Cass it was mostly because another year was almost gone, her freedom to return to Eagle Forge that much closer. But she never spoke of it. She had learned how to keep peace and happiness in Maria's house. She had only to remember not to mention Robert, not to say she wanted to be a teacher, and especially not to turn down an invitation from Jacob, even if it were only a sleigh ride he offered.

"Jacob is so very nice to you," Maria would say, "and so very fond of you! And you know how sensitive he can be. You must never hurt him. He is a wonderful man."

Which was another true thing to remember. Jacob was so kind, so thoughtful. So, determined to be thoughtful and kind in return, Cassie agreed to every request Jacob made, right up until Christmas morning, when his gift to her was a diamond ring and his request was for her hand in marriage.

They were alone in midmorning, admiring the decorated tree, when he handed her the small velvet box that contained the ring. Opening it, she gazed at the large, brilliant-cut diamond, aflame with cold, dancing fire on a slender circlet of gold. It was as big, or bigger, than any gem Maria owned.

"Why . . . why, Jacob, you know I cannot accept something so valuable as this. It must be worth a fortune . . ." Her voice died away, for in his burning eyes and flushed face she saw why he had given her the ring. "Oh, no," she whispered then, "please, Jacob, no. You are like a brother to me. . . ."

Trembling, Jacob reached for her, holding her loosely in his arms. "Don't say that, Cassie. You . . . you don't need a brother. You need a husband. And I need you . . . very, very much. Say you'll marry me." His face was scarlet by now, beaded with perspiration even in the cool air. Cassie looked up at him helplessly.

"I can't," she said in a low tone. "I can't, Jacob. I wish I could, for you've been wonderful to me." She pressed the box back into his hand and broke away to run, crying, from the room.

"She'll come around," Maria told a dejected Jacob later. She had come in and found him alone in the back parlor, and his crestfallen air had given him away. It had been easy to get the story out of him, for he was looking for advice and reassurance. "She's very young and inexperienced, Jacob. Had I known you planned to propose so soon I would have prepared her a little. As it is . . ."

"I should have waited," Jacob said, straightening. "I know that now. I think I shocked her badly. She probably knows nothing about marriage. Perhaps you should talk to her, Aunt Maria."

"I will." Remembering what Cassie did know about marriage, Maria knew the most important part would be to convince her that other marriages weren't like the one between her mother and Willie Harmon.

"Cassie? It's me. Can I come in?" Lily's blue eyes were round, her face tense as she peered around Cassie's bedroom door.

"'It's I,'" Cassie corrected wanly. "Or just say your own name. 'It's Lily' sounds fine and leaves no doubt. Besides, it's easy to remember."

"Yes, Cassie. But . . . *can* I come in?"

"Oh, I'm sorry, dear. Of course you may." Cassie was sitting in her window seat, and she moved to make room for Lily, who came and curled in beside her.

"I heard Adah tell Sallie and Maud that you turned down Jacob," Lily said without preamble. "What did she mean?"

Cassie started. "She meant she'd been listening at a closed door," she said sharply. "I'll tell her to stop her snooping!"

"You know she always does," Lily said, "and anyway, I want to know what happened." She leaned against Cassie and looked up adoringly. "Did Jacob propose to you? Are you going to marry him, Cass?"

"Yes, he asked me, and no, I'm not going to marry him. I'm not going to marry anyone. I'm going to keep house for you and Robert. How will you like that?"

"I'll like it fine! But won't you be lonesome when Robbie and I get married?"

Cassie almost smiled. "You are a goose. You can't marry your half brother."

"Oh, Cassie, don't make fun of me. I knew that. I meant when he married someone and I married someone. You'd be all alone then."

Cassie turned her face away, pressing her forehead to the window and looking out at the bare trees and snow. "I suppose so. But . . . I still don't want to be married. If I have no one to live with, I'll live alone."

"You won't have to," Lily said comfortingly, and put her arms around Cassie's waist. "I'll stay with you, Cass. If some man wants to marry me, I'll just say no like you did."

Cassie went on staring at the bleak winter scene. It had taken no more than Lily's questions to show her the decision would affect the future for Lily and Robert. Not that she thought romantic Lily would sacrifice her desires to stay with her—when Lily fell, she'd fall hard and toss the world away for the man she loved. But Robert was a different story. Would he deny his own wants to stay with her? She was very much afraid he would, or if not that, would he insist on her living with him and his wife? She tensed, and felt her heart twist in an agony of jealousy.

"I'd *hate* that!" she said fiercely, and Lily jumped.

"You would? Why? D-Don't you like me?"

Cassie whirled and saw the woebegone young face. "Oh, Lily! I didn't mean *you*, darling. I was thinking of someone . . . something else." She hugged Lily hard. "Of course I like you—no, I love you, and I always will. You must never doubt it."

An hour later Maria found Cassie still sitting in the window seat, pale and silent. She came in, pulled up the rocking chair, and sat down.

"I know you're upset, darling, and I'm sorry. But I thought you surely must know Jacob was going to ask you."

Cassie shook her head. "I didn't know. How could I? He never gave me even a hint of his feelings. He . . . he was just friendly. He never has acted like the other young men."

Maria looked at her curiously. Jacob had, on occasion,

puzzled even her by his reticence around young women. "What do you mean by that? How do the other young men act?"

"Oh, you know." Cassie went back to staring at the snow outside. "You must know. Even the old men act like that around you."

Startled, Maria swallowed a nervous laugh and sat straighter. Cassie wasn't as unobservant as she had supposed. "You mean he isn't flirtatious?"

Cassie shrugged. "Not with me. That's why I like being with him. When we dance he doesn't get that—that sort of eat-you-up look and the hot, sweaty hands the others have." She met Maria's eyes. "When they get like that, they try to rub against you, or touch the side of your breast." She paused. "That's passion, isn't it?"

"Yes. But it isn't always love." Maria spoke gently, wondering at Cassie's misery. For she was miserable, that was plain.

"I know. But it's what makes men want to marry, and Jacob doesn't feel any of it, at least for me. He seemed more embarrassed than anything else when he proposed. So, why did he?"

Maria didn't know, and all at once she didn't want to know. She stood up, smoothing down her gown distractedly. "Cassie, I think you're overwrought. Jacob wouldn't ask you to marry him unless he loved you and wanted you. As for the way he acts, you know very well he's shy. He'll get over it soon enough, once you're married." She turned to leave, stopping at the door to add: "Think it over very carefully. Many a man wouldn't repeat the offer once you'd refused, but Jacob will. He has thought deeply about it, and he realizes he was too abrupt. He means to give you time to get used to the idea."

Cassie nodded, her face downcast and serious. For the last few hours she too had been thinking deeply. She knew now that what she decided would affect the whole family, the whole future. Oh, Lily wouldn't care one way or the other now, though it might make a difference to her later. But it was easy to guess that Aunt Maria wanted her to say yes, and probably Jacob's mother and father had been consulted and had agreed. They would be insulted if she refused. Even

Violet might be angry with her if she refused her brother. And Jacob—she had already seen him tremble and turn red as fire. Poor Jacob, who was always so sweet to her.

She sighed, wishing she could talk to Robert. He knew how she felt about belonging to a man, about being a wife. He could tell her whether she should marry at all when she dreaded it so. Besides, she thought suddenly, he's the head of *our* family, and he's grown-up now. He has a right to give us advice, and we have a right to ask for it. If Jacob proposes to me again, Robert shall have his say about it. *And I shall pray to God that Robert will say no, no, Cassie shall never wed.*

That decision cleared her mind. She left the window and went to wash her face and brush her hair, then hurried downstairs to open the rest of her Christmas gifts. She was rewarded by a package from London, sent by Robert on the Black Ball packet boat and containing Charles Dickens's latest novel, *David Copperfield.* And, as if that weren't enough, there was a note inside wishing her a Merry Christmas and asking her to please write to him more often. "I'm lonely," the note ended, "and I miss you."

Chapter 16

Walking along Spruce Street through a lightly falling snow, John Kendall fished his chased gold watch from an inner pocket and glanced at it, then turned to mount the steps at the Andelet house. He was early, but not too early, and today he felt the cold. He looked tired and haggard, his high cheekbones and strong arch of nose standing out from a thinning face.

Dickon opened the door to let him in, took his hat and muffler, his heavy outer coat and his cane, and distributed them on table, racks, and umbrella stand. He gave John a look of mournful sympathy as he ushered him down the hall.

"We are all very sorry to hear that Mrs. Kendall is ill," he said, "and hoping she will soon be well. The cook has prepared a special beef broth, very strengthening, for you to take home to her."

Walking slowly toward the study, John nodded. "Thank you. Tell Sallie it's extremely kind of her." He shivered, for the hall was drafty today, but there would be a coal fire in the study. "I'm early," he added, "but don't disturb Mrs. Andelet. I'll be glad to wait."

"No need, sir," Dickon replied, opening the study door, "as you see, she's waiting for you."

Maria, wearing an expression of sympathy mixed with apprehension, rose from the desk and came forward quickly to take both of John's hands. Behind John, Dickon closed the door discreetly, and John, though he had never touched Maria before in this house, let go of her hands and wrapped his arms around her tightly, bending, burying his cold, distraught face in her warm neck.

"Oh, God," he said hoarsely, "I didn't know this would be so difficult. She's dying, Maria. Sweetly and calmly *dying,* and there's not one damn thing anyone can do. I feel like going on my knees to her and asking forgiveness."

Maria pulled back to look at him, her face stricken and pale. "Johnny, please don't say that. We stole nothing from her."

He turned away, rubbing both hands over his face. "I know. I didn't mean that. I don't know what I do mean, except I feel guilty for being well, for living on, while she must die."

"In many ways," Maria said gently, "you have been a kind and thoughtful husband. More so than most. Stop blaming yourself."

John shook his head. "I keep thinking I could have given her a better life. A happier life." He turned back again, his eyes reddened. "She wants you to come to the house, Maria. Will you go?"

"She asked for me?"

"Yes. She has no family left, you know. She mentioned your little girls, and something about a kitten. Perhaps she was wandering in her mind . . ."

"No. I remember that. And yes, I'll go. I'll go today. I should have gone before."

Over the years Maria's visits to Alice Kendall had dwindled, first to one each fall when they returned from Eagle Forge, and then, as Alice grew weaker and slept a great deal, to none at all. This time Maria went alone in a hired coach, with instructions to the driver to pick her up again in an hour.

The draperies at the broad living-room window where Alice always lay on her lounge were closed; the house looked deserted and forlorn in the snow, which now fell thickly. But as the coach came to a stop the maid opened the door and hurried out in her hooded cloak to help Maria into the house.

"Oh, ma'am, it is so good of you to come. My poor lady is in a terrible bad way." Vera's teeth were chattering, her nose red from crying and the cold. Closing the door, she took Maria's fur-lined cloak and galoshes. "She is in the small room at the back, Mistress Andelet. She is no longer strong enough to be taken from her bed."

Maria nodded, gathering her courage and turning down the hall. The smell of carbolic acid and medicines hung in the overheated house, the shadows in the dark hall menacing and oppressive. Fear was a stranger to Maria, but she felt an instinctive awe of approaching death.

Going into the small room that had once been used as a study similar to her own, she found it stripped of the cozy furniture and bookcases and fitted out like a hospital room. Alice lay motionless in the high bed, so emaciated that the shape beneath the white counterpane was as small as a child's. But she raised a hand at sight of Maria and smiled, her pale lips curving sweetly.

"You came . . . thank you." Her voice was very weak, her breath faltering, and Maria hurried to the side of the bed to clasp the thin hand.

"Dear Alice! Of course I came, once I knew you wanted me here. I am so sorry to find you weak and in pain."

"I am . . . in no pain." She raised a hand again and waved Vera away, waiting to speak after the door closed. "A faithful creature she is," she whispered with another smile, "but so apt to weep. You look wonderful, Maria. Sit down . . . tell me about your girls . . . and . . . and wasn't there a boy?"

Maria pulled up a chair and sat. Condensing the past five years into a short list of triumphs and anecdotes, she watched Alice closely for fatigue. "And the kitten," she concluded, smiling, "has a regiment of kittens of her own. They all live in Eagle Forge and police our barns and granaries for mice and rats. You did us all a tremendous favor with that cat."

"Good." The voice was even weaker, but clear. "For I would ask a favor of you."

Full of pity and sorrow, Maria swallowed before she could answer. "Anything, Alice."

Alice's hot, bony hand pressed hers. "Then . . . please, do not allow John to turn away from happiness to grieve for me . . . or to do penance. He . . . he is shamed now, thinking his love for you is wrong. But I . . . know differently. All these years . . ." She was panting for breath, but as Maria, shocked, started to speak, Alice shook her head. "W-Wait . . . let me talk . . . while I can. All these years he has been able to . . . to keep on . . . being kind and sweet to me, being happy and . . . and whole, because he had the love he needed. Because of you, Maria . . ."

"Alice—" Maria barely got the word past stiff lips, and then her face crumpled and her hands flew up to cover it. "You knew. Oh, God, now I too am shamed. I—I wouldn't have hurt you for anything in the world. . . ."

"You *didn't*. That is what I'm trying . . . to say. I was so relieved! I . . . am *thanking* you, Maria. How could I not? His sad patience became a . . . a shining happiness, and I . . . was so glad for him. Please, don't leave him alone. He will need you . . . more than ever. He—" She began to cough, a racking spasm that brought Vera running in with a dark bottle of syrup and a spoon.

While Vera administered the medicine and soothed her patient, Maria pulled herself together. Rising, she went to the window and stood there, wiping her eyes. She had never felt so humbled, so aware of her faults. When the coughing had ceased she turned and went back to the side of the bed, standing there and watching as Vera straightened the bedclothes and punched up the pillow. Vera's red-rimmed eyes were full of love as she fussed over Alice.

"There," Vera said at last, "she's comfortable again. But she's very tired, Mistress Andelet."

"I know," Maria said softly. "I'll not stay long now, Vera." She waited until Vera left the room and then leaned over, her eyes wet, and kissed Alice's thin cheek, looking into the steadfast eyes, seeing the question still there.

"I will do as you ask," Maria said. "I'll not leave him, nor will I let him believe he has sinned beyond repair. And I will love him as much as I am able to love. But some day I will tell him that he has been loved with a far greater love than I am capable of feeling. You are a wonderful, wise woman, Alice Kendall."

"She is a saint, Sallie. Every thought was for John's happiness." Sitting at the kitchen table, Maria's usually vivid, determined face was pale, washed with emotion. "God knows," she added with unaccustomed humility, "how I would behave under the same circumstances."

"Better than you think," Sallie said. "Only a fool or a coward rails in the face of certain death. You are neither." She smiled as she rose from the table and went to check the bread she was baking. "However," she added, taking out the browned loaves, "there was a lesson there for you. Now that you've seen love, perhaps you will stop pushing your niece into a loveless marriage."

Maria gasped. "How can you say that? Jacob adores Cassie!"

"Armand adored you."

"Armand was *old!* Jacob is young and handsome."

Sallie sighed and settled her bulk at the table again. "Then why did she refuse him, Maria?"

"Damn it, I have told you! She saw the drunken brutality of her stepfather wreaked on her ill mother. She is afraid, that is all. One night with Jacob will prove to her that a man can be gentle and considerate in bed as well as in company."

Sallie's deep eyes slid into a narrow, sidelong glance at Maria's flushed face and slid away again, dropping to her folded hands. "Cassie is a young woman who has not yet discovered her passionate nature. But it is there, only waiting to be kindled. Jacob will never light that fire. He is gentle and kind, but he is not a man."

"Oh, don't be so critical of the boy," Maria said. "He's a charming and sensitive person. You sound like Benedict. Just because he doesn't go blustering around, you think he's not manly." She rose, gathering up her gloves and small purse. "Actually," she added, "he's perfect for Cassie. She is too much like me to want a domineering husband. With Jacob she will have her own way."

"Mon Dieu!" Sallie blew out a disgusted breath. "Her own way, is it? The child will never have her own way until she escapes from you, Maria Gerard! You would breathe for her if you could! You would *be* her!"

Maria stared and then laughed nervously. "Such drama," she said, turning to the door. "You've put far too much meaning into my natural concern for my niece. I admit to being perhaps a little too protective, but that's all. You'll see, Sallie. She will be happy with Jacob."

Ten days later, on a miserably cold February morning, the Bradfords and Andelets attended the funeral of Alice Kendall, held, because of the large number of mourners, at Holy Trinity. John Kendall sat alone, looking as cold and gray as the scene outside, and left alone after the burial service in the family vault. Maria's large eyes followed him in silent concern, but she said nothing. Watching, Cassie felt she understood. Riding home again in the hired coach, she held Maria's hand and tried not to listen to Geneva's rude and heartless remarks.

"A blessing, of course. Poor Alice was nothing but a problem to herself and to John, and I expect he's relieved if the truth were known. Heaven knows he's got nothing to blame himself for—there was never a kinder nor more faithful man, and I suspect she was bitter and complaining. I know I would be . . ."

"You might be," Maria said, staring through the window at the gloomy day, "but she wasn't. She was a generous, loving woman, and John will miss her sorely."

Cassie's hand curled in hers and squeezed tightly. Maria glanced at her in surprise and saw the eyes so like her own looking at her in warm admiration.

"Well," Geneva said, taken aback, "I have to admit you knew her better than I did. But she would have to be a saint not to have some bitter feelings about her situation."

Maria smiled at Cassie and settled back contentedly, letting Geneva's voice drone on.

* * *

"What? Writing to Robert again?" Maria had come into the study quietly and found Cassie scribbling away at the desk. "It seems only yesterday that I took a letter to the carrier for you."

"A week ago today," Cassie corrected, smiling, "not yesterday." She folded the sheet of paper, put it into an envelope and rose to allow Maria to sit at the desk. "I wish the time went as quickly for me as it does for you. Robbie would be home a great deal sooner." She realized as she saw Maria frown that she had spoken unwisely, and spoke again, hurriedly. "How is Mr. Kendall? He waved at me as he was leaving this morning, and he looked so much better today than he has since the funeral."

Maria's frown eased away. "He does indeed seem to be recovering from his loss." Taking the desk chair, she looked suddenly younger, her skin flushed pink. "Perhaps warmer weather will hearten us all. Is Jacob well?"

"He seems very well." Leaning over the desk from the opposite side, Cassie kept her gaze on the envelope she held, closing it and sealing it with a dab of wax. Maria watched her, conscious that she was purposely hiding her thoughts, and then spoke again.

"Didn't I see him in the back garden with you this morning?"

"Yes," Cassie said, still avoiding Maria's eyes. "I went out to see the purple crocus Sallie said had come up, and he came over through the gate. We . . . we talked for a few moments."

"That is all?"

Cassie glanced quickly at Maria's intent face, wondering what she might know. "Yes, except he brought me a—a poem he thought I might like. And he asked me to go to the Westons' party with him."

"Alone?"

"Violet was to attend with us."

"Oh. Then of course you agreed?"

Cassie's gaze came around and leveled on Maria's eyes. "No, I didn't. I thanked him for thinking of me and said I had other plans."

"That was neither gracious nor truthful," Maria said, an edge to her voice. "Why did you lie?"

Cassie turned red. "Would you rather I said I didn't want to go because he might ask me to marry him and I'd have to refuse again?"

Maria leaned back in her chair and threw up her hands in disgust. "Cassie, for heaven's sake! What *is* the matter with you? The other young women flock around Jacob like bees around honey! How could you ask for anyone better—or even half as good? Young, handsome, wealthy, and likely the nicest man you'll ever know, and you won't have him! *Why?*"

"Because," Cassie said carefully, since she knew Maria was going to be angry, "because I'm waiting for Robert to come home. I thought about marriage for a long time, and I decided I must ask him first what I should do."

Maria could feel rage blooming behind her eyes. A noise between a groan and a growl rose in her throat. She managed to suppress it, clamping her lips shut and turning away from Cassie's stubborn face. *Robert.* Damn Robert! Cassie had seen him only three or four times in the past five and a half years, yet it was still Robert she turned to, Robert she depended on, Robert she *loved.* In that moment Maria wished with all her heart that Robert had drowned on the way to China. The effort to speak in a reasonable tone brought beads of perspiration to her forehead.

"I see. Isn't that rather foolish? I seriously doubt that Robert will ask for your opinion when he wishes to marry."

Cassie swallowed and gazed at her feet. "Perhaps not. Nevertheless, I will ask him. If he believes I should marry Jacob, I . . . well, I suppose I will." She waited patiently for Maria's next objection. When the silence grew long, she glanced up and found Maria's large eyes fixed on her speculatively.

"I can think of no reason why Robert would dislike Jacob," Maria said slowly. "Can you?"

"Oh, no. I already know he likes Jacob. But he—he's the only one who really knows how I feel about being a wife, and he may not think I should marry at all."

So that was it. Maria felt a sudden, tremendous relief. The child was still too frightened by the physical side of marriage, and needed Robert's word that it would be all right.

And Robert could give her that reassurance as no one else could, for she would believe him. Maria's anger fled away as quickly as it had come. She rose and came to Cassie, putting her arms around her and kissing her cheek.

"Now, I really do see," she said softly, "and I regret my arguments. Of course you must ask him, darling. But why wait until he comes home? You can write another letter."

"I suppose I could. But . . . well, I wouldn't want to marry anyway until after Robert came home."

Maria laughed and hugged her. "Why, you couldn't! After your engagement is announced, it will take six months at least, and likely more, to schedule the parties that will be given for you and Jacob. Robert will be home long before that. You should write soon."

March winds and weak sunshine combined that afternoon to melt the last, dirty-gray snow on the cobblestone streets. Bundled against the still sharp cold, Maria was lighthearted as she drove her gig through the alleys and byways that led to the hidden house. The clip-clop of the horse's hooves on the wet stones was welcome after months of deep, muffling snow. A sound of spring, she thought, and her smile came, lighting her face, putting a glow in her eyes. Spring was a time of renewal, and she was more than ready for that. John had kept to himself since Alice died; he had been like a stranger when he came to the house to discuss business affairs. Nothing she could say or do had penetrated his frozen gloom until this morning, and then it was the sight of Cassie and Jacob in the muddy garden that finally broke through his reserve. John's eyes had softened, watching them.

"They are very good friends, aren't they?" he had said.

"Yes," Maria had replied, "and I hope more than friends soon. I would like to see them marry."

"Oh? Then your dislike of marriage doesn't apply to your niece?"

Looking at him, Maria could see no trace of mockery. He simply wanted to know. "Marriage is for the young, John. Making a home and having children takes precedence over other things. Perhaps freedom is a luxury only the old can afford."

John had nodded slowly. "That may be so. But freedom is also a lonely state."

"It doesn't have to be."

He had said nothing more until he was ready to leave. Then, his long, caped coat over his shoulders, he had turned at the door and spoken abruptly.

"Will you meet me, then? Say at two?"

Warmth had flowed into her heart, dislodging a small but very cold fear of losing him. She took a deep breath and smiled, touching his hand with a feather-light caress.

"You know I will, Johnny."

And now she was there, driving into the stable with her heart suddenly pounding, her mind in a whirl of conjecture. Somehow, it was like meeting a different man. Someone she hardly knew. There was excitement in that too. Her hands were shaking as she gave the reins to the stableman and went in, seeing the glow of lamplight at the end of the dark entry hall. Then John's lean body, in fitted trousers and silk shirt, was silhouetted in the doorway, his arms opening and reaching. She ran, her slender legs thrusting against her heavy skirts, her arms rising to encircle his neck, her lips parting eagerly for his kiss.

"Johnny . . . oh, Johnny . . ."

"My love. My little love." His deep voice, taut with feeling, reverberated in her heart. She was lifted in his arms, carried inside, and there were suddenly tears in her eyes, tears of joy because she was still loved, still ardently desired, by the only man she had ever truly wanted, or truly needed.

He undressed her slowly, kissing and caressing each newly exposed bit of rosy flesh, and for once she submitted to his wishes, allowing him to remove every stitch. She was rewarded by seeing his ardor increase until his hands trembled and his pale eyes smoldered with dark passion. When he turned away and rapidly discarded his own clothing, she saw his engorged shaft shining like taut silk, tightly straining, and she felt her thighs move apart involuntarily, felt the aching glow of heat between them. But he remained standing, looking down at her, extending the moment.

"So beautiful," he whispered, and saw her slow smile, the tenderness in her large eyes. As she lay before him he could see the flutter of her rapid heartbeat in the shadowed valley between her breasts. He lay his palm there, feeling the pulsing life and warmth.

"I love you," he said unsteadily. "God help me, I love you too much to ever let you go. Please . . . love *me*, Maria. Love me, my darling . . ."

In answer she drew him down over her, took him inside her welcome heat, wrapping her arms and her slender legs around him until he felt enclosed by warm flesh, by love. And then, as their bodies surged into the ancient rhythm of mating, he knew she had stolen him away from the grip of winter and death and brought him back into life.

Chapter 17

April 1849

The sound of Cassie's laughter came clearly through the kitchen window of the manor, and both Noonan and Sallie, having morning tea together, turned to look.

Dawn, the bright chestnut mare, was dancing off the dull confinement of winter and celebrating spring. Cassie on her back, Dawn reared up on her hind legs, whinnied sharply, blew and pirouetted, punching the air with her front hooves.

"That girl sticks to a horse like a burr," Noonan said, grinning. "I think she likes to cut loose as well as the mare does. Listen to her laugh!"

"And watch her go," Sallie added as Cassie brought the mare down and sent her through the garden path at a gallop, heading for the meadow. "She's off for another full day, running away from Maria's fussing about an engagement party. I saw her stuff a sandwich for herself and carrots for the mare in her pocket before she left the house."

Noonan nodded, still grinning. "She's a country girl, Sal. The mistress will have her hands full getting that one city broke."

"No, I won't," Maria said from the doorway, and laughed

with as much delight as Cassie when both of them jumped and turned to look at her. "So this is what you do when I'm not around—talk about me and my problems."

"Eavesdroppers never hear anything good," Sallie said. "You're lucky it wasn't worse. Where are you going?"

"To the forge. John will be here today to go over the records, and I want them handy. When Cassie comes in, tell her I said to spend some time on her embroidery. Those hope-chest linens will never be finished if she doesn't get started."

"Embroidery is for winter," Sallie said. "This is April. Don't tie her down, Maria."

Maria heaved a resigned sigh. "You're worse than she is, Sallie. Just forget it. I'll see to it myself tomorrow."

Once out of sight, Cassie turned north and pulled Dawn down to a trot. Straightening her linen skirt, she settled into the saddle and breathed a huge sigh of pleasure. The sights and sounds and smells of spring were all around her in the crisp air. Pink blossoms covered the apple trees, violets nestled in the grass along the beaten path, the rich, sweet smell of fertile earth drifted from the plowed fields. Sunshine and blue sky. Birds. Birds everywhere, scolding, singing, hunting insects, carrying wiry grasses and leaves to the crotch of a limb or a crossing of branches to begin a nest. Cassie was drunk with April, joyous for no reason except for the feeling of wonders beginning, of life bursting forth, the promises of unknown glory to come.

When she came to the narrow road that led from the highway to the village, she turned again and rode west, as she did every day. Before she reached the village she would branch off on a lane that led past the hut where she had spent the first ten years of her life, and continue on until she came to the old Thompson farm, deserted since Caleb Thompson died.

There the fields were choked with weeds, the long lines of fences wavering along unevenly, falling into piles of decaying logs. The dam that crossed the wide creek running through the farmland had been breached, the pond drained, the beams and stones of the dam scattered.

When she had first ridden to the farm some days ago,

Cassie had been fearful of finding everything in ruins. But the big farmhouse, the three-story barn and stable, the chicken house and pigpen, were all in fine shape, the roofs and siding repaired and glistening with new paint, soft gray and white for the house, dark red for the barn. She had heard from a farmer hired to plow the Andelet fields that when Uncle Caleb died, Robert had sent money to old Henry Tilburn, along with a good sum for Tilburn himself, to see that the house and outbuildings were set to rights. Robert knew, as all the villagers knew, that Tilburn, who was stingy and biased, was also honest. He had seen to the job as if it were his own place. It was ready, Cassie thought, for the three of them to move into and begin the long task of bringing a farm back to life. Now, if only Aunt Maria would listen . . .

She had just turned off on the lane when she heard the rapid hoofbeats and spinning wheels behind her. Turning her head, she gasped and slowed.

"Aunt Maria!"

Maria pulled up beside her, her usually smiling face pale and grim. "I'm glad I found you. The *Sea Sprite* has been badly damaged, and John has driven all night to bring me the news. We're leaving immediately for New York. Do you want to go with us?"

Cassie hesitated. "Take Lily instead, Aunt Maria. You won't need me there, and she's always wanted to see New York."

"Won't you be bored here alone? We may be gone for a week or more, seeing if the cargo can be salvaged and the ship repaired."

"I'll be fine. I just hope the damage isn't too great. I'll ride back now and help both of you pack."

Some of the grimness went out of Maria's taut face and her smile appeared. "You're a dear, thoughtful girl, Cassie. I will be glad of the help."

In two hours they were ready to go, with fresh horses for John's coach, and Noonan helping with the driving, for John was worn out. They would go to Philadelphia and take the train for New York. Lily was too excited to talk, and Adah, who was going with them to watch over Lily when Maria was busy, was pale with a matching excitement, her freckles standing out as she looked through the coach window and waved at Cassie.

Hurrying out to join the others in the coach, Maria kissed Cassie's cheek and glanced back at Sallie's huge presence in the entrance door.

"Keep her safe, Sallie."

Sallie grinned, a wide, white slash in her dark face. "No strangers get past me."

"I'll be back in a day or so to help," Noonan said, loosening the whip on the driver's box. "I reckon the two of us can hold the fort, Sal. Gee up, boys!" He cracked the whip in the air and the coach jolted forward, rocked, and settled into a swaying run down the drive.

Two days later, in early afternoon, Sallie Fernod heard hoofbeats outside and looked through the kitchen window. She had been expecting Noonan, but this was not a coach. A single horse cantered into view, heading for the stableyard with a big, broad-shouldered and hatless man on his back. Even at a distance his thick tawny hair, blowing in the spring breeze, told her who he was

Sallie's first thought was for Maria. She would be furious when she heard Robert had come home months before he was expected. Her second thought was more of a feeling, welling up from a heart that understood a great deal more about other hearts than ordinary people's did. Here was a crisis, here was a great change, and no one was around to prevent it but herself. She put down the spoon she'd been using to stir a pan of soup, moved the pan from the stove and went silently and quickly through the door and down the steps, hurrying as Robert dismounted and tied his horse to the fence. Dragging a strapped leather baggage roll from the back of his saddle, he looked up and saw her coming toward him. A wide smile lit his tanned face.

"Sallie Fernod! Here, take charge of this." He tossed her the leather roll and laughed as she caught it in one hand. "I'm home for good, Sal! There will be no more roaming the sea for me. Just tell me where she is!"

She knew who he meant. She gave him her brilliant white smile, but her eyes slid away from his. "Mistress Andelet isn't here, Master Robert. She's in New York, seeing to the damage on the *Sea Sprite*. Since that was your ship, you might be of help there . . ."

Robert waved a dismissing hand, as if the ship had nothing to do with him. "But I meant Cassie! Where is she?"

For the first time since she had grown to her present size, Sallie Fernod felt helpless. It was impossible to lie to him, impossible to keep them apart. And, deep in her heart, she didn't want to try. But still she could warn him.

"More than likely she's in her room, Master Robert. She rode all morning and went up afterward to take a bath. I suppose you know she's to marry Jacob Bradford this fall . . ." Her voice faltered and was still, for Robert had brushed past her and was taking the steps two at a time. She followed slowly, hearing his quick, heavy stride in the front hall, on the stairs, his deep voice calling.

"Cass! Cass, where are you?"

Cassie's heart gave a great leap; she stood stock-still in the middle of her room and listened. That couldn't be Robbie's voice, but it was. Oh, it *was!* She ran, heedless of her disarray, the thin shift and soft robe, her tangled hair, still wet from a bath. Into the old schoolroom, to the door that led into the hall, hearing him call again, feeling her heart close to bursting. She flung the door open and saw him striding toward her, opening his arms.

"Robbie! Oh, *Robbie!* You came home! How did you know I n-needed you . . . I . . ." She was half crying, she was babbling, and then she was in his arms, in the air, her feet off the floor as he lifted her up and swung her back inside the rooms.

She cried because he felt so good, so big and strong, so wonderfully familiar, so much her own dear Robbie. She clung to him like a drowning man clings to a lifeline, her arms tight around his neck, her cheek on his shoulder, trying her best not to sob out loud.

"Cass," he said, letting out his breath. "Thank God." He felt his heart swell until it seemed to fill his chest; tears came to his own eyes. He let her slide down to her feet and hid his face in her damp hair. He kissed the hair and then her face, her eyes, cheeks, lips. His mouth was hot, his big hands and hard body insistent, uncontrollable, straining her to him. He felt her give to him, lean into him, sweetly innocent. He reached for control over his rampaging emotions, drawing back to look into her eyes.

"Listen to me, Cass. When I got your letter I couldn't believe how I felt. I read it over and over, the part where you said you'd marry Jacob Bradford if I told you to. I felt awful and I thought I must be crazy. I went out and got roaring drunk and sick as a horse. When I sobered up I knew what I must do, for both of us. I closed up the office there and came home to tell you. You can't marry Jacob, Cass. You can't marry anyone but me."

She gasped. *"You?* But . . . but everyone thinks you're my *brother!"*

He laughed, his eyes shining "Who cares what they think? *Am* I your brother, Cassie? Are you my sister? Are you even my half sister, as Lily is to us both? Or—now think, Cass!—haven't you always been my own true friend, my own true love, as I have been yours? Oh, Cass, my darling, darling Cass, we should have known! There's never been anyone else in our hearts, and there never will be, never in all our lives."

Cassie closed her eyes and swayed with the delicious shock of what he had said. To her, it was as if they had been waiting forever for happiness in a cold, barren place with nothing to hold on to but each other, and now, suddenly, the world around them was blooming with trees and grass and flowers, with a house that looked remarkably like the Thompson house, with real love inside for a man and a woman. And it wasn't a dream; it was true. They loved each other and they always would.

"Yes," she whispered, opening her eyes. She felt swept by a tremendous happiness. "We should have known! Maybe inside we did know, and that was why I didn't want to marry. Because I loved you. Only you." She pulled his tawny head down and reached to kiss him, full and open on his mouth. "But I will marry *you,* Robbie. I will *be* yours, right now."

He bent and lifted her again in his arms, trembling. Her soft, heated body beneath the gaping robe and thin shift gave off a faint but irresistibly erotic scent. "I—I want to make love to you, Cass. I have wanted you since the day I left you crying there in the city. But we must marry first."

"No! I want to belong to you while . . . while no one can stop us. So no one can stop us later . . . please, Robbie."

He understood. He drew a deep breath and nudged the door closed with his knee. Then he carried her in to her bed and sat down on the edge of it with her in his lap. She watched him, her face serious but calm, as he untied her robe.

"I—I promise I won't cry, Robbie."

His hands stilled and some of the light went out of his face. "I'd forgotten," he said slowly. "How could I forget? You're scared of this, aren't you, darling?"

"No! No, I'm not! Not with you."

He smiled slowly. "You don't have to be scared. I'm not drunk. I'll never be drunk when I make love to you. Kiss me again, Cass."

She kissed him, and felt his lips move, his tongue touch hers, sliding in and out of her softness. It thrilled her, deep inside. She lay back on the bed and grasped his wrists, breathing deeply. Then she pulled his hands to her breasts. "Hold them," she said, "they ache when we kiss . . ."

He began again to undress her, and this time she helped. She rose and took the robe and shift off and carried them to a chair, draping them over the back. When she came back he was taking off the last of his own clothes. Naked, they looked at each other with awe and longing.

"You're beautiful, Cass. I didn't know you were so perfect underneath your clothes."

"Look at you," she whispered, running her hands over his wide chest. "Just look at you. You're like the pictures of Roman gladiators in my history book. And, there . . ." Her hands stroked down and touched him gently, intimately, and she was awed again. "Oh, Robbie, you'll never get *that* into *me.*"

He groaned and swept her up again. "A man and a woman are made to fit," he said gruffly. "It'll work. But you might not like it at first."

Cassie felt dazed, lightheaded. "I don't care. I want us together. I ache there, now. Please hurry up, Robbie, and do it. Then I'll never feel alone in my body again. I'll belong to you."

He turned down the bed, for it was growing cool in the

room, and got in with her. Under the covers they made heat of their own, their bodies burning as they kissed and caressed. Cassie trembled with an innocent, unknowing passion, a slender flame that arched and urged and pleaded with him. Obstinate, Robbie shook his head. If the truth were told, he knew very little more about this than Cassie did. He'd never before made love to a virgin.

"I'm supposed to wait," he told her, "as long as I can. It will make it easier for you."

"But I told you," she insisted, "that I don't *care!*" She was vehement, full of desire, but when at last he forced the joining, she clapped her hand over her mouth to mute a cry of pain, and tears rolled from her eyes. Shocked, he held still, afraid to move for fear of hurting her more.

"I'm sorry, darling. I'm so sorry."

She managed a smile and put her arms back around him, pulling him close. "I'm not. I'm what I wanted to be. Yours. And the pain is going away."

His body drove him, but still he was careful, holding back his full strength, keeping a tight rein on his passion. Then he felt the frightened stiffness of her body begin to leave and felt the first, timid movement of her hips rising to meet him. It made him melt with tenderness. His Cassie. His own true love. Forever and ever his love.

Later, his passion gloriously spent, he held her and promised solemnly that soon she too would feel the wonderful magic of lovemaking. Cassie smiled, stroking his back.

"I know I will. I felt the first tremors inside me. And I want it, Robbie. But why hurry? We will have all our lives."

They slept, and while they slept, Sallie Fernod came upstairs and along the hall, soundless as always. She entered the schoolroom and listened at the unlocked bedroom door. Then she pushed it open a little and looked in. Closing it again, she went back down to the kitchen, where Noonan, who had finally come home, was waiting to hear what she had to say.

"It's too late to roust them out," she said, "even if I were willing to try. They're asleep and naked in her bed."

Noonan groaned. "We're both likely to lose our jobs," he said. "The mistress will blame everyone in sight when she finds this out. Why didn't you stop them?"

Sallie smiled. "There are things no one can stop, old man. Like the tides of the sea, like the winds of a storm, like true love. This time, Maria must lose."

Long after Noonan had left for his quarters over the stable and Sallie had retired for the night, Cassie and Robert woke and were hungry. They came down to the kitchen and made thick sandwiches of ham and pickle, heated water for tea and talked far into the night. They would farm—they had decided that long ago—but now they saw their whole future shining before them.

"When Aunt Maria hears that we love each other," Cassie said serenely, "she will understand why I could not marry Jacob. And once we are married and in our own house, we can take Lily off her hands. Perhaps, now that John Kendall is free to marry again, Aunt Maria will also begin a new life."

Robert smiled without much humor. He was sure it would not be that easy to explain to Maria; he was also sure there would be a major battle over Cassie before they were through. Not between himself and Jacob, though. Jacob was not at all aggressive. But Maria Andelet was. She could be sweetly persuasive, she could be subtly demanding, but if that didn't work, she could and would be overbearingly aggressive.

Robert had come to understand Maria during the past few years; he knew she combined the best of both masculine and feminine ways of fighting for what she wanted. And, though he didn't know exactly why, he knew without doubt that what she wanted was to control Cassie's life.

"Aunt Maria will not give up that easily, Cass." He said it more as a warning than a complaint, but Cassie brushed it away with a warm, teasing smile.

"But what can she do, Robbie? I have been compromised, and I hope to be even more thoroughly compromised before she returns."

Surprised, Robert met her eyes, misty soft, newly sensual, intriguingly playful. At once he felt the shock of new desire rise hot and hard in his loins. He drew in a deep breath and laughed unsteadily. "How lucky I am," he said, reaching for her. "The woman I love is seducing me. I surrender, darling. Take me back to bed."

In the morning they were up at dawn and on their horses soon after, riding toward the Thompson farm. It was the kind of spring day that wrings the heart and soul with beauty, with the exquisite blue of its sky, the champagne sparkle of its air. But Cassie and Robert had the eyes of new lovers, seeing only each other, talking as they had always talked, words falling over themselves in an effort to share thoughts.

"I've thought myself happy at times during the past few years," Robert said as they rode along. "When the trading went well, when the storm at sea had been weathered, when we turned our bow toward home. But that happiness was a pale shadow compared to what I feel now."

"I know. I—"

"Why didn't we know before?"

"I think we did, deep inside. I was jealous just thinking of you marrying. . . ."

"I could have killed poor, gentle Jacob!"

They were both silent for a moment after that outburst. Then Robert spoke again, painfully.

"I like him, you know. I'm sorry he will be hurt by this."

"He might not be too upset," Cassie said thoughtfully. "I know he likes me, and I like him. But I think Aunt Maria and Aunt Geneva put the idea of marriage in his mind." She glanced up at Robert, riding beside her, and smiled. "It won't break his heart to lose me, Robbie."

He searched her upturned face, the smile on her firm lips, the clear, glowing skin, and the love in her great eyes. His own face softened, the hard bronze of his cheeks relaxing, the bright blue eyes suddenly misty. He looked away and swallowed before he spoke.

"It would break mine."

Chapter 18

"By heaven," Noonan said, his round, red face wrinkled with distaste, "I don't think they even saw me. Walked right by, they did, got on their horses and left. Heading for bed again, I'd wager. He ought to be horsewhipped."

Sallie chuckled, her eyes on the stableyard outside, where Robert was saddling his horse and Cassie was mounting her mare, with a thick bundle of cloth already tied on the back of the sidesaddle. The sun was hardly above the trees on the rise to the east, its rays striking through to turn Robert's tawny hair to gold, to light his bronze face as he said something to Cassie and laughed. It was near a week now since Robert had come home, and though they ate and slept at the manor—slept in Cassie's room together—they were gone from early to late every day.

"That bundle of cloth Cassie has tied on her saddle is a collection of old lace curtains Maria set aside to throw out," Sallie said. "Cleaned, and the holes darned. I suspect Cassie's taking them over to hang at the Thompson house."

"The money Robert's made, he could buy China silk."

"Of course. But those two have had lessons in thrift. They'll not waste money."

"They'd better not," Noonan grumbled, watching through the window as they left. "It wouldn't surprise me if the mistress disowned them both."

Sallie shrugged. "It's hard to say. She'll be very angry. Her heart is set on Cassie marrying Jacob Bradford."

"He's no better," Noonan said perversely. "He's woman-ish. The place would be better off with Robert."

"She won't allow that." Sallie grimaced, picking up the tea kettle and bringing it to the table. "I will warn you, old man, don't get in the way when she comes home. You've never seen Maria Gerard in a real fury, but you might— when she finds Robert has been in Cassie's bed."

As if called by the mention of her name, Maria arrived in late afternoon, accompanied by Lily and both Adah and her sister Maud. They were driven by a hired coachman who was to take back John Kendall's coach to the city. Looking tired and harassed, Maria came to the kitchen with Lily and asked for a cup of tea for her and cambric tea for Lily. Taking off her gloves, smoothing back her hair, she sat down and Lily sat with her. Sipping her tea, Maria told Sallie of the trip.

"The damage was extensive," she said. "I've decided it will be cheaper in the long run to build another clipper than to try to repair the *Sea Sprite*. And we have the time. After all, we still have *Sea Racer* and *Moon Racer* to keep our share of the trade. Where's Cassie?"

Sallie Fernod never beat around a bush. "Over at the Thompson farm," she said, "with Robert."

The teacup clattered and sloshed tea into the saucer as Maria put it down, and Lily flinched, alarmed.

"Robert?" Maria asked, and stared up at Sallie. "He's supposed to be in London!"

"He came home almost a week ago, and he's been here ever since." Sallie waited, puzzled for once by the look on Maria's face, by her sudden silence. It couldn't be fear in those determined eyes; Maria was never afraid. It was more as if she saw something she didn't want to see, and dreaded looking any closer. Lily, whose young face seemed pale and unhappy, kept her eyes lowered. "They will probably be coming in soon," Sallie added, turning away. "It's getting close to dinner time."

"Yes," Maria said vaguely, and let out her breath in a long sigh. "Yes, it is. I . . . I'll wash my hands." She rose from the table, pushing herself up awkwardly, as if her back hurt. "Come along, Lily. Adah will help you unpack."

Sallie watched them leave the room and was troubled. Now Maria was acting as if some terrible disaster had come into her life, and surely it was not the ruined clipper. She had spoken with confidence about rebuilding. But she couldn't know yet that her plans for Cassie had been ruined. *Or had she guessed?* Sallie frowned, turning back to her cooking. She herself had known there was a strong but unawakened passion between Cassie and Robert. It had always been there, mixed into their solid love for each other—like tinder waiting for a spark. But Maria did not usually see, or care, how others felt. As for Lily, just turned twelve and full of burgeoning emotions and new problems, who could say what made her look so worried?

Curled together beneath a rough blanket on a bed upstairs in the Thompson house, Robert and Cassie watched the sunset through lace curtains and planned the rest of their lives.

"We'll have a place in the city, Cass. We'll want our children to go to the schools there. To the university."

"Yes." She sounded careless, which she was. Without care. Her mind was dazzled, her slim body deliciously heavy with satiation. After that first time, when the pain and shock of invasion had kept her from feeling the climax of lovemaking, she had learned rapidly, discovering a natural sensuality that thrilled them both. They had made love twice in the last hour, and the last of the joy still thrummed faintly in her loins. "Whatever you say," she added placidly, and Robert chuckled.

"After we're married, how often will you say that?"

She smiled and snuggled closer. "As often as you're right."

He laughed and then he sighed, tightening an arm around

her, watching the red rim of the sun drop below the rolling hill to the west. "It's time to go, and past time," he said, "and I wish to heaven that wasn't right. Come on, Cass. It'll be dark when we get there."

She yawned. "We can find our way in the dark. And no one will care. Sallie doesn't worry about me when I'm with you." But in spite of her words she slid out of bed and began dressing. Sooner or later they would go back and find that Aunt Maria had come home. It would be better then to be on time.

They rode fast in the gathering dusk, but passing the last farmhouses, they could see lamps being lit inside, see families sitting to supper. And when they came in sight of the manor, the number of lamps shining inside, both downstairs and upstairs, told them Maria had returned. Cassie shivered suddenly.

"I suppose she'll be angry at first," she said, slowing her mare and glancing over at Robert. He seemed huge in the darkness, quiet and forbidding, his face stern. "We must remember that she's probably upset about the ship as well."

Robert heard the tremor in her voice. He caught her reins and stopped both horses on the path, looking at the glimmer of her pale face. "No matter how angry she is, no matter what she says, remember that we will be together in the end. But we must try our best to convince her now that we should marry. We need her permission."

Cassie raised her chin. "If she refuses, I will leave with you."

"Of course. But don't anticipate the worst. Come on, Cass, we'll beard the lioness together."

They rode on, and out of the darkness a slender figure in a light gown materialized, waving them down before they came to the corner of the house.

"It's me, Cassie! I mean, it's Lily!"

Cassie laughed softly and stopped. "Welcome home, dear. Did you have a nice time?"

"Ye-es, but I'm glad I'm home. I . . . I . . ."

Robert leaned down and rumpled the golden hair, gleaming even in the darkness. "What are you doing out here, honey?"

"I came to warn you," Lily got out in a dramatic rush.

"Aunt Maria is . . . is very upset. And she's drinking too much wine. I think she's angry with you, Robbie. And maybe Cassie too. Be careful."

"We will," Robert said. "Don't worry, Lily. It will be all right. Go inside now, before she gets mad at you."

"Yes," Lily said breathlessly, "I'd better." She ran off, toward the front door.

"Poor child," Cassie said quietly as they rode toward the stables. "Ever since Maria let Mrs. Brooke go, Lily has felt alone."

"She will have a home with us now," Robert said, and Cassie nodded, silent as they rounded the house. Lamplight and the odor of roasting meat poured from the kitchen window. She was sharply reminded of the first night they had come to this house, hungry and frightened. That night Sallie Fernod had laughed her rich, dark molasses laugh, and they had looked at each other and smiled. It had seemed so wonderful, like heaven. Food and warmth and love. What had happened that it all went wrong?

At the stables they both worked quickly, removing the saddles, rubbing down the horses, filling their mangers with oats. They washed their hands at the outside pump before they went in.

"Courage," Robert whispered as they started up the steps, and Cassie, looking up at him, saw his grin. "She can't kill us."

Maria was still in the immense dining room of the manor, seated alone at the heavy, carved table with a plate of half-eaten food before her and a nearly empty bottle of wine. Her face was a trifle flushed, but she smiled as they came in and held up her cheek for Cassie's kiss.

"Well, Robert," she said then, offering her hand, "you do keep surprising me. I had no idea you'd come home for Cassie's engagement party. I thought you'd write your congratulations and then come home for the wedding."

Robert took her hand for a moment and then stepped back, putting an arm around Cassie's waist.

"Perhaps I might have done just that, Aunt Maria, had I approved of the engagement. However, I didn't. I am sorry to disappoint Jacob, but there's no help for it. Cass is not going to marry him, she is going—"

"Not marry Jacob!" Maria broke in sharply, and rose to her feet. "Don't be ridiculous! *You* have nothing to say about it, Robert! I am her guardian, and I have decided she'll marry Jacob! It's all arranged."

"That can't be so," Cassie said, bewildered. "I told you plainly I wouldn't promise anything until Robbie had his say. . . ."

"It's all right, Cass," Robert said, and took her hand. "She can't force you to obey her in this case." He turned back to Maria. "Arrangements or not, she'll not marry Jacob. She's going to marry me."

Maria stood motionless, the color draining from her flushed face, her eyes enormous. Suddenly she gave a loud and shaky laugh. "For heaven's sake, Robert, don't say that in front of anyone else. They would be utterly disgusted that you could even think of marrying your sister! Why, it's not only immoral, it's illegal!"

"It's neither," Robert said levelly. "Cassie and I are not related, and you well know it. Don't be unfair."

Maria glared at them, her small hands clenched, her eyes glittering. "You were raised as brother and sister, and everyone believes that's what you are. When I took on the three of you, I took you as a family. This is indecent—"

"It is *not* indecent," Cassie said hotly. "We love each other! I want Robbie to be my husband and the father of my children!"

"Oh, dear God," Maria said prayerfully. "Who has filled your innocent mind with such ugly thoughts? It must have been you, Robert! How did you dare? Don't listen to him, Cassie. It's perverted for your brother to even speak to you of such things. . . ."

"He's not my *brother!*"

"It's the same thing. You were raised with him. . . ."

"It is not the same thing! Not at all! I'm closer to being related to Jacob, since he's your nephew and I'm your niece! You just don't want me to l-l-love Robbie. You never have!" Tears in her eyes, Cassie turned and flung her arms around Robert. "Let's go home, please."

Robert's face was grim as he turned to the door, his arm tight around Cassie. "She loves you too, you know," he said to Maria. "But if you want to see her, you'll have to come to the farm."

"You step out of this house with her," Maria said tightly, "and I'll have you arrested for kidnapping."

Robert swung back, white with rage. "You'd push her into a marriage to someone she doesn't love, but you won't let her leave your house with *me?* She's only a—a possession to you, Maria! Something you own! You don't care for her at all."

"I care enough to keep her from committing a sin with you," Maria flashed back. "You'd have her in bed with you before morning, I'd wager."

Robert looked at her bitterly. "If making love is a sin, Maria, Cassie and I are already sinners. We were sure we would marry soon, and we didn't wait."

Maria's mouth opened but no sound came out. Her huge eyes fastened on Robert, horror-stricken. "You took her?" she asked in a wavering whisper. "You came here to my house and violated Mark's daughter—" She tried to say more, but her eyes went blank and rolled back until only the whites showed. She crumpled, going down suddenly, heavily, her temple striking against the corner of the table, her face hitting the edge of the chair before she dropped limply to the floor. Cassie rushed to kneel beside her, grabbing up a hand and rubbing it. Maria's white forehead was gashed and bleeding. Her breath made a harsh, rasping sound, her skin was gray. Cassie began to tremble, holding Maria's limp hand to her cheek.

"Oh, Robbie . . . what have we done? I'm afraid she's going to die! Call Sallie, please!"

"I'm here," Sallie said from the door, and came in. "I was listening." She knelt, feeling Maria's pulse, then picked her up, cradling her like a child. "She'll be all right," she said to Cassie, "her heart is fine. She's fainted from shock and exhaustion. Rest and time to heal that cut is all she needs."

"Thank you," Robert said, and reached for Cassie's arm. "We're leaving, then. We'll be at the farm."

Sallie had turned toward the hall and stairs, but now she hesitated. "She'll be asking for you, Cassie."

"I'll visit her in the morning," Cassie said, meeting Sallie's dark eyes, "and I'll do what I can to help. But I'll not stay where Robert isn't welcome."

Sallie inclined her head, looking from one to the other gravely. "Take food for the night from the kitchen," she said to Cassie. "You will need strength before this is over."

An hour later Maria opened her eyes, winced, and gazed around at the familiar, quiet luxury of her bedroom, the shaded lamps and silken hangings, the crystal and silver on her dressing table, the paintings on the walls. For a moment she wondered at the throbbing pain in her forehead and cheek, and then it all came back. She sat up jerkily, grasped her head and groaned.

"Lie down." Sallie's soft voice came from beside her. "Give yourself a chance to heal. There's nothing you can do now anyway. It's done."

Maria lay down and twisted to look at Sallie's bulk in the big armchair, an enormous dark pyramid of strength. "You knew. Why didn't you stop him?"

"You knew too," Sallie said. "Didn't you? You knew it was only a matter of time until they found they belonged in each other's arms. Yet you planned to marry her to someone else."

Maria's slim jaw tensed into rigidity. "I will still marry her to someone else! I'll not let her throw herself away on Robert Harmon." She put out a hand, reaching toward Sallie. "You, my friend, will help. You will get rid of Robert for me."

"No."

Maria was silent, staring at Sallie, her large eyes gleaming from the light of flickering lamps. "So," she said at last, "the time has come when the past is forgotten and your loyalty wavers. What is it about Robert that stays your hand?"

"He has done you no harm, and much good."

Maria closed her eyes and lay down again. "He has stolen from me the one thing I wanted, Sallie. I ask you again—get rid of him for me. I don't want him dead, you know. Just keep him away long enough for me to see Cassie wed to Jacob."

"She'll not marry anyone else, Maria. She'll wait."

"Provide me with the time. I'll think of something." Her eyes opened again, staring unseeingly at the silken canopy overhead. "The *Moon Racer* is loading now at the Philadelphia docks and heading for Hong Kong in three days. If Robert sailed with them, that would give me nearly a year."

Sallie sighed soundlessly. "It could be done. But why make the two of them unhappy? I tell you, she will wait. In the end it will make no difference. . . ."

"There are ways," Maria said distinctly. "You do your part and I'll do mine."

Riding back to the manor alone the next morning, Cassie had no real hope of a reconciliation. Listening to Maria the night before, she had seen at last how Maria twisted facts, hurled false accusations and ignored the feelings of others, all simply to compel others to agree with her. The only way to avoid it, Cassie thought, was to give in to her, and this time there would be no giving in. Robert hadn't wanted her to return to the manor today, even to get their clothes. He had said they could buy what they needed at Lynfield. But he hadn't forbidden the visit.

"I know you're concerned," he had said, "so you may go if you wish. Do not let her make you unhappy, darling."

Cassie had smiled and kissed him. "No one could do that now. I am happier than I ever dreamt I would be."

She was thinking of that and smiling again as she tied her horse in the stableyard. Noonan was inside, standing in the wide corridor between the horse stalls, harnessing a team to the heavy coach that was usually used only for a trip to the city.

Cassie spoke to him, wishing him a good morning, and then added: "You must be planning a long trip, Mr. Noonan."

"I take my orders," Noonan said gruffly, "and I mind my own business." It was clear that he felt he was setting an example she'd be wise to follow. Her cheeks red, Cassie said no more, only walked briskly away and into the house, stopping in the kitchen when she saw Sallie.

"Is she awake, Sallie?"

"Yes. She's having a cup of tea and some seed cakes."

"In pain?" Cassie's eyes were wide and dark, fearful of the answer. Sallie smiled reassuringly.

"Some, I imagine. But Maria doesn't let pain bother her. Go on up, she's anxious to see you."

Reluctantly, Cassie went on. She wanted somehow to assure Maria of her gratitude and affection, but at the same time to convince her that there would be no wavering of her love for Robert. She was going to marry him.

Lifting the hem of her riding skirt enough to clear the shining tips of her boots, Cassie started up the stairs. She was well aware that if she and Jacob were married, combining the financial assets of both Andelet and Bradford fortunes and reflecting the tremendous prestige of the Bradford name, they would move into the highest of high Philadelphia society. And that was all Maria really wanted. She doesn't care a whit whether I'm happy or not, she thought.

The thought made it easier to keep up her resolve when she entered Maria's room and saw her poor face. She looked at the cut and bruises in genuine distress.

"I'm so sorry you're hurt, Aunt Maria. Is there something I can do to make you feel better?"

Maria held out her hand, taking Cassie's. "Yes, darling. Sit with me awhile and talk. I'm sorry too. I shouldn't have lost my temper so completely last night. I suppose I was too tired to think properly."

"I'm sure you were exhausted. We should have put off telling you about our plans until you were rested."

"Very possibly." Maria's eyes flickered, the lids dropping as she glanced down at the lace-trimmed counterpane and smoothed it nervously. "Where's Robert?"

Cassie stared at her, uncertain. She had been sure Maria wouldn't want to see Robert again under any circumstances. But she didn't seem nearly as angry as she had been before. "He's at the farm. There is much to do there. He has kept himself busy ever since he came back. Why? Did you want to talk to him too?"

Maria shook her head. "No, darling, I only wondered if he had come along. I really believe it's better for just the two of us to talk at this time. Later, of course, he may wish to give us his own thoughts on the matter."

"Perhaps—" Cassie began, and suddenly thought better of it. She knew what she wanted to say, and she would say it. "To be honest," she said, "neither of us need give the matter any further thought. There is no possibility that we will change our minds. Both of us are very thankful for all you have done for us, and we hope very much that in our new life together we can remain friendly and loving with you, and in fact repay your kindness in the years to come."

Maria was silent, surprised by Cassie's new confidence, the look of quiet determination on her young face. That morning she had almost told Sallie to forget the agreement they had made in the middle of the night. At the time, she had thought she might be able to talk Cassie out of this wholly unsuitable match. Thank heaven, she thought now, she had let it go as planned. The child was adamant. She sighed and pushed herself up on the pillows. It was necessary to keep her here and talking for a time.

"That was a very clear statement, Cassie. You seem quite grown-up for your age. And now I wonder if you'd be good enough to call Maud in for me—I could use refreshment."

"I'll go down, Aunt Maria."

"No, I'd rather you stayed. Just ask Maud in."

Puzzled but willing, Cassie complied, and was grateful a few minutes later for a hearty meal of fruit, sandwiches, and milk. There had been nothing for breakfast on the farm, a situation she would remedy this afternoon in the village.

Maria ate little, but waited for Cassie to finish before going back to the discussion.

After Maud cleared the dishes and left, Maria said, "If you are determined to go through with this, Cassie, I must ask you a few questions. I feel it is my duty to make sure you understand what you are giving up, and also what you may expect from others. You know, of course, that the name of Harmon will mean absolutely nothing in the city."

There were several answers to that, but Cassie held herself down to a quiet: "Yes, Aunt Maria, I do know, but I don't mind." She hadn't really thought of that before, but now she did, and the blessed anonymity of being nobody in a big city dawned on her—all the sights to see, the museums, the libraries, the soaring architecture to enjoy, all without the constant care of being on display yourself, of always trying to be the best dressed, the best looking, the best hostess, the best of everything . . . She smiled at Maria and added: "I truly *don't* mind, you know."

"Then," Maria said again, an edge of steel in her voice, "perhaps you won't mind either that both you and Robert will be cut out of my will."

"Not a bit," Cassie assured her quickly. "We both feel you've already done more for us than you should have. And Lily too. We'll take her and see her educated. There will be plenty for us, with the farm and the money Robert made in the trade."

Maria clenched her teeth, setting up a throbbing in her swollen cheek, but she managed a smile. "It's kind of you to offer to take Lily, my dear, but at least give the child a choice. She may wish to stay with me." Even as she said it, Maria knew Lily would far rather live with Cassie and Robert. She looked away from Cassie's lovely face and swallowed the sudden hurt, reminding herself that none of this had happened yet, and wouldn't, if her own plans were realized.

"Yes, of course Lily can choose," Cassie said, surprised, "if you like. It's wonderful to have this settled, then. We'll talk more tomorrow, after you've had more rest. Now, if you don't mind, I'll gather up some clothes for Robert and me."

Glancing at the ormolu clock on her dresser, Maria nodded. "All right. But . . . don't overburden yourself on horseback. I can't offer Noonan to help you today."

"I know," Cassie said, leaning to kiss Maria's unbruised cheek. "I saw him harnessing the horses to the coach when I came this morning. I suppose he's gone for the day."

"Yes," Maria said, "he's gone for the day—perhaps even longer. I'll see you tomorrow, my dear."

Chapter 19

Going downstairs later with Robert's strapped leather bag full of clothes for them both, Cassie found Maud in the kitchen peeling vegetables for a stew. Maud, unlike Adah, was a fair cook and often helped Sallie with the dinners served in the Philadelphia house. This time Sallie was nowhere in sight. With Maria laid up, Cassie thought, no doubt Sallie had gone for supplies. Which reminded her she had shopping to do herself. Robert had given her money for food.

Hurrying out, she tied the leather bag to her saddle, untied the mare and mounted, turning at once toward the farm. She would leave the clothes there and tell Robert how much kinder Aunt Maria was than they had thought she would be after last night. And then perhaps Robert would go shopping with her in the village. In any event, he'd be pleased with the news.

The air was cool, the road dry and hard, and the mare very willing to run. Cassie held her to a gallop nearly all the way to the farm, arriving pink-cheeked and breathless, her eyes scanning the empty yard. She got down and tied the mare, snatched the bag from the saddle and went inside; not calling out, for no farmer would be in the house at this time of day. In moments she had the clothes shaken out, hung up, and was back outside mounting Dawn again.

It was two hours before she gave up. She'd gone back to the house at the end of the first hour and searched for a note Robert might have left, but found nothing. Surely, she thought, if he'd decided to go to the village he would have left word. But still, when she gave up finding him in the fields she went on to the village herself and looked for him there. She looked in the barbershop and in the general store, where she bought a few staples, and then asked for him at the livery stable where she'd left her own horse.

"Robert Harmon?" the hostler asked. "Why, no, though I'm not sure I'd know him now if I did see him. I heard he went to sea and made himself a fortune. He's back, then?"

Cassie nodded numbly and went home, arriving at dusk. She made herself a skimpy meal, double bolted the doors and went to bed, determined not to give up; not to think of what might have happened. Tomorrow she would search again and ask questions of the neighbors. Someone might have seen him. Once or twice the image of Noonan and the coach came into her mind, but she saw no possibility of an old man overpowering Robert. It couldn't be that, and yet . . . and yet . . . only Maria would want him gone.

By noon the next day she was at the manor. There was no sign of either Noonan or the coach as she dismounted in the stableyard. Walking up to the back door, she saw Maud in the kitchen alone, preparing a noon meal. She went in, closing the door quietly.

"Where's Sallie?"

Maud jumped, dropping a fork. "Heavenly days, Miss Cassie, you did startle me. I don't know where Sallie is, and I wish I did. I wish I knew she was right here in this kitchen. I can't seem to suit the mistress at all. . . ."

Her voice faded from Cassie's ears as Cassie went into the hall and up the stairs, fear closing her throat. There was no polite knocking at Maria's door, no waiting for questions and answers and by-your-leaves. Cassie threw the door open and went in and up to the side of the bed.

"What have you done with Robbie?" she asked Maria loudly. "Where is he?"

Maria sat straighter, staring at her. The bruises on one side of her face gave her a look of having two opposite natures, one loving and sweet, one ugly and angry. "What do you mean, darling? Surely you know Robert wouldn't come here?"

Cassie's soft mouth twisted. "He's disappeared, and you're the only person I know who doesn't want him around. Where are Noonan and Sallie?"

"Now, that I can answer intelligently. Noonan drove into the city to bring John Kendall here in case John's new coach isn't finished this week. And Sallie—well, Sallie wanted to buy a few things for herself, so she went along."

"I don't believe you. Robert wouldn't leave me by his own choice."

Maria smiled slightly. "Sometimes they do, darling. Young men are very changeable. Perhaps Robert isn't entirely ready to be tied down by marriage. He wouldn't be the first man to run away on a pair of cold feet."

Watching Maria's eyes, Cassie felt a shock of intuition. "This is why you were so nice to me yesterday! So I would stay and talk to you—long enough to give your servants time to get rid of Robert." She was trembling now; her fear had permeated her whole chest so she could hardly breathe. She reached forward suddenly and grasped Maria's shoulders, shaking her hard, making her head snap back and forth.

"You tell me! You tell me right now where Robbie is! If you've hurt him I'll kill you!"

Adah's long, skinny arms grabbed her from behind and wrestled her away, leaving Maria gasping and holding her head. Cassie struggled a moment and then sagged, knowing her threats were useless. She could no more kill than she could fly.

"Miss Cassie, are you crazy? You mustn't treat the mistress like that." Adah's freckles were standing out like tiny copper pennies on her frightened face. "She couldn't have done anything wrong. She's been right here in bed! And as for Noonan and Sallie, surely neither of them would think of trying to hurt a nice young man like Robert." She loosened her hold, and Cassie straightened, looking at Maria.

"I will give you a week to fetch Robert back," she said coldly. "If you cannot, I will bring charges against you and tell the whole story in court."

Breathless, in pain from the shaking, Maria snapped back. "Including the fact that you were spending your nights sporting in bed without the benefit of wedding vows?"

"Indeed, yes," Cassie said, suddenly furious. "I shall tell the judge we learned the habit from Maria Andelet and John Kendall, who've been practicing adultery for many years. At least Robert wasn't cheating on a poor, sick woman."

There was a dead silence, and into it a faint, barely heard whisper from Adah.

"Oh, Miss Cassie . . . you should *not* have said that. . . ."

Maria's pale, bruised face took on an iron hardness. "You may go now, Cassie," she said, "and see how you like living alone in a farmhouse. If I hear anything about Robert I will let you know. You may return only when you are ready to apologize to me." She watched Cassie leave the room. The slight figure was ramrod straight, her chin was up, the eyes that were so much like Mark's eyes were hot with unshed tears. Maria's own eyes were suddenly bleak, filled with regret. But still she swallowed the impulse to call Cassie back, and turned to Adah, who had kept her gaze on the floor.

"I want to know the instant that Sallie Fernod arrives," Maria told her. "Bring her to me immediately."

"Yes, Mistress." Relieved to escape, Adah was nearly to the door when Maria spoke again.

"No, wait. Before you go, bring me the blue folder of letters from my desk. I . . . wish to go through them. Give me a half hour and then send Lily to me. I must assure the child that she is still welcome in our house."

A week later Noonan came back to the manor alone. Tight-lipped, he came in and asked Adah to tell the mistress he wanted to talk to her, and was ushered upstairs as soon as Maria heard he was there. Dressed and out of bed, Maria received him in her sitting room and excused Adah, asking Adah to see that they were not disturbed while they talked.

"Now," Maria said when they were alone, "tell me at once where Sallie is and why she didn't come home with you."

Standing in the middle of the room, Noonan looked ill. "I wish I knew, Mistress. I never thought Sallie could get into something she couldn't handle, but I guess she did. She got word to me by a dockhand that she was on the run. Here . . ." He pulled a dirty piece of paper from his pocket and handed it to her. "She says you'll know who the man is who spotted her on the docks, and why she can't come back here."

The name Titus Hammand leaped from the crumpled paper to Maria's eyes, and her heart plummeted. There was only a line scrawled: *Titus Hammand heard the crimp call me by my old name.* Drawing in a sharp breath, Maria dropped into a chair and motioned to Noonan to take the one beside it.

"This is the worst thing that could have happened," she said. "Hammand is a slave hunter."

Noonan nodded, staring at her. "I figured as much, ma'am. Maybe you can buy her back."

Maria shook her head numbly and tears suddenly flooded her eyes. "Never. She's . . . wanted for killing her owner." She stood up, wiping her cheeks with both palms, beginning to pace back and forth. "God knows, I wish now I had never sent her to the docks. Nothing is worth losing Sallie."

Distressed by her tears, Noonan looked ready to cry himself. "She did what you sent her to do, ma'am, and she did it well. Harmon never knew what hit him, and before he come to, she'd got drugs down him that made him act drunk. The crimp who was raisin' a crew for the *Moon Racer* bought him like a shot and paid good."

Maria stopped her pacing and looked at Noonan thoughtfully. "Then at least she has some extra money. She'll need it. A woman her size needs help to hide. I'll send you back with more funds in a day or so, and you can try to find her. Did you see Mr. Kendall?"

"Yes, ma'am. He should be here early tomorrow."

"Thank you." Maria had recovered her control, but sadness and regret showed plainly in her expression. "I hope you realize that this must all be kept from Mr. Kendall and anyone else in the family. If anyone asks about Robert, you don't know, and if they ask about Sallie, you must say she's on a trip."

"I understand, Mistress. If Sal can make it back, we don't want anyone to know there's a price on her head."

"Exactly. And that's all, Noonan. I'm sorry you had to bring such disturbing news."

"Yes, ma'am," Noonan said heavily, rising to leave. "I'm going to miss Sal."

"So will I," Maria said, and turned away, clenching hands into tight fists. This time her determination to have her own way had cost far more than it was worth, and she knew it. She had lost her best and perhaps her only real friend.

Two days later, Maria stood at her bedroom window and looked down as a team of matched grays trotted up the lane with the new, fancy, black and silver coach that John Kendall had bought. The coachman was also new, a good-looking young man wearing matching black and silver livery. As Maria left the window to go down and greet John, she smiled at the rather ornate display. John had always liked being well turned out, and now, since he had only himself to indulge, everything he bought was of the finest.

Embracing her minutes later in the hall, John pulled back and looked at her face, touching the fading bruises tenderly. "Noonan said you'd had a fall," he said, "and from the looks of this it was very painful. How did it happen?"

Maria smiled. "Don't embarrass me. I hate admitting to awkwardness, especially to such a fashionable man. Your new coach is very handsome indeed, Johnny."

He smiled, pleased. "I'm glad you like it. Young Terence is an excellent driver also." He turned at a sound on the stairs and smiled again. "Ah, there you are, Lily. You're looking very well. Where's Cassie?"

"She's . . . she's not here," Lily said, giving Maria an uneasy glance. "She's over at the Thompson farm. I ride over to see her in the afternoons, so I . . . I'll tell her you asked about her."

Puzzled, John turned to Maria, who shook her head,

smiling. "I'll explain later, Johnny. A bit of family trouble, you know. It will work out, I'm sure. And Cassie is safe enough there."

"Uncle John, can I take your new horses some sugar lumps?" Lily asked. "I saw them from my window, and they're beautiful."

John laughed. "Indeed you may, and then you may show Terence where the stables are." He put an arm around Maria's waist and led her toward the conservatory as Lily ran to the kitchen for sugar. "I've missed you, my sweet. I've mail for you in my baggage that I'm sure will please you. For one thing, the insurance on the *Sea Sprite* paid off handsomely. You don't stand to lose a thing from that accident . . ."

But she had, Maria thought. She'd gone off to see the ship in New York, left Cassie alone and lost her. Now it was nearly time to see if she could get the child back. So far, some things seemed to be falling into place.

Adah had to be sent out for Lily when the midday meal was served. She came back and explained to Maria that Lily was helping young Terence rub down the grays and polish the dust off the harness and coach, but would be in soon.

Maria laughed as Adah left. "That child is fascinated by horses," she told John. "It's hard to drag her away from them."

John cocked an eyebrow. "Sure it's the horses? Young Terence is a good-looking lad, and he likes to flirt."

"Good heavens, Johnny! Lily is only twelve."

"Not too young to notice a handsome boy, and certainly pretty enough to attract a roving eye."

Maria looked at him thoughtfully. "That's true. Lily will be as beautiful in her way as Cassie is in hers. They're in no way alike, but I imagine Lily will cause as big or a bigger stir when she comes out. Her hair is as remarkable as Geneva's, and her features are perfect."

John shook his head and laughed. "You sound like a doting mother, darling. Surely beauty isn't that important."

"True again," Maria remarked with a small laugh. "In our society, it's definitely second to the name."

"As a sister to Mrs. Jacob Bradford," John said, "Lily will

have no worries on that score. She'll come out at an Assembly dance if that is her choice."

"When it's even a remote possibility," Maria said, "it becomes the choice. A girl would be insane to turn it down."

They were all three through with the meal when Lily sought out Maria to say she was leaving to visit with Cassie for an hour or so. John had retired to his usual bedroom to rest from the trip, and Maria was in the small study, going through the mail he had brought her from the city. She smiled at Lily and held out an envelope, a new one and blank, which was closed with a blob of wax.

"Please take this letter to Cassie for me," she said. "I put it in a new envelope for her. It was sent to me, but Cassie will find something in it that she needs to know."

Lily took the envelope and looked at it curiously, then, minding her manners, she stuck it in her pocket without any questions. Maria gave her a look of approval. "Thank you, dear. If you'd like, you can take along some of Maud's dried apple pie and a jar of thick cream for the two of you."

Lily's face lit up. "Thank you! Cass will like that." She leaned over and kissed Maria's cheek. "I'm glad you aren't mad at her anymore, Aunt Maria."

Maria smiled. "I think you'll find that Cassie was the one who was angry," she said gently. "I've just been giving her time to get over it."

Alone at the farmhouse, Cassie vacillated every day between hope and despair. Her faith in Robert told her that somehow he'd manage to come back to her; her new knowledge of Maria's iron will frightened her into nightmares about the dire circumstances he might be in. But her own will was strong, and she was determined not to give in, go back and apologize. She would wait.

Food was scarce, except for the eggs her own chickens laid. But it hardly mattered, for Cass had little appetite. She was losing weight, and when her clothes felt loose she realized she should eat whether she wanted to or not. She had money, for Robert had kept a store of coins in the house, and she rode his horse into the village to buy what she needed. The villagers stared and wondered, but none dared ask impertinent questions of someone connected with the Andelets.

She waited each afternoon for Lily's arrival on the old bay gelding, in hopes of hearing news about Robert. Today she thanked Lily for the pie and cream, set it on the counter and asked her what was in the envelope.

"Aunt Maria said it was a letter that came to her, and she wants you to read it."

Cassie shrugged and turned away. "Why should I read her letters? Take it back to her still sealed so she'll know how I feel."

Lily regarded her seriously. "I think you're wrong. She said there was something in it that you—wait, I'm trying to remember—something you needed to know."

"I already know too much about Aunt Maria," Cassie said bitterly. "I don't need to know any more. Want to go with me to gather the eggs?"

Lily laughed. "You know I do! After I broke those two last time, I thought you'd never let me in the coop again. But listen . . . maybe what's in the letter isn't about Aunt Maria. Maybe it's about something else . . . Cass! Maybe it's about Robert!"

Cassie sat still, staring at Lily's flushed face, recalling Maria's words: *If I hear anything about Robert I will let you know.* It couldn't be. If Robert could communicate with anyone, he'd communicate with her, not the enemy. But still her hand trembled as she held it out.

"All right, I'll look at it."

Unfolding the page, Cassie gasped. "It's *from* Robbie," she said weakly, tears starting to her eyes. "He . . . he's alive, Lily. At least he's alive . . ."

"Oh, Cass! Did you really think he wasn't? I never did!"

Cassie was silent, reading down the short page, her face losing even the faint color it had, her eyes going from hopeful to utterly lost.

"Oh," she said in a husky whisper, "how could he? How *could* he? We . . . we . . . oh, Lily, none of what happened between us meant anything to him!"

Confused, unable to understand, Lily gazed at her pitiful-ly. "Cassie, please tell me what's wrong. You look like you're dying! What hurt you so much? I know it had something to do with Robert . . ."

"I love him," Cassie said, "more than anything. And I thought he loved me. We were going to be married."

"Married, Cass? *Could* you?" Lily's eyes went wide. "Why, you could! You're my half sister, but you're not his. Oh, that would be grand! Then . . . why did he leave?"

"I thought Aunt Maria somehow forced him to go, Lily. But he . . . he left on . . . on *purpose*. Here, read it for yourself."

Lily took the page quickly and began to read.

"Dear Aunt Maria, I am writing this—"

"Not out loud, Lily. I don't think I can stand it."

"All right." Lily went on reading silently.

I am writing this in haste before I go aboard, for I can't leave without offering my apologies to you. It was very rude to argue with you and cause you pain. I sincerely regret it. After thinking it over, I am sure you were right in what you said.

Tell Cassie I love her and I'll miss her a great deal, but I really feel it is best to leave. And tell Lily I love her too, and that I said to listen to her Aunt Maria and do what she says, for I know you have their best interests at heart.

I must go now or miss the sailing. My best regards,
Robert

Lily glanced up over the sheet of notepaper and shook her head. "I don't think Robbie wrote this, Cassie. He would have written to you instead."

Cassie sighed and stood up, carrying their dishes to the sink. "I wish I could think that too. I wish it with all my heart. But I'd know Robbie's handwriting in hell."

"Cassie! Don't say that word. You're likely to go there if you do."

"I feel as if I already have. I've been a fool, Lily. Aunt Maria was right all along. She said he wasn't the first man to run away on a pair of cold feet."

"What does that mean, Cassie?"

"I hope you never find out, darling. One fool in a family is more than enough."

Apologizing to Maria was the hardest thing Cassie had ever had to do, but in the end Maria made it easy for her. She opened her arms and took her in, cried a little and welcomed her home. And, within two weeks, she was again discussing Cassie's marriage to Jacob.

They were sitting together in the conservatory, making the fashionable drawn work embroidery on linen pillow-cases and talking. The conservatory plants were all bloom-ing at once, and the odor of tuberoses hung cloyingly in the air, heavy and too sweet. It had always reminded Cassie of funerals. Now, with both of them dressed in white lawn and lace, dark hair in thick knots on top of their heads, pearls in their ears and their delicate embroideries in their laps, Cassie was reminded of the subdued family members who sat with the remains of the dear departed during the time when friends called to offer sympathy. She had no idea why her thoughts were so morbid, except that perhaps she was mourning her dead happiness.

"As I was saying," Maria went on, "I really think you should announce your engagement soon and marry in the fall. No one waits a year now."

"I am sure," Cassie said without looking up, "that somewhere in Philadelphia there is a young woman who would love and cherish Jacob the way he should be loved and cherished. I cannot."

"Jacob has set his heart on you, Cassie. He won't mind if you aren't head over heels in love with him. He'll be satisfied just to have you for his own."

Cassie laid down her work and stared off into space. She constantly reminded herself that Robert did not want to marry her; that he had, in fact, taken a coward's way out of any chance of it. And yet . . . and yet . . . there was a foolish place in her heart that kept insisting that wasn't true. That there had been some terrible mistake. That kept on repeat-ing a litany of the things Robert had said. *There will never be anyone else in our hearts, never in all our lives.*

She turned back to Maria and frowned. "I can't marry Jacob, Aunt Maria." She hated making Aunt Maria feel sad these days. She was sad enough about Sallie Fernod. The whole house was different without Sallie and Sallie's laughter. "I'm truly sorry," she added, touching Maria's arm gently. "But even if I wanted to, Jacob might not want me, once he heard what I have done."

"True," Maria said stiffly. "Which is the reason we will not tell him. Don't be a fool, Cassie. Look how close Melainie came to losing Arthur."

Cassie laughed and went on with her embroidery. "How silly we are," she said, "arguing about it when it's not going to happen. I will probably never marry."

"Then I will leave it to Jacob to convince you. He and Violet are coming out next week to stay for a while."

Maria herself had changed more than she realized. She told herself she had no intention of giving up her plans, but losing Sallie had hurt her badly, had made her wonder if her ambitions were worth the cost; certainly they were not worth losing her best friend. Glancing at Cassie's shining head bent over her work, she thought to herself that if it weren't for Robert, who would undoubtedly survive another dangerous voyage and turn up again like a bad penny, it would work out quite well if Cassie stayed single. She was very easy to live with, and without Sallie, it was lonely here. And there could still be a brilliant, fashionable wedding in the future—Lily would make a lovely bride for some wealthy man.

Three weeks later, not quite a week after the arrival of Jacob and Violet, Maria found a note pinned to Cassie's pillow. Her bed did not look slept in, and once Maria read the amazing note she understood why.

Dear Aunt Maria:

I am sorry to do this in this way, but I am sure you'll forgive us both. Jacob and I have eloped. We plan to marry in Hazleton and stay there for a few days. Neither of us wanted a big wedding. Please tell Jacob's mother as soon as you are able to get in touch with her.

There was no use now to follow them, nor could she risk Jacob Bradford's ire if she did. Maria went to find the rest of the family with tears in her eyes, whether of happiness or complete frustration, she didn't know. The brilliant marriage she had planned for Cassie and the extremely eligible Bradford heir was being conducted in some dusty little room in the dusty little town of Hazleton. But there was some consolation, after all. She had missed a social triumph she longed for, but now, with Cassie married into the Bradford family, she would have her close to her for the rest of her life.

Chapter 20

It had all begun on the third morning of the Bradfords' visit.
It was late May, and the weather perfect, the air soft as silk,
full of the sound of honeybees in the clover. Jacob, avoiding
Violet's incessant chatter and seeking out Cassie, mentioned to her that he'd like her company on a ride. Cassie,
who had let out the farmhouse to an old man, agreed readily
because she wanted to ride there and see how the old man
was getting on.

"Would you like to include Violet and Lily?" she asked
Jacob. "Or would you rather we go alone?"

"Alone, by all means. That is, unless you have some
objection . . ." Jacob was trying to sound offhand, but he
was blushing again. It wasn't fair, Cassie thought, for nature
to curse such a shy man with clear white skin that showed
his every emotion in shades from pink to dark red.

"I have no objection at all," she told him, leading the way
to the stableyard. "In fact, I too prefer it. It's easy enough for
two to talk on horseback, but with four it's nigh impossible."

"I agree," Jacob said, relieved. "Besides, I have something I want to say to you in private."

After that remark, Cassie was positive Jacob meant to bring up the subject of marrying. She was also positive he would rapidly change his mind when he heard what she had to say. For she had more than one confession to make now. It was possible, though not probable, that Jacob would forgive her lack of virginity—but she was quite sure neither he nor any other man would accept a woman carrying another man's child. Which she was. There was no longer any doubt, and she marveled at herself, for she felt absolutely no regret. She decided she must be entirely shameless, for each time she thought of Robert's child growing inside her, she felt a leap of joy in her heart.

They rode first to the farm and found old Hans Blucher hard at work putting in a kitchen garden. A widower, he'd lived with his son's crowded and noisy family and was glad to move into a place of his own.

"You don't mind, Missus? I've not much to do, and I like to watch the cabbages and onions grow."

"Use the land as if it were your own, Mr. Blucher. It's a shame to let it go to waste."

The old man grinned. "Ja, it is. It's fine land, Missus. I will take good care of it. You look fine yourself, ma'am. Blooming like a rose."

Cantering off, Jacob glanced over at Cassie and smiled. "You have an admirer there, I believe. You do look well, by the way."

Cassie looked down at herself and laughed. The same old heavy blue linen riding skirt with its wide black belt cinched at the waist, the same white lawn blouse, the same scarred boots. Her hair pulled up and back to a thick knot, tangled strands hanging down her nape. "You must be exceedingly easy to please," she said, teasing. "I look like someone's washerwoman in these clothes."

Jacob glanced away. "You're beautiful, Cass, in anything you wear. You're beautiful inside too. Loving and kind. I—I wish you weren't quite so perfect. It would make it easier for me to say what I need to say to you."

"I'm far from perfect," Cassie said wryly. "As you will find out. Say whatever you please."

"Not here," Jacob said. "Not yet. Where can we find a good place? Some private spot where we can sit and talk without others coming along."

She had been watching his face as he spoke, and now she didn't know what to think, except that she'd been wrong. He surely didn't have the look of an ardent lover about to propose. There was misery in his dark eyes, and something close to shame.

"I have something I must tell you too," she said, "and there's a place like that on Durmont Creek. We'll go there." It was one of the places she had often gone with Robert, one of the places she now guarded jealously from others. But Jacob's look of misery had touched her heart.

From even a short distance the break in the trees that grew along the creek was hard to see, but wide enough when they got there to accommodate both horses and a wide pathway of sunlight. They rode in and to the bank of the creek and dismounted, tying the horses on long lines to graze. Then they found a sunlit space of thick grass and sat down, Jacob hunched over his knees and staring at the rapid water of the creek, Cassie leaning against an old log. They were both silent, both waiting, conscious of strain. Then Jacob turned, his black eyes troubled and full of regret.

"I suppose the simple way to begin is to say I must take back my offer of marriage. I'd like to be able to leave it at that, but in all fairness to you, I've decided to explain."

"That isn't necessary, Jacob." At once, Cassie was sure he knew about her affair with Robert. What other reason could he have? "Please," she added, "do leave it at that."

"No! I told you I loved you and wanted to marry you, and I do love you, very much. The fault isn't yours, it's mine, and I'll not leave you wondering why I changed my mind. You see, I—I'm a man who should never marry."

Cassie sat up straight. "Now, that's foolish. You're a wonderful man, Jacob. There are dozens of young women who—"

"I'm impotent!" The words burst forth, and Jacob was red as fire. "I'm sorry to shock you, but there it is. I should never have asked you to marry, but I always thought—no, hoped and prayed—that when I met the right woman I would

somehow, magically, be cured. And then you came along, so beautiful and so kind to me, and I . . ."

This was why he had been so upset when he proposed. So terribly unsure of himself. Shocked and sympathetic, Cassie leaned forward and put a hand over his. "Don't, Jacob. Stop blaming yourself. If you want to be cured, see a doctor and ask—"

"I did. I finally got up my courage. He said I'd been born that way and there was nothing anyone could do. I wasn't surprised. I've never had any of the physical reactions other men have."

"I'm sorry," Cassie said, "because of your feelings. But you are my valued friend and always will be. I'm glad I know you, Jacob. You're an exceptionally fine, honest man."

"Thank you." The red was gradually draining from his face, a small hint of humor appearing in his black eyes. He wrapped his arms around his bent knees and smiled at her with wry affection. "I suppose there are compensations. No irate husband will ever challenge me to a duel. Now, what was it you felt you had to tell me?"

Cassie opened her mouth, shut it again and sat looking at him for a moment. "I don't really have to tell you now," she said, "but I will. I must tell someone, and you'll be kind."

She told him all of it, from the beginning to the end. What had happened between Robert and her, how she felt about it, how he had disappeared, and how she was going to disgrace herself, she supposed, by having Robert's baby. And then Jacob insisted on marrying her, or at least appearing to marry her. He said they could pretend to elope and then live together as if they were married, but really like a brother and sister. They even smiled at how ironic that was, after the years she had been like a sister to Robert.

"I'll claim the baby," Jacob said. "And no one but you will know it couldn't be mine. This will solve everything, Cass. No disgrace for either of us. And we'll have each other as true friends."

At first Cassie hesitated. "But what will we do when Robert comes home?"

Jacob stared at the ground. He didn't know what to think of Robert or of what had happened to him. But he did think that if he were going to come back, and if he still lived, he would have already done so. "I suppose," he said, "we'll have to work that out if and when it happens. We'll do whatever is best for you and the child, then."

In two days they'd made the arrangements, hiring Hans Blucher and his wagon to take them to the nearest station on the Little Schuylkill Railroad, spiriting their baggage out wrapped in a disguise of more old curtains for the farmhouse, then sneaking out themselves in the middle of the night and meeting Blucher on the lane. Hans Blucher was having the time of his life, aiding the two crazy young people who were, as Jacob confided to him, only saving the bother and expense of the big society wedding her aunt was planning. Blucher understood, for, as he said, he was a saving man himself.

The whole idea seemed wild to Cassie, who clutched Jacob's arm in the darkness and held down laughter as the wagon rumbled off to the east.

"Aunt Maria will want to kill me," she whispered. "She has grand dreams of us in Philadelphia's biggest church."

"My mother feels the same," Jacob said, but thinking of it afterward, he knew better. His mother took social prestige for granted and cared little for it. What she wanted from the wedding was only the Andelet money Cassie would have.

During the morning of the next day Cassie was lost in wonder at the scenery. The little railroad followed the Schuylkill River, here a rushing, foaming, narrow stream that dashed over rocks and tumbled through gaps in the mountains. The sides of the mountains were covered with silver pine and hemlock, with thickets of bright green maple and dark, massive oak. Mountain laurel was covered with bloom, masses of pink and white softening the rocky slopes. But when they arrived at Tamaqua, which Cassie had pictured as a charming mountain village, she found it a tawdry town ringed by innumerable mines and black with coal dust.

There the railroad stopped, and they went with other travelers on a stage, glad to leave Tamaqua behind. For nearly ten miles now the stage labored upward through the gorges of mountains covered with giant evergreens, and finally emerged on a vast, high plain as flat as a plate, where tall, gaunt pines towered over an undergrowth of scrub oak as far as the eye could see.

"Over that way," Jacob said, gesturing off into the distance, "is Hazleton. There's a rather comfortable old inn there. I think you'll like it."

Once freed of his shyness by his own confession, and completely comfortable now with Cassie, Jacob became an excellent actor. He signed them into the Hazleton Inn with the endearing flourishes expected of a new husband, took Cassie walking on the clean, cobblestoned streets with his arm around her waist, and once he'd had a cot brought in, he shared her room. They were carefully modest, and yet there was no awkwardness between them in this intimacy. It was as they had decided—like brother and sister, like boon companions. They talked, trusting each other to respect the confidentiality of what they said, far into the night.

The second day Jacob went out alone and found a printer who made fancy handbills and such. He came back minus a good sum of money but bearing a beautiful scroll, decorated with handpainted violets and roses, ivy vines, and a cherub with a trumpet. Cassie stared at it in disbelief, her eyes following the flowing script that centered this profusion of art.

United in Holy Matrimony this Day . . . It went on, proud and officious. Cassie shook her head in wonder. To the eyes of any who might read it, she and Jacob were man and wife. Only the names of the minister and witnesses were false, and who in Philadelphia would know that?

"Jacob! Isn't this against the law?"

Jacob smiled. "How could anything that pretty be against the law?"

She began to laugh, helplessly. And then to cry, holding on to his lapels. "You're so wonderfully kind, Jacob. I know you're doing this so I'll be free if Robert comes home. But there would be scandal then, even so."

"To hold someone against their will is worse than any scandal, dear Cassie."

She leaned back and looked up at him, brushing the tears from her eyes. "I feel so awfully selfish," she said. "It's as if you're disrupting your whole life for me. What in the world are you getting out of all this?"

"A close and wonderful friend," Jacob said, smoothing back her glossy hair, "and a charming companion. Besides, I've wanted a place of my own, and now I've a reason to get it."

Cheated of the grand wedding she had envisioned, Maria still insisted on giving the new Mr. and Mrs. Jacob Bradford a lavish wedding trip. First to New York to buy a proper trousseau and then to Newport and the bridal suite at the Ocean House.

"It is important to begin well," Maria told Cassie. "See that you pay attention to Jacob when you are in the company of others in Newport. All of the best people go there, but there are also a number of upstarts with money but no breeding. Jacob will tell you which families are worth knowing."

"Must we go to Newport?" Cassie asked Jacob in private. "I'm afraid I'm not too interested in society. Besides, I've heard that Cape May has a much better beach and nicer hotels."

Jacob laughed out loud. "Never let Maria hear you say that, my dear. What you heard is true; Cape May is better, yet the proper Philadelphian sneers at its middle-class clientele. But come, it won't hurt us to please your aunt. She's been very patient with us over the elopement."

"And you've been very patient with me. I shall be ready to leave tomorrow."

Before they left, Maria gave Cassie directions to her own favorite shop for clothes in New York, which was Alexander T. Stewart & Company, on Broadway and Reade. Visiting the place on their second day there, Cassie was overwhelmed. The shop was like a palace, a very large marble building of Grecian architecture, with five huge and beautifully decorated halls, filled with wonderful clothes in silks, velvets, and laces, all terribly expensive. Jacob accompanied her and insisted on buying several gowns for her. When Cassie objected in a low tone, saying they were too expensive and would soon be too small, he only smiled and said it was his pleasure to dress her well and she was not to interfere.

They crossed to Newport on the *Bay State,* a steamer noted for its fine appointments. They had a stateroom to themselves, but spent a good deal of the cruise wandering through the ship and looking at the splendid furnishings in the saloons and cabins. Brilliant carpets, marble tables, sofas and armchairs covered in the richest of upholstery; even the machinery of the ship was polished to a silver sheen and put on display behind plate glass set in gilded frames.

"I suppose the age of sailing ships is over," Cassie said, peering through the plate glass as the machinery chugged and hissed.

"Not for the long haul," Jacob said. "Too much goes wrong. The East Indiamen and the clipper ships are still best for that . . ." His voice died away and his black eyes met hers, struck by thought. "I suppose," he said in a different tone, "that must be what happened to Robert. He is probably on his way to Canton or Hong Kong. It's strange that I hadn't thought of that before. When we return from our trip and you are settled, I will make inquiries in New York."

"What good would that do?" Cassie battled new hope, new despair. What good would anything do? If Robert didn't want her—but it was hard, hard to convince herself of that. "Who would remember now, even if they had seen something?"

Jacob smiled faintly, taking her arm and moving away from the other passengers who had stopped for a look at the engine. "I wouldn't look for a witness, Cassie, for I don't know what to ask about—a struggling man or a willing one. I will look at the harbormaster's records of ships sailing for the Orient. If Robert went willingly, he would, naturally, go as a captain. Any owner would be glad to put him on. And the captain's name is listed with the name of each ship on the sailing records."

"Willingly?" Suddenly the icy doubt that enclosed Cassie's heart broke free and her faith in Robert came flooding back and filling her with absolute certainty. Letter or not, she knew Robert wouldn't have left her *willingly.*

"You won't find his name," she told Jacob. "If he's aboard a ship bound to the Orient, he was shanghaied."

"But the letter—" Jacob began dubiously, and Cassie raised her chin.

"Damn the letter! I don't believe it!" She looked startled by the loudness of her own voice, and so did several of the other passengers. Subdued, she glanced at Jacob and muttered an apology. He smiled.

"Never mind. I rather doubt the thing myself."

In Newport Mr. and Mrs. Jacob Bradford were welcomed like royalty and given the best suite of rooms in the Ocean House. They unpacked, put on their bathing costumes, and went for a dip in a cold, gray, roiled sea. Later, bathed and dressed—Cassie in her new finery—they went downstairs to the pleasant gathering room and the wide porch that overlooked the shore. Jacob was hailed by members of several groups, and, nodding at others, he steered Cassie toward the nearest set of smiling faces. The Middletons, who were close friends of Geneva's, immediately invited Jacob and Cassie to a dinner party at their cottage the following evening.

"The 'cottages' here are very large and planned particularly for parties," Jacob told Cassie on the way in to dinner. "But some of them are now being sold. The Philadelphians are moving out as the New Yorkers move in. They're considered pushy and garish."

Cassie looked at him curiously. "Do you like this kind of entertainment, Jacob?"

Jacob laughed. "So far, I haven't lied to you, so, at the risk of causing you disappointment, I must admit I think Newport a complete waste of time. But we will stay as long as you think you will enjoy it."

"We'd best stay longer than that," Cassie said, slanting an upward glance at him. "Aunt Maria would feel we had slighted her gift if we went back tomorrow."

The other diners smiled indulgently as the newlyweds came into the dining room arm in arm and laughing together.

* * *

Returning to Philadelphia, Jacob and Cassie stayed at Maria's town house, which was empty now except for the servants. Geneva, who was leaving in a week for Newport herself, came over for breakfast the first day and offered them a house she owned on Rittenhouse Square.

"It's handsome enough," she said, sipping tea and looking at Cassie doubtfully, "but it will need refurnishing. You're very young for a task like that, so I will help you."

"Unnecessary," Jacob said, accepting another slice of ham from Dickon. "I'll take care of that myself."

Geneva shrugged. "Your taste is excellent, Jacob, but I doubt you'll have the time. Now that you're married, I'm sure your father will want you to join his legal firm."

"I hope you're wrong. I would hate to disappoint him, but I have no intention of working. I've money enough for a life of leisure and writing, and, in this case, time enough to pick out the furniture for our new home."

Geneva shrugged again. "Benedict said you'd feel that way, but I couldn't imagine anyone refusing to make more money. Evidently your father knows you better than I do." She rose, smiling at Cassie. "I do hope you'll like the house, my dear."

"I'm sure I will, Mother Bradford. I appreciate your kind offer to help me, as well as your generosity with the house."

Gratified, Geneva patted her arm. "I've always said Maria did a marvelous job in teaching a little country maid manners, Cassandra. You are remarkably gracious."

Cassie watched her leave, noting the stout, corseted figure in swathes of rustling silk as blue as the marking on a teal's wing, and the golden-red hair that glowed in the dim hall. "I like your mother," she said suddenly. "In spite of her obsession with money, she's very good-hearted. And your father is not only kind, but very sensible under his bluster."

"I'm glad to hear it."

Cass looked up, seeing his half-teasing, half-amused smile. "Sometimes I wonder," she said, "just what I've got you into. I truly dread hurting your parents or causing a scandal. And poor Violet would be absolutely mortified if she discovered our marriage wasn't real."

"Don't worry. It's not likely anything like that will come out, and if it does, it will soon blow over. Now, for plans.

First, I'll take you back to Eagle Forge, where it's cooler, and leave you there with Maria while I return to New York and George Platt's shop on Broadway to see to the furnishings of the house. He has the newest French wallpapers and everything else, from carpets to picture frames, all of the finest quality. And while I am in New York I'll look into the sailing records, though, like you, I doubt I'll find Robert's name."

"Even listening to you plan your next few weeks is confusing, dear Jacob. What can I do to help you?"

"Stay in the country, eat and sleep, and don't worry about anything. They say a calm, happy woman has a calm, happy baby. If there is to be a child around, and it seems there will be, I'd like a calm one."

The night breeze that swept the fields at Eagle Forge, bending the growing corn and flax, blew in the open windows of the manor and across the wide bed where Maria and John lay, their bare bodies relaxed in the aftermath of lovemaking and sheened with a glisten of perspiration.

"Johnny?" Maria spoke low, nearly in a whisper, in case he was sleeping. His sculptured profile, outlined against the lesser darkness of the night, turned toward her. His hand came over and palmed the soft oval of her belly.

"I'm awake. And I could become very loving, in case of need." There was a teasing humor in his low, pleasant voice, but Maria knew he meant it. It was one of the traits that made him such a satisfactory lover. But there was something else now that she needed, and she was uncertain about it, almost frightened to ask for his help.

"I know. But what I want is to talk a moment or two. I'm worried about Sallie Fernod. She should have been back long ago, and . . . well, I've sent Noonan several times to look for her, but—" She stopped, breathless with apprehension. She would have to tell him about Sallie's background, and she had no idea how he would take it. She plunged on. "I remember that you said once that Sallie's past might be more interesting than I admitted. I should have told you about her then, but I'd promised secrecy. Now, I must tell you if you are to help. Sallie is an escaped slave."

John sighed in the darkness. "I thought as much. And I think I see now what you want me to do. Find her, and find out what amount of money will buy her back. It would have been much simpler to negotiate while you still had her in your house."

"I'm afraid it isn't quite that simple. She . . . killed her owner. He was a very cruel man."

"My God, Maria! What difference will an owner's cruelty make in a southern court? In fact, it would be difficult to make anyone believe Sallie could be beaten. She'd likely snatch the whip away."

"She did. And strangled him with it."

John let out his breath in a near groan. "I hate to say this, darling. If they caught her a month ago, she's dead. She would be given a quick trial, or none, and executed at once."

"I know that." Maria's voice was suddenly trembling. "And if she's dead, it's my fault. I should never have sent her to the city. But there is one chance. Noonan says that Sallie told him that a slave hunter named Titus Hammand had seen her there. Hammand knows Sallie lived with me, and he may be waiting to hear how badly I want her back."

"I see," John said, his voice flat. "You think this slave hunter can be bribed."

"Anyone can be bribed," Maria said, "with money, love or power. You just have to find out what they want the most. With Hammand, I'm sure it's money."

"Then you know him?"

"I've met him. I can give you a complete description. That is, if you decide to help me."

"You know I will. You bribed me long ago with the second item in your list of favors. If I can possibly manage it, I'll bring back your black Hecate."

Maria was suddenly still, staring at him through the darkness. "Hecate?"

John chuckled and pulled her close. "Don't you know your Greek goddesses? Hecate ruled night, witchcraft, and the underworld. It seemed appropriate to your Sallie."

And of course it did, Maria thought. But . . . had it been a slip of the tongue instead? John might have done some investigating on his own. She waited now for his breathing to deepen with sleep, and then moved away, seeking a cooler spot, stretching her small, curved body to the touch of the night wind and thinking back to the days when she and John had first become lovers. Before she had taken the children; before she had become so . . . so intent on Cassie. Back then she and John had shared every thought with each other, trusted each other. Counted on each other for the understanding every lover yearns for.

She sighed, remembering. It was no longer true, for the trust was gone. She had hidden too much; he sensed it and was troubled. She knew that it was her fault, both if she'd lost Sallie and if she lost John. But this time she knew she would have Mark's daughter. Jacob was gentle and charming, but very weak. Cassie would need strength as she faced motherhood. She would learn to love and depend on her Aunt Maria.

Chapter 21

August 1849

"Lily doesn't mind changing her room, Aunt Maria, and I do think Jacob and I would like having our own suite here in the manor." Cassie smiled, secretly amused at her own wifely pretensions. "Also, it will give me a chance to practice my homemaking skills before we move into a house of our own."

Maria didn't blink an eye as she agreed. If Cassie wanted the old schoolroom and the two bedrooms to make a suite in the manor for her and Jacob, that was fine. Nor was she surprised that the newlyweds chose to have separate bedrooms. Her own instincts had told her long ago that Jacob would not be a demanding husband. There was no hint of strong sexuality in the whole Bradford family. "You'll probably enjoy fixing the schoolroom into a private lounge for you and Jacob," she said, smiling at Cassie. "And as you say, the practice will help when you furnish a house of your own."

"Yes, and thank you. I'll start on my plans." That had a fine sound, Cassie thought, watching Maria go lightly down the stairs. My plans. Just what are they? We need so little. Two comfortable chairs, with good reading lights, and bookcases, all of which were already there. A nice rug. She wandered to the window and looked out, thinking of the first night in this room. She had stood here with Lily in her arms, awed by the fiery light of the furnace in the darkness. She remembered now how the red light had shone on Robert's young face, how serious he had looked as he watched the furnace. They had been amazed that night by the good fortune that had come their way. Having lost everything and having been threatened by separation, they had been saved in a single day by Maria Andelet, who took them all and poured pure luxury over them in a flood of good food and wonderful clothes, servants and governesses and education.

Suddenly ashamed of the critical thoughts she often had about Maria, Cassie turned from the window and put her mind to practical things. Draperies, for instance. The old schoolroom curtains were fine for a schoolroom, but as a decoration for a private sitting room, they lacked style. Perhaps Aunt Maria would let her take a look at the draperies in her own sitting room on the second floor. In the meantime, she'd get Adah to help her and they'd take these curtains down and wash the windows.

Adah was gone with the curtains to wash and Cassie was scrubbing the sills when she heard a familiar footstep in the hall and ran out to greet Jacob with a hug. She had come out to the manor this time with Geneva and Violet, and Jacob had stayed behind to see to the final furnishing of the house, which had taken much longer than either of them had expected. She had missed his company a great deal. She led him into the bright room and pointed out what she had been doing. Jacob laughed.

"Nesting? I've heard of that phenomenon. It's supposed to be common in young women at a certain time. I approve of the arrangement, but I think you can leave Adah to finish the work. Come ride with me."

"But you've been riding for the best part of two days," Cassie pointed out. "Aren't you ready to rest?"

"I'm ready to ride on a horse and talk to you, not in a

jiggling, bumping coach with a man who had absolutely nothing to say. I've never seen John Kendall so grumpy before."

"I'll change." She hurried off, glad to have company for a ride. She rode every day, but it was seldom she was able to coax Violet or Lily to ride with her. Violet hated the sun on her skin, and Lily, thirteen now, had developed a terrific crush on young Terence Gilpin, John Kendall's coachman, and would never leave the manor while he was in the stables. No one minded, for Terence was extraordinarily kind, and careful not to take advantage of her adoration.

"I suppose he finds it pleasant to be so admired," Cassie said as she and Jacob rode away, leaving an enthralled Lily hanging on a stall door and watching Terence groom his team of grays. "Especially by a young girl who is plainly on her way to being a raving beauty."

"She is that, indeed. I see Maria looking at her with ambition in her eyes."

Cassie chuckled. "Maybe she expects better luck the next time she plans a big wedding. Now, you said you wanted to talk . . . ?"

"Let's find our place on the creek."

Cassie's smile disappeared. It was serious talk, then. Perhaps, after all this time of coming up against one blank wall after another, he actually had found news of Robert. She put Dawn into a rocking canter toward Durmont Creek, anxious now.

When they arrived at the break in the trees, Jacob was silent and thoughtful, tying his own horse and then coming to tie hers and take her arm to walk down on the grassy shore. He was so careful with her now, so quick to protect her from stumbling or falling. She was a little heavier, her waistline thicker, but she was still agile and strong, and often she laughed at him. But he persisted, and she let him. It was nice to feel cherished by a friend.

Seated on the sunny bank, Jacob drew up his knees in his familiar hunch and wrapped his long arms around them. "I have been looking in the wrong place all this time," he told her. "I should have been on the Philadelphia docks, not New York's. I still have no facts, though. Only a strong suspicion. Robert's name doesn't appear on any sailing records, and there is no trace of him in any of the usual places frequented by sailors. It's possible, of course, that he's turned to some other line of work. But—and this is something you must keep to yourself—an old friend of my father's is one of the Philadelphia dockmasters, and he had an interesting tale of mischief to tell."

"About Robert?"

"About John Kendall, mostly."

"Oh, no, Jacob. John Kendall would never be party to anything underhanded."

"True. But Kendall has been investigating someone else, and from what I heard later, it may well be connected to Robert. Where is Sallie Fernod, Cassie?"

"Why, I don't know. Aunt Maria said she was on a trip. I suppose she's visiting her family this summer."

"Not unless her family lives in China. It seems she was on the Philadelphia docks, and a slave hunter named Titus Hammand was following her when they both disappeared."

"But why would a slave hunter be following Sallie?" Cassie asked.

"No doubt Sallie has a past that few of us—perhaps only Maria—know about. At any rate, Ben, the dockmaster, saw Sallie later on the stern deck of the *Moon Racer* as it left before dawn for Hong Kong. As he said, it's impossible to mistake the woman even in dim light, and in any event, Ben knew her well. Later, Hammand was found in the shallows near the shore with a broken neck. Ben suspects Hammand tried to take Sallie and regretted it."

Cassie shuddered. "Sallie could have done it, if she felt threatened. She's strong as a man, and stronger than many. Have you talked to John Kendall about this?"

"No. I doubt he knows I've even been down there. Ben said Kendall had been hanging around the docks all summer, asking questions. Until last week, when he met a crimp who knew him, no one would tell him anything, not even Ben. They're afraid of lawyers."

"I see. But what has that to do with Robert?"

"Perhaps nothing. But the *Moon Racer* belongs to the Andelet line, and that was the same night that Robert disappeared."

It was a long time before Cassie spoke. "Then that's it,"

she said, trembling. "Sallie and Noonan managed it between them, by trickery and force. May God keep Robert safe until he returns."

Jacob shook his head. "It's hard to believe Maria would go so far, but I suppose she thinks she was doing her best for you."

"She was doing exactly what she wanted to do, Jacob. For herself. For her own ambitions. Here, on her own land, she's an empress with her own empire, and her whim is law." Cassie leaned back on one elbow, staring at the shining surface of the creek. "I suppose I should hate her for her lies and her treatment of Robert, and sometimes I do, but how can I keep it up, Jacob? I was thinking today, just before you arrived, of how much she has done for me—for Robert too, and Lily. You would have to be poor, threadbare, hungry, and nearly hopeless to understand what a miracle it was."

"Half angel," Jacob said, "and half devil? Don't we all have traits of both good and evil? It's only that Aunt Maria never holds back on her desires, whether good or bad. She doesn't try to control them, either from conscience or fear of God. She simply puts all her available powers to work to accomplish what she wants."

Cassie stood up, straightening her skirt and dusting it off. "I believe you. And, for that reason, I'm going to keep what you've told me a secret. She feels safe now, since she believes we are married, and I doubt she'll make an effort to keep Robert from coming back. But if I accused her again . . ."

"Exactly," Jacob said with a rueful smile. "Robert would be in danger." He scrambled to his feet and helped her mount, then handed her reins to her. "Cassie, do you ever see the evil in me?"

Cassie reached over and pushed away the black lock of hair from his forehead, her touch soft and maternal. "I don't think it's there, Jacob. You're almost too good."

"No. I confess to you now that I'm every bit as selfish as Maria, inside. If I gave way to the devil in me, I'd be helping her keep Robert away."

It was hot, miserably hot, even at near midnight. With the windows open and only one lamp lit in the sitting room on the second floor, John Kendall had unbuttoned his shirt and let it hang open, exposing his lean middle and muscular chest. He was pouring a fruited wine from a crystal pitcher which also held a few precious shards of ice, taken from the fast-dwindling cache in the springhouse.

Watching him from her lounge, Maria wore only a thin linen and lace robe, sleeveless and low-necked, exposing her white shoulders and the tops of her rounded breasts. She was comfortable enough physically, but her large eyes were puzzled and doubtful, fixed on John's somber face. He had arrived at noon and had not touched her once, not even her hand. After an absence of over two weeks, that meant something was terribly wrong.

Bringing her glass from the serving table, John set it on a stool beside her and took his own to his chair. Seated in the flickering shadows, he was still silent and preoccupied, keeping his eyes averted from Maria's questioning gaze. He had drunk nearly all his wine before he spoke.

"I have finished my investigation of Sallie Fernod," he said. "There are no charges against her at this time."

Maria sat up abruptly, startled. "Oh, wonderful! How did that come about?"

"The government never pursued the question of who killed Jack Pelham," John said grimly. "If they thought about it at all, which is doubtful, they were probably grateful. It was Jack's gang that set the slave hunters on her, wanting vengeance, and they have all been caught and executed, some years ago. Why didn't you tell me she was owned by a pirate crew?"

Maria met his icy gaze openly. "Because I thought if I did you would consider her a criminal and refuse to help her."

John stared at her, then stood up and turned away, walking to the window and standing there with his back to her.

"I suppose she is, for she's killed twice. That is, twice that I know of, since she is blamed for the death of Titus Hammand while she was on the docks." He turned again and looked at Maria, who stared back at him, shocked. "I also suspect one more. Tell me the truth about Payne Regan."

Maria drew in her breath. "She killed him, but she did it for me. She would kill anyone who attacked me, let alone tried to murder me. Payne Regan was like a rabid wolf that day."

John's cold eyes flickered and moved away from her face. "You didn't trust me enough to tell me the truth, I take it. Not then nor later, when other of your plans were made. Tell me now—why did you send Sallie to the docks?"

Maria swallowed. He knew. There was something in his voice, something cold and judgmental, that told her so. "I—I asked her to—to see that Robert was aboard when the *Moon Racer* left for Hong Kong. I was . . . extremely angry with Robert at the time."

"Damn it, Maria, don't pretty it up! You had him hog-tied and drugged and sold to a crimp!" John came back across the room in long strides and stood over her, looking down savagely. "Who do you think you are? God?"

"I'm Cassie's guardian, aren't I?" The words lashed out like a snake striking. Maria's face suddenly thrust forward, flushed with fury. "That lecher was *sleeping* with Cassie while I was in New York, and the two of them had the nerve to tell me they were going to marry, when half the people in Philadelphia thought they were brother and sister. What kind of a wedding would that be?"

"A damn good one! One in which the two participants married for love instead of money or name."

"What? Don't tell me you think I should have allowed . . ." Her voice trailed off as John grasped her arms and jerked her to her feet.

"Even I could see what those two meant to each other, Maria." John was so angry his voice trembled. "And you—you saw it from the beginning. You were *jealous*. Meanly, hatefully jealous of a love too deep for you to understand."

Maria struggled against his painful grip and tears came to her eyes. "You're the one who doesn't understand, John. I love her too much to let her make a mistake."

"You don't even know what love is!" John shouted, and then, realizing he was losing control, let her go and turned away again, trying to calm himself before he went on.

"All right, there's more you must know. The crimp told me one other thing. He said Sallie was also on the ship when it sailed. She evidently feared the police would blame her for

Hammand's death, even though the crimp says he saw Hammand come up behind her and try to knock her out."

Sitting now on the edge of her lounge, Maria felt dazed, and then, as John's words became clear to her, shocked again. It seemed to her that her whole, carefully planned world had crumbled and fallen around her.

"My poor Sallie. For though she grew up on a French brigantine, she hates the sea."

"She is likely to hate it even more, and Robert too will find it inhospitable. Do you remember the captain you hired for the *Moon Racer*, Maria?"

She looked up, her huge eyes damp and sad. "I believe so. I think his name is Trenton. I remember he brought his mate with him, a big man named Rudy Blenheim."

"Bloody Back Blenheim."

"What?"

"That's the mate's nickname, Maria. Not because he has a bloody back himself, but because he makes so many with his cat-o'-nine-tails."

"Oh, dear God." Maria covered her face with her hands. "What have I done, Johnny?"

"I suppose we'll find out when the *Moon Racer* returns. In the meantime, I hope you'll excuse me. I'm tired, and I want to make an early start for the city tomorrow."

Maria looked up again and then away, her worst fears realized. John Kendall was through with her; his gaze was bleak and cold, his stern features set hard. He had made her happier than she had ever been, and now she'd lost him. She wanted to fling herself at his feet and beg him not to leave her, but that was not her way, nor would it be.

"Yes," she said gently, her eyes on her slippers, "of course. Don't let me keep you."

John stood there and looked at her for a moment, biting his lip. Then, with a palpable effort, he turned away with a gruff "good night." He went at once to the west bedroom and shut the door. Maria sighed, got up, and slowly made her way to her own bed. She was closing her door when she thought of the other three-room suite, upstairs. Frowning, she turned down her silken covers and got in, lonely, unhappy, and thinking of Cassie and Jacob, also lying apart in their separate rooms. Well, they hadn't begun that way at least, for her eyes had told her in these last weeks that Cassie was carrying her first child. She'd been quick to conceive, which would enhance her place in the Bradford family, for they needed an heir to carry on the name.

She lay back, pushing the covers away and frowning again, thoughtfully. Geneva would be pleased and Benedict would be ecstatic if the baby was a boy. Remembering Cassie's patience with Lily when she was small, Maria was sure she would love having children. But Jacob, gentle and sweet and always attentive to Cassie, showed none of the desire common in a new bridegroom. Maria had noticed that during the time they had been together in her house, he had stayed up hours each night after Cassie had gone to bed, reading and writing in the study. It was puzzling, and almost frightening. Had she finally gotten the husband she wanted for Cassie, only to damn Mark's daughter to a lonely and passionless life?

Chapter 22

December 28, 1849

The changes had been quiet but definite. They had moved back to town in early fall and Lily began attending a new school for young ladies. In less than a week she took on a more mature and fashionable air. She was like a chameleon, Cassie thought fondly, who had been moved from green leaf to brown bark and immediately changed colors to match. Lily would always be at home anywhere, for she loved people and wanted to be like her companions.

Cassie's small body became burdened. She settled into maternity as if it were her natural state, not bothered at all by any of the usual complaints. She and Jacob moved into the house on Rittenhouse Square, hired servants, and gave a series of small parties at the beginning of the Christmas season. Jacob was greatly relieved when that obligation had been discharged, and Cassie more so. But then, as Jacob's supposed wife, she had known she would have a certain role to play and it would do no good to try to avoid it.

"It seems impossible that I am a settled, married man with a home of my own and a beautiful wife," Jacob said a few days after Christmas, "when only a year ago I was a miserable, lonely misfit."

"You were none of those things," Cassie told him. "That's a pure bit of dramatic imagining." She looked up from her sewing and laughed at the startled expression on his face. "Did you think I would commiserate with you? Nothing ailed you last Christmas but embarrassment. Otherwise, you were as happy as you are now."

Jacob grinned. "I suppose you're right. But I truly did enjoy the past few months decorating the house and playing husband, even though I didn't have time to devote to my writing. Now that the holiday is over, I hope that will change."

They were seated in the front parlor of the place in Rittenhouse Square, which was exquisitely furnished in the newest rococo style. The sofas and chairs were made with the cabriole legs and oval backs of the Louis XV era, covered with the finest of velvets and tapestry weaves. The woods used were heavily carved in patterns of leaves and fruits, including the table aprons and a mirrored display cabinet. Jacob had chosen to use the same style throughout the house, lightening the effect of the dark woods with cream walls and cream Persian rugs with brilliant designs woven in. His flair for decorating was sharply accurate—there was never too much in any room, and the accessories of paintings, lamps, and bits of art were never fussy. Still, Cassie was used to the plain Quaker styles and found the rococo a bit overwhelming, though she never said so. Now, going back to her sewing, she thought of the *Moon Racer*. If all had gone well on the trip, and there had been no delays either for cargo or weather, the ship should be arriving in a matter of weeks. Or days!

"Jacob."

He had picked up a book, but when she spoke he laid it on his lap and looked at her attentively. She glanced up and then down again, plying her needle nervously. "If—If I leave you, will you still keep this house?"

He looked away. He knew what she meant, of course. If Robert came home; if Robert still wanted her, she would leave him. It had been understood from the first, but he now felt it very unlikely that Robert would return. Still, he had to accept it as a possibility.

"Yes," he said calmly, "I believe I will. I love my parents, but I like living apart from them, having my own home and maintaining the kind of life I want to live. And I like this house. It suits me well, and will be fine for entertaining friends and family."

"I'm glad. You've put so much of yourself into it, and you will be happier here, I can tell."

Jacob nodded and went back to his book, staring at it unseeingly. After a moment he spoke again. "Maria told me this morning that she's going to spend the month of January in New York, attending a number of important social functions. She'd like us to move into her house then and look after Lily. What do you think?"

Cassie bit off her thread and smoothed the small garment she had made, thinking. Maria had changed perhaps more than any other in the family. She no longer saw John Kendall except on business, she was quiet and sometimes morose, her bright spirit dimmed. She seemed happy only when she was with Cassie and Lily, and even then she seemed to have lost that vivid charm, that touch of arrogance she wore so well. Perhaps it would do her good to be away for a while, indulging her love of high society.

"I'm willing, if you are. But if you'd rather have Lily stay with us, I'll arrange it."

"No." A peculiar expression came over Jacob's face, half determined and half shamed. "It's ridiculous, I know, but I'd rather not have her here. She . . . well, she's extremely fond of you, and she might want to make it permanent. I'd hate to have to refuse her."

Cassie gasped. "Why, Jacob! Don't you like Lily?"

"Of course I like her. It's just that the very young are always so energetic and noisy. I need a more peaceful life to pursue my literary efforts."

"I see. Then the best solution will be for me to go there, and you must stay here and write during the days. In the evenings you can join us for dinner. How would that be?"

"Perfect!"

Cassie smiled and bent again to her sewing. It was easy to

263

please him now, she thought, but how will he take to the noise a baby creates? For a moment a vision of the farm-house she owned came into her mind. Compared to this house in town, the farmhouse was very large, with plenty of rooms where Jacob could write. Besides, it was pleasant and cool in the summers. It would solve part of the problem, at least.

Having Cassie in the house made Maria feel better than she had in months. Twice she delayed her departure for New York on one pretext or another and stayed to talk and plan.

"I'm almost afraid to leave," she said as Cassie came in the third morning, "for fear your baby will be born while I'm gone. Sometimes the first one arrives early, you know."

Taking off her heavy cloak and fur tippet, Cassie nodded. "I've heard that. But you mustn't worry. I'll be fine." She handed her things to Adah and smiled, smoothing her gown over her rounded, protruding belly. She could feel the baby moving and stretching, and she knew, though she couldn't say so, that the birth would be soon. "If anything happens, Adah and Maud will look after me, and Noonan will go for the doctor. What more can anyone do?"

"Come," Maria said, taking her arm. "I've something to show you in the back parlor. Something for the newest Bradford, when he arrives."

When Adah came in they were still there, examining the white wicker carriage with its plush pillows and lacy covers, and Cassie was exclaiming about the sturdy wheels and the springs that would ease the bumps.

"A gentleman to see you, ma'am. He gave his name as Captain Felton Coxe of New York."

Maria frowned. The name was unfamiliar to her. "Did he state his business?"

"He said he had news of one of your ships."

Maria caught her breath. There was nothing in the words or in Adah's expression to account for the cold wind of premonition that swept her in that moment. She was suddenly badly frightened, and, as always, it angered her to be afraid. She frowned and straightened, her mouth grim.

"What an hour for business, indeed. Show him into the

front parlor, then. If you'd like tea, Cassie, you can go through into the kitchen and ask Betty to serve you."

"Thank you, I will. I need an extra cup this morning."

Cassie stayed in the kitchen for a minute or so, talking to Betty, then wandered back into the back parlor to gaze again at the fancy white wicker baby carriage. Standing there, she could hear the deep voice of the man who had come to talk business at such an odd hour.

"I came myself, not wishing you to hear of it from someone who didn't know the facts. Sam Trenton was a friend of mine, and I wouldn't want him blamed. The *Moon Racer* left Hong Kong in fine weather, not a cloud in sight. It was late the next day when we heard the thunder of storm waves on the shore. Trenton would never have set sail if he'd seen those waves. He would have known, like the rest of us did, that a typhoon was brewing out there."

"I understand," Maria said stiffly. "I wouldn't have blamed Captain Trenton in any event. Storms will happen, and ships will be lost. It's all a part of the gamble. Tell me of the loss. Was anything . . . was anyone . . . rescued?" Her heart seemed to have swollen with fear until it filled her chest and thumped painfully against her ribs.

Captain Coxe shook his head. "Ma'am, the storm was terrible. Even the ships in port were damaged, two of them beyond repair. Aside from a crushed lifeboat and a few floating spars that I came across on my third day out, nothing remained of the *Moon Racer*. Everything went down together, ship, cargo, and men."

And Sallie Fernod. A wave of shock and terrible sorrow swept over Maria. "I . . . I see," she breathed, and heard behind her the tinkling crash and clatter as a vase and table went over, and then a soft thud. She turned, then was out of her chair and rushing to the half-open door.

"Cassie! Oh, my dear child! Adah! Adah, come quickly!" Dropping to her knees, Maria loosened the high lace collar around Cassie's neck, gazing at her paper-white face in an agony of doubt and apprehension. Could it be possible that Cassie knew Robert had been aboard the *Moon Racer?* Oh, surely not! No one who knew would be cruel enough to tell her.

"Here, ma'am, allow me." Captain Coxe bent down, his blue coat straining over broad shoulders as he picked up Cassie's limp body. "Just show me where to take her, ma'am, and then, from the looks of things, I'd say you'd better send for a doctor."

John Kendall followed close on Dr. Winstead's heels, for after summoning the doctor, Noonan had gone directly to Kendall's offices and asked him to come along. Noonan knew, as all the household knew, that Kendall and the mistress had had a falling out, but, as he said to John Kendall, a man was needed at the house. It was indicative of Noonan's opinion of Jacob that he never thought once of going for him.

Inside, John took the doctor's hat and overcoat and handed them to Dickon, taking off his own but holding them as he watched Maria lead the doctor up the stairs to Cassie's room. Maria looked terrible. Sad, desperate, and frightened. That last jolted John's heart, for he had never before seen her frightened. He had always thought she had more courage than most men. When she was out of sight he asked Adah what had upset her.

"Oh, sir, Miss Cassie fainted dead away," Adah said shakily. "The captain had to carry her up to her bed."

"What 'captain,' Adah? Who was here?"

"A . . . a Captain Coxe, sir. I—I heard a bit of what he said. He was telling the mistress about the *Moon Racer* ship and how it sank in a storm, with . . . with all lost, cargo and men." Tears glinted in Adah's eyes. "And then Miss Cassie just keeled over on a little table and everything went down."

Shocked, John grasped Adah's wrist. "Cassie heard what he said?"

Adah directed her gaze to the floor. Like John himself, she knew more than she cared to admit. "Yes, sir. And when the captain got her into her bed, she . . . she came to and started weeping fit to break your heart." She turned away, crying herself.

John stared at her, aghast. Then Cassie knew. He strongly suspected even Adah knew. "Oh, my God," he said, "this is terrible. And in her condition . . . where's Jacob?"

"I don't know, sir," Adah got out. "Maybe at . . . at Rittenhouse Square."

"I'll find him. Tell your mistress I'll be back as soon as I can."

Wiping her eyes, Adah gave an acquiescing mumble.

Upstairs, Dr. Winstead spoke in a low, comforting tone and exhorted Cassie to bear with the pains and think of the child to come. Cassie stared at him silently through the tears that kept welling up and rolling down her cheeks. She had no real understanding of what he said or why he said it, for the first, rippling spasms of labor, though now increasing in strength, had not yet penetrated her encompassing grief. When the doctor took her hand, her fingers closed on his tightly.

"I fell, didn't I?" she whispered.

Winstead smiled. "Yes, but I believe you're all right. Your baby will soon be born."

"I want Lily," Cassie said faintly. "Please."

Winstead released her hand and stood up, looking at Maria. "Is there someone named Lily?"

Maria was under an iron control, though guilt and sorrow gnawed at her ferociously. She still couldn't believe Cassie knew Robert had gone down with that ship, but she knew profound shock when she saw it. "Yes. Lily is her young sister. Leave us a moment, please. I'll try to find out what is troubling her."

"Yes. I expect that's best. I'll wait in the hall."

Winstead left with alacrity, conscious of the strange tensions in the room. Maria went to the bedside and sat down, reaching for Cassie's hand.

"Please don't touch me, Aunt Maria."

Maria flinched as if from a blow, but she withdrew her hand. "Now, Cassie, I want you to listen to me—"

"No, please. I am very tired. All I want is Lily, and Adah if you can spare her."

"Of course I can spare her! But I want to help too."

"No. When Robbie's child is born, I want only love in this room."

Maria gasped. "Robbie's child?"

The huge eyes so like her own stared up at Maria with a heartbreaking look of loss. "Yes. I thought you knew."

"B-But Jacob . . ." Maria was stammering, staring in fearful wonder. "Good God," she added in a hurried whisper, "don't say that in front of him!"

Cassie's body suddenly tensed, her knees drew up and her hands clutched at her belly. A sheen of perspiration appeared, dewing her flushed skin. She breathed deeply, her attention now on what was going on inside. Relaxing as the pain receded, she looked back at Maria's distraught face. "Go," she said firmly. "Send Lily and Adah to me."

Maria grasped Cassie's hand and held it, ignoring her effort to pull away. "First you promise me one thing! Promise you'll never let Jacob find out the baby isn't his! That would ruin everything I have planned for you. Promise!"

"I know," Jacob said behind her. "I've always known." He grasped Maria's arms as she whirled, drew her away from Cassie's bed and knelt there himself, taking the hands that reached up for him. "My poor darling," he said. "John told me about the *Moon Racer*. I am so sorry, so very sorry." He gathered her into his arms as she wept again and held her close. There were tears in his eyes as he turned and looked at Maria. "Do go away, Maria. Let her grieve for him in peace."

Dazed, Maria drew herself up, pushing away a strange feeling of loss. She told herself that nothing either of them said made sense. They were young and foolish.

"I will leave," she said reasonably, "so she can settle down. But I'm coming back when you finish your talk. She needs me, Jacob."

Jacob's soft dark eyes suddenly smoldered with anger. "Needs you? After the things you have done? She needs to be rid of you!"

Maria turned and felt blindly for the door, unable to see through blurred and aching eyes. When the door opened she felt the familiar, comforting warmth of John Kendall's hand on her arm, heard him murmur something to Dr. Winstead. Then John was leading her to her own room, his arm across her back. Maria was crying uncontrollably, tears coursing down her cheeks, her skin splotched red.

"She hates me, John. H-Hates me! She cannot bear my

touch. All I ever wanted was the best for her! How could it turn out like this?"

Perhaps there was someone, John thought, who could take a grim pleasure in telling Maria Andelet just how selfish and thoughtless—even criminal—she had been. Someone who could say to her that she was only reaping the heartache she had sowed. But it wasn't him. He felt her pain as if it were his own.

Inside her room he pulled her into his arms and stroked her hair. "Shhh, darling, you'll make yourself sick. Cassie will realize in time that you didn't deliberately send him to his death. But she loved Robert with all her heart, and she's grieving now. Don't hold her accountable for what she says."

Maria pulled away and covered her face with her hands. "I don't. Believe me, John, I *don't!* I am at fault, not Cassie. You were right when you said I was jealous of their love for each other . . . God help me, I still am! I'd give my soul to be loved like that. To know I was truly loved and my faults accepted. I have no one, I can trust no one."

"You have me," John said, and took her into his embrace again. "I love you. I've never stopped loving you. Trust your heart to me, Maria, as you did when we began."

Robert Harmon Bradford was born on January 3, 1850, in the fashionable Spruce Street home of his mother's aunt, Maria Andelet. He weighed six pounds, a bit more than most premature babies, and had blue eyes, with dark, curly hair like his mother's.

A week later the young family moved back into the house on Rittenhouse Square. Cassie parted from Maria with polite formality and told her she would be welcome if she cared to visit the baby. But she turned away from the offered embrace. She still couldn't bear Maria's touch.

Birth announcements went out and visitors arrived to see the heir apparent to the Bradford fortune. To those who asked where the Bradfords found a name like Robert Harmon, it was explained that the baby was named for a family member recently lost at sea.

Chapter 23

In early April, a month unseasonably chilly this year of 1850, Cassie announced at breakfast one morning that she was ready to move to the farmhouse for the summer. "Soon," she added. "I've already sent a message to Mr. Blucher saying I need the house for myself, but if he can find a room in another house nearby, he can keep on using enough of the land for a garden."

Jacob stared. Cassie continually amazed him by making detailed plans and carrying them out before mentioning them to him. He didn't mind; it was only that in his family the least thought of doing something different was examined carefully by everyone, and then, usually, discarded.

"Are you sure? It may be too cold for an infant. He might catch something."

"He's much more likely to take a fever in the city."

"True." Jacob leaned back, studying Cassie. It was a pleasure that grew with time, for Cassie was now coming into the full flower of young womanhood, and Jacob was a true connoisseur of feminine beauty. Her skin, delicate as a peach blossom, her glossy hair, her graceful figure, all delighted him. To his poetic mind the hint of sadness in her wonderful eyes only deepened the lovely, generous nature within. He loved to look at her, especially when she sat quietly in these surroundings he had chosen himself. They seemed a proper setting for such a jewel. "But," he added, remembering the subject, "there's no real hurry, is there?"

"Actually, no, dear, not for your move, which can be made at your leisure. Aunt Maria has offered me Adah, and Noonan will take us to the farm in Maria's coach. Adah likes the countryside, and she and I will get along fine together." She smiled at his dubious expression. "You know you'd like a quiet house for a time. Bobby is quite loud, I'm afraid."

Jacob gave her a singularly sweet smile in gratitude for her understanding. "No louder than any other baby, dear Cassie. He's really a handsome young chap, and I expect to enjoy him thoroughly once he's old enough to talk instead of yell. But you're right, as always. I do need a week or so of quiet here to finish my latest essay. Then Frederick will drive me out to join you. Is there a decent place there with room for the coach and team?"

"The barn is very large, Jacob. There is room for eight horses and certainly room for a coach. Even Frederick will have quarters of his own in the loft."

"I see," Jacob said, startled. "This must be quite a farm you have now. I'm looking forward to seeing it."

"It's the best farm in the valley," Cassie said with a touch of Maria's arrogance. "You'll see."

That afternoon Cassie left the baby with Jane Lee, the nursemaid, and went to visit Maria and tell her the plans. Maria and John Kendall had married a month ago in a small, quiet wedding held in the Spruce Street house and attended only by family. Maria was much happier, but, like Cassie, could not bear to speak of the disaster at sea. The wall between them remained, though they both tried to ignore it.

"I'll miss you and the baby," Maria said when Cassie informed her she was leaving soon. "I wish we were going along. But John wants to stay in the city through May and finish his legal affairs before we begin our summer." She smiled. "It suits me well, for once we're there he won't need to travel back and forth as he has before."

The arrangements were made for Noonan and Adah, and a week later Cassie left, with Adah and Jane Lee accompanying her in Maria's big coach and vying for a chance to hold the baby. Leaving the city behind, seeing the rolling land and the forests in the distance, Cassie was caught up in a flaring, nearly painful excitement. She felt free for the first time in months. She was thrilled, yet confused, her heart a bird loosed from a cage and half afraid of freedom. She saw that Adah too was staring out at the faint new green of leaves and thrusting shoots, her freckled face alive and yearning, hungry for more signs of spring. Cassie laughed shakily.

"Oh, Adah, I never want to go back."

Adah smiled, her gaze slanting over to Cassie's glowing face. "Nor I, ma'am. It's country I like."

But young Jane Lee sniffed scornfully, straightened her modish cap and cuddled the sleepy baby. "The country is fine for a visit," she said, "but no one who is anyone actually lives there."

It was nearly the end of May before Jacob left the city and traveled to Eagle Forge, and even then, though looking forward to seeing Cassie again, he admitted to himself that he would have put it off longer if he could. Having Cassie as his supposed wife had been grand. Gentle and quiet, she had been a wonderful addition to his life as she waited for her baby to be born. But it was quite different now, for there was always some turmoil. He foresaw a life in which he would be forever looking for a place to think and write, and seldom finding it.

The day after Jacob left for Eagle Forge a Portuguese ship, marked by gaudy red and green paint and colorfully patched sails, came into the Delaware River cautiously, steering clear of the shoals near Windmill Island and finding a place to tie up at a Philadelphia wharf.

Hungry for fresh food instead of salt meat and moldy bread, the sailors poured down a hastily rigged gangplank and headed for the Jersey Market, where there were rows of stands full of fresh vegetables, milk and butter, and game. The last man down the gangplank was tall, broad-shouldered, and deep-chested, his shaggy hair the color of a lion's mane, his skin the color of teak. The Portuguese captain came with him and paused on the dock to shake his hand.

"If the big woman want to stay, I pay her well, Captain Harmon. A good cook, that one."

Robert grinned. "Someone will come for her after dark. She prefers not to be seen on these docks."

"Ah! I think maybe you be careful too. The mate from the *Moon Racer* see you, he put you in irons."

"Not without a fight this time, Juan. Anyway, I see no sign of the ship. Perhaps she went in at New York. And now, once more, I thank you and wish you a fair wind home."

They shook hands again, and then Robert strode toward the market, in search of a gig or wagon with a driver for hire. Over the months when they had been part of the *Moon Racer* crew, bedeviled and harassed by a sadistic mate, Sallie had told him nearly everything about Maria's desperate jealousy and her great desire to marry Cassie off to Jacob Bradford. Robert had been furious at first, but now he had no thought of revenge. Too much had happened since then, and in any event it would be impossible to prove that he had been shanghaied at Maria's request. Sallie would never testify against her, he knew.

Home again, breathing the free air of America, he didn't care about the past. After he and Sallie had jumped ship in Hong Kong and escaped to Portugal's colony in nearby Macao, he had had to wait a very long time for passage back to the States. Now he hungered mightily for a sight of Cassie. Heaven to him was Cassie in his arms and the quiet acres of his own land around him instead of the restless ocean.

But he needed money. The mate aboard the *Moon Racer* had stolen every penny he had the first night, while he still lay drugged and helpless in the hold. Before they jumped ship, Sallie had broken open the ship's strong box and shared with him what she found, but most of that had been used for their escape to Macao and the voyage home. Thank God, he had plenty of money near at hand—on deposit in the mid-city Bank of Pennsylvania.

Hiring a gig and driver, he set out for the bank. There, while trying to withdraw a good sum of money, he discovered he was listed as lost at sea, his funds put in trust for an infant named Robert Harmon Bradford, the order signed by Cassandra Bradford of Eagle Forge, the same being his personally appointed heir, the former Cassandra Harmon.

Summoned by a confused clerk, the president of the bank, Philip Holt, restored the accounts to the name of Robert Harmon and told him of the *Moon Racer* sinking with all aboard. Robert listened in silence, nodded, withdrew the sum he wanted and left, his ears ringing with the name Cassandra Bradford. He could have understood it if she'd wed after the sinking was reported, but if she'd been married to Jacob long enough to have a child, they had married as soon as he left. He supposed it was nice of them to name the child after him. A sort of memorial, he thought, after the ship went down. He felt numb, as if he had died.

Outside, he gave the driver the number of the house on Spruce Street. He was sure that by now the whole family would be at Eagle Forge, but Dickon and one of the maids would be at the Spruce Street house. He would use Maria's town coach for picking up Sallie that evening, and he'd bring her back here. They'd both be comfortable for a night or two, until he figured out what to do.

It was close to noon when Robert climbed out of the gig and paid the driver. Then, carrying his roll of baggage, he went up the familiar steps and rang the bell. John Kendall opened the door. For a moment he stared, and then he grabbed Robert's thick arm and dragged him inside, yelling loudly and incoherently for Maria and pounding Robert on the back.

"By God, it's a miracle! Maria, come down! Robert is *alive!* He's here!"

Maria ran down the stairs. Her face was pale with shock and her large eyes brimmed with tears when she saw Robert, but she gave him a kiss and hugged him. "Robert! They told us all on the ship were drowned. Thank God, thank God it wasn't true! When I heard, I—I couldn't forgive myself."

It was as near as she would ever come to admitting her part in his abduction, and he knew that. But he still didn't care. There was nothing now to care about. He thought how ironic it was, considering the unhappiness she had caused him, that he was about to give her real happiness in return. But he wasn't doing it for her. He was doing it for Sallie Fernod.

"Tonight you and John will go down to the docks," he said, looking down into the eyes that were so like Cassie's, "and find a Portuguese trade boat tied there. Stop your coach as close to the boat as possible, and wait."

"What trick is this?" John asked, laughing. "We're still trying to believe you're alive, and you're plotting tomfoolery against us."

"He's not," Maria said slowly, staring at Robert's dark face. Her eyes begged him to say what she wanted to hear. "At least I hope he's not. It . . . it isn't a joke, is it, Robert?"

Bitterness rose in him, and for an instant he wanted to hurt her—hurt her badly. Tell her to stop hoping, tell her Sallie wasn't coming back from the dead; only the man she had tried to get rid of had returned. Then shame overtook his bitterness and he turned away.

"No, it's no joke. Sallie Fernod is afraid to be seen on the Philadelphia docks. I told her there would be a coach waiting when the night grew dark enough to match her hide."

That night there was no formality. They sat around the table in the kitchen and talked. Sallie, in one of her old black silk gowns and a tall, violently colorful turban, rose occasionally and brought more food to the table, then sat with them again. She had added to her usual costume with large gold hoops fastened in her ears. If anything, she was bigger than when she had left, a mountain of flesh that flowed across the floor as silent, and almost as gaudy, as a sunrise topping a dark, rolling sea.

Robert ate, but not enthusiastically. He answered John's questions, described the insanely cruel treatment the mate of the *Moon Racer* had visited on the crew, and told how he and Sallie had escaped and made their way to Macao. He asked no questions about Cassie or even about Lily, for to mention her would bring Cassie in, and he was afraid if they began on that subject he wouldn't be able to stand it. He had made up his mind to go back to sea for as many years as it took to forget her. It still didn't seem possible that Cass would marry anyone else, but he'd seen her signature today and he knew she had.

Maria fell silent, her eyes moving over Robert's still face and shuttered eyes. He knows Cassie is married, she thought, and felt a chill run up her spine. But how? She was afraid to ask, afraid to even mention the girls. Then, when John laughed and said it might be a good thing for Robert to have himself declared alive again, Robert described his visit to the bank.

"Fortunately," he said, "Philip Holt knew me. Otherwise, I suppose it would have taken days to straighten things out."

"Ah, yes," Maria said, seizing the opportunity. "Then you know Cassie and Jacob have married. She handled the disposition of your accounts, so you must have noticed her changed name. They and the baby are in Eagle Forge right now, living in her house there."

A wave of intense hurt and anger crashed over Robert. How could Cassie lie abed with another man in the Thompson house! "I may want to buy that house from her," he said abruptly. "It's on my land, you know." He watched all three of them lower their eyes, as if he'd said something improper, and his anger grew. He pushed back his chair and got up, feeling the first dizzying rush of senseless rage. "What about Lily, Maria? Doesn't she live with you?"

"Why, yes. But she missed Cassie so much I sent her out for a visit when Jacob went out yesterday. Robert, I know you're upset, but I wish you'd—you'd—" Watching the fury building in his burning blue eyes, Maria felt her throat closing, her voice fading away. She swallowed. "I mean, it's not far. If you'd—"

"What? If I'd *what?* Smile and congratulate Jacob?" Big as he was, Robert could hardly contain his fury. He was barely holding it in, his voice rising to a near shout. "You knew she was mine, Maria! But you'd never let up, would you? By the way, how was the wedding? As fancy and fine as you wished? Was the wedding gown extravagant and the wine from France? Tell me, damn you, were *you* satisfied?"

"No," Maria said stiffly. "They eloped."

That knocked the breath out of Robert. He stared at Maria while the last tiny bit of hope in his heart wavered and died. Then Cassie hadn't been coerced and pushed and driven into a wedding she didn't want. She had eloped. Lovers eloped. She had wanted to marry Jacob, wanted it bad enough to run away with him. Suddenly Robert felt the heat of tears start in his eyes and he grabbed his chair and shoved it screeching across the floor, banging it into its place at the table.

"All right! That finishes it. Tell her—tell Lily too—they can have all the land to go with the house. I'll never put a foot on it. And, I'll promise you I'll never see Cassie again, because if I did I'd have her, married or not!" He turned and flung himself toward the door, crashing into a chair on the way.

"Robert!" Maria's imperious voice came clearly to his ears and he stopped, his hand on the door.

"Go to hell!"

"She had to get married."

Robert's jaw dropped. "She what?"

"She had to get married. She was pregnant with your child."

In a moment Robert's tense body sagged, his face crumpled. He went on out, stumbling on the doorsill. Drawing a hissing breath through tight teeth, Sallie rose and glided out behind him, frowning. Dimly illumined by the light from the windows, Robert was sitting on the steps with his face in his hands, his whole big body a curve of dejection. Sallie sat down, squeezing into a space beside him with an impatient sigh.

"Why are you sitting here weeping, Robert? Why aren't you up and fighting for what you want? There were times on that blasted ship I thought we couldn't make one more day, but you never gave up. And don't tell me you're afraid of Maria Andelet, for I won't believe it."

Robert shook his bent head silently, then rubbed his face, hard, with both hands. "It's not her, Sallie. It's Cassie. There she is, married—a proper wife. She's raising my—raising a child—and she's got a proper husband and a respected place in the world. I'd . . . well, I'd ruin it. I meant what I said in there. If I saw her I'd take her. I'd take her to bed and then I'd take her away from Jacob. And she'd go, Sallie. We . . . we're different. We're . . ."

"A match," Sallie supplied. "Lovers. It's a rare thing, Robert, two like you. A glorious thing. Too rare and too glorious to sacrifice on the altar of propriety. To be fair, I'd think you should ask Cassie what she wants to do before you close the door. . . ."

She sat there, smiling and alone, listening to his footsteps, quick and hard, traveling through the black night toward the nearest livery stable. When the sound died away in the distance, she got up and went in, her dark eyes warm as she met Maria's gaze.

"So, Maria, when at last you could have rid yourself of Robert by simply keeping your mouth closed, you changed your mind. Now that he knows Cassie only married for protection, he'll take his woman and his child. No one will be able to stop him."

Maria smiled faintly. "Why do you think I told him?" She leaned back into the arm John had draped over her shoulders and sighed. "I've learned a little more about real love lately. And somehow I doubt Jacob will be heartbroken."

Lying in a feather bed on the second floor of the Thompson homestead, Jacob Bradford contemplated the faint light coming through freshly laundered curtains and reckoned the time at around six A.M. He listened to the various and muffled noises that had been going on for around an hour and tried to sort them out.

The rooster was easy enough to identify, and so was young Bobby, letting the world know he was hungry and wet. Someone had dropped a heavy pan on the stone floor of the kitchen, and it rang like a bell. Having thought of a bell, Jacob thought further, glancing around for a bellpull like the one that hung by his bed at home. There was none, which meant when he wanted hot water to shave, he would have to go down and get it himself. It was only a minor inconvenience, but from the voices murmuring below, the kitchen was full and he'd be in the way. Perhaps he should ask Cassie about putting in a bellpull.

Recognizing the ridiculous amount of thought he was putting on something so small, he got out of bed, found his robe and slippers and went downstairs, passing young Jane Lee in the hall with Bobby in her arms.

"If you're looking for Miss Cassie," Jane said brightly, "she's just gone out to the barn. Adah will give you breakfast, sir."

"Thank you. What is Cassie doing in the barn?"

"Why, I suppose whatever one does in a barn, sir. I've never been in one."

"I see." Jacob went on, reflecting that he'd been in a barn several times in his life, but only to speak to a sutler or a blacksmith, which seemed quite enough. Still, if he had to spend part of his time here, he should find out.

"Why is Cassie out in the barn, Adah?"

"Good morning, sir! The boy who does the milking didn't come today. Would you like to have a tray, sir?"

"Cassie is *milking?*"

"Yes, sir. It isn't hard. There's only two cows and only one is fresh. Will ham suit you with your eggs?"

Jacob gave up, prudently. Who knew where the questioning might lead? He certainly didn't want to have to help with the milking, however that was done. "Ham will be fine. And if I could have some hot water . . . ?"

"Right away, Mr. Bradford. Next time, bang on the floor with your shoe. I'll hear it down here."

It was an hour before Cassie came in, and then she didn't stay, only ran up to her room to nurse Bobby and rock him to sleep. Before she went out again she changed to her old blue linen riding outfit and hunted Jacob down, finding him in the parlor and asking him if he'd like a ride.

"I've a spare horse," she told him. "A nice gelding with an easy gait. I think you'd enjoy it."

"Another time perhaps." Jacob was slightly aggrieved. "I'm still tired from the trip, for I wakened too early."

Cassie laughed. "I know! That rooster is a nuisance. I'd have Adah cook him if we didn't need chicks. Have patience, Jacob dear. A farm takes a bit of getting used to."

Yes, Jacob thought. Yes indeed. Quite a bit of getting used to. He went back upstairs and found his writing materials. It seemed sensible when observing a different way of life to keep a record.

Cassie was in and out all day, for no matter how many things there were to do on the farm, or to oversee, Bobby had to be fed and loved. But finally it grew late, the shadows of the big trees growing long and the sun laying orange-red paths on the lane.

"Sure you wouldn't like a walk before supper?" Cassie asked Jacob. "You've been in the house all day."

"I've been pondering over a poem," Jacob said, looking self-conscious. "It's becoming clearer in my mind. I think I'll go up to my room and write a bit before dark."

"Wonderful! I'll look forward to reading it when it's done." Smiling, Cassie picked up a shawl and left, heading out into what she thought was the loveliest time of day, with the satisfaction of work done, the cool air of evening coming on, the rolling hills burning gold in the sunset. She had asked Lily to come along and received another refusal, for there were puppies being born in a corner stall of the barn, and Lily was not persuaded that the mother—after only three litters—could manage without her.

Cassie walked briskly west, where men she had hired to plow and sow flax had worked all day and left the fields smooth and dark, the fertile seed snug inside the fertile earth.

Swinging along, the old blue skirt fluttering in the evening breeze, Cassie admitted to herself that she was just as glad the others hadn't come along. It left her free to remember, and if the remembering brought an ache to her heart, it also brought warmth and pride, for she was doing now what she and Robert had planned to do with this land. He had even told her which fields would be used for the various crops, and she hewed to that plan exactly. When the farm passed down to Robert Harmon's son, it would be the farm his father dreamed of.

She turned at the end of the newly plowed field and started back more slowly, her own dreams in her eyes as she scanned the distances. In her mind Robert was there and she was pointing out what she had done. Over there were the oats; strong, healthy shoots springing skyward and already half grown. On the left a planting of cabbages needed thinning, and that reminded her she needed crocks for putting down sauerkraut. She could see the house and hear the racket as one of the dogs ran out to bark at a horse, and she frowned, thinking she'd use a bit of discipline there, before the dog ended up with a broken jaw from a good kick. Slowing, she looked more closely at a break in one of the fences, and while she stood considering whether to repair or replace, she heard Adah let out a long, sustained, and trembling screech.

"Ohhh, thank the blessed mercy of our gracious God! Cassie, Cassie, Cassie! Come quickly!"

Shaken and frightened, Cassie picked up her skirts and ran, her legs flashing beneath the blue linen, her hair bouncing loose and falling down her neck, her straining eyes on the front of her house, where a horse was tied and a man was turning away from Adah, standing in the door. Turning and then starting toward her, head up and looking, then running, running fast, his tawny hair bright in the evening sun, his thick arms opening, his big body so familiar, so solid and real! She gasped, her own arms flying up and open, her eyes full of unbelievable joy; her voice, sputtering, babbling, incoherent, then suddenly whole words tumbling out. "Robbie! My Robbie! Alive! *Alive!* Ah, my own darling . . . my own dear love . . ."

They met in the middle of the road, Cassie half hidden by Robert's flapping coat as he grabbed her up and swung her around, her loose hair streaming out, a banner floating triumphantly. They were kissing and crying and laughing, and in the doorway behind them Adah was grinning like a freckled child, rubbing her eyes with her apron. Jane Lee, holding Bobby, came to peer over Adah's shoulder, and in the wide window above, Jacob stood for a moment watching and then turned away, amazed and shocked, to find a chair.

He sat there, listening to the turmoil below—Adah's trembling voice bidding Jane Lee to find Lily, then Lily's scream, more laughter, more tears, the baby crying.

It was very noisy, Jacob thought, but he understood. After all, it was like a miracle. He'd want to congratulate Robert, of course, but he'd give them a while before intruding. He'd rather Cassie explained a bit first. Robert's temper was usually even, but this time he might think he had reason for anger.

Below, Cassie took the baby from Jane Lee and handed him to Robert. "Your son," she whispered, and tears of joy ran from the downtilted corners of her eyes. She wiped them away, watching Robert cradle the infant in his arms, gazing at him in awe. How wonderful it was to see those big, muscular arms holding their baby. She smiled around at Adah and Lily, both frankly weeping and smiling, holding on to each other. She looked back at Robert and saw that beneath his bronzed skin he was now ashen pale. She moved forward, grasping his arm.

"Robbie! Are you ill? Were you injured in the shipwreck, after all?"

Robert shook his head and handed the baby back to her. "I wasn't in it. Sallie and I had jumped ship in Hong Kong, and I didn't know the *Moon Racer* was sunk until I came home and tried to take money out of my bank account in Philadelphia. I was hurt worse right then in that quiet room than I had ever been aboard any ship."

Cassie's eyes went wide. He'd seen her signature, he'd seen the baby's name. *Bradford.* "Oh! Oh, no! That was just something that—that had to be done, Robbie! It means nothing! It was only because—"

"I know," he said almost sternly. "You don't have to explain. Maria told me." He stood looking at the two of them with first heartbreak in his face and then a sudden, steely determination chasing it away. He straightened, his broad shoulders squaring. "Somehow," he said, "I'll make this right. I'll have you and my child for myself, whether or not the Bradfords agree to a divorce. I came here thinking I could let you choose, but I can't. I'm sorry if you're going to be shamed when it comes out, but you're part of me, and so is the baby. I'll kill to keep you."

Jane Lee uttered a little scream and Adah grabbed her arm. "Get in the house and be quiet," Adah said sharply. "Come on, Lily, let's all go in and give them time to themselves."

Cass had reached out again and caught Robbie's thick arm with one hand. "Don't, Robbie! Don't even say that! Jacob and I aren't really married—only pretending . . ."

"Whaaat? That bastard! I'll beat him within an inch of his life—"

"No! He did it for *me!* So I could have the baby! He's never—I mean, we don't! Share a bed, I mean. Oh, Robbie, did you really think I'd take another man to love me?"

Looking deep into her eyes, Robert found the truth. His face lost its stern look and reddened with emotion. "My Cass," he said unevenly. "Still my own, my darling Cass . . ." Opening his arms, he pulled the two of them against him and held them close, whispering his love into her ear and letting his tears dampen her fragrant hair.

Above, Jacob had come to the window again to watch. Seeing Robert take Cass and Bobby into his arms, Jacob smiled faintly and went back to his chair. There would be many compensations to being a bachelor again. For Cassie, he'd managed to put up with noise and confusion, and he would have gotten used to this damnable farm too, but it would never have been his choice of a summer place. His choice, as it always had been, would still be the Andelet manor. In fact, it might not be a bad idea to move over there now. Noonan was there, and Maud. They'd take care of him, and, for that matter, they'd be glad to hear the exciting news. Robert Harmon had returned from the dead.

After a time Jacob rose and began collecting his things, packing them neatly. The noise outside had moved inside and moderated a little, though it still rose and fell in bursts of laughter and wonder. He felt a bit lonely, yet satisfied that while his own life would be less interesting, it would also be considerably smoother. Finally, his jacket on, he straightened his shoulders and left the room, going down the steps and toward the big parlor. From the sound of things, that was where everyone was. He opened the door and stepped in, quietly.

Across the room, holding the baby and surrounded by Cassie and Lily and young Jane Lee, Robert looked huge and strange, his deeply tanned skin and rough, sun-streaked hair like that of the foreigners around the Philadelphia docks. Then he looked up and his clear, bright blue eyes met Jacob's. A smile spread over his dark face. Handing the baby to Cassie, he came forward, grabbed Jacob's hand and wrung it emotionally.

"When I heard yesterday you'd married Cassie, I could have killed you, but Cassie has told me the truth, including how kind and unselfish you've been, Jacob. I'll be everlastingly grateful to you."

And I, Jacob thought, heaving a sigh of relief, will be

everlastingly grateful to Cassie. He had forgotten just how sizable Robert was.

"I was glad to do it, Robert. I judge Cassie to be a wonderful friend, one I hope I never lose. Then . . . she told you our elopement was a ruse?"

Robert grinned. "Yes. But our elopement will be real. We leave in the morning for Lynfield and a minister. Would you care to join Lily and be one of the two witnesses?"

Jacob laughed and clapped him on the shoulder. "I wouldn't miss it. In fact, I am deeply honored."

Lily took over the planning. Pink-faced, excited, waving her hands, she insisted on a memorable occasion. "You must be your most beautiful, Cassie! And Robert his most handsome. And don't say you haven't time to buy new clothes. There are plenty of good summer clothes packed away in the closets at the manor. We'll all ride over tonight after supper and find outfits for each of you!"

"But they'll never fit, Lily! You forget, I've had a baby, and just look at Robert—he's bigger than ever."

"We'll squeeze you in! Besides, you've gotten thin again, working so hard. Pleeease, Cassie! I—I've never been in a wedding before!"

Cassie laughed. "Neither have I," she said, and relented, turning to Jacob. "Do you mind driving us over?"

"Not a bit! And we'll use my coach tomorrow, if you like. I'll go tell Frederick."

Chapter 24

Finally, after hours of talk, after supper in the big kitchen, after Jacob had departed for the Andelet manor and all the others in this big house had gone to bed, Robert and Cassie were left alone. Sitting on the small, curved and carved tapestry-covered love seat in the parlor, they held hands and looked at each other.

"Tomorrow," Robert said, "we say our vows. At that moment we will become a family. We'll take our place as part of this community, and our children will grow up here. It's a good feeling, after a life at sea."

"Yes." Cassie rested her head on his shoulder, only half hearing what he said but approving of it. He was the man, he was supposed to think of those things. She was thinking of tonight.

"I think we should begin right," Robert went on, rather sternly. "We made a mistake last year that we won't repeat. This time, we'll wait until we're married to sleep together. Do you agree?"

Cassie sat up straight and stared at him in astonishment.

"Why, if that's what you want . . . yes, of course I agree. After all, it's . . . it's only one night." She drew away and stood up, rather pink. "And no doubt you're very tired too. Come, I'll heat some water for you, and make up the bed in the front room with . . . with fresh sheets. . . ."

He would have said, as tired as he was, that he would drop right off to sleep. But he lay there, the night around him a-live with images of their lovemaking from the past. That first time, when they had stripped themselves in her room at the manor and then had been almost too awed to touch each other. How beautiful she was! How trusting—when all she had ever known of physical love had been the agony of an invalid and the lust of a drunken fool. Then later, when her joyous sensuality had revealed itself, how passionate she was! Lord, they'd made love on the creek bank and in the fields. And here, in this bed, over and over again. Even when he had been satisfied she had ways of touching him with her hands, with her lips, that set him afire. Remembering, he felt his loins react strongly, heating and springing into readiness. He moved restlessly in the crisp, sun-dried sheets and told himself to stop thinking so he could sleep.

"Robbie?" The door creaked and a glow of candle light appeared in the narrow opening, illuminating the curve of Cassie's cheek, the long, glossy fall of her hair over one shoulder. Her huge eyes were shadowed and secret, but he could see the tilt of a small smile. "Are you awake?"

He raised his knees, hiding the evidence of his erotic thoughts inside a billowing linen tent. "Yes. Is something wrong?"

"No. Not exactly . . ." She pushed the door back and came in, closing it behind her. She was wearing a thin white cotton gown with a single wide ruffle around the hem, a low scoop of neckline trimmed in lace, and small puff sleeves. Above the neckline the tops of her high, full breasts gleamed in the light of the candle with a texture like warm, thick silk. Robert's eyes fastened on them and his mouth went dry. He tried to speak, coughed and licked his lips, noting a well-remembered look in her eyes as she came closer, a look that made him quiver with desire.

"I said we would wait, darling."

"I know." Her little smile slipped slightly but stayed, undimmed. "I heard you. And I agreed. It's only that I . . . I cannot sleep."

Robert smothered a groan. "Nor I," he admitted. "But it won't be the first sleepless night I've spent thinking of you."

Cassie sighed and sat down on the edge of the bed. "It won't be the first for me either. But I do hope it will be the last." She leaned forward and set the dripping, smoking candle on his bed table, an action that brought her breasts within a foot of his eyes and swept the sheaf of her silky hair across his chest. Then, wriggling into comfort, she leaned back against his upraised knees. "There. As long as we're both awake, we may as well keep each other company."

Robert stared, first at her mouth, slightly parted so that he caught the shine of her small white teeth, then at her eyes, where deep in the gray-green depths something danced. Mesmerized, he kept on looking while he slowly rose to a sitting position and took her into his arms.

"Is it possible," he asked in a whisper, "that you think we can be here together, like this, and not kiss?"

"Oh, no," she whispered back, gazing innocently into his eyes, "I didn't think that. I was sure we would kiss." Her mouth opened under his and received the moist fire of his tongue, sweetly surrendering to its thrust.

Robert took his time, slowly licking the soft inside, gently sucking her lips into his mouth. The pressure and exquisite pain in his loins increased until it forced another anguished groan from his wide chest. Suddenly his failing resolve melted in the heat of desire. No longer holding back, he slid a hand beneath the twisted gown and found her silky thighs. Pressing between them, he followed the soft curves up to the heated apex and cupped the mound of tight curls in his hot palm. Cassie drew in a long, ragged breath and widened the space between her thighs, giving him access to the damp satin path hidden there. She closed her eyes and trembled as he explored.

"Robbie . . . oh, Robbie. I don't want to wait . . . I can't."

He made some inarticulate noise in answer and swung her over his body, pulled up her gown and pushed down the sheet, baring his tremendous, tautly shining erection. Cassie's eyes went wide, and then she was panting, struggling to rid herself of her gown, stopping to kiss him, laughing and half crying as they both fought the enveloping clothes. Then, as she settled over his loins, Robert pressed her down, slowly and gently, careful not to force a full joining.

Gasping, Cassie gripped his narrow flanks with her slender legs and eased down to lie against his wide, muscle-ridged and hair-roughened chest. His thick arms wrapped her and held her, his heartbeat beneath her ear like thunder.

"Yes," she breathed. "Oh, yes, this is right." She felt rather than heard a rumble of agreement under her cheek. "We must never be apart again," she added, raising her head. "Promise me."

Robert smiled, cupping her small buttocks in his hands and holding her tightly as he moved inside her. "Tomorrow I will promise you all the days and nights of my life, my darling. Will that be enough?"

Moving with him, Cassie closed her eyes with the sweetness of his solid heat pressing in, with the thrill of his first careful entry which only fed her raging hunger for more. "No," she whispered, "one lifetime is not enough. Promise me eternity."

"Forever, then. Oh, my love, my Cassie . . ." His powerful thrust filled her, completed her, and she argued no more.

Trooping into the small Anglican church in Lynfield the next day, the wedding party was decked out in finery and in flowers, since the roses were magnificent this year and the manor garden was full of them. The bride wore a long-sleeved white lace jacket over a pink silk gown the color of dawn, a choice made by the maid of honor, who had loved the gown passionately ever since Cassie had come out in it at the Dancing Class evening.

The bridegroom wore fitted trousers of cream-colored suede and a matching vest beneath the deep blue, gold-buttoned captain's coat. The maid of honor, standing demurely beside the bride, wore a sunny yellow, ruffled dress and matching ruffled pantalets, which showed beneath the ankle-length skirt. And the best man was highly fashionable, for his suit had the new short coat and his shirt the narrow, short stock that seemed no more than a silk wisp around his neck.

All in all, they seemed a likely group, and the rector, encouraged by a large donation from the best man, gave them the full celebration and blessing of a marriage. So caught up in a sonorous speech on the meaning of marriage, in the end Cassie was awed by the beauty and strength of the vows they made.

Leaving with the rector's earnest good wishes ringing in her ears, Cassie was whispering part of the blessing, anxious to remember it. "Let their love for each other be a seal upon their hearts, a mantle about their shoulders, and a crown upon their heads. Bless them in their work and in their companionship; in their sleeping and in their waking; in their joys and sorrows; in their life and in their death." She glanced up at Robert and found his blue eyes on her, full of the same steadfast love he had always given her, and more. She sighed and then laughed, pushing her forehead against his thick arm.

"My happiness is spilling out, Robbie. I can't hold it all."

"I know. I see it. It's like a fountain of rainbows, rising from you and splashing on everyone around."

Helping the ladies into the coach, Jacob laughed. "Let's go back to the farm and open that bottle of wine I stole last evening from Maria's cellar. And then I'll be gone. Maud and Noonan are taking me in."

"And I," Lily said, making room for Jacob beside her.

"But we're leaving Jane Lee to take care of Bobby, and Adah to cook for you. And—" she hesitated, and then went on in a spurt of words. "I do have to ask you this, Cass. If Aunt Maria arrives, what in the world do I tell her?"

"The truth," Robert said. "She won't be upset. I think she expects it. She's had a change of heart."

Cassie smiled secretly. She wouldn't have blamed Robbie if he'd hated Aunt Maria, but she knew, she always had known, there was no hatred in him, no lasting bitterness. Robbie's heart was as big as he was; he forgave without being asked.

At the farm Adah had made and decorated a wedding cake, baked two chickens and put wine to cool in the springhouse. But not the wine Jacob had taken from Maria's cellar. Instead, two bottles of French champagne sat neck deep in the cold, flowing water, and as the wedding party came in, laughing and talking, Maria rose from a seat beside John in the parlor and looked straight at Cassie. Her chin was up, her face stiff with effort, and her lips trembled as she said words she had thought she would never say to anyone.

"Forgive me," she said into a shocked silence, "if you can. I was very wrong, and I am sorry."

Deeply touched, Cassie went to her with open arms. Hugging her, and feeling the slim arms trembling as Maria hugged her back, the last of her anger melted away.

"It's over, Aunt Maria, and forgotten. Will you and Uncle John celebrate our wedding with us?"

"Bless you, of course we will." She put a hand out to Robbie. "Have you forgiven me, Robert?"

Her hand disappeared in his; he bent his handsome, tawny head and kissed her cheek. "How could I not? I haven't forgotten how you took us in when we were hungry, ma'am."

Maria smiled faintly, remembering. " 'Ma'am'?"

"Aunt Maria," Robert said meekly, and grinned, catching Cassie's shoulder and pulling her close. "Tell Lily to go get the wine, darling, and we'll start the celebration."

"Let's go with her, love. Come along, Lily."

Maria watched them from the window, seeing their hands

clasped as they ran down the slope to the spring. In her memory she saw them again, shabby children with serious faces marching up the hill to the manor. I love them, she thought, surprised. I love them all. Mark is long dead, and they have filled my heart. "Thank God," she whispered to John. "My children have forgiven me."

Epilogue

Eagle Forge, July 4, 1850

Geneva Bradford, dressed in white linen, a straw hat trimmed with red and blue ribbons on her golden curls, stepped out of the big Bradford coach, followed by Violet, dressed in blue trimmed with white ruffles at the low neckline and a corsage of red roses. Following Violet was her fiancé, Martin Bosley, wearing a sedate business suit, but in honor of the occasion, a red, white, and blue cockade in his lapel.

After greeting both Geneva and Violet with an embrace, Maria turned to Martin and extended both hands. "So you are Martin, and soon to be my nephew. Our family is growing, indeed. So nice to have a congenial crowd to celebrate."

"There is no holiday so peculiarly Philadelphian as Independence Day," Martin said gravely. "The first Independence Day celebration took place in Philadelphia in 1776, and every year since they have celebrated again. It behooves us all to remember to give our great city credit for that."

"Ah, yes, I suppose that's true," Maria said blankly. "In

the meantime, do come in, all of you, and settle yourselves after your long ride. Noonan and Terence will see to your luggage."

Geneva put a staying hand on her arm and looked around before she spoke. "Tell me first, while we're out here alone—has the scandal died down at all?"

Maria stared. "Why, Geneva, I should think you could tell me more accurately than I could tell you. After all, I haven't been to the city in months."

"Oh. Why, no one speaks of it any more in Philadelphia. I meant here, in Eagle Forge."

"Come, Martin," Violet said, irritated. "Let's go in and have some refreshment. Let them gossip about old, tired news if they wish."

"But this is interesting, my love. Shouldn't I learn something about the Eagle Forge branch of our family?"

"Martin!"

"Oh. All right, sweetheart."

Maria waited until they left. "Frankly, Geneva, if the farmers and tradespeople are gossiping about Cassie, it hasn't reached my ears. Nor hers, I would warrant, since she seems happy as a lark."

Geneva's eyes bored into hers. "Are they coming here today?"

"They are here, and so are Bobby and Lily. Wait until you see how our Bobby has grown. He's sitting up now, as handsome as he can be."

Geneva sniffed. "And looking more like Robert every day, I wager."

Maria had the grace to look embarrassed. Up until now she had gone along with the illusion that the baby was Jacob's, since Benedict seemed to want to claim him for the family. "I'm sorry," she answered stiffly. "I was as surprised as you are about that."

Turning, Geneva started for the house, her lips pressed together. Maria followed, smarting a bit but glad it was over. Neither Robert nor Cassie would have let Benedict's claim stand in any event. And besides, what she had said was true. She had been surprised, in spite of knowing they'd slept together. She stopped on the top step, in order not to run into Geneva, who had stopped in front of her and turned around.

"*I* wasn't surprised," Geneva said flatly. "It's time I admitted that. I knew the baby couldn't be Jacob's. Do you remember when you asked me if Jacob's 'mistress' would object to his marriage? I should have told you then that Jacob had no mistress, and told you why. He's impotent, Maria. He always has been. I suppose that's why he only pretended to marry Cassie."

Maria gasped. "But . . . but . . . why, Geneva! *You* asked for the match between Jacob and Cassie! How could you?"

"Benedict wanted someone to carry on the Bradford name. Surely you can understand that."

"What? That's ridiculous! There wouldn't have been any children."

Geneva blew out her breath in scornful disgust. "In Philadelphia? Don't be naive! Of course there would have been children." She nodded her head thoughtfully and turned to the door again. "Maybe some with old family blood, at that. Don't you remember the way Harry Wharton took to Cassie? Why, I'd wager—"

"Don't bother," Maria said stiffly, reaching for the door. "It didn't happen, and now it can't, thank God."

Sailing through into the wide foyer, Geneva gave her a suspicious glance and sniffed again. "It's just as well. Cassie's a lovely, warmhearted young woman. But I seriously doubt one could ever make her into a real Philadelphian. As I've told you before, it's all in the breeding."